"Do you have any idea [...] Joseph Romano were in Vienna asking questions about a bloodline, Rennes-le-Château, and the Hapsburgs? I'm afraid she's found something."

"That's why I urged you to leave immediately."

Michael felt a twinge in his stomach. "They're involved?"

"Brittany interviewed Uriel and Raphael the day before their bodies were found. I thought that was sufficient cause to get you out of Vienna and up here immediately. I'm sure the Council is investigating every possibility."

"She was very interested in Rennes-le-Château. You don't suppose she knows about this place."

Gabriel opened the elevator door and stepped inside. "I doubt that. I'm sure her research brought up the issues surrounding Rennes-le-Château, but I think we'll be safe here until the Council resolves this crisis."

As the elevator descended, Gabriel locked Michael in his gaze. "We must also be prepared for the possibility that the deaths may be an act of God. They could be preparation for the Second Coming."

A sudden chill surged through Michael's body. . . .

———————

"Dan Brown fans will not be disappointed as [the novel] climbs from the bowels of Grand Central to the streets of Rome to an incendiary conclusion high in the French Alps."
—Andrew Gross, *New York Times* bestselling coauthor of *Lifeguard* and *Judge & Jury*

Patrick / McAleer -

continued . . .

UNHOLY GRAIL

D. L. WILSON

BERKLEY BOOKS, NEW YORK

THE BERKLEY PUBLISHING GROUP
Published by the Penguin Group
Penguin Group (USA) Inc.
375 Hudson Street, New York, New York 10014, USA
Penguin Group (Canada), 90 Eglinton Avenue East, Suite 700, Toronto, Ontario M4P 2Y3, Canada
(a division of Pearson Penguin Canada Inc.)
Penguin Books Ltd., 80 Strand, London WC2R 0RL, England
Penguin Group Ireland, 25 St. Stephen's Green, Dublin 2, Ireland (a division of Penguin Books Ltd.)
Penguin Group (Australia), 250 Camberwell Road, Camberwell, Victoria 3124, Australia
(a division of Pearson Australia Group Pty. Ltd.)
Penguin Books India Pvt. Ltd., 11 Community Centre, Panchsheel Park, New Delhi—110 017, India
Penguin Group (NZ), 67 Apollo Drive, Mairangi Bay, Auckland 1311, New Zealand
(a division of Pearson New Zealand Ltd.)
Penguin Books (South Africa) (Pty.) Ltd., 24 Sturdee Avenue, Rosebank, Johannesburg 2196, South Africa

Penguin Books Ltd., Registered Offices: 80 Strand, London WC2R 0RL, England

This is a work of fiction. Names, characters, places, and incidents either are the product of the author's imagination or are used fictitiously, and any resemblance to actual persons, living or dead, business establishments, events, or locales is entirely coincidental. The publisher does not have any control over and does not assume any responsibility for author or third party websites or their content.

UNHOLY GRAIL

A Berkley Book / published by arrangement with the author

PRINTING HISTORY
Berkley edition / April 2007

Copyright © 2007 by David L. Wilson.
Cover illustration by Gallucci Imaging Inc.
Cover design by Richard Hasselberger.
Interior text design by Kristin del Rosario.

ISBN: 978-0-425-21478-7

BERKLEY®
Berkley Books are published by The Berkley Publishing Group,
a division of Penguin Group (USA) Inc.,
375 Hudson Street, New York, New York 10014.
BERKLEY is a registered trademark of Penguin Group (USA) Inc.
The "B" design is a trademark belonging to Penguin Group (USA) Inc.

PRINTED IN THE UNITED STATES OF AMERICA

10 9 8 7 6 5 4 3 2 1

For Miki,
my muse.

ACKNOWLEDGMENTS

My heartfelt thanks to the wonderful people who made this book a reality:

Matt Bialer at Sanford J. Greenburger Associates, agent extraordinaire, who spotted the spark of potential in my initial manuscript and guided me through the tough reality of getting published. Samantha Mandor, senior editor at The Berkley Publishing Group, for believing in me and keeping me and my book on track through the complex publishing process. Your work ethic and dedication to the publishing world was a true inspiration.

My writer friends and family who read countless versions of this book. Especially the editorial guidance of Bill and Glo Delamar, Doug and Lucia Deaville, Terry Friedman, Molly Cochran, and Bill Kent who spared the editors at Berkley from having to burn the midnight oil.

The priests, ministers, theologians, and professors who shared their expertise, knowledge of scripture, and opinions with me. Hopefully their sage advice allowed this work of fiction to contain enough content to give readers the feeling that they may have actually learned something woven within the fictional elements of the plot.

Finally, my wife, Miki, whose support, dedication, and sage advice kept me going through the rough spots and made the trials and tribulations of writing a first novel all worthwhile.

AUTHOR'S NOTE

Many things in life are not black or white, true or false, right or wrong. Much of what we accept as fact is based upon theories, claims, beliefs, and the level of science at the time. One misquote, misinterpretation, or misread can confuse fact and fiction. What is accepted as fact today doesn't always stand the test of time.

Unholy Grail is a work of fiction with content. The plot draws on generally accepted facts, legends, myths, and conspiracy theories. Many of the concepts are based upon extensive research; interviews with priests, ministers, theologians, and professors; as well as the fictional creativity of the author.

PROLOGUE

"FORGIVE ME, FATHER, FOR I HAVE SINNED." THE muffled voice came from the darkest corner of the confessional in St. Patrick's Cathedral.

Father Edward Byrne poked a finger under the cuff of his jacket, lifted it, and checked his watch. Two more minutes till the end of confession.

"It has been seven days since my last confession." The man cleared his throat, paused, and continued in a loud whisper, "I am about to commit a mortal sin."

Byrne stiffened. He knew it was bound to happen. A despondent soul contemplating suicide coming to confession seeking a spark of hope. He tried to swallow but couldn't. His dry tongue stuck to the roof of his mouth.

"Mortal sin robs the soul of . . . of sanctifying grace." Byrne's voice cracked. He struggled searching for his next words. He closed his eyes, straining to focus his thoughts. "Nothing . . . nothing on God's earth can justify taking your own life. I know life must seem hopeless to you now—"

"Father, please, you don't understand. Not *my* life. I must kill. Kill to save the very sanctity of the Church."

Byrne leaned toward the confessional screen. He tried to make out the shadowy figure in the dark recess of the confessional. All he could see was a dim white square standing out against the center of a black collar.

PART I

THE
ENCOUNTER

ONE

Father Joseph Romano moved closer to the aluminum easel and held a magnifying glass over the reproduction of Poussin's *Les Bergers d'Arcadie*. The seventeenth-century painting depicted three shepherds and a shepherdess gazing in bewilderment at the inscription carved into a stone tomb perched on the edge of a rocky landscape. The Fordham University professor focused on the Latin inscription, *Et in Arcadia ego* (I am in Arcadia). He chuckled, thinking of the number of conspiracy theorists, researchers, and code breakers who had spent countless hours analyzing the phrase, searching for secret messages or a key to the location of the Holy Grail. To him it was obvious. The inscription referred to the Early Modern perception of Arcadia as a lost world of idyllic bliss. The stone was simply a hopeful reminder that whoever was buried there was now living in the kingdom of Utopia.

Romano put down the glass and searched through a stack of folders on the table next to the easel until he found a packet marked "Arques, France." He sorted through the contents and clipped two photos next to the lithograph. He focused the magnifying glass on the backgrounds of the photographs. Yes! The painting was definitely of the tomb in Arques.

Romano rapped his knuckles against the large letters scrawled across the top of the flip chart on the wall: *Et in arca Dei ago*. Then he called to two graduate students huddled around a computer on the second desk crammed into the office, "Have you young geniuses come up with anything?"

The young man looked up from the computer screen and tugged on the bill of his Fordham Rams cap. "Father, I'm sorry, there are no other rational anagrams in Latin. Unless you want us to try eliminating some of the letters?"

Romano shook his head. "No, Charlie, that's creative, but it would be going too far afield. Remember, this is an academic work."

"That doesn't stop the heretics from stretching the truth when they make these ridiculous assumptions," the other student said. Her dark, close-cropped hair and skin the color of bleached mahogany contrasted with Charlie's ocean of freckles and the sandy fringe poking from under his cap.

"Carlota, remember, social scientists must always err on the side of caution when refuting historical claims." Father Romano underlined *Et in arca Dei ago* (And I act on behalf of the ark of God). "If this is the only anagram that makes sense, then we concede the benefit of the doubt . . . at least for now."

The phone rang, and Carlota scrambled to get it while Charlie turned back to the computer. Romano began organizing the mounds of notes surrounding the spate of magazine articles that had turned up in France three months ago. Like many before, they claimed the existence of Jesus' bloodline. Some of them actually provided genealogies through to the present—including some very distinguished names. Of main concern to the Church, however, was a reference to a secret scripture, which one of the authors claimed had been written by James, the brother of Jesus, only days after the Crucifixion.

"Father, it's for you." Carlota put her hand over the mouthpiece. "He won't give his name," she whispered. "Says it's about some original documents. He'll only talk to you."

Romano took the receiver. "This is Father Joseph Romano."

"Be at Grand Central Terminal tomorrow morning at eight thirty." The man's voice was low and gravelly.

"Who is this?"

"Just be inside the entrance at Forty-second and Park by eight thirty. Wear your collar."

"I'm a Jesuit priest, a serious researcher, not some journalist looking for sensationalism."

"What I'll give you is serious research. A box containing original parchment written by the hand of Jesus' brother, James. It describes in detail what really happened at the Crucifixion." The line went dead.

"What was all that about?" Carlota asked.

"Someone claiming to have a section of the James Scripture." Charlie looked up from the computer and shook his head.

"Don't tell me these people are serializing this ridiculous secret manuscript."

"No, no, this isn't another alleged translation." Romano hung up the phone. "The caller claims to have the original manuscript."

Charlie put his hands behind his head, leaned back in his chair, and raised his eyebrows.

"Wow," Carlota said. "If it really exists, that'd put a different spin on your book."

Charlie's eyes narrowed. "If actual proof of a bloodline of Christ exists, what'll it do to the Church?"

Romano smiled at his grad assistants and stroked his neatly trimmed dark brown goatee speckled with flecks of red as he searched for the right answer. As a rule, he avoided discussions on the subject of "unquestioning faith." He decided to skirt the issue rather than attack it head-on.

"You're very bright students. You'll come up against some tough tests of faith in your lifetimes. Christianity's been around for almost two thousand years and nothing's been able to shake its foundation. I'm writing this book because it's important for us all to review the Crucifixion and Resurrection based upon evolving scholarship and the latest technology. As a scholar and a priest, I've spent a large part of my life analyzing every nook and cranny of Christian canons. I haven't found any critical faults that could undermine my faith." Romano smiled and waved a finger. "Let's not jump to conclusions because of an anonymous phone call."

Romano glanced at his watch. "You better get to class or we'll have Monsignor Lochner down on us."

Charlie and Carlota grabbed their books and were out of Romano's office before he realized he'd forgotten to tell them he wouldn't be there when they returned in the morning. He'd be watching the commuters at Grand Central, waiting for a stranger to hand him a box that could send shock waves through the Church.

FATHER ROMANO GAZED OUT THE WINDOW ON Sixty-second Street overlooking Damrosch Park and, beyond it, the Metropolitan Opera. The view was breathtaking, one of the perks of being on the Fordham faculty. He thought of Marta. She had really enjoyed the opera.

At eighteen he'd sneaked her into his family's box seats while his mother hosted one of her charity events. Marta had been awestruck by the grand scale of the opera house: the glass colonnaded arches, the enormous Chagall murals alive with color. She held his hand during the entire performance and didn't move a muscle. After the opera she insisted they sit on the broad rim of the fountain in the quadrangle. She dipped her fingers into the cool water, splashed him, and graced him with one of her smiles of pure innocence . . . it seemed a lifetime ago. Since then he'd dedicated his life and his substantial trust fund to research and the Church.

Romano left his office and headed for the Metro-North train to the Bronx—and his lonely room at Spellman Hall.

TWO

GABRIEL TURNED OFF NORTH CHURCH ROAD AND through the high wrought-iron gate marking the entrance to the Jesuit Center for Spiritual Growth. He glanced at the molded faces staring out from the top of the ornate ironwork. How ironic, he thought. They could depict Greek gods or even disguised versions of the pagan fertility god, Baphomet. To many, his horned head was the devil incarnate. To the enlightened few, Baphomet was a cipher for Sophia, ultimate wisdom.

Shadows bathed the tree-lined drive as the last vestiges of daylight filtered through the thick foliage. There were no cars or grounds crews this late in the day. Gabriel felt a sense of nervous anticipation as he drove toward the magnificent former novitiate for Jesuit priests and brothers. He slowed as he approached the massive brick structure perched on a hill overlooking the quaint town of Wernersville, Pennsylvania. The shape of the building resembled an early version of the seal of the Society of Jesus. The four-level east and west wings connected by long central halls formed an H from IHS, the first three letters of the name Jesus in Greek. In the center of the H was a structure in the shape of a cross that served as the main entrance.

Gabriel pulled into a lower parking area that gave him a clear view of the upper lots and the grand stone portico. He slouched down in his seat, took out a small pair of binoculars, and focused them on the two tiers of stone steps leading to the front entrance of the Jesuit center. Since 1971 the center had provided retreats and programs based on the *Spiritual Exercises of St. Ignatius Loyola*, the order's founder. Today they were hosting a silent retreat. Gabriel would blend in with the participants and wouldn't have to worry about nosy questions. He'd be in, out, and long gone before anyone even thought about an intruder.

He waited patiently until he spotted a car with New York

plates pass the lower lot. He swung his binoculars and focused on
the blonde behind the wheel as she turned toward the main entrance to the center. He couldn't mistake her dark brows and wide
olive eyes. She was beautiful, and memorable. In a way, he felt
guilty using her, but she was the perfect ruse. She'd buy him critical time. Timing was everything and nothing could be sacrosanct
in his religious quest. After all, he was chosen by God . . . and
therefore so was she.

Gabriel prayed for guidance as he watched the car continue
around the circular drive and park in front of the Jesuit center. By
the time the blonde reached the second flight of steps, the door to
the center opened and a priest emerged with a big smile and a
beckoning wave. The two shook hands, chatted for a moment,
and went back to her car.

As they headed down the drive, Gabriel saw a second car with
New York plates pass them, turn around at the first parking lot,
and follow them out of the center. He tried to focus his binoculars
on the driver, but all he could make out in the dwindling daylight
was a man with dark hair. Had Interpol and the FBI worked that
quickly? Did they have someone following her? Even if they did,
he knew she'd still be their primary focus, giving him the critical
edge he needed. Then again, maybe the Council had already
picked her up in their sights. He smiled. It really didn't matter.
He was way ahead of them all. He was in control.

Gabriel took a black leather cigar case out of his shirt pocket.
He pulled off the top and checked the contents of each of the tu-
bular compartments; everything was prepped and ready. Then he
walked nonchalantly across the grassy lawn to the center.

He opened the main door and stepped inside. An eerie silence
pervaded the dim entryway. He took a deep breath. It was the
smell of age, as if the air had used up all its vibrancy. He peered
down the dark hallways lit only by occasional lamps on small
side tables. Not a soul was around. Gabriel glanced at his watch.
The priests and retreat participants should be at dinner. He made
his way to the residence of the priest who had left with the
blonde.

Minutes later, Gabriel returned to the first floor and settled in
an overstuffed chair in a private waiting room near the entrance.
On one end table was a delicate porcelain lamp and on another a
box of tissues and a well-worn Bible. That's when he felt it once
again, the same sensation he'd experienced in Spain. The heat

started from deep within his chest, radiated through his arms, inching up his neck like flames caressing his face until it seared his brain. Beads of sweat erupted above his upper lip and in a band across his forehead. It was as though he were engulfed by a raging fever.

Gabriel reached for the Bible sitting on the end table. He opened it to Ephesians, then flicked the pages until he came to 4:23. "And be renewed in the spirit of your mind." He read it over and over and over. It was that renewal, that regeneration, that had come to him while deep in prayer; he was the chosen one, the one to eliminate the evil, the one to return Christianity to its original state of innocence. The heat faded as quickly as it had come.

Gabriel settled back into the chair and waited patiently for the return of the only person who could recognize him. That priest was probably in a restaurant with the blonde enjoying his last supper.

THREE

FATHER ROMANO'S TRAIN ARRIVED AT GRAND
Central Station at the height of the morning rush hour. He wore
his religious collar as requested by the caller but stuck with his
usual khakis and a soft-shouldered sport coat and Nikes. One of
the things that had drawn him to the Jesuit order and teaching was
not having to wear formal religious garb. He felt self-conscious
whenever he was out in public wearing his priest's collar.

Thousands of commuters poured out of the suburban lines
into the labyrinth beneath the station. He negotiated the nearest
set of stairs and entered the main terminal. It was nearly the size
of a football field. The signs of the zodiac swept majestically
across the arched ceiling.

Romano made his way through the mass of people and up the
ramp to the Forty-second Street entrance. He went outside and
walked along Park Avenue, then up and down a block of Forty-
second Street, in case the caller thought he'd be coming from his
office at Lincoln Center Campus, but he saw no one searching the
crowd except a panhandler with a coffee can.

He stood under the Park Avenue overpass and glanced across
the street at the Pershing Square Central Café. No one was standing around scrutinizing the early-morning rush of humanity, so
he went back into the terminal. The caller had specifically said
he'd meet him inside the Forty-second Street and Park Avenue
entrance. He jockeyed to find a place to stand without blocking
the steady stream of commuters rushing to work. As the minutes
ticked away, he glanced nervously at the giant lighted clock
mounted between two massive columns. He felt stupid. This had
to be some crackpot . . . or a joke. Were his students somewhere
in the station watching him—laughing? He wouldn't put it past
Charlie to do something like this.

The sound of a shot was deafening even in the din of the

crowded terminal. It echoed off the vaulted ceiling and seemed to come from all directions. People ran for the exits, jostling Romano. A man shoved something into his chest, almost knocking him to the ground. When he regained his balance, Romano found himself clutching a manuscript box. He turned and looked for the stranger, but the man had disappeared into the panicking crowd.

Romano fought his way to a ring of onlookers congregating around a young woman lying on the stone floor. An MTA police officer shouted instructions into a radio and knelt down beside the victim. Blood oozed from a wound in her left shoulder. Her head thrashed from side to side. She opened her mouth as if to scream, but no sound emerged.

Romano grabbed a handkerchief from his pocket and gave it to the officer, who pressed it against the woman's shoulder, looked up, and nodded. "Thanks, Father."

Romano knelt down next to the woman, laid down the box, and held her hand. The woman stared at him, silently pleading. He slipped off his jacket and tucked it under her head. She winced and stopped thrashing. The officer continued to apply pressure to the wound. In seconds the handkerchief was soaked and his hand smeared with blood. Romano prayed in silence.

"Don't worry, miss. The medics are on their way," the officer said as two soldiers in camouflage uniforms and more MTA police pushed through the crowd.

Romano heard the undulating wail of an approaching ambulance. Shortly, a team of EMTs arrived and took over. Before Romano could catch his breath they had the woman stabilized and on a stretcher.

One of the EMTs patted him on the shoulder. "She'll be okay, Father," he said as they wheeled her through a path cleared by two officers.

The Metropolitan Transportation Authority police were everywhere. A Lieutenant Garret started to question Romano about what he'd seen. A porter tapped Romano's shoulder, pointed to blood on his sleeve, and handed him a towel. Romano was sweating and his hands still trembled as he wiped off the blood. He told the lieutenant he was at the entrance when he heard the shot and hadn't actually seen the shooting. Rushed to the scene to help or pray, whatever he could do. After a few more questions, Lieutenant Garret thanked Father Romano, gave him his card, and told him to call the station if he remembered anything more.

On his way toward the ramp out of the terminal, Romano noticed blond hairs matted on the breast pocket of his coat. The victim's, poor woman. He prayed she'd make it, then brushed them off.

"Father, isn't this yours?"

Romano turned to see an MTA policeman holding the manuscript box. "Sorry, with all the confusion I forgot."

Before he got to the door, he stepped into a small alcove and lifted the box flap. The odor of gunpowder seared his nostrils. Nestled in a foam cavity was a gun.

Father Romano stared in disbelief at the gun. Without thinking, he closed the box and clutched it to his chest. Lights flashed behind him. He spun around and almost dropped the box. A giant image of a fashion model strutting down a runway covered the wall. He let out a nervous breath. It was a promotion for a fashion show. His mind was spinning. Why would somebody try to frame him for the shooting? He thought of the woman who had been shot. There was something familiar about her, as if he'd seen her before. He just couldn't remember where.

Romano stepped next to the wall, away from the dazzling light of the changing slide show. He thought of leaving, but looked down at the box and realized that wouldn't be wise. He was probably holding the weapon used in the shooting. When his mind settled, he knew there really was only one sane option. He reached into his pocket for Lieutenant Garret's card and headed back into the main concourse.

Officers had cordoned off the area where the woman was shot. Romano approached a uniformed MTA policeman. "Excuse me. I need to speak with Lieutenant Garret."

The policeman looked askance at Romano. "Is it about the shooting?"

"Yes. I . . . I have something to add to my statement."

The officer's eyes widened. "You were the priest who assisted Harvey. You forget something?"

"Actually, it's something I found." Romano held up the manuscript box. "This might be important evidence."

The policeman reached for the box. Romano pulled it away.

"Sorry. I'd prefer to explain this to the lieutenant."

"Father, if that's evidence in the shooting, you should hand it over to me now."

The policeman hesitated when Romano didn't give him the

box. With his eyes fixed on him, he pulled out his radio and made a call. When he finished, he nodded to Romano.

"Father, please follow me to the lower concourse." The policeman pointed to the stairs. "Lieutenant Garret wants to see you at our substation."

When they arrived at the food concourse, an electric police cart met them with lights flashing. The policeman motioned for Romano to sit next to the driver. As soon as he was seated with the box held tightly in his lap, they drove off past track entrances until Romano saw "Police Lost & Found" on the crossbeam over a passageway. The cart slowed, entered the narrow passage, and stopped in front of a glassed-in waiting room. POLICE was printed in huge vertical letters on either side of a door emblazoned with the bright blue-and-yellow insignia of the MTA police.

The officer escorted Romano inside the empty waiting room. A few posters and a glass case filled with police patches adorned the otherwise bare walls. An American flag on a stanchion stood in one corner. The officer behind the counter turned from a bank of video monitors and pointed to a door. "Lieutenant Garret's expecting you. He's in the conference room with a city detective."

The officer opened the door and they went down a short hall to a brightly lit, stark room. Sitting at a gray steel conference table were Lieutenant Garret and a man in a rumpled blue suit with thick, dark, wavy hair and a tangled fringe of gray that curled over his ears. Romano felt a twinge of anxiety as he entered the room. He was concerned about how they would respond to him handing over the weapon and explaining that someone jammed the box into his hands during the bedlam that ensued after the shooting.

The man flipped the brown folder in front of him closed and looked up at Romano over a pair of narrow black reading glasses. His face was etched with deep lines. A small scar over his right eye gave Romano the impression that he was probably more street smart than book smart. This detective could no doubt handle himself in any situation.

Lieutenant Garret stood and gestured to the man next to him. "Father Romano, this is Lieutenant Renzetti of NYPD. His department will be assisting in the investigation." Renzetti nodded and continued to stare over his glasses at Romano.

Garret pointed to a chair across the table from them. "Please, have a seat. One of our officers said you had some evidence related to the shooting."

Romano sat down and placed the manuscript box in the center of the table. He told them about the mysterious phone call and what happened when he arrived at Grand Central Station. When Garret asked if he remembered what the man looked like, he closed his eyes and saw the blur of bodies rushing past him. He couldn't be certain, but he thought the man had been wearing a dark jacket. He squeezed his eyes tighter. Was it a Windbreaker? Sport jacket? He couldn't remember. He tried again and again to recapture that moment, but everything had happened so fast. In the commotion, all he could recall was a flash, a flash of what could have been a scar.

Romano opened his eyes. "I think he had a—" He stopped short when he found his eyes fixed on the scar cutting across Renzetti's right eyebrow. He shook his head and continued. "All I can remember is dark hair, dark jacket. Sorry, I can't be certain about anything more."

Renzetti looked skeptically at Garret, then pointed to the box. "And what, pray tell, Father, does this secret box have to do with the shooting?"

Romano took a deep breath and returned Renzetti's gaze before responding. "I think this is the weapon."

Garret and Renzetti glanced at each other, then at Romano. Renzetti used his pen to slide the box toward himself. With the tip, he lifted the flap, revealing the gun nestled in the foam cavity. He leaned toward the box, sniffed, shook his head, then pulled out his cell phone and called a crime scene investigator.

The two detectives grilled Romano, with Renzetti taking the lead. The NYPD lieutenant didn't seem to buy Romano's story about some mystery man tricking him into coming to Grand Central, then jamming the box into his chest. He had Garret bring in the MTA officer first on the scene, and the officer who returned the box to Romano, and questioned them in another office. When he came back, his questioning softened somewhat.

A Crime Scene Investigation team finally arrived. Renzetti asked an investigator to test Romano for gunshot residue. The test was negative. After revisiting every detail of what Romano did that morning, they told him they would contact him if they needed additional information and he was allowed to leave.

Romano didn't waste any time rushing out of the station. He

actually felt relieved when he hit the pungent air of Manhattan's Midtown East. As he headed toward his office, he tried to put the past hour into some kind of perspective. He couldn't, but took solace in thinking it certainly couldn't get any worse.

FOUR

A tall, slender doctor stepped into Brittany Hamar's room. He stared intently at a file folder clutched in his veined hands. His hair was mottled in dramatic shades that reminded her of fireplace ash. He looked up from the folder and smiled. "Ms. Hamar, you're a lucky woman. A few inches lower and we'd be talking in our trauma unit, or we might not be talking at all."

Britt noted the bright red "Dr. Henry Faulkner" embroidered on the doctor's white jacket. "Somehow I don't feel lucky, Dr. Faulkner. Someone shot me."

The doctor's smile dissolved into a more professional demeanor. "Sorry, Ms. Hamar, I didn't mean to be flippant. It's just that the gunshot wound to your shoulder didn't damage any bones, organs, or major blood vessels."

"What exactly does that mean?"

"There was only an entrance wound." Dr. Faulkner tapped his lips with a forefinger. "Actually, that was odd. You were shot at close range. The bullet didn't hit any bone. It should have gone through your shoulder. You must be tough-skinned." He grinned, then seemed to realize Britt wasn't amused. He became serious. "I was able to extract the bullet and stitch you up. Other than a small scar, you're going to be fine."

"When can I go home?"

"Well, I'd like to keep you here overnight for observation. I want to make sure there's no infection. That's why we have you on intravenous. We can release you first thing in the morning."

Before Britt could respond, there was a loud rap on the hospital room door and a man in a navy suit strode in. He had a hard face and a look of all business as he walked up to Dr. Faulkner and flipped open a leather case showing a badge and ID.

"Lieutenant Renzetti, NYPD. I need to ask Ms. Hamar about the shooting."

The doctor glanced at Britt, then back at the detective. "She's undergone quite a traumatic event but should be able to answer your questions." He turned toward Britt and smiled. "Ms. Hamar, I'll leave you to the lieutenant. Just push the call button if you need anything." He turned and left the room.

Lieutenant Renzetti pulled out a notepad and jotted something down. He looked at Britt with calculating eyes. "Ms. Hamar, do you have any idea who shot you?" His deep voice made the question sound like a command.

Britt was taken aback by his gruff manner. But maybe that was the type of person who could find out who shot her, and why. She didn't want whoever did it to have a second chance.

"Lieutenant, I wish I did, but I have no idea. To be honest, I can't even describe the shooter. It was surreal. There was a horrendous noise. It felt like somebody punched me in the shoulder. Next thing I remember, I was lying on the floor. That's about it."

Renzetti tapped his pen against the pad. Britt couldn't tell if it was a nervous tic or frustration. He dropped his head for a second, then gave Britt a feeble attempt at a smile. "Did you notice anyone paying special attention to you as you were walking through the station? You know, anyone staring at you? Any looks that gave you a creepy feeling?"

Britt tried to create a picture in her mind, but everything seemed hazy. She finally shook her head. "To be honest, I can't remember much about this morning. I don't think I could describe anyone I saw while I was in the station."

"Do you know of anyone who might want to harm you?"

"No one specific. But I'm sure it has to do with why I was at Grand Central."

Renzetti's eyes narrowed. "And?"

"Yesterday I received a call telling me to be at the information booth at Grand Central Terminal precisely at eight thirty this morning. Someone was going to give me an ancient manuscript."

Renzetti jotted something on his pad and stared at Britt. "Who?" he asked.

"The caller didn't identify himself. It was a male. Spoke in a low voice."

"Have any idea who it could've been?"

Britt hesitated. She thought about *The Messenger*, but was certain it wasn't him. His language had been more refined, his voice more genteel. Calm. This guy was direct, demanding. "No, I can't say that I recognized his voice," she finally said.

"What about this manuscript?"

"You've got to understand. I'm a professor of religion. I'm on sabbatical, writing a book about Christianity. It questions some of our accepted beliefs about Christ. I'm sure the Roman Catholic hierarchy and many religious zealots are not happy with some of my findings."

Renzetti stopped writing and looked at Britt with a questioning stare. "Are you insinuating the Church might want to kill you?"

"I really have no idea who would want to kill me." She shrugged. "But I suppose in this day and age, you can never be sure."

Renzetti shook his head. "Believe me, in my business I've seen it all. Now what about this manuscript?"

"The caller said it was a secret manuscript written by James, the brother of Jesus."

"You're saying Jesus had a brother?" Renzetti looked dumbfounded.

"Are you a Roman Catholic, Lieutenant?"

"Yes. Even went to Catholic school."

"Whether Jesus had brothers and sisters is debatable among religious scholars. The Roman Catholic Church believes strongly in Mary's perpetual virginity." She paused. "They downplay any historical or religious implications about Jesus and siblings. The Virgin Mary is too important to them."

Renzetti looked at her skeptically. "You're serious? It's the twenty-first century and we don't know for sure if Jesus had brothers and sisters?"

"Don't take my word for it," Britt said. "Take a look at Saint Mark, chapter six, verse three. It refers to Jesus teaching in the synagogue in Nazareth on the Sabbath. The worshippers say, 'Is not this the carpenter, the son of Mary, the brother of James, and Joses, and of Juda, and Simon? And are not his sisters here with us?' "

"That's in the Bible?"

"Even in the versions approved by the Roman Catholic Church." Before Renzetti could respond, Britt added, "But it's a little more complicated than that."

Renzetti shook his head in disbelief. "We never discussed that verse in parochial school. But son, brother, sister. Seems pretty clear to me."

"The terms 'brother' and 'sister,' even though they were translated from the Greek, can become confusing if you apply Semitic usage from the time of Jesus. In that perspective, those terms apply not only to children of the same parents but to nephews, nieces, cousins, half brothers. But in the case of the James manuscript, it doesn't matter. If James was Jesus' brother, or an apostle, or the head of the Jerusalem Church, he still would have had firsthand knowledge of the life and death of Jesus."

"And who would have this secret manuscript?" Renzetti asked as he jotted something in his notepad.

"It could be anyone," Britt said. "Antiquities dealer, researcher, archaeologist . . . or a wacko. I have no clue. But I'd say there's a good chance the person who shot me either doesn't like the concept of my upcoming book or didn't want me to get my hands on the manuscript."

FIVE

FATHER WILLIAM SHELDON LOOKED OVER THE AS-
sembled priests finishing breakfast in the rear of the large dining
hall at the Jesuit Center for Spiritual Growth. Portable partitions
separated their tables from the front, which was filled with the
participants of a silent retreat. The silence was disturbed only by
the occasional clink of a utensil against china or the scrape of a
serving spoon against a stainless chafing dish.

The spiritual director got up from his table, walked over to
one of the other priests, and whispered, "Thomas, have you seen
Ted Mathews this morning?"

The priest looked up at the ceiling for a moment, then shook
his head. "That's strange, I haven't. I usually see Ted at least a
half dozen times before breakfast."

"Did you hear him at all in his room this morning?" Sheldon
asked.

"You know, I didn't hear a sound. Although, he is a quiet
neighbor." Thomas nodded toward the priest sitting next to him.
"It's Jack who's always banging around. But I usually hear some
activity from Ted. It's not like our rooms are soundproof."

"I'm going to check on him." Sheldon turned and left.

Father Jack Gannon slid his chair closer to Thomas and leaned
toward him. "I hope Ted didn't run off with that blonde."

"What blonde?" Thomas asked.

"The one he had dinner with at Stouch's Tavern. I saw him
meet her out front on the steps. A very attractive woman." Gannon raised his eyebrows.

"Jack, you need counseling. Ted told me he was meeting a
professor of religion who's writing a book and wanted to interview him. All very professional."

"There you have it, Thomas, smart and beautiful. A dangerous
combination for a lonely old priest."

Thomas slowly shook his head. "You, I'd worry about. Of any of us, Ted is one of a kind. He really does walk in the footsteps of Jesus."

FATHER SHELDOП MADE HIS WAY DOWП THE DIMLY lit hall in the wing that housed the resident priests. He felt a sense of foreboding as he passed the rooms, rooms that had housed former residents. Close friends who had died. Some had departed quietly in the night, and some had struggled through prolonged illnesses. The center was not only a retreat house and a place for spiritual programs and workshops, but also served those priests who were getting up in age. It was home for those priests no longer physically or emotionally able to function in education, mission work, or directing retreats. Their final ministry was to pray for the Church and society. Jesuits never retired.

Sheldon tried to block out thoughts that something may have happened to Ted Mathews. Even though he was getting on in years, Ted was in good health and a vibrant contributor to the retreats.

As Sheldon approached Ted's room he listened for any sound, any indication that he was up and about. At first he thought Ted might be under the weather and had decided to sleep in that morning. But then he looked at his watch and realized Ted was scheduled to meet with a client in ten minutes as part of a directed retreat. And Ted Mathews was never late for anything.

Sheldon rapped three times on the door. "Ted, Ted, are you in there? It's Bill." He waited and heard no response. Then he knocked again. "Ted, it's Bill. You okay?" Nothing.

The spiritual director grasped the cool brass knob and slowly turned it. The door inched open. "Ted, Ted," he called.

He leaned in as the door opened and peered inside. A ladybug lit on Ted's marred oak desk, flexed its wings, rubbed its legs along the edge of its shell, and settled in. A pewter Christ hung in limp repose from a rosewood crucifix Ted had been gifted years ago during a stint as a missionary in Central America. The floor creaked with each step as Sheldon approached the open door to the bedroom.

Sheldon breathed a sigh of relief when he saw Ted Mathews in white boxers, eyes closed, hands folded in prayer, lying on his neatly made bed. Ted was known to be especially focused during prayer as he contemplated the greater glory of God. Some of the priests said his depth of prayer bordered on the mystical. But this was way beyond anything Sheldon had ever observed. Ted must have totally shut down his senses and entered an extreme state of meditative prayer.

A chill settled over Sheldon as his eyes focused on Ted's skin. It was a pale shade of blue purple. His eyes locked on Ted's hands folded in prayer. He had seen his share of dead bodies, but he was not prepared for what he saw next.

SIX

Father Romano's breathing reached a steady rhythm as he approached Fordham University. He had jogged from Grand Central to the Lincoln Center Campus to clear his head and to get to his office before Charlie and Carlota gave up on him. He bought three spring waters from a hot dog vendor then pulled out his ID as he sprinted to the main entrance. He passed through security and dashed up to the second-level elevators just in time to jam his arm between the closing doors. When the doors reopened, he promised himself he'd try to stop that stupid habit before a defective elevator won. He stepped inside and slumped against the wall. His grad assistants wouldn't believe what he'd just been through. For that matter, neither did he.

As the elevator jerked into service and headed toward the ninth floor, Romano tried to find a connection between a supposed secret manuscript, a woman being shot, and a Jesuit priest who teaches religion and validates ancient manuscripts. He wondered who the woman was. That he somehow knew her or had at least seen her before nagged at him. He should have mentioned that to the police but realized he had nothing to base it on, and Lieutenant Renzetti already seemed to have doubts about him.

And the scar? He thought the guy had a scar on his face, but then he saw Renzetti's scar and feared his mind was playing tricks on him. The whole thing was becoming a mental blur. At this point he'd be a sorry excuse as a witness. The elevator bounced to a stop.

Charlie was hunched over the small conference table that served as the grad assistants' makeshift desk, his eyes glued to the monitor when Romano arrived in his office. Charlie banged away on the keyboard for a few seconds, then hit the Enter key forcefully with his forefinger before straightening up and looking at Romano.

"You miss your train, Father?"

"I wish I had, Charlie."

"What's with the priest garb? You have a big meeting today?" The grad assistant spun around in the chair and jerked the bill of his Rams cap to the back of his head, then screwed his lips into a questioning look.

"I should have worn my usual polo shirt. You won't believe what happened." Romano brought Charlie up to date on his morning drama. All Charlie said was "wow" when Romano mentioned the shot ringing out, the manuscript box, the gun, and the police interrogation.

When Romano finished he handed two bottles of spring water to Charlie. "For you and Carlota," he said as he twisted off the cap from the third and took a few gulps. "By the way, have you heard from Carlota? She's always here before you come trailing in."

"You know, that's strange, she always beats me here. That's how she gets first dibs on computer time."

"That's bull," Carlota said as she rushed into the office. "You're always late for classes, too. It's your style, Charlie."

Charlie raised his eyebrows. "But I get the job done, don't I, Father?"

Romano smiled. "Both of you are first-rate. I couldn't ask for better grad assistants."

"Tell her about the shooting."

"Actually, Charlie beat me to the office this morning," Romano said. "You'll never guess what happened, I—"

"Shooting?" Carlota cut him off. "That's why I was late. You don't mean the professor from Hunter College."

"What? What are you referring to?" Romano asked.

"It's all over the news," Carlota continued. "Brittany Hamar, the professor at Hunter who's writing *The Jesus Fraud*. She got shot at Grand Central Station."

Romano felt a rush of adrenaline. It was the same feeling he got when he heard the shot and when he opened the box.

"It's the manuscript!" Charlie shouted. "Didn't she say in the interview about her book that she thinks those French magazine articles could have some merit?"

"She did," Carlota said. "She specifically referred to the secret manuscript that started the whole rash of articles about a bloodline."

"If I recall, she never mentioned any evidence validating the so-called manuscript." Romano paused. "Or that she ever even saw it."

Carlota shrugged her shoulders. "She did say she had some physical evidence that could relate to a possible bloodline."

"The key words are 'could relate' and 'possible,'" Romano pointed out. "Remember my cautions about jumping to conclusions."

"What do you think, Father?" Charlie asked. "Could the manuscript be for real?"

"You both should know my position on that. We've often discussed my concerns even about the canonical Gospels. Matthew, Mark, Luke, and John weren't originally attributed to any particular authors. The Gospels were actually anonymous works regarded as 'the gospel' of a particular Christian sect. Only later did they acquire the names of their supposed authors. They were written in capital letters, with no headings, no chapters or verse divisions, and practically no punctuation or spaces between words. They were not even written in the Aramaic of the Jews of the time, but in Greek. But after almost two thousand years of scrutiny, no one has come up with verifiable evidence to discount them. They are still the official word of all Christian religions."

Romano stopped and stared at Charlie and Carlota. When he thought his words had sunk in, he added, "Do you still wonder if I think a manuscript that has never been officially produced for analysis, interpretation, or any validation could be real?"

Charlie shrugged. "It would be interesting to know what this Professor Hamar thinks."

"For once, I agree with you, Charlie." Romano pointed to Poussin's *Les Bergers d'Arcadie* on the easel. "Why don't the two of you see if you can dig up some more data on the inscription. I think I'll check on Professor Hamar and ask her."

SEVEN

TALL, WEATHERED BRICK TOWERS JUTTED MAJESTI-cally into the gardenlike entrance to Bellevue Hospital. Romano was impressed as he headed through the tree-covered setting highlighted by antique lampposts, concrete planters, and a tiered fountain. This was his first visit to Bellevue, and he wasn't even sure he should be there. But he and Brittany Hamar had too much in common for all that had happened to have been coincidence.

Romano had been to maybe two or three conferences that Brittany Hamar had attended. They hadn't been on any commit-tees together, and he didn't recall ever talking to her, but he re-membered her and should have recognized her. The main reason he hadn't was her hair. She had dark brown hair then, not like the blonde whose head he had cradled with his jacket.

The long portico leading to the entrance was jammed with visitors and medical staff. Romano joined the queue for the infor-mation desk. Rows of brightly colored pennants hung across the entry hall ceiling, lending a festive air to the usually somber hos-pital atmosphere. A subtle disinfectant scent left no doubt, how-ever, that this was a hospital.

A chill shot down Romano's spine. He never felt comfortable in hospitals, not since he was startled awake in the middle of the night by sirens at the age of twelve. His mother had rushed him in his pajamas to the local hospital, where they huddled together in a waiting room as an emergency team tried to resuscitate his fa-ther. It was to no avail. He lost his father to a massive heart attack at the time when a boy needed a father the most. It was at the fu-neral service that his father's best friend, Father Ted Mathews, a Jesuit priest, became his close friend and mentor. Through Joseph's formative years, Father Ted was always there for him, a shoulder to lean on, especially during those times when a mother just couldn't understand.

It was Father Ted who guided Joseph to the priesthood during the second most traumatic time in his life. The time he hated—despised—his mother for doing what he felt was unthinkable. She had taken Marta from him.

"Father. Father, may I help you?"

Romano realized he had moved to the head of the line and was staring, but not seeing. He blinked. A perky elderly woman at the information desk was looking up at him with a congenial smile. She quickly located Brittany Hamar in the directory and pointed to the proper elevator.

When Romano finally found Hamar's room near the end of a long beige hall, her door was open. He looked in and saw her lying in bed, her head propped on a pillow, and her eyes closed. Her left arm was on top of the blanket. A catheter connected to an IV was taped to her forearm. She looked pretty good considering she had been shot only a few hours ago. He had forgotten how attractive she was; seeing her as a shooting victim, he hadn't really focused on her esoteric beauty. Now, as she slept peacefully, he noted the proud line of her nose, the fullness of her lips, and the gentle wave of ash-blond fringe across her forehead.

Romano was about to leave when Hamar's eyes opened. She stared at him. She shook her head as if to clear the cobwebs, then her face contorted into a look of suspicion.

"What are you doing here? I didn't ask for a priest or a pastor." Hamar's voice was far from friendly.

"I'm not here as your priest," Romano quickly replied.

"You certainly fooled me." Hamar looked disgusted. "I don't want to talk to any priests."

"I'm sorry, Professor Hamar. I was there when you were shot. I helped the officer who stabilized you. I was concerned about how you were doing."

Brittany Hamar's expression wilted to a look of confusion. "I do remember you. You held my hand before the medics arrived. But I know you from somewhere else. Without the collar." Her eyes widened. "You're a professor at Fordham. Professor Romano. I've read some of your books."

"Guilty on both counts. But, please, call me Joseph."

"Only if you call me Britt."

"Britt it is. I hope you didn't find my writing too cumbersome."

"No, not at all. I found *The God of the New Testament* to be fresh and enlightening. You presented many diverse interpretations." Britt seemed to force a smile but the corners of her eyes turned down slightly, giving her a pensive look. "You did open the question of the role of Paul in the emerging Christianity, but in the end you held a bit doggedly to the bureaucratic Church line."

"Well, what do you expect from an old priest?"

"But I thought you liberal Jesuits draw your own lines in the sands of history."

"We can debate that in the halls of academia when you're back on your feet." Romano gave Britt a quick grin; then his mouth formed a hard line. "There's something more important I came here to discuss." His gaze locked on to hers. "Would you mind telling me why you were at Grand Central Station this morning?"

Britt pushed herself up in the hospital bed. "Why are you asking?"

"Because yesterday I received an anonymous call instructing me to be there to receive a manuscript written by James. An original manuscript."

Britt appeared shocked, but she quickly recovered. "And did you get the manuscript?" she asked.

"Someone in the rush of people running out of the station after the gunshot shoved a manuscript box into my arms and—"

"Where's the manuscript?" Britt interrupted.

"There wasn't a manuscript."

"Then what was in the box?"

"It's in the hands of the police. After they rushed you to the hospital, I opened the box. There was a gun in it."

Britt's jaw dropped. "Do you know who called you? Have you received calls like that before?"

"No, unfortunately I don't, and didn't. I wasn't able to give the police much to go on. That's why I came here to ask you if there's any connection other than our vocations."

Britt appeared ready to answer, but instead she looked down and ran a finger over the tape holding her catheter in place. When she looked up, her face had tightened into a look of determination. "The only thing I know for sure is that I'm writing a book that could devastate the Church and you're a priest with ties to the Vatican."

"Don't you want to find out who shot you?"

"I certainly do. But I don't think it would be wise to discuss the shooting with anyone but the police." She reached over and pressed the call button. "I'm having a bit of discomfort. If you'll excuse me, I need to see the doctor." Britt smiled weakly and continued, "Thank you for coming by, Joseph. I look forward to that debate. I'll stop at Fordham soon."

There was no doubt in Romano's mind that he had been dismissed. "I wish you a speedy recovery, and you're welcome to visit whenever you feel up to it." He gave Britt a short wave, turned, and left.

As he strode down the hall to the elevator, he sensed there was a lot more to Professor Brittany Hamar than he had observed in that hospital room.

EIGHT

Britt Hamar closed her eyes and tried to visualize the large iron cross Romano had been wearing. Something about the cross gave her a strange feeling of déjà vu. Maybe she was still rattled by the shooting. Changing thoughts kept flashing through her mind. What was Romano's role in all this? He knew about the manuscript. Could he be *The Messenger*, the one who sent the manuscript fragment? Or was he the one who lured her to Grand Central? She had to be sure. A stupid mistake could cost her her life.

She had almost been ready to confide in Joseph Romano. His reputation as an expert in interpreting and validating ancient manuscripts was impeccable. She had actually considered contacting him to validate the manuscript fragment alluding to children of Jesus and Mary Magdalene, but had hesitated because, after all, he was a priest. Then she received the carbon-dating results verifying the fragment was from the time of Jesus' Crucifixion. It had to be authentic. Romano would have been perfect to work with, but when he asked why she was at Grand Central Station, a warning triggered. What if the Church was somehow involved? What if Romano was involved?

It had all started with the French magazine articles referring to *Le Serpent Rouge*, a bloodline of Christ winding through history like a "red snake." Many of the assertions in the articles matched Britt's research and her conclusions that there really could be a bloodline of Christ. Unfortunately, they provided no verifiable evidence to support their claims other than vague references to a secret gospel. Most of the magazines were French versions of *Star* or the *National Enquirer* and only served to bring the subject into the mainstream rumor mills for café and dinnertable discussion. Academics found the articles amusing but gave them little credibility. That was, until her interview. When the interviewer asked what she thought about the articles, she said they could have some merit. Then she dropped the bombshell that she had physical evidence that would be presented in her up-coming book, *The Jesus Fraud*. The comment and the book title generated a lot of media attention and pressure from her pub-lisher to get the book done yesterday.

Since then she'd been scrambling to put the finishing touches on her manuscript. The fragment of the supposed James Gospel locked in her safe-deposit box was the linchpin that supported some of her conclusions, but she'd need more to satisfy the ma-jority of religious scholars. She desperately wanted the whole manuscript or whatever portions survived after two thousand years. She'd thought that the evidence was minutes away as she waited in Grand Central Station—then she was shot!

NINE

FOR THE FOURTH TIME IN LESS THAN TEN MINUTES, Philippe Armand passed the massive Doric columns lining the front of the church. It was odd seeing a big old church tucked away in the middle of Manhattan among apartments, businesses, and restaurants. He wondered if the Church had anything to do with the secret group that employed him. Many of his assignments had religious overtones, and he often wondered who was really behind the bizarre requests that sent him all over the world. One thing he was sure of, it involved big money. Just as they had paid his father before him, they paid him to be available 24/7. And they paid him well.

Philippe continued on to the brick apartment building in the middle of the block that he had carefully scoped out the day before. A low wrought-iron fence hemmed in the shrubs along the face of the building. This time as he passed the canopied entrance, there was no one in the vestibule. He looked up and down the street and saw only one woman halfway up the block pushing a baby carriage. It was time to go in.

He turned back to the stairs leading to a basement entrance at one end of the building. A child's bike was chained to the chipped, white iron railing lining the sides of the stairwell. He descended the concrete steps and put his ear to the graffiti-stained metal door. No sounds came from the basement laundry room. He had chosen this way in because he figured no one would be doing laundry this early in the morning. It took him only seconds to pick the crude lock and enter the dimly lit room. He went through the open inner door that led to a narrow central courtyard surrounded by tall, weathered brick ells. Fire escapes leading from the upper-story apartments spiderwebbed the wings of the building.

Philippe surveyed the windows overlooking the courtyard. He

was relieved most of the blinds and drapes were still closed and that no one was peering out of the few that were open. His navy Windbreaker, khaki pants, and black case would give any wandering eyes the impression he was doing routine maintenance. He located his target fourth-floor apartment, grabbed a trash barrel, turned it upside down and stood on it, pulled down the fire escape ladder, and climbed up to the window.

Philippe took a cordless Dremel tool out of his jacket pocket, drilled the spiral cutting bit around each screw holding the inside window latch in place, and poked out the screws. He lifted the window and crawled inside. He wasn't worried anyone was in the apartment. The tenant lived alone, and right now she was in an emergency room being patched up for a bullet wound to the shoulder. He lowered the window, squeezed a generous amount of Super Glue Gel onto each screw, and inserted them back through the latch into the window frame. When he was finished, he'd leave through the front door, which would lock behind him. From the inside, there'd be no evidence of a break-in.

He twisted his Mini Maglite to a narrow beam and shined it down the hall. A colorful painting on tin shimmered in the flashlight's glow. It was a strange, almost primitive oil, depicting what he first thought might be a costumed merrymaker at a Mardi Gras parade. When he aimed the light on the artist's signature, he saw an inscription identifying the piece as *The Virgin of Guadalupe*. During a quick check of the apartment, he noticed a number of sculptures, paintings, and mounted fabrics that appeared to be from Mexico and Central and South America. The beautiful blond religious professor must have spent a lot of time south of the border.

Philippe checked the drawers and cabinets in each room. The apartment was immaculate and orderly almost to the point of obsession. He discovered what he was looking for in her study— two file cabinets, a computer, and a desk drawer filled with carefully labeled folders of research notes. He was sure the black Dell computer held the primary object of his search, the data files for *The Jesus Fraud*.

While he waited for the computer to boot up, Philippe sorted through the file folders and took digital photos of pertinent pages and notes listing source names and addresses. He then checked the hard drive and breathed a sigh of relief when he saw that the contents of the entire drive would fit on one of his flash drives.

He connected a portable Microdrive to the USB port and downloaded the contents of her hard drive. Then he shut down the computer and packed his equipment back into his case.

After double-checking that he hadn't missed anything and that everything was back in place, Philippe left the apartment building. He headed for the airport and his flight to Monte Carlo and a $200,000 cash bonus. Not a bad payday for three days' work. He found it odd that his paymasters just wanted Hamar wounded. If they wanted her out of the picture, it would have been a lot easier to put a bullet right through her heart.

TEN

—

When Father Romano entered his office, two pairs of eyes locked on to him as he walked to his desk and plunked into his chair.

"Well?" Charlie and Carlota asked in unison.

"I guess I flunked Interrogation 101."

"Don't tell us you didn't even get to talk to her." Charlie gave Romano a puzzled look.

"No, I did talk to her." Romano looked down at his desk and slowly shook his head from side to side. He looked at his grad assistants and grinned. "She even admitted she had read some of my books. I believe 'enlightening, but doggedly following the bureaucratic Church line' sums up her review."

Carlota shrugged. "For someone quite left of center, I'd say that sounds like a compliment."

"Unfortunately it went downhill from there. When I asked her what she was doing at Grand Central Station and if she knew of any connection between us other than being professors in religion departments, she basically sent me packing. Said she's writing a book that could harm the Church and I'm a priest with ties to the Vatican."

The phone rang before Charlie or Carlota could respond. Charlie grabbed the receiver. "Professor Romano's office." He shot a serious glance to Romano. "One moment, please, Father." Then he clamped his hand over the mouthpiece. "It's a Father Sheldon from the Pennsylvania Jesuit center. Says it's urgent."

Romano took the receiver from Charlie. "Bill, what can I do for you?"

"Joseph, could you come to Wernersville right away?"

"Please don't tell me something happened to Ted."

"I'm sorry, Joseph. Ted passed away. We just found his body."

Romano felt a wave of nausea sweep through him. He swallowed hard before replying. "I'll be there in a few hours. Was it his heart? I spoke to him last week. He sounded great."

There was a pause on the other end of the line. "He had been fine. We're . . . we're not sure of the exact cause of death. The coroner's on the way."

"I'll be there as quickly as I can."

"There's something else, Joseph." There was another pause, then Father Sheldon continued, "The police are also on the way. I think you'll want to see for yourself. I don't know how to even begin to explain it. We think his death may not have been from natural causes."

ELEVEN

BRITT FELT HER LIFE WAS STARTING TO UNRAVEL again just when she thought she had regained at least a semblance of control. She couldn't believe someone had tried to kill her. The only plausible theory that made a shred of sense was that it was related to her book. It all started when she announced in the interview that her book analyzed the possibility of a bloodline of Jesus. And that threatened only one group, Christian Churches, especially the all-powerful Roman Catholic Church. But even she didn't think the Vatican would resort to murder. That left an untold number of religious fanatics who might think they were doing God's work.

She sure as hell had experienced her share of confusion during the research for the book. She uncovered countless fringe groups that laid claim to bizarre theories of bloodlines, cults, clandestine organizations, and ancient secrets. The frustration had come when she tried to find sufficient evidence to support or discredit their claims. The Internet had brought a new dimension to her research, but unfortunately the easy access to good data had also brought with it a wellspring of bad.

The interviews with the two Jesuits had proven to be just as confusing. *The Messenger* had identified them as having direct knowledge of *Le Serpent Rouge*. He had warned her they wouldn't volunteer information. She'd have to carefully draw them into providing bits and pieces she could use to support her theories. He also provided a code word for each of them, the names of archangels. The first was Uriel, meaning fire of God and watcher over the world and lowest part of hell. The second was Raphael, God's healer or helper. He assured her the names would trigger definite responses. But she should only use them as a last resort.

Father Juan Matteo had been very evasive. The Spanish priest had spoken in a low monotone with an even cadence that punctuated each word. But those eyes. She'd never forget his eyes. The irises were so dark they merged with his pupils into large black orbs. She asked how he thought a bloodline of Jesus would affect the Church. He told her it was a moot question, since there was no bloodline of Christ. When she said she found numerous historical references to a bloodline, he accused her of heresy. That's when she asked him how Uriel would respond to that question.

She couldn't tell whether it was fear or rage but his eyes bore straight into her with an intensity that caused her to tremble. He stared at her for what felt like an eternity, stroked the large cross that hung around his neck. The cross—she pictured it clear as day. It was the same cross Romano wore. She was certain the Jesuits didn't have any specific dress code or cross common to the order.

Britt rubbed her hand across her forehead and closed her eyes. She tried to remember last night. The priest she had dinner with wasn't wearing a cross, unless it was under his shirt. And he was nothing like Father Matteo. He was extremely pleasant and answered her questions like a professor to a student. When she brought up a bloodline, he gave her a good-natured smile and stressed that man was blessed with a creative mind. An unfortunate by-product of that creativity was a torrent of theories about everything and everyone. He also reminded her not to forget that faith was the real glue that held Christianity together.

But even Father Ted Mathews had seemed stunned when she mentioned Raphael.

TWELVE

FATHER ROMANO WAS STILL IN SHOCK AS HE DROVE along Interstate 78 into Pennsylvania. Ted had always been so full of life, one of those guys who never got sick. High blood pressure, but he was on medication. Romano couldn't accept that Ted was dead. And the final shocker—that Ted may not have died from natural causes. Bill wouldn't elaborate on the phone.

Trees flashed past the car. Romano glanced at the speedometer. Ninety. He eased off the gas pedal. He wanted to get there as soon as possible, but it was too late now. Ted was gone.

Romano turned off the interstate at the Hamburg exit and headed down Highway 61. He could almost drive the route on autopilot. He had visited Ted so often he lost count, and the Jesuit center was also a place where he could reflect, focus, get his head on straight. The former novitiate was perched on a magnificent forested crest surrounded by rolling hills and lush meadows. The air was fresh, clean, invigorating. In the early morning and late afternoon, sunlight filtered through the foliage of grand old oaks, pines, and maples, dappling the buildings and grounds in shades of gold.

Ted's words of wisdom and the tranquility of the center had pulled Romano through some rough bouts of depression. They always grew out of guilt for resenting his mother. He was a priest entrusted with the sacred duty to forgive the transgressions of others, yet deep in his heart he couldn't even forgive her. Sometimes he doubted his worthiness to be a priest. He feared he entered the priesthood as retribution against his mother rather than from a true desire to follow a higher calling.

Father Ted knew the right words to quell Romano's anxiety, his fears. *It's natural to have doubts. What you're experiencing is guilt about your feelings. That in itself shows you care. You can't change what happened or your response. There was a wound.*

Wounds take time to heal. You're in the healing process. That's forgiveness. Romano always found something in Ted's words, maybe only a thought, but something that started his climb out of depression. Now there'd be no new words to help him through tough times. The sounding board for his research and the shoulder to rely on when hit with new challenges, like today's shooting, was gone forever. He was on his own.

When Romano arrived at the center, two police cars were parked at the top of the curved drive. He pulled in behind them and bounded up the steps two at a time. He shoved open the large entrance door and rushed up to Ted's floor. When he got to the hall, he saw a police officer in front of Ted's door, surrounded by a group of priests.

"Joseph." Bill Sheldon emerged from the group and reached out his hand. "I'm so sorry."

Romano grabbed Sheldon's hand and pulled him into an embrace. "I came as quickly as I could. Dear God, what happened?"

The men hugged for a moment, then Sheldon leaned his head back and sighed. "Take a look for yourself." He put a hand on Romano's shoulder and guided him to the door. The other priests stepped aside, offering condolences.

Sheldon opened the door. Inside, another uniformed officer was talking on a cell phone.

"Just a sec," the officer said. He held up a cautioning finger. "Please, Father, don't disturb the body or touch anything in the bedroom. I'm on with the FBI. Agents from New York will be here shortly."

"The FBI? I don't understand," Sheldon said.

The officer looked up. "They'll brief you when they get here."

Romano walked to the open bedroom door. Ted was lying on his bed wearing only boxer shorts. At first glance, he looked so serene. He was perfectly positioned on the center of the bed, hands folded across his chest in prayer. His body was covered with a mass of kinky salt-and-pepper hair matching his closely cropped head and bushy goatee. But the unnatural pallor of death had replaced his normal ruddy complexion.

When Romano focused on Ted's hands, pain stabbed his gut and sent waves down his legs.

Dark red holes punctured Ted's wrists. And his feet. A slash pierced his side. And not a drop of blood stained the pale green blanket.

Romano stared dumbfounded at his mentor. It was as though the sound was suddenly shut off during a movie and one frame locked onto the screen.

A hand suddenly grabbed Romano's shoulder. "Joseph, Joseph, I'm sorry." Sheldon was by his side.

The officer stepped in front of the priests. "Unfortunately, Fathers, we can't allow anyone in the room until the FBI specialists process the scene."

Romano closed his eyes and said a silent prayer for Ted. Then he turned to Sheldon. "What happened? Do you have any idea?"

Sheldon motioned toward the hallway. "Let's go to my office. There's not much more to say. You've seen what we have."

When they settled into the office, Sheldon shrugged his shoulders. "I have no idea," he said, shaking his head. "Ted went out to dinner last evening. When he returned, he was seen going into his room alone. No one heard a thing all night. I checked on him this morning when he didn't show up at breakfast. You saw what I found. The local police and the coroner couldn't determine any obvious cause of death. The coroner thinks the wounds were made after his heart stopped beating. But he thinks, even then, there'd be some evidence of blood on the blanket. They're totally baffled. I don't know what to think."

Two knocks and the office door opened just enough for a woman to stick her head inside. "Two FBI agents here to see you, Father."

Sheldon slid back his chair and stood. "Please, send them in."

The woman leaned in, opening the door farther as two men in gray suits edged by her. The lead agent was lanky, with a large nose featuring a slight hump that could have been the result of a fight gone bad. He had thick, dark, wavy hair and sparse eyebrows mottled with wisps of gray. His weathered skin had a leatherlike patina. "I'm Agent Tom Cutler," he said, then motioned toward the younger man with him. "This is Agent Brian Donahue."

The second agent nodded. He was taller and well-groomed with quick and friendly blue eyes. His tailored suit emphasized time spent in the gym. He looked like the pressure of the job hadn't yet taken its toll as it had on his partner.

"I'm Father William Sheldon, spiritual director here at the Jesuit Center for Spiritual Growth. This is Father Joseph Romano. He's from your neck of the woods. He's a professor at Fordham and was very close with Father Mathews."

Romano stood and shook hands with the agents. "Do you have any idea how Father Mathews died?"

Agent Cutler shook his head. "There's no obvious physical injury that could have caused his death. The wound in his side was superficial and most likely made postmortem."

"Please, have a seat." Sheldon pointed to the two chairs facing his desk.

The agents sat down and Romano slid another chair up to the desk and joined them.

"I'm afraid we'll have to wait for the results of an autopsy to determine the specific cause of death," Cutler continued.

"I don't understand why the FBI is here," Romano said.

"Two days ago another priest was found dead in Bilbao, Spain, under similar circumstances," Cutler replied. "The authorities there determined he met with someone from New York the day he died. In his notes from that meeting was a reference to Father Ted Mathews. We were following up when we called the center and heard of Father Mathews's death. Do either of you know if he knew Father Juan Matteo?"

Sheldon pursed his lips for a second then shook his head.

"I've heard mention of Father Matteo," Romano said. "Father Mathews may have studied with him in Innsbruck many years ago."

"Father Ted was originally from Switzerland," Sheldon added. "He came to the States sometime in the fifties."

Agent Donahue paused from taking notes. "Was he a U.S. citizen?"

Sheldon nodded. "Since the early sixties."

Donahue jotted in his pad, then looked at both priests. "Do either of you have any idea of what may have happened to Father Mathews?"

Romano glanced over at Sheldon. Both priests looked bewildered.

Sheldon shook his head. "I have no idea what may have happened. No one here heard or saw anything out of the ordinary."

"And there's no reason why anyone would want to kill Father Mathews," Romano added.

Cutler cleared his throat. "Do either of you have any opinion on the stigmata?"

The office got very quiet. Sheldon and Romano looked hesitantly at each other. Finally Sheldon raised an eyebrow and said,

"I'll defer that question to Father Romano. He's the academician."

Now it was Romano's turn to clear his throat. "As Jesuits, we certainly are not looked upon as coming from the solid right of the Roman Catholic Church. We've been known to be the doubting Thomases when it comes to the more esoteric elements of Church dogma or the area of miracles."

"Are you saying you don't believe in the stigmata?" Donahue asked.

"I wouldn't go that far," Romano said. "Let's say that I have never seen the stigmata and don't personally know of anyone who has. That doesn't mean they don't exist. St. Francis of Assisi was the first example of the miraculous infliction of stigmata. In 1224 while fasting for forty days at a mountain retreat, St. Francis beheld a man in the embodiment of a seraph, a six-winged angel, come toward him from the heavens. His arms were extended and his feet conjoined, and his body was fixed to a cross. Two wings were raised above his head, two were extended as in flight, and two covered the whole body. As the vision disappeared, it left St. Francis marked with the stigmata, the five wounds of Christ. Hands, feet, and side."

Cutler looked skeptically at Donahue. "Is there any scientific explanation for the marks?" he asked Romano.

"From the fourteenth to the twentieth century, more than three hundred persons were identified as having been stigmatized. Many claimed to have experienced periodic bloody sweats. Some scientists maintain the phenomenon could be produced by a red glandular liquid, not blood, oozing from the body. Overactive imagination. Autosuggestion. There are many theories. But there has been no solid scientific evidence to prove or disprove the phenomenon. It's important to note that the Church has never authenticated a stigmatic while he or she was still alive."

Donahue looked up from his notepad. "Father Mathews has wounds on his wrists. In every picture and sculpture I can recall, Christ is nailed to the cross through his hands. Should we assume . . ." Donahue glanced at Cutler. "That is, if we determine Father Mathews didn't die of natural causes, that whoever caused his death was not very familiar with Christianity?"

"To the contrary," Romano replied. "Early artists interpreted reports that spikes were driven through Christ's hands and feet literally to mean through the palms of his hands. In the language of the day, the wrists were considered part of the hand. If the spikes had been driven through his palms, his weight would have caused the skin to tear and he would have fallen off the cross. The spikes went through the wrists where the median nerve runs. This largest nerve going out of the hand would have been crushed by the spike, causing extreme pain. This unbearable pain was literally beyond words to describe. They actually invented a new word, excruciating, to describe it, which comes from the Latin *ex*, meaning out of, and *cruciare*, meaning cross."

The agents appeared engrossed by Romano's explanation. "Then I would assume that if someone inflicted the wounds, that person would be well versed in religion?" Cutler asked.

Romano nodded. "I'd say that's a safe assumption."

"Is there any reason someone may have marked Father Mathews after his death?" Cutler looked at both priests. "You know, as a symbol or to give him special religious significance."

"I can't think of any reason," Sheldon replied. "Our priests are rational, stable men, dedicated to the Church. What you're suggesting would require someone who had severe delusions. I can assure you there's no one fitting that description at this center."

"Father Romano, do you know of anyone who might want to hurt Father Mathews?"

Romano shook his head. "These priests have devoted the greater part of their lives to the service of God and the Church. I doubt if anyone here would be capable of something like that. Father Mathews was a leader. Everyone respected him. Came to him for advice."

"What about the lay staff? The people participating in the retreat?" Cutler asked.

"The staff all adored Father Mathews. He was the kind of man everyone looked up to," Sheldon said. "As for the members of the retreat, they're usually very religious people looking for direction to enhance their spiritual lives."

"How well do you know the people at this retreat?"

"Some have been here before. Some are first-timers."

"Could you provide us a list of the people at the center last night and today?"

Sheldon stood. "Let's go to the main office. They'll give you a roster of the current participants and a list of staff."

"If you don't have any more questions, I have some calls to make." Romano held out a business card to Agent Donahue. "You can reach me at the university. I should let some people know about Father Mathews's death."

Cutler took a card out of his jacket pocket and handed it to Romano. "Thank you, Father. We'll give you a call if we need anything more. And if you think of something, no matter how trivial it might seem, please, call us."

The agents followed Sheldon out of the office, leaving Romano staring out the window at the sunlight flashing through the trees and thoughts flickering through his mind. Thoughts of death . . . murder . . . stigmata.

THIRTEEN

THE PHONE RANG ONCE, TWICE. AFTER THE THIRD ring, Romano was about to hang up when he heard, "Good afternoon, the Regina Romano residence." The voice was that of Victoria, his mother's live-in maid of ten years.

"Victoria, this is Joseph. Is my mother available?"

"Father Romano, it's great hearing your voice. Please hold while I check."

Romano heard the click followed by silence. His mother was probably standing right next to Victoria. She insisted the maid put the phone on hold when she announced who was calling so she could decide whether to grace the caller.

"Joseph, I'm surprised. It's not my birthday. What's the special occasion?"

Romano took an extra breath to quell his sudden surge in blood pressure. He should have waited until he was back in Manhattan to personally bring her the sad news. She could get quite emotional, and Ted had been like a brother to her. And he had also been the only stable link between mother and son after the incident with Marta's family.

"Joseph, why are you calling? Something happened, didn't it?"

"I've got some bad news. Ted passed away. I'm at the—"

"Oh my God. Oh my God. I spoke with him last week. How? Why? No! No! No!"

Romano could hear her gasping for breath. He knew Victoria would calm her down. "I'm at the center. We're not sure how he died. There'll be an autopsy."

"Autopsy?" His mother let out a shriek. "God, please spare my son."

"Mother, calm down. I know you're upset."

"No, you don't. You don't understand. You can't." Her voice switched from hysteria to an almost controlled anger.

"What do you mean?"

"Joseph. Joseph. Promise me." Another loud outburst. "Promise me." Regina was back in hysteria mode. "Pray to God. Pray to God. Your safety. God, don't take my son."

"Mother, get control of yourself. I'm not in any danger. Ted is dead. I'm as crushed as you are. He would want us to celebrate his life, not get hysterical over his death."

Romano heard his mother's gasping slow, then stop. He waited for a response. He knew his boundaries with her, and he was perilously close.

After a long pause Regina let out a low moan. "When is the funeral?"

"Don't worry, I'll take you to the service. It may take them a week to complete the arrangements. There's the autopsy, and many priests will be coming from great distances. I'll let you know as soon as things are finalized."

There was another pause. Then Regina said, "Let me know as soon as you find out how he died."

"Don't worry. He didn't suffer. It looked as though he died peacefully while he was praying." Romano wasn't about to bring up the stigmata or the FBI.

"I'm relieved. I'll wait for your call. Be careful."

Romano heard a click. As usual, his mother had the last word.

FOURTEEN

FATHER ROMANO PULLED THE SEAT BELT ACROSS his chest and snapped it into place. He wasn't looking forward to the drive back to New York. He was still shaken by Ted's death. Crime scene investigators had taken the body away for autopsy. He and Father Sheldon had contacted the father rector and started the arrangements for the funeral service and burial. They agreed the service should take place at the center, where Ted had spent his last twenty years.

Before Romano could turn the key, he heard his name. He looked out the window and saw Father Sheldon waving an envelope as he hurried across the grassy embankment toward the car. The director's thick chest and ample waistline reduced his effort to jog to more of a waddle. During his tenure at Wernersville, Sheldon had grown too attached to the rich Pennsylvania Dutch cooking and too detached from the small gym in the basement of the center.

Romano lowered the window. "Take your time, Bill. What's the rush?"

Sheldon was huffing when he got to the car. He leaned against the roof and took a few deep breaths before handing the envelope to Romano. "I was afraid you'd driven off. Sorry, Joseph, with all the commotion, I totally forgot. Shortly after you entered the priesthood, Ted gave me this envelope. Told me that upon his death I was to give it to you. He gave me the impression it had something to do with your family. He never went into details, and I didn't ask."

Written in bold calligraphy across the front of the envelope was "Joseph Romano, SJ—Personal and Confidential." On the back was a bright red seal imprinted with a symbol resembling the steel cross Ted had given him after he took his final vows. Romano stared at the seal. He had never seen Ted use or even mention something like that in all the years he'd known him. The letter looked awfully important. He was about to tear it open, but hesitated. Maybe it contained something Ted wanted kept confidential.

Romano slipped the envelope into his jacket pocket. "Thanks, Bill. I'm Ted's executor. It's probably instructions for notifying distant relatives back in Europe." He started the car, then reached out the window and squeezed Sheldon's hand. "Bill, I really appreciate all you've done. Please let me know the moment you find out what happened to Ted. I'll keep in touch with the FBI and let you know if I hear anything."

Sheldon's jaw slackened, blending his face and neck into one thick mass. His eyes dissolved into a blank stare. "Joseph, I know you're the skeptic when it comes to things like this, but . . ." He paused, then his mouth turned up slightly into a cautionary smile. "Ted was the very ideal of the priesthood. Of our order. His ability to focus in prayer was remarkable. Do you think? Is there any possibility that those marks were caused by some religious or mental phenomenon?"

Romano shook his head. "You're right about my skepticism relating to miracles or unexplainable phenomenon. When it comes to Ted, I'd say very little is impossible. But I'd have to put stigmata into the realm of highly improbable." Romano smiled at Sheldon. "Let's just say we'll be in a better position to delve into that subject when we have the results of the autopsy."

Romano slid the gearshift into drive and slowly pulled away from Sheldon while waving good-bye. He headed down the curved lane, out of sight of the main buildings. When he got to the iron gates at the entrance to the center, he pulled off to the side and carefully opened the envelope. Inside was a two-page handwritten letter. It began with a poignant thank-you to Romano for allowing Ted to become a part of his life. Then Ted devoted half a page to urging him to repair his relationship with his mother, if he hadn't already done so. He alluded to Romano's mother having only his best interests in mind and referred to factors outside her control that someday he hoped Romano would understand.

Then the letter abruptly switched to Romano's father. Ted had written that they had been more than friends. Their relationship had gone much deeper than that. There had been a lot more to his father than he could have appreciated up to the tender age of twelve. *I pray that the day will come when you will be blessed with the knowledge of your father's good deeds. God works in mysterious ways, but is wondrous to perform.*

The letter then concluded with instructions to contact Scottish Father Nathan Sinclair, SJ, who was also a close associate of his father and Ted. He was urged to use Father Sinclair as a mentor and confidant in the same way he had with Ted. *Do not hesitate to share anything with Father Sinclair. I have kept him up to date on all your accomplishments as well as your value to the Church as a priest and outstanding researcher and educator. Notify him immediately of my death. When he comes to my service, the two of you can begin your adventure where ours left off. May the Lord bless you, and keep you. May the Lord make his face shine upon you, and be gracious unto you. May the Lord lift up his countenance upon you, and give you peace. This I ask in the name of the Father, the Son, and the Holy Spirit.*

It was signed with the bold strokes of Ted's signature and what looked like a teardrop-shaped stain. A stain that Romano realized could be—blood.

FIFTEEN

FBI agent Tom Cutler finished entering the notes on Father Ted Mathews's death into his laptop and checked his latest e-mails. Brian Donahue's eyes were riveted on the road ahead as he kept the bureau car well above the speed limit on their ride back to New York.

Cutler shut down his computer and glanced over at Donahue. "Brian, are you a good Catholic?"

Donahue jerked his head toward Cutler. "Whoa—what brought that up? Are you a little spooked by the dead priests?"

"Nah. We've seen our share of dead bodies under worse conditions than this one. It's just the whole religious angle that concerns me. This could be a tough case to crack." Cutler groaned. "If there is a Church connection, we'll have our work cut out for us."

"How so?"

Cutler raked his fingers through his hair. He couldn't recall when he had picked up the habit; he rationalized it might stimulate brain cells. At least it distracted the other person so he could organize his response. In this case, he knew his partner well enough that he could be frank about his feelings concerning the Church. "If there's any hint of someone involved from inside the Church, they'll close ranks. Just look at their track record."

"I see your point."

"Brian, I know you're a Catholic. I was just wondering if you're tight with any priests."

Donahue chuckled. "I'm probably not your good Catholic. I'm an okay Catholic. I go to church on all the right holidays, but I'm usually out too late on Saturday nights to show up as a regular on Sunday. The priest wouldn't even know my name. To him I'm a nod and handshake parishioner."

"I guess that's what I get for having a young stud for a partner.

Maggie and I are Lutherans of about the same level as you. If we had kids, we'd probably be more involved." Cutler flipped open his cell phone. "I'm gonna call the office. The bureau must have someone we can consult on Church policy."

"What's bugging you?"

"The latest info I just got from Interpol on the Spanish priest. The crime scene was identical to Wernersville. Priest found in his room positioned on his bed in his underwear with the stigmata. Even down to the wounds in the wrists."

"Then we've probably got the same killer. Or at least some weird conspiracy."

"They promised autopsy results later today or first thing to-morrow."

"That should be the clincher," Donahue said.

This time Cutler raked both hands through his hair, then gave his partner a puzzled glance. "What do we do if the deaths of those priests are determined to be from natural causes?"

SIXTEEN

GABRIEL SETTLED BACK INTO THE PLUSH SEAT as the jet leveled off and headed for New Orleans. He deserved first-class accommodations. After all, he was on a religious quest destined to save the sanctity of the Church for the final phase of Christianity—the Second Coming. How could those fools think they could control destiny. Only God would determine when, where, and how. And it was clear in the Gospels that the Son of Man would be seen coming through the clouds of heaven with great power and glory. Not from some human sham here on earth.

Gabriel would succeed where Pope Clement V had failed on Friday, October 13, 1307, when the soldiers of King Philip the Fair of France opened their sealed instructions and arrested many of the Knights Templar throughout Europe. Unfortunately the Pope failed to capture the secret protected by the Knights Templar. Many Templars were killed and the order was discredited, but the secret survived.

The FASTEN SEAT BELT sign blinked off. Gabriel unsnapped his belt, reclined his seat, and let his eyes drift closed. He knew he wouldn't fail. After all, he himself was a key part of the secret that threatened the sanctity of the Church. It was only a matter of time and the clock was ticking down.

He mused about the irony of using Britt in his quest to save Christianity. In a way he felt saddened by what she had been through. But it really didn't matter. And it didn't justify her response. She had lost her faith, doubted her religion, and was writing her heretical book, *The Jesus Fraud*. If only Britt knew how close she was to the truth—figuratively and literally.

SEVENTEEN

FATHER ROMANO TURNED OFF FIFTY-SIXTH STREET just before Sixth Avenue and pulled up to the gate next to the America House. The huge sign left little room for error: PRIVATE DRIVEWAY, DO NOT BLOCK, ACTIVE 24 HOURS. He unlocked the gate, parked the black Chevy belonging to the order in the reserved space, and started unloading cartons and suitcases.

He had gone from Wernersville directly to the Rose Hill Campus in the Bronx to pick up the first load of his belongings. It was almost as if Ted had planned his death for the day Romano had reserved the car for his move to the Fifty-sixth Street Jesuit residence. The thought caused him to shudder. What if Ted did plan his death? Impossible. Ted had a zest for life. What about the priest in Spain? And the stigmata? Today's mind-boggling explosion of events left Romano with questions and no answers.

The America House was only a few blocks from Romano's office. He'd been commuting from the Bronx for two months since he had become chair of the new Fordham Lincoln Center Department of Religion. He'd been a little apprehensive of the move. He wasn't eager to have to adjust to spending full-time in the fast-paced, noisy Manhattan scene. Most evenings he looked forward to returning to the peace and quiet of the main Rose Hill Campus after a hectic day in Manhattan. Now he'd have to rely on his collection of contemporary and New Age CDs to help him unwind. He hoped the soft piano melodies of David Benoit and Jim Brickman and his Bose headphones could compete with the Manhattan traffic.

Romano lugged his bags and cartons up to his new living quarters. He plugged in his laptop and checked his e-mails. There was a streaming video message from Father Dante Cristoforo, the assistant to the father general in Rome. When he clicked on the link, a video image of Father Cristoforo sitting at his desk at the Vatican dressed in his typical all black filled the screen.

A few of the Jesuit professors at the university joked that Cristoforo had his sights set on being father general someday so he could rekindle the concept of the Black Pope. Two hundred years after Saint Ignatius of Loyola had created the Society of Jesus, the ordinary people of Rome referred to the Jesuit father general as the Black Pope, comparing his power to that of the Pope himself. The reference was based on the all-black cassocks worn by the Jesuits in comparison to the all-white robes of the Pope. In 1773 Pope Clement the XIV abolished the Society of Jesus, disbanded the twenty-three thousand Jesuits, and put the father general and his advisors into papal dungeons. It wasn't until 1814 that Pope Pius VII resurrected the order. Since then the Jesuits hadn't shed their cloak of controversy, but they had been careful not to come into direct conflict with the papacy.

Cristoforo's somber face gazed from the screen. His hands were folded on top of his massive desk. *Father Romano, I was so sorry to hear of Father Mathews's death. I know he was a close personal friend. As you may be aware, a second priest, Father Juan Matteo, died under similar circumstances in Bilbao, Spain, only a few days ago. I want to assure you that the Vatican will do everything in its power to find the causes of these deaths. Please e-mail me any information that could assist us in getting to the bottom of these tragic events. My thoughts and prayers go out to you.* With that the screen went blank.

Romano was puzzled by Cristoforo's request. What information could the Vatican think he might have? He sent a response to Cristoforo, assuring him that he would provide the father general's office with any information that could help with their investigation. He included the names and contact numbers of the two New York FBI agents who were on the scene at Wernersville.

Romano then did a Google search on Brittany Hamar. She was a professor at Hunter College teaching Modern Theories in Religion and Faith and Disbelief. There were references to two books she'd written on Christian origins, as well as notations about her numerous articles on New Testament exegesis. The latest Internet postings referred to her comments on the news program about her upcoming book, *The Jesus Fraud,* supposedly supporting a bloodline of Christ. He wondered what set her off in that dubious direction. His years of research showed no solid, or even reasonably shaky, ground for a bloodline theory—only rank speculation.

Romano tried to think of what could possibly link him to Britt. Someone, somehow must have connected them. But why? The only obvious common denominator was their religious research and publishing relating to the New Testament. If anything, the book he was working on now would probably contradict Britt's book. And he was just getting started. His book wouldn't be finished for at least another year or two, and it sounded like hers was in its final stages. It didn't make any sense.

So far the only solid evidence was the anonymous telephone call concerning the James Gospel. It had to have been from the shooter. Maybe the police would be able to track the caller? Romano doubted it. Whoever targeted Britt for execution had it planned down to split-second timing. The shooter wouldn't call from a traceable phone. It all revolved around why someone would want to kill Britt and frame him. He decided the answer must be linked to her book. He needed to find out more about Brittany Hamar—and *The Jesus Fraud*.

EIGHTEEN

"BRIAN, YOU WON'T BELIEVE THIS," TOM CUTLER shouted to his partner. He almost couldn't believe the results of his computer search. He hit Print to get a hard copy of the report.

"What'd you find?" Brian Donahue asked as he rushed into Cutler's office.

"I'm glad we stuck around to get the latest from Interpol." Cutler pulled the first two sheets from the printer and handed them to Donahue. "The woman who visited the Spanish priest the night before his body was found has been a busy lady. And that's not all."

Donahue scanned the report. "She's from right here in Manhattan. It'll be interesting to find out where she was last night."

Cutler handed Donahue another sheet. "We sure as hell know where she was this morning."

Donahue looked down at the sheet, then up at Cutler. "This is a police report from Metro."

"Check the name of the victim."

Donahue held a page in each hand, glancing back and forth. His eyes widened. "You gotta be kidding. The woman who visited the Spanish priest was shot in Grand Central this morning?"

"That's what it says." Cutler handed him another sheet. "Check the witness list."

Donahue scanned the list, then looked up at his partner in stunned silence.

"That's right." Cutler cocked his head and grinned. "Father Joseph Romano. The same priest we met today in P-A. Now don't try and tell me that's a coincidence."

NINETEEN

BRITTANY HAMAR STEPPED THROUGH THE HOSPI-
tal door and took a deep breath when she saw the first glint of
sunlight across the tops of the buildings. She hadn't wasted any
time checking out of Bellevue. She wasn't a fan of hospitals, especially when she was the patient. She adjusted the sling on her
left arm, then raised and lowered the arm a few times. The pain
was negligible. The doctor had said she could get back to most of
her normal activities immediately as long as they didn't include
extreme movement of her shoulder. He did recommend that she
hold off working out with weights at the gym for a few weeks.
She'd probably ditch the sling before the day was over.

She headed to First Avenue to flag down a taxi, but when she
got there she decided to walk to her apartment. She needed the
exercise. She'd been on her back for almost twenty-four hours.
As she started walking, she took in the early-morning sounds of
the city. Revving engines, squealing brakes, beeping horns, people shouting into cell phones. Manhattan was anything but bor-
ing. The noises helped block out the thoughts that had rampaged
through her mind while she was stuck in the hospital. Especially
the nagging fear that whoever had shot her might try to finish the
job.

By the time Britt reached Sixth Avenue, she was feeling her
old self again. She hurried along the last block to her apartment
building and was relieved the elevator was on the ground floor.
When she got into her apartment, the first thing she did was flip
the power switch on her computer. While it booted, she kicked
off her shoes and took off the clothes she had been wearing when
she was shot and the knit top she bought at the hospital gift shop
to replace the one with the bullet hole. She changed into gray
slacks and a pale blue cotton blouse.

Britt sat in front of her computer, pulled out the keyboard

drawer, and reached for her mouse. She fumbled at first, then realized the mouse wasn't on the mouse pad on the right side of her desk. She glanced down and saw it directly in front of the monitor stand. She grabbed the mouse and opened the research folder on *The Jesus Fraud,* then scrolled to the file containing the notes on the message she received from the mysterious caller. There it was. She had even highlighted the note in bold. The voice of the caller who told her to meet him at Grand Central Terminal seemed different from that of *The Messenger,* who provided the manuscript fragment. She had noted that he never referenced the previous calls, was very abrupt, and hung up before she could respond.

As Britt scanned through her computer files, she was nagged by the thought of the mouse not being on the pad. *What if someone accessed her computer while she was in the hospital?* She remembered checking her e-mails before she left for Grand Central. She was right-handed and always left the mouse on the pad. She began to panic. She checked her doors and windows and found no sign of a break-in. There was even a ten-dollar bill still lying in a decorative bowl on the narrow table just inside the front door. Her jewelry was in the two cases on top of her dresser. She checked her file cabinets, then pulled open the file drawer under the desk. The files looked undisturbed.

Maybe she was being paranoid, but she had never taken the mouse off the pad. If the shooting had to do with her book, someone could have tried to destroy her manuscript. But all her files were still there. Maybe someone wanted to find out what her research had revealed. They wouldn't have found anything. All of the physical evidence was locked in her safe-deposit box. Somehow she had to find out if someone had accessed her computer. She thought of Bruce Leonard at Hunter College. He was the ultimate computer geek; he always got to work early and left late.

Britt dialed Bruce's direct line at the college. True to form, he answered before the second ring. "Bruce Leonard, computer central."

"Bruce, it's Britt Hamar."

"Britt, I thought you were on sabbatical, writing a shocker of a book."

"I am. That's sort of why I'm calling you. I need to tap the mind of the computer guru."

"Don't tell me you forgot to back up and crashed your hard drive."

"Dear God, no. I learned the backup lesson a long time ago. This may sound stupid, but I found my mouse had been moved while I was out of my apartment. I'm afraid someone has accessed my computer. I know it sounds paranoid."

"It's easy enough to check. Are you at your computer?"

"Yes."

"Let me know the version of your operating system and double-check your date and time to make sure they're accurate."

Britt gave Bruce the information, then waited while he got onto the same opening screen on his computer.

"This will be a piece of cake," Bruce said. "Your version of Windows logs application access times. Right-click My Computer, then click Manage. A window should open for Computer Management."

"Got it."

"The window has Event Viewer that offers a choice of Applications, Security, or System. Under Applications you should be able to see the Type, Date, and Time an application was accessed. Check your Startup files and you can see when they were loaded."

Britt scrolled to the files and saw that her computer was booted up while she was in the hospital.

"What did you find?" Bruce asked.

"Bruce, you're a genius, as usual. I guess I'm not just paranoid after all. Somebody was on my computer."

"Sorry to hear it. Hope they didn't delete any important files."

"No, I already checked that. But I guess they could have copied just about anything."

"Unfortunately, you're right. And I hate to be the bearer of bad news, but if they accessed your personal data, you could end up a victim of identity theft."

"That's where being lazy comes in handy," Britt replied. "I still do all my financial dealings the old-fashioned way. Snail mail."

Bruce snickered. "When you finish your vacation—sorry, I meant sabbatical—we'll have to talk about that over lunch. In the meantime, think about logging on with a password. At least until you find out who got into your computer."

"Bruce, you came through as usual. That lunch will be on me. Now I better find out who got into my apartment. Thanks again."

Britt hung up and dug her weekly appointment book out of her purse. She looked up Lieutenant Renzetti's number and was about to dial when she noticed a note about *Ordo Templi Orientalis*. The shooting had caused her to lose a day. She couldn't miss the ceremony. It might provide new information useful for her meeting with Felix in Vienna. She glanced at the lower corner of her computer monitor and saw it was only 8:32 a.m. She'd have plenty of time to get to Gramercy Park. She put the handset back in the base. This wasn't the time to have police all over her apartment; too much was riding on the next two days. She shut down her computer, went back to her bedroom, and changed clothes again. This time she dressed all in black.

TWENTY

CHARLIE AND CARLOTA STROLLED INTO FATHER Romano's office, side-by-side and half an hour early. Romano chuckled. "Have you two started choreographing your entrances?"

Carlota gave Charlie a short nod.

"I decided to do something about my tardiness." Charlie held up his cell phone. "From now on, Carlota's my punctuality meter. She calls when she heads for the office and I scramble to be in the lobby when she arrives. And we're going to alternate who gets to be first on the computer."

"Well, it's obvious the two of you are locked firmly into the digital age. You notice I don't carry a cell. I had one a few years ago but found myself controlled by the phone. I even carried it when I jogged and took calls. I finally decided my time is my time, so it had to go."

Charlie's eyes lit up with a smirk. "You know cell phones do have an off switch."

Romano shook his head and smiled. "You should know by now I'm too compulsive for that. Have you ever seen me let the answering machine take a call if I'm in the office?"

Charlie smiled. "We know that only too well."

"We're really sorry about Father Mathews." Carlota lowered her eyes. "How'd it go?"

Romano shook his head. "It was tough. He was like a father to me."

They both looked at him with pained expressions.

Romano debated how much to tell them. They were, after all, grad students at the top of their class, and his partners. Charlie had a unique combination of intellect and keen intuition, which caused him to stray beyond the normal research boundaries. Carlota was highly intelligent, well organized, and acted as a stabilizing factor for Charlie. The two were an ideal team. Romano had already decided they could be a great help in looking into the Brittany Hamar scenario, especially since he didn't know where Ted's death would lead him. He told them enough of the details to get dual wide-eyed responses as they settled into the chairs at their desk.

"The police don't have any idea what happened?" Charlie asked.

"It all depends on the outcome of the autopsy," Romano replied.

Charlie slouched in his desk chair and started rotating it slowly back and forth. "Yesterday was like right out of the *Twilight Zone*. What do you think's going on, Father?"

"There are a lot of possibilities. But I think I'll hold off on speculating until there's more solid information." Romano ran a finger across his ragged mustache. "There is one thing I can tell you at this juncture. I don't like where this is heading." He leaned toward his grad assistants. "Now, why don't you tell me what the two of you dug up yesterday while I was gone. Then I have a surprise for you."

Carlota edged her chair in front of the computer, grabbed the mouse, and scrolled through a screen of data. "We found an amazing number of references to 'possibility' scenarios for how Jesus could have survived the Crucifixion. This is the most interesting." She highlighted a paragraph on the screen.

"It's the substitution theory. Someone was crucified in place of Jesus. We found a reference to it in one of the Nag Hammadi texts. It was in a Coptic tractate called the Second Treatise of the Great Seth. It refers to a substitution of Simon the Cyrene for Jesus at the Crucifixion. The text maintains that Jesus did not die on the cross. Jesus is quoted as saying after the Crucifixion, 'As for my death—which was real enough to them—it was real to them because of their own incomprehension and blindness.' "

"Good work." Romano nodded. "The Gnostic Gospels found near Nag Hammadi in 1945 revealed a much wider range of Christian groups than we realized had existed. I definitely plan on referencing them in the book. The only problem is we don't know what true firsthand knowledge the authors had of what really happened during the time of Christ. Everything was passed down through oral tradition, which introduced a lot of bias. There were numerous comments relating to revealing mysteries and things hidden in silence in these writings. Many sayings in the collection criticize common Christian beliefs as naïve mis-understandings. They could have been the work of doubters trying to discredit the early Orthodox Christian Church. The Nag Hammadi texts and others like them were denounced as heresy by Orthodox Christians in the middle of the second century."

Romano waved a finger of caution. "Don't get me wrong. I'm not recommending you ignore those texts. I suggest only that you look for supporting materials."

Carlota scrolled to another page. "We did find a few more references." She pointed to the monitor. "The Islamic Qur'an in chapter four, entitled 'Women,' says, 'Yet they slew him not, neither crucified him, but he was represented by one in his like-ness . . . They did not really kill him.' "

"That's an important factor to add to our database," Romano replied. "But keep in mind that Islam evolved in the seventh century as a new religion and as such had to compete with existing religions. The Qur'an came to Muhammad as a series of revela-tions, some while he was alone in a cave. We'll judge it accord-ingly when we accumulate all our research."

Romano saw Carlota and Charlie exchange skeptical glances. "In all fairness," he continued, "I include material in my books using the same criteria as a court of law. Everything will be judged relative to the preponderance of evidence and preferably beyond a shadow of a doubt. And that's where you come in. I'm relying on you to bring me a balanced body of evidence."

Carlota's face seemed to relax as she scrolled to another cita-tion on the screen. "We also found second-century references from the historian Basilides of Alexandria and the Gnostic leader Mani, who wrote that the Crucifixion was manipulated to use a substitute for Jesus."

"You two are really attacking this scenario from all angles. Keep going. We want to have a full spectrum on which to base our conclusions." Romano stood behind his grad assistants and patted their shoulders. "Remember, those references come from people who were not present when Christ was crucified and resurrected. Think about your response in this day and age if you heard for the first time that someone supposedly had been resurrected and was walking freely in Manhattan, days after being executed."

Charlie threw up his hands. "You're right, Father. I'd think it was bull."

"This time, I'd probably agree with Charlie," Carlota added.

"That's why we want to look at the whole body of evidence before we jump on any bandwagon," Romano said as he returned to his desk. "I recall seeing some references that imply Simon the Cyrene was a substitute for Simon Zelotes, not for Jesus. Look into that aspect. I'm sure you'll find a lot more data on the substitution theory. Our job is to weed through the 'possibility' scenarios and determine the 'probability' that they have any merit."

"This is gonna be tough, Father." Charlie shook his head in frustration. "During our research, we also found a few ambiguities in the New Testament. In John eighteen, chapter thirty-one, Pilate said to the Sanhedrin, 'Take him yourselves, and judge him according to your law.' The Jews answered him, 'We do not have the right to execute anyone.' From what I could find, the Jews were empowered to implement the death sentence. Stoning to death was a common occurrence."

"There are many ambiguities in the Gospels," Romano replied. "Most are due to idiosyncrasies in translation. As I've said many times before, the Gospels were also originally passed on through oral tradition. Many Christians think they were actually written by Matthew, Mark, Luke, and John even though every version of the New Testament clearly states the Gospel According to Matthew, According to Mark, Luke, John."

Carlota looked up sheepishly. "I must admit I didn't realize that until I took my first course on the New Testament."

"Ditto," Charlie added.

Romano picked up a Bible from his desk. "What we are reading today went through Aramaic, Greek, and Hebrew before ending up in English. 'Sanhedrin' is a Hebraic form of a Greek word meaning a council, and refers to the elders, chief priests, and scribes who met under the high priest to decide legal and religious questions that did not pertain to Rome's interest."

Charlie looked up at Romano. "Then couldn't they have put Jesus to death?"

"Not necessarily," Romano said as he sat in his chair. "By now you know religion's not a piece of cake when it comes to validating historical information. That's probably why you chose the field. Both of you like a good challenge." Romano leaned back with his hands behind his head, imitating Charlie. "Jewish sources are not clear on the competence of the Sanhedrin in Jerusalem at this period to sentence and execute for political crimes. I'm sure the Jewish leaders were concerned about the repercussions if they killed Jesus. And, remember, the Romans were running the show. But it's an important point for us to consider. See what historical data you can find from Jewish history."

There was a knock. The door opened and a man rolled in a cart holding a Mac identical to the one Carlota was using.

"Here's the surprise." Romano beamed. "Now you won't have to keep track of who gets first crack at the computer. But"—he waved a cautionary finger in the air—"now I'll expect twice as much research output. You can start by finding out some background on Professor Hamar and *The Jesus Fraud*."

TWENTY-ONE

FBI AGENT TOM CUTLER PUT DOWN THE PHONE and focused on the computer screen. The cursor flashed. *"C'mon, damn it."* Finally the report started downloading. He looked up as Agent Donahue hurried into the office clutching a stack of files.

"What did Metro have to say?" Donahue asked.

"You thought the stigmata thing was bizarre. Wait till you see the detailed report on the Hamar shooting."

Donahue dropped the files on the corner of the desk. "Don't tell me she had the marks of the stigmata."

"No, but you're close. I just got off the phone with Lieutenant Renzetti of NYPD, who's handling the case with Metro. You won't believe how this Father Romano's involved."

Donahue plopped in one of the black-suede-and-chrome chairs in front of Cutler's desk. "Try me."

"Renzetti interviewed Father Romano in the Metro office at Grand Central. The priest had helped one of the Metro officers stabilize Hamar until the EMTs arrived. During the interview, Romano handed him a manuscript box he said someone jammed into his chest after the shooting. In it was the damn gun."

Donahue gave Cutler a bewildered look. "Did he shoot her? How the hell did he get to Wernersville?"

"Renzetti claims they're convinced he didn't. Romano's story holds up. He insists he got an anonymous call to be at the station to get some ancient manuscript. Two witnesses recall a man in the area before the shooting clutching a box, but their descriptions were definitely not of Father Romano. The guy didn't have facial hair and had on different color clothes. Romano was wearing a priest's collar and a large steel cross. Not easy to miss."

"Could Romano have been disguised when he shot her, run out, pulled it off, and returned to the scene?"

"They tested Romano for gunshot residue and powder from

surgical gloves. Both negative. They also checked all the trash
bins in the area for discarded clothes, gloves, mask. Nothing."

"Did Hamar see the shooter?" Donahue asked.

"Renzetti interviewed her in the hospital. She claims she has
no clue who shot her. Her memory's pretty hazy about the whole
thing."

"If she had anything to do with the priest deaths, this Father
Romano'd have a good motive."

Cutler shook his head. "One of the MTA officers confirms he
saw Father Romano running toward the scene only ten or twenty
seconds after the shot was fired while the crowd was still running
away."

"What if Romano had an accomplice?"

Cutler hadn't thought of an accomplice. He grabbed his ma-
roon paisley tie, yanked on it, then stuck a finger under his collar
to loosen it. This case was getting tricky. "We'll have to take a
careful look at both Father Romano and Brittany Hamar. You
check out Hamar. Maybe she's still in the hospital. I'll see what
I can get on Romano."

TWENTY-TWO

Agent Donahue spotted the red brick apartment house in the middle of the block. Air-conditioning units protruded from many of the white-framed windows scaling the front of the building. A navy canopy jutted out between white columns framing the main entrance. Two guys in jeans and T-shirts sat on the corner of the concrete front stoop, sipping from cups emblazoned with a stylized orange sun on a pea green background.

Brittany Hamar had checked out of Bellevue early that morning. Donahue hoped she had gone to her apartment and was still there. He stepped into the vestibule and located the apartment buzzers on the left-hand wall. As he scanned the row of names, the inner lobby door opened and a very attractive blonde dressed in all black strode across the black-and-white marble floor. An earthy, alluring scent filled the air as she passed Donahue. He noticed she held her left arm across her stomach.

Donahue stepped to the entrance and watched her turn up Thirteenth Street and head toward Sixth Avenue. One of the guys on the stoop let out a whistle. "That's the prof on the fourth floor. Has she gone Goth?"

The other guy craned his neck to watch her. "Doubt it, but I still wouldn't mind being in her class."

"Was that Professor Hamar?" Donahue asked.

"Yeah," one of them said. "You a friend?"

Donahue shrugged. "I know her from the college." He turned and nonchalantly followed her up the street.

Donahue was about to catch up to Hamar and question her but decided to see where she was going dressed in a look that bordered on someone headed to a costume party. Her hair was pulled back into a tight French twist held in place by a large black clip. He remembered her face when she had passed him in the lobby.

Her eyes were highlighted with black eye shadow. Her lips were
dark red, outlined in black. She wore a short, black, robelike
dress sashed at the waist, black stockings, black short boots, and
carried a black fabric bag that matched the robe.

Donahue was afraid she might flag down a taxi when she
headed up Sixth Avenue. He breathed a sigh of relief when she ignored two in-service taxis that slowed to gawk as they passed.
She turned onto Fourteenth Street, then up Irving Place, and
headed toward Gramercy Park. She stopped in front of a brownstone facing the park and looked up and down the street. Donahue wasn't sure if she was meeting someone or had become
suspicious of being followed. He'd kept his distance and was on
the opposite side of the street when he passed her and continued
on to the next corner. He glanced her way before crossing and
saw a small group dressed in similar colors of the night arrive
and head up the steps into the building. Hamar followed them inside.

By the time Donahue got to the brownstone, more people had
arrived. Most were dressed in dark clothes that could represent
evil or the somber colors of a wake. Donahue was certain this
was no wake. He didn't feel like a total outsider in his charcoal
gray suit and burgundy rep tie, so he buttoned his jacket and followed a group inside. Each person paused in the foyer, made a
strange symbol in the air with the right hand, and entered a large
room dimly lit by wall sconces and dozens of candles at the base
of an altar. The windows were covered in thick blackout drapes
and the walls were sponge-painted a faux marble in shadowy
tones of gray.

Donahue focused on the altar at the far end of the room. A
stone slab rested on a pedestal rising from the center of a three-
tiered platform. Halfway to the altar on either side of the room
were smaller pedestals, each holding an incense burner, books,
and a stone mortar and pestle. The right-hand corner behind the
altar was shrouded by layers of semi-sheer curtains. Donahue
could make out a dark rectangular shape behind them. He
couldn't tell if it was a table or a casket on a stand. He hoped it
wasn't a casket.

A center aisle separated rows of folding chairs, their backs
covered with black satin sheaths. Donahue found an aisle seat
near the back, scanned the congregation, and spotted Hamar a
few rows in front of him. He estimated there were over fifty

people in the room, but it was quiet as a tomb. No one spoke. Everyone seemed to be focused on the altar. He slid his cell phone out of his jacket pocket and switched it to vibrate. This was not the place for his cell to start playing the James Bond theme.

A chime sounded and all heads pivoted in unison to the back of the room. A tall man with Christ-like, long brown hair and closely cropped beard walked down the aisle. He wore a loose, white satin robe tied at the waist by a red sash. As he approached the altar, he crossed himself at the forehead, chest, and shoulders. Then he said something in a language that sounded to Donahue like Hebrew and traced a pentagram in the air with two raised fingers of his right hand. This guy was certainly not a priest of any order Donahue was familiar with.

When the priest reached the altar, he dramatically raised both arms, spread them wide, and intoned the names Gabriel, Michael, Raphael, and Uriel. He then recited something that reminded Donahue of a takeoff on the Nicene Creed. Donahue noticed Hamar stiffen when he said, "I believe in the Serpent and the Lion, Mystery of Mystery, in His name Baphomet." At the mention of Baphomet, Donahue noticed Hamar's head jerk.

The priest faced the congregants and another chime sounded. Everyone turned as a woman in a flowing white gown followed by a young man in a red robe came down the aisle. After receiving some sort of blessing by the priest, they parted and walked around opposite sides of the altar and headed to the draped corner of the room. The man in red pulled aside the curtains and they both entered the dark void.

The congregants stood and started to chant. Donahue couldn't understand the sounds repeated in unison over and over and over. The pulsating voices reached a crescendo that had a mesmerizing effect on Donahue. He stared at the curtains, but all he could see were dark shadows moving to the rhythm of the chant. Then the shadows seemed to mount the rectangular object.

An eerie sensation surged through Donahue. The two were either having sex or doing a damn good job of faking it. The chanting got louder and louder as the bodies throbbed to the erotic rhythm. Donahue's eyes were glued to the shadows behind the sheers and he found himself humming to the strange chant. It rose to a climax and stopped suddenly when the two forms collapsed in a heap.

Most of the congregants started hugging the people around

them and some filed out. Donahue mingled with the first group through the door. He grabbed a pamphlet from a table in the foyer and headed across the street to the park, where he could watch for Hamar to exit. He scanned the pamphlet. He had just experienced a ritual ceremony at an *Ordo Templi Orientalis* temple. He didn't know if this was an oddball religion, cult, or what.

Just then Hamar left the brownstone and started up the street in a hurry. Donahue followed her to Park Avenue South, where she hailed a cab. He jotted down the cab number. By the time he flagged a cab, hers was long gone. He called Cutler and headed back to his office at the Federal Building. It was time to check into Brittany Hamar's background and find out more about *Ordo Templi Orientalis*.

TWENTY-THREE

BRITT HAMAR RUBBED A MOIST TOWELETTE ACROSS each eyelid, grabbed another one from her purse, and scrubbed off the lipstick as the cab bobbed and weaved its way through the late-morning traffic. She couldn't wait to get back to her apartment and change out of these clothes. She felt dirty, debased by the ritual ceremony.

There must be a connection between the esoteric society and the Order of the Knights Templar. After all, the Templars were accused of worshipping the idol Baphomet. And the mention of the archangels. The Messenger had given her code words for the two priests, Uriel and Raphael. Felix had also mentioned the archangels but wouldn't tell her the exact relationship to Le Serpent Rouge. Now she might have enough information to press Felix for the details. It was all starting to fit together like the pieces of a delicate puzzle.

Britt decided she had nothing to lose. An uneasy calm drifted over her. She wasn't afraid of dying anymore. The initial fear that ravaged her after the shooting had faded, replaced by visions of Tyler and Alain. Visions that vacillated between fond memories and horrid nightmares.

Someone leaned on a horn. The picture in Britt's mind switched to an image of Father Romano's large cross, and then to the same cross on Father Juan Matteo. She needed more pieces of the puzzle to make the case for her book. She decided to change clothes and go to Fordham. In Romano's office she'd be safe, even if he were somehow involved in her shooting. Maybe he could shed some more light on the Jesuit connection.

The cab screeched to a halt in front of her apartment. The two young men were still sitting on the stoop sipping their coffees from the corner Così Café. She pulled the clip out of the French

twist and shook her hair free as she entered the apartment building.

By tonight she'd be out of the country. Whoever shot her
would have a tough time tracking her down. But that didn't
dampen the shiver of fear that slithered down her back.

TWENTY-FOUR

"SORRY I'M LATE." AGENT DONAHUE BURST INTO the MTA conference room at Grand Central. "Had to grab some new info on Brittany Hamar."

Agent Cutler waved Donahue to the seat beside him and introduced him to Lieutenant Nick Renzetti of NYPD and Lieutenant Frank Garret of the Metropolitan Transportation Authority.

"You're just in time," Cutler said. "I just brought the lieutenants up to date on the Mathews death. We should be getting the autopsy results later today. We were just starting to go over the report on the Hamar shooting."

Renzetti slid a folder to Donahue. "Here's a copy of the latest report. I just got a medical update from the doctor at Bellevue. The bullet didn't go through her shoulder. The doc says it didn't hit any bone and the penetration was only four and a half centimeters. This was a nine millimeter at close range. I don't buy it."

"Low-velocity ammo or maybe the guy loaded his own," Garret said. "You know, contract killer. Weak load. Didn't want to take anybody else out."

Cutler looked to Donahue, who rolled his eyes. Then Cutler shook his head. "If he was a hit man he sure as hell needed to work on his aim. Missed her heart by six inches at close range."

"Could it have been staged?" Donahue suggested. "To keep her off the radar for the priest deaths."

"Can't rule that out," Renzetti replied. "And I'm still not sure about this Father Romano. MTA is convinced he couldn't have been the shooter, but that doesn't mean he didn't participate. If the bureau thinks she could be involved in the priest deaths, he'd sure have a motive."

"I'm looking at Brittany Hamar," Donahue said. "She's a real piece of work." He shared the details about the *Ordo Templi*

Orientalis ceremony. Then he pulled a computer printout from his briefcase. "A bureau investigation shows that the organization is eccentric and delves into some questionable rites, but, until now, they seem to be nonthreatening."

"We can't forget about the book," Renzetti added. "Hamar's convinced the only reason she could be targeted is this Jesus book. She claims there could be a Church connection."

"Gentlemen." Cutler pushed himself erect in his chair. "At this point we don't have any concrete evidence pointing to who killed the priests or who shot Hamar. The purpose of this meeting is to make sure we're all on the same page and to set guidelines for moving forward."

Everyone nodded but Renzetti. He'd slipped on a pair of reading glasses and was scanning Donahue's printout on Hamar. He slid the glasses farther down his nose and looked over them at Donahue. "I just found out a little more about Hamar this morning that's not in here. Something we should keep in mind."

"What'd you find?" Cutler asked.

"She's had a rough year. Enough to make anyone go off the deep end. Her son died. The kid wasn't even a year old."

"I didn't find any reference to a husband," Donahue said.

"There isn't one—now," Renzetti replied. "That's how I found this info. It was in a police report on the husband."

All eyes snapped toward Renzetti.

"Evidently the kid died from a horrendous genetic disease. When the husband found out he carried the defective gene, he couldn't handle it. Shot himself."

Cutler nudged Donahue. "Brian, get copies of those police reports. We better take a real close look at Brittany Hamar."

TWENTY-FIVE

BRITT HAMAR PULLED THE SMALL CARRY-ON BAG out of the cab and tried to hike it onto her left shoulder. A sharp pain convinced her she still needed a lot more rehab time. She stared up through the green foliage on the trees lining the sidewalk at Sixtieth and Columbus Avenue. A towering concrete structure rose into the skyline and took up most of the block. Dark shadows slashed the concrete like majestic rows of dominos accenting the myriad windows. Britt headed for the annex entrance to the Fordham Lincoln Center building. The single-story structure, accented in French blue, exuded an almost Art Deco style. Wide stairs wound up and around a checkered block tower supporting a steel walkway leading to the flat roof of the annex.

While Britt had been packing for tonight's flight, she'd had second thoughts about seeing Father Romano. *Why was he at Grand Central when she was shot? Did he really get the same call about the manuscript?* And there was the cross. *Could the cross link him and Father Matteo?* She'd also thought about the fact that in three days she'd run into three Jesuits. *Was there a Jesuit connection?* She couldn't decide whether Romano was a threat or the key to unlocking more secrets about her bloodline research. She had finally decided she had nothing to lose by meeting with Romano.

When Britt entered the annex, she found herself in front of a well-manned security desk. A female security officer dialed Romano's number. As soon as she mentioned Britt's name, the officer nodded, then directed Britt to the elevator leading to Romano's ninth-floor office.

Romano was waiting for her in the reception area in front of a bank of offices. "Well, Professor Hamar, you've made a remarkable recovery." He motioned toward the first door. "I wasn't expecting you to come by to debate the liberal nature of Jesuits so quickly."

"They tell me I was lucky. The bullet didn't do any major damage. I'll have an aching shoulder for a while. Thank you for seeing me on zero notice." Britt smiled at Romano. "I thought we agreed on Britt and Joseph."

"Sorry, Britt, for the formality." He escorted her into his office. "And for the mess."

Besides Romano's desk, the office was crammed with a conference table serving as a second desk with two desk chairs and two Mac computers with large LCD monitors, two horizontal file cabinets, an easel, a bookcase, and a couple of well-worn side chairs. Books and files were stacked everywhere and two flip charts next to the side wall were filled with notes in bold black marker. This was definitely a working office.

Britt had to squeeze by the makeshift desk. Romano moved one of the chairs so she had more room and took her bag as she sat down. He placed the bag on the other chair. Britt was impressed.

"I'm not here to debate your religious convictions, Joseph," Britt said.

"What did you come by to debate?"

"Actually, I came to discuss what may have brought us both to Grand Central yesterday." Britt noticed Romano kept his eyes on her as he made his way behind his desk. She had remembered looking up into those eyes while lying on the floor of the station. They were the soft color of cappuccino. Piercing, penetrating, but with a subtle hint of compassion. As he sat and smiled at her, she noticed two faint lines crossing his forehead and emerging crow's-feet. Romano was probably still in his late thirties, but those features gave him the discerning look of a seasoned academic.

"For me it was simple," Romano said. "As I told you in the hospital, I got a call here the day before from someone claiming to have the original James manuscript. Told me to meet him at eight thirty inside the station at the Forty-second and Park Avenue entrance."

"I received a similar call," Britt replied. "Except he told me to be at the round information booth in the main lobby. Said he'd find me. He sure did."

"Do you have any idea who it could be?" Romano asked.

"No. Do you?" Britt stared at Romano, waiting for his response.

He shook his head a few times. "Not a clue."

"Are you researching the bloodline theory?" Britt asked.

"Not really. I just started working on a book dealing with the birth, Crucifixion, and Resurrection of Jesus. It's a follow-up to *The God of the New Testament* I wrote years ago. This one is taking a look at the story of Jesus in light of the evidence and technology of the new millennia."

"Then you must be giving consideration to a bloodline theory."

Romano frowned. "Not really," he said. "My grad assistants find the recent news coverage fascinating, so I'm showing them my liberal side by allowing them to look into some of the claims. It lets them satisfy their whims of fantasy."

Britt's lips tensed.

"I don't mean to downplay your research," Romano added. "Or your apparent conclusions. But I haven't found any substantive evidence to support a bloodline. I'd think a secret like that could not have survived a couple millennia of rumor mills."

Britt detected no bravado or tension in his voice. His eyes didn't even blink. No signals of deception. She tried to suppress a smile, but by his response she knew she failed. "I guess I'll just have to send you an advance copy of my book," she said.

"I look forward to reading it." Romano maintained a serious professorial expression. Britt didn't discern even the slightest glint in his eyes.

"Will you promise me a few honest comments from a respected academic?" she asked.

"Absolutely."

"Strictly academic. Not jaundiced by your priestly vows."

"I see you don't know me well enough." Romano touched the fingertips of both hands together. "When it comes to research, I look for one thing, the truth. No matter what shape it comes in." He stroked his goatee. "Sometimes interpretations require instinct and inventiveness. Unfortunately, as far as the Church is concerned, there is no room for instinct and inventiveness, only the facts as described in the biblical canon. I follow all facts wherever they come from and wherever they lead."

"You're a more liberal Jesuit than I thought."

"Don't get me wrong. I wouldn't challenge the Church unless

I had solid reason to. As I tell my grad students, don't try to establish any new precedent unless you have a preponderance of evidence on your side. They've got to pass my 'beyond the shadow of a doubt' rule." Romano raised his eyebrows. "Especially if you intend to challenge Church canon. For two thousand years, Christianity's held up pretty darn well."

Britt smiled. "I follow George Iles's adage that doubt is the beginning, not the end of wisdom."

"Point well taken," Romano replied.

Britt noted a momentary gleam in his eyes. She was gaining a refreshing respect for Professor Joseph Romano. *Maybe it was time to ask him about the two Jesuits.* She decided the cross would be a good segue.

"Sorry to change the subject," Britt said, "but I was fascinated by the cross you wore to the hospital. Does it have any special significance?"

Romano looked like he was taken off guard. He stared at Britt for a few moments with a rather blank expression. "It was a gift. From another priest after I took my final vows." He looked askance at Britt. "Why do you ask?"

"I saw another one like it a few days ago. On another Jesuit priest I interviewed in Spain. Father Juan Matteo. Do you know him?"

A strange expression flashed across Romano's face. A blend of surprise and puzzlement. "Father Matteo is dead."

Britt's jaw dropped. She stared at Romano, stunned.

"So is my friend who gave me the cross," Romano continued. "Father Ted Mathews."

Britt felt an electric surge flash through her body, then a sudden numbness. She tried to speak, but couldn't find words.

Romano looked shocked. "What's going on?" he asked.

"I also interviewed Father Mathews. It was only two days ago. What happened to them? How did they die?"

"They found Father Ted's body yesterday morning. Why did you interview them?"

"They were recommended. It was for my book."

"My God. The FBI is involved," Romano replied. "They think there may be a connection. Why them? Who recommended them?"

Britt lowered her head and grabbed her temples. She felt faint. "Can you get me some water? Please."

"There's a cooler down the hall. I'll be right back."

Britt lifted her head and took a few breaths to recover before he returned. She had to be careful. She had to get her wits together. She was too close to the end. In just three days she was promised she'd have the ultimate evidence. The truth behind the Holy Grail. But the deaths of the priests, her shooting . . . this was far more than she had ever bargained for. And somewhere out there was—*The Messenger*.

As Romano filled a cup for Britt, he wondered why she had almost gone into shock when she heard Ted and Matteo were dead. He figured the death of priests would affect most people. But she had just interviewed them. Why? And what was the connection?

He hurried to his office with the water. Britt gulped it down, rolled her head back, and took a deep breath. He gave her a moment to compose herself, then asked, "Why did you meet with Father Matteo and Father Mathews?"

"I was following up on leads that indicated they may have had some connection with *Le Serpent Rouge*."

"What kind of connection?" Romano asked.

"That they were aware of the bloodline and could provide me with valuable information."

"No way," Romano responded. "Father Mathews was my mentor. A close friend. Like a father. He had no knowledge about a bloodline of Christ. It was something he wouldn't even give a second thought to. He was a dedicated priest. If anything, he had conservative views on religion. Very conservative."

"Did he have access to the secret Vatican archives, confidential Church research?" Britt asked.

Romano couldn't figure out where this was heading but decided to appease Britt. Maybe one of her questions would lead him to an answer. An answer to why Father Ted was being sliced open in a morgue.

"He did spend some time at the Vatican when he was a young priest," Romano replied. "That was over thirty years ago. He may have been in the archives. I really don't know. Believe me, Father Mathews didn't have any secret knowledge of a bloodline."

"You don't know that," Britt said. "You said he was a very pious man. If he knew something that could hurt the Church, he'd protect the Church."

"Look, this whole concept of a bloodline is ridiculous. If you're a serious researcher, you can't actually believe there is any validity to this nonsense."

"My theory's based upon solid evidence, not nonsense." Britt pointed to the Poussin print. "And what do you call that? Are you researching the nonsense theories behind that painting and the Holy Grail?"

"I'm using that as an example," Romano said. "To show students how extraneous theories can evolve from bits and pieces of information and grow into absurd speculation. To me, it's pretty straightforward. *Et in Arcadia ego* on a tombstone means just what it says: I am in Arcadia, the lost world of idyllic bliss."

Britt raised her eyebrows. "What happened to instinct and inventiveness?"

"That's why my grad assistants are looking into it. To follow their instincts and use their inventiveness to reach their own conclusions. But conclusions based upon valid facts. What solid evidence supports your bloodline theory?"

Britt looked down, sighed deeply, and seemed to collapse into herself. She rubbed her forehead then looked up at Romano. "I have a portion of the manuscript."

"The original James manuscript?"

"Verified by carbon dating." Britt's eyes locked on to Romano's. "It came from the time of Christ. The papyrus document I have describes twins born to Mary Magdalene. A boy and a girl."

Romano was stunned. He had been fairly certain the whole James manuscript claim was pure fabrication. Something dreamed up by the tabloids. "How did you get it?" he asked.

"The same way you had hoped to get it," Britt replied. "From an anonymous source."

"That could be the person who shot you. The one who may have killed Father Ted."

Britt shook her head. "I don't think so. The man who sent me the manuscript page called me a few times. I could recognize his voice. It was low-key and refined. He recommended I interview Father Matteo and Father Mathews. The call that led me to Grand Central—that voice was totally different. Gruff. Crass."

Romano thought about his call. "You know, that's how I'd describe my caller." He tried to remember the exact words. "And there was something else. He said, 'Be at Grand Central Terminal.' Did your caller say 'Terminal'?"

Britt closed her eyes. "You know, he did." She opened her eyes and stared at Romano.

"A New Yorker'd say Grand Central Station or Grand Central." Romano shook his head. "He's probably not—"

"There has to be a connection to the Church," Britt interrupted. "Think about it. A priest from Spain. A priest from Pennsylvania. We're researching the life of Christ. Everything points to the Church."

"I doubt it," Romano said. "Did you involve the Church in any of your research? Present your findings to any Church officials?"

"Not directly," Britt answered. "No one but my editor knows the details of my work."

"Then I don't necessarily see a Church connection. After your interview, there are lots of people out there besides the Church who know you support some outrageous theory about a bloodline. I'm sure there are many fundamentalists who wouldn't take kindly to you referring to their Jesus as a fraud."

"That's your opinion," Britt snapped. She leaned back, her eyes full of anger. "Don't judge my work until you've seen it. The book discusses many theories about Jesus. It presents a balanced spectrum of religious ideology."

"I'd say that *The Jesus Fraud* doesn't sound like the title for a balanced approach," Romano replied.

"It does if you apply a literal translation of 'fraud.' " The tone of Britt's voice left little doubt Romano had touched a nerve. "A deception deliberately practiced in order to secure unfair gain. I'm not claiming Jesus was a fraud. I'm focusing on how the early Church defined Jesus. That's where I think the fraud was perpetrated. They overlooked much of what Jesus said and focused on what they wanted Jesus to represent for their own gain."

"The early Church was very careful in establishing the canons," Romano said. "The three criteria of apostolic authority, conformity to the rule of faith, and continuous acceptance and usage by the Church at large were excellent safeguards."

"Sure, for the Church at large. Don't tell me you've never questioned the motives of the early Orthodox Church leaders. They wanted clear-cut, hard-and-fast criteria to create boundaries, which gave them power and control. I don't think that's what Jesus wanted."

"What did Jesus want?" Romano asked.

"I believe Jesus was sent to earth to present the word of God.

To teach us to find God in our own hearts and minds." Britt brushed a few strands of hair off her forehead. "I know you won't agree, but I think Jesus clearly invites us to a process of exploration—not simply a set of beliefs that we either accept or reject."

"You've been reading too many Gnostic texts," Romano said.

Romano could see the muscles tensing along Britt's jaw. Then she shook her head. "Joseph, I came here to find out if there was a connection between you being at Grand Central and me being shot. And now I think both of us also want to know why two Jesuit priests I interviewed are dead. We can debate my religious views another time."

"I want the same answers," Romano replied. "I think you're too focused on blaming the Church. If there is some mysterious bloodline of Christ, and for some reason the bloodline kept this secret for two millennia, they'd have plenty of reason to keep you from exposing them."

Britt's eyes took on a dark, sad, worldly look. She stared past Romano out the window behind his desk. "I never even gave that a thought. I guess I was too caught up in my own convictions, focused on blaming the Church."

"That's why I always try to have a sounding board when I'm working on a book. Right now I've got two great grad assistants who aren't afraid to step outside the box and tell me they don't buy my premise." Romano felt his stomach muscles twitch. His eyes suddenly burned. He saw Ted lying on the bed, his hands folded in prayer. And the marks. "And my best editor, Father Ted. Now he's gone. I want to know why. Did you find anything during your interview?"

Britt sighed as if she sensed his pain. "Not really. But he did live up to your description. When I asked him about a bloodline, he said it was an unfortunate by-product of man's creative mind."

Romano felt the tension in his body suddenly relax. That was Ted. He could always find the right words. "I told you," Romano said. "But there has to be a reason you were sent to him. What did the caller say?"

"He gave me the two names and how to contact them. Said they could provide further proof of *Le Serpent Rouge*, but they wouldn't give it willingly. I'd have to draw them out. He gave me a code word for each of them that would convince them I knew their involvement. Father Matteo was Uriel and Father Mathews was

Raphael. They denied knowing anything about a bloodline. But they both seemed shocked when I mentioned the code names."

The names of the archangels didn't register anything with Romano. He couldn't remember ever discussing archangels with Ted. He couldn't think of anything about his mentor that could link him to any secret conspiracy. This whole thing was bizarre. It didn't make any sense. But then, why had Ted been targeted? Why was he drawn into the shooting of Britt Hamar? Maybe the cross was the key? He only wore it on special occasions and kept it in his office. He slid open his desk drawer and removed the cross from its velvet bag. He noticed Britt cringe.

"You know, we could be missing the obvious," Romano said as he laid it on the desk. "Maybe we should give this some consideration. It's the only thing that directly links all three of us." He stroked his index finger along the contours of the heavy steel cross. "Father Ted did say it's a relic. He said it was given to him when he took his final vows in Switzerland. He never told me the details. Always said something vague about it being passed down through many generations of priests. He didn't know the actual origin."

"Isn't there some way we can track it?" Britt asked. "Doesn't the Church have some registry of official relics?"

"I'm ahead of you on that one," Romano said. "I tried once. Couldn't find anything close to it. I doubt if this was ever worn by a saint. Especially not if you saw an identical cross worn by Father Matteo."

Britt leaned over and looked carefully at the cross. "This is unique. I'm fairly certain it's the same one I saw on Father Matteo."

Romano noticed the envelope from Father Ted on the corner of his desk. He wondered if Father Nathan Sinclair might know something about the cross.

There were two quick raps on the door. It opened and two faces peered inside. "Sorry, Father, we didn't know you had company."

"Come in," Romano said. "We could use two fresh brains to help sort this out."

Romano introduced Britt to Carlota and Charlie. They muttered hellos and stood by the door glancing at each other. When Romano explained that Britt had recently interviewed Father Matteo and Father Mathews, the grad assistants seemed stunned.

"Your timing's perfect," Romano said to Carlota and Charlie. "Professor Hamar, if you have the time, Charlie and Carlota can take you downstairs to get lunch, my treat. Bring it back here and we can continue looking for a common denominator for these tragic events."

Britt nodded. "Sounds like a good plan," she said as she stood and turned toward Carlota and Charlie.

Romano reached into his pocket and pulled out a few bills and handed them to Carlota. Britt followed the grad assistants out of the office. Romano stared at the letter from Father Ted. As he picked up the telephone, he wondered if Nathan Sinclair might shed some new light on Ted . . . bloodlines . . . archangels . . . stigmata.

TWENTY-SIX

Father Nathan Sinclair stuffed the last of his clothes into a black duffel bag. He positioned the wooden crucifix on the pillow and smoothed the navy cotton blanket across the bed. Then he checked the room one more time to make sure he had everything. He scribbled a note explaining he had a last-minute change in flight plans and had to leave in a hurry. He ended it with a thank-you to the New Orleans Jesuit center for their usual hospitality, placed the note on the desk, and left the room.

The call had been a shock Sinclair hadn't expected. Father Mathews and Father Matteo were dead. He could be next. The Council was taking steps to protect him and his remaining brethren, but time was critical. Minutes could mean the difference between life and death.

Sinclair rushed down a side street, ignoring a taxi driver waving at him on the corner. He passed a store advertising erotic cakes, chocolates, and adult toys. A little farther a tattoo parlor flashing red neon lights claimed it was "Red Cross Certified with Hospital Sterilization." Storefront restaurants touted authentic Cajun and Creole cooking. He was definitely in the heart of New Orleans.

Another taxi slowed and the driver tried to entice Sinclair with promises of the hottest bars in the French Quarter. He ignored the taxi and picked up his pace. He'd walk all the way to the Royal St. Charles Hotel, where he had been told to book a room. It would give him a chance to take stock of what was happening.

Sinclair had been warned this was always a possibility but thought it would never happen. He had thought the levels of security were impenetrable. Only the Council of Five knew the names of the Inner Circle, and they only referred to them by their ritual names. The breech must be related to the news accounts in

France. Someone discovered a connection, a list, broke a code, or sold out the cause. He initially thought the stories of a bloodline were based upon mere speculation. There had been numerous accounts over the years, mostly the work of creative minds and conspiracy theorists. But now he feared someone had discovered the truth.

Sinclair had thought he'd be able to live his life in anonymity like so many of his brethren before him following in the footsteps of Christ—but now one phone call had destroyed that dream.

TWENTY-SEVEN

FATHER ROMANO HELD DOWN THE DISCONNECT button and debated whether to call the FBI. He realized he really had nothing to tell the bureau until he spoke with Sinclair, who was now on his way to Guatemala for his annual missionary work. But then there was Britt, and her meetings with both dead priests. *Was she connected to their deaths? Why was she shot?* She had been totally shocked when she heard of the deaths, and she didn't seem like a cold-blooded murderer. But he couldn't erase the thought—if Britt hadn't visited Ted, he might still be alive!

He decided to wait until after he had a better handle on Britt and this bloodline connection or had reached Sinclair. He slid his finger off the button and hung up the phone.

Romano thought of Ted lying on the bed. He had looked like he was praying. *Maybe he had been.* Then he remembered the wounds. They had looked fake, almost no blood. Romano picked up the phone to call Bill Sheldon and see if there was any word on how Ted died. Just as he punched in the area code, Britt came into the office, followed by Charlie and Carlota carrying two huge bags and a tray of drinks. He put the receiver back in the cradle.

"I hope there's something in there for me," Romano said.

"Your usual oriental chicken salad and a whole-grain roll," Charlie said as he put the two bags on the table. "The green tea was Carlota's idea."

Romano got up to help them slide the computers to the back of the conference table and make room for lunch. After they ate, he'd take a stab at finding a common denominator. Britt needed to be more forthcoming about her book and the research that may have led to the deaths of two priests.

TWENTY-EIGHT

GABRIEL RUSHED DOWN TO THE FIRST LEVEL OF THE Armstrong New Orleans International Airport and hailed a cab. His flight had been late and timing was critical. He instructed the driver to take him to St. Louis Cathedral at Jackson Square. He didn't want a record of a cab driving someone from the airport to the Royal St. Charles Hotel. He'd make the six or eight blocks from the cathedral to the hotel on foot.

Gabriel settled into the backseat of the cab and pulled a rumpled cap out of his shoulder bag. He tugged it down over his immaculately trimmed jet-black hair and ran his hand across the stubble on his cheek. He felt uncomfortable in rumpled khakis, polo shirt, and cotton Windbreaker. This was a far cry from his usual manicured persona.

The air conditioning was blasting away. Gabriel rubbed a palm against the cool cracked leather and felt an eerie sense of relief. There was only one more phase after today. The meeting at the Holy Site would finally bring it all to a close. This was his test from God to erase the blasphemy that had evolved from the mind of man through ignorance and greed.

In a few days the Church would continue bringing hope to the faithful without any threat from the *Rex Deus*. The Council of Five were the only ones initiated with the oral history of the *Rex Deus* and its holy cause. They and the Inner Circle would be gone for eternity. The Second Coming would be as God had meant it to be all along. The words of the Gospels would be fulfilled—*They will see the Son of Man coming upon the clouds of heaven with power and great glory.*

TWENTY-NINE

OVER LUNCH FATHER ROMANO AND BRITT brought Carlota and Charlie up to date on their discussion about the shooting and the deaths. They decided their focus would be to search for feasible links tying Britt and Romano to motives for someone to kill her and the priests.

Romano finished his cup of green tea and looked over at Britt. "I think the most obvious factor is your research for the book."

"The calls about the James Gospel prove it," Charlie said. "It's what brought you and Father Romano to the station, and the guy who sent you the fragment referred you to Father Mathews and Father Matteo."

"But I'm sure it wasn't the same person," Britt replied.

"But they referred to the same secret gospel," Carlota reminded her. "It relates to your concept of a bloodline. It's threatening someone or some organization. Or maybe someone assumes you know something you really don't."

"Or it's a wacko," Charlie added.

Britt recalled Romano's comment about a sounding board. She had already developed a respect for the quick minds of Carlota and Charlie. She decided she had nothing to lose and everything to gain by sharing what got her to this point. Maybe there were some details she had failed to connect. But she didn't trust Romano. Maybe it was because he was a priest. And she wasn't about to share her final chapter.

"The whole premise for *The Jesus Fraud* is based upon trying to present a balanced view of historical data, folklore, mythology, as well as the canonical version presented by the Church," Britt said. "The news reports on my book focused on sensationalism, not a balanced perspective."

"But it sounds like you're trying to debunk Christianity," Charlie said.

"Not really, Charlie. My intention is to present a broader view of the possibilities surrounding Jesus Christ outside of the Church's very biased perspective."

"But by giving justification to views contradicting Church doctrine, aren't you really debunking?" Charlie asked.

"Whoa, Charlie," Romano interrupted. "Let's not debate Professor Hamar's book or her theories. There'll be plenty of time for that later on. Why don't we keep the discussion focused on her bloodline research and the James document. I agree with you and Carlota. That's where we may find a link."

They looked at each other and nodded.

"That's fair," Britt said. "Some of my concerns about the claims of Christian beliefs evolved from research I was doing on the *Kohanim*, the high priests of the Temple of Jerusalem at the time of Christ. I had done considerable research for previous works in the area of the Gnostic Gospels and the writings of Saint Paul. That led to the basic question, did Jesus come to reveal or to redeem?"

"What about the *Kohanim*?" Carlota asked. "I did a paper on them. There are some interesting theories relating to the *Kohanim* and Jesus Christ."

"I assume you're referring to the theory that Jesus might have been the son of Mary and one of the Temple high priests."

"Exactly," Carlota replied. "I read that to be a *Kohan*, a member of the *Kohanim*, a man could only reach that level of the priesthood by being a male descendant of another *Kohan*. Some historians believe that the twenty-four high priests of the Herodian Temple in Jerusalem were responsible for a lot more than teaching the female students. When selected females reached childbearing age, the priests impregnated them and paired them up for marriage with respected males in the community. When the offspring of the priests reached age seven, they were required to attend the Temple school. This is how the *Kohanim* maintained the purity of their bloodlines."

"Don't forget the ritual names of the high priests," Charlie piped in.

"That's right," Carlota said. "The code names Uriel and Raphael for Father Matteo and Father Mathews. That could be a link. On ceremonial occasions, the high priests stood in order of rank on the Temple steps. They were known by ritual names. Melchizedek, Michael, Gabriel, Raphael, Uriel. The names of archangels."

"And some of the theories have Mary being impregnated by Gabriel, one of the high priests," Charlie added. "They even support it by the Gospel accounts of the angel Gabriel coming to Mary and telling her she found favor with God and would conceive a son to be called Jesus."

Britt nodded. "I wish I had the two of you around when I started working on the book. I've been writing it while on sabbatical and haven't had the luxury of two such research whizzes."

"Are you saying you actually believe Jesus was the son of Mary and a high priest?" Carlota asked.

Britt noticed that Romano sat calmly at his desk soaking up the conversation. She hesitated answering Carlota but finally decided to be candid. They'd either accept that she could have differing beliefs or that she was a quack. She didn't really care.

"I personally believe that it is a possibility. I also believe that Jesus could have been separate physical and spiritual entities. God could have merged the spiritual Christ with the physical being. Possibly through John the Baptist. The spiritual being could have been resurrected, met with the disciples and followers, and ascended into heaven. The physical Christ could have had children with Mary Magdalene."

Charlie and Carlota glanced nervously at each other, then looked to Romano. He maintained a poker face and didn't respond. It was as if he wanted Britt to keep going.

"I also give credence to the early Christians seeking spiritual enlightenment through the mysteries, which were beyond the understanding of mere mortal man," Britt continued. "God is supernatural. Why should we accept the paradigm presented by the Church describing Christ's virgin birth, Crucifixion, Resurrection, and ascension? Couldn't what really happened be beyond our comprehension?"

"I laud you for being honest," Romano said. "And I think, as professionals, we can agree to disagree. Carlota and Charlie are free to develop their own beliefs."

"I'm curious," Britt replied. "Your students have obviously done a lot of research into alternative theories about Jesus Christ. Why haven't you given more credence to any of them or questioned the orthodox point of view?"

Romano motioned to Carlota and Charlie. "I'll let them handle that one."

"For me it's simple," Charlie replied. "From the time of Jesus through the first few hundred years after his Crucifixion, there have been numerous sources supporting what became accepted as the New Testament scriptures. There is no evidence from eyewitnesses or those close to eyewitnesses to support those alternative suppositions."

Carlota nodded and said, "I agree with Charlie. And I'd stress the criteria of continuous acceptance. Those people who were members of the early Church accepted the Gospels and passed them on for generations. If there were any serious errors in the stories, don't you think someone would have set the record straight?"

"Don't forget," Britt replied, "many texts from the beginning of the Christian era were denounced as heresy by the evolving Orthodox Christians in the middle of the second century." She noticed Romano perk up. "By the time the Roman emperor Constantine the Great made Christianity the official religion in the fourth century, Christian bishops commanded the authorities to make possession of books that were denounced as heretical a criminal offense. Copies of such books were burned and destroyed."

"But we've got the Nag Hammadi texts," Charlie blurted. "Don't they confirm that during that time there was no real evidence to contradict the Christian canons?"

"Sorry to interrupt," Romano said, "but I'm afraid this is going to get us into a real quagmire—real quickly. There have been thousands of books, articles, and reviews concerning the Nag Hammadi texts. All they have been able to really confirm is that there was a very diverse mixture of Christian, pagan, and Jewish tradition being espoused during that time. Since Gnosticism is involved with spiritual truths and self-knowledge, it contains mystical qualities that make accurate, meaningful translations very difficult. Those texts have become the *chronique scandaleuse* of contemporary academia. Ravaged by scholarly jealousies."

"So, where does that leave us?" Carlota asked.

"I think we have to go back to Carlota's question of 'Don't you think someone would set the record straight?'" Britt said. She looked at Carlota, Charlie, and then at Romano, who seemed a bit ill at ease. He may have sensed what she was about to say.

"It looks as though someone may have actually done that," Britt said while keeping her eyes focused on Romano. "As I told you, I have a fragment of papyrus that has been carbon-dated to the time of Christ. James, the author, claims that his brother, Jesus, was the father of twins."

Britt noticed a faint halo of sweat on the underarms of Romano's shirt. With just the hint of a smile she said, "This may be the first step in setting the record straight."

THIRTY

CHRISTIEN FORTIER took in the view from his penthouse apartment at Le Parc Palace. It was truly one of the most beautiful vistas in the world. He scanned the horizon as the last rays of sunlight shimmered over the rocky peaks surrounding Monaco and washed across the deep blue Mediterranean. A few waning spears of light illuminated the glistening white hulls of the private yachts docked in Port de Monaco. To his left, the International Meeting Centre jutted out into the sea from the Spélugues complex built on concrete pilings hugging the shoreline. A brilliant spectrum of colors radiated from its hexagonal mosaic terrace.

Fortier had lived in the Principality of Monaco for almost thirty years. He'd originally moved his permanent residence there from France as part of a tax shelter for the vast wealth he'd accumulated through the Council's banking empire. But within a few years he found Monaco to be more than a mere haven for his riches. He became intoxicated by the quiet elegance and lingering perfume from the sea and gardens of the small principality nestled along the Côte d'Azur.

The video intercom announced the arrival of the other members of the Council of Five. Fortier buzzed them in. They had flown to Nice from their residences in Munich, Glasgow, Moscow, and London. The Council helicopter had been waiting to take them for the seven-minute flight to the Monte Carlo heliport. From there, two dark gray Bentleys rushed them to Le Parc Palace.

Fortier opened the door as the men arrived in his private elevator. He had sent his servants out for the evening. "Gentlemen, I apologize for the inconvenience." Fortier escorted the men into his private study. A magnificent rosewood table stood in the center of the room beneath a Venetian-cut crystal chandelier. Deep mahogany Italian leather chairs, crystal wineglasses with individual decanters, and laptop computers awaited the men.

After they were seated, Fortier took his place at the head of the table. "The catastrophic events of the past few days have caused me to consider drastic action."

"Never before have members of our Inner Circle been assassinated. What in hell do you plan to do?" Moscow asked.

"Are we certain they were killed?" Glasgow added.

All heads snapped toward the Scot.

"What in bloody hell are you insinuating?" London asked.

"I'm not insinuating a damned thing," the Scot replied. "We're responsible for protecting a holy order. We are servants of God. There are things beyond our comprehension and control."

"Gentlemen, gentlemen." Fortier rapped his knuckles against the table. "We will find out soon enough how Uriel and Raphael died, but for the moment we must do everything in our power to protect the remaining members. If this is an act of God, so be it. It will be out of our hands."

"What do you recommend?" Moscow asked.

"I found out that Brittany Hamar visited Uriel the day before his body was discovered, then flew back to the United States."

The members' expressions tightened. They glanced questioningly at each other.

"I immediately dispatched Philippe Armand to follow her and put her temporarily out of service," Fortier added.

"And?" Moscow asked.

"Philippe was to wound her—"

There was a united gasp.

"He assured me he would not kill her," Fortier continued. "While she was hospitalized, he was to copy the materials relating to her book and bring them to Monaco for our review. Just before you arrived, I received word Philippe is at the Hôtel de Paris. The materials are on their way here via courier."

"You think Hamar could be behind this?" London asked.

"We don't know for sure, but don't forget, we've got two things to worry about," Fortier said. "The deaths and preventing any leaks that could jeopardize our holy order. The recent press reports and Hamar's *Jesus Fraud* put her at the top of the list. And don't forget Father Joseph Romano. Philippe was instructed to plant evidence that would implicate Father Romano in

Hamar's shooting. That will keep them both out of the picture for the time being."

"Raphael promised us Father Romano was no threat," the Scot replied. "He knows nothing."

Fortier glared at the Scot. "Raphael's dead. That changes things, doesn't it?"

"I say we bring in the remaining members. Split them up. Isolate them until we are assured the threat is neutralized," Moscow said.

"But we must do it without bringing undue attention to them," London added. "Someone may be watching and waiting. A person with too much knowledge could be more dangerous than a person with a gun."

A chime broke the tension in the room. Fortier stood. "That must be Philippe's report and the copies of Hamar's research materials."

As Fortier went to the intercom, he had another thought. *Could someone in the Council or the Inner Circle have found out the truth about the manuscript? Could he, in his zeal to shore up the foundation of their holy order, have started its downfall?*

THIRTY-ONE

ROMANO WASN'T SURE HOW TO RESPOND TO BRITT. He stared at the notepad he'd been doodling on. He didn't want to directly challenge the authenticity of her manuscript fragment but had serious doubts about it. There had been many instances of "supposed" artifacts and documents that had passed initial aging tests and later were proven to be frauds. And he still had his doubts about Britt. There were times in the way she looked at him when her eyes retreated behind an unnerving squint, as if she were hiding something. She seemed to be genuine in her odd beliefs but had really gone off the deep end by giving serious credence to so many unconventional concepts. Something about her raised a red flag.

Romano looked up and saw three sets of eyes converged on him waiting for a response. "I'd be very interested in taking a look at this manuscript fragment," he said. "I've done my share of interpreting and validating ancient manuscripts."

Britt perked up immediately. "I'd appreciate your professional evaluation," she said. "But on one condition. That I may quote your conclusions in my book."

Romano really didn't look forward to the possibility of being caught up in a media controversy that questioned Church doctrine. But then, he always stressed that his students should search for the truth wherever it may lead them.

"I always stand behind my work," Romano said. "When and where?"

Romano saw Britt glance at the worn leather bag on the chair in front of his desk.

"How about early next week?" Britt asked. "Monday or Tuesday. I'll bring it here. You can analyze it in your lab."

"Monday's fine," Romano replied.

"Father, do you think that's a good idea?" Carlota asked.

"What's your concern?"

"Whether the shooting and deaths are some nut or a conspiracy doesn't matter. We agree they definitely have something to do with the manuscript. Maybe Professor Hamar's right. The original caller who sent her the fragment is not involved in the shooting. What if someone is following her? They killed Father Matteo and Father Mathews. They knew how close you were with Father Mathews. If he knew something, you could too. Then they set up Professor Hamar to be shot."

"Where is the fragment?" Romano asked.

"Right now it's in a safe-deposit box," Britt said. "But Carlota brings up an interesting point. While I was in the hospital, someone accessed my computer in my locked apartment."

"Then someone definitely thinks you know something you shouldn't or they want to get that fragment," Romano said. "It should stay in the safe-deposit box until the authorities get a handle on who's behind this."

"I've been inputting notes on this whole weird scenario," Charlie said. He scrolled through some highlighted passages on his computer monitor. "The obvious link is the telephone calls. I'll bet the FBI can find out where those calls originated."

Romano pulled out his billfold and fumbled through it for Agent Cutler's card. He pushed his phone to the front of the desk and handed the card to Britt. "Charlie's right. You should notify the FBI immediately and tell them about the calls and your meetings with the dead priests."

Britt put the card on the desk, stood, and grabbed her bag. "Sorry, I can't do that. Not now." She turned and walked to the door.

Romano picked up the phone. "If you don't call the FBI, I will."

THIRTY-TWO

Father Sinclair entered the lobby of the Royal St. Charles Hotel and stood in line at the circular registration desk. A large silver column rose up from the center of the desk and disappeared into the recessed ceiling through a wide silver halo containing spots that bathed the counter in pale yellow ovals. He wondered why Gabriel had chosen the boutique hotel one block from the French Quarter. It was a lot more upscale than Sinclair was accustomed to, especially the accommodations he would have as a missionary in Guatemala. But then, Gabriel was used to a more luxurious lifestyle.

The check-in went smoothly, and Sinclair felt a rush of relief as he clicked the lock on the door to his room and slid the safety chain in place. He stashed his duffel bag in the closet niche and started a pot of coffee in the coffeemaker on top of the minibar. While it brewed, he settled into a plush armchair and waited for the telephone call from Gabriel. After all, if anybody had the resources to protect him until the Council put a stop to the killings, it was Gabriel.

THIRTY-THREE

BRITT FROZE IN THE DOORWAY. THE TIMBRE OF
Romano's voice had suddenly changed. There was a hard edge to
it she hadn't heard before. She knew he'd make the call to the
FBI. She turned back to Romano. His soft eyes seemed uncom-
monly dark.

She couldn't let another priest interfere in her life. The parish
priest had urged her to pray for Tyler. "God answers our prayers,"
he had told her time after time. She had prayed again and again
and again every day. When she awoke in the middle of the night
she had prayed herself back to sleep. What did it do? Tyler suffered through a long, painful death. After Alain she was visited
by another priest. He also recommended prayer, to ease her suffering. It hadn't. She'd given up on prayer, priests, and the hollow
teachings of the Church. It was then she had met Felix. His story,
as bizarre as it had sounded, convinced her to "set the record
straight." She'd risk her career to do it, her life if she had to. She
couldn't let Romano call the FBI.

"Please don't," Britt said. "I'm scheduled to fly to Vienna in a
few hours to meet someone who may have answers to the deaths
and my shooting. I can't afford to get sidetracked by the FBI."

"Don't tell me you're meeting another priest who's going to
end up dead," Romano said.

Britt put her bag down, leaned against the doorjamb and
shook her head. "No, this is different. I'm seeing the man who
provided me the initial data on *Rex Deus*. I met him a year ago at
a meeting of the Saunière Society in London."

"Dear God," Romano protested. "They're a group of conspiracy nuts. And if you're including references to *Rex Deus*, you
might as well include King Arthur, Sir Lancelot, the Holy Grail."

Britt sensed anger welling up inside her but also felt the urge
to smirk. Romano didn't know how close he was to the truth. She

was tempted to tell him the ultimate purpose for her trip but knew before she finished he'd be dialing the FBI.

"I'll admit some of these theories go off in tenuous directions," Britt replied. "But they all contain some threads of historical credibility."

"Very tenuous threads," Romano stressed.

"Threads are threads."

"Let's get back on track," Romano said. "Who are you meeting?"

"I only know him as Felix. It was his information that got me started on the bloodline theory. He referred to *Le Serpent Rouge* and secret documents that could support a bloodline of Christ. And then a few months ago the articles began appearing in French publications referring to a secret James Gospel. That's when I was contacted by the caller who sent me the manuscript fragment."

"Did the caller indicate any link to Felix?" Romano asked.

"Not at all. I asked him if Felix had directed him to me. He had no idea who Felix was."

"Why are you meeting this Felix?"

"Felix had warned me I could be in danger if I pursued leads on *Le Serpent Rouge* and included references to it in the book. I haven't been in touch with him since. He may be able to tell me who could be behind the deaths and my shooting."

"Then you definitely should inform the FBI," Romano insisted. "He could be the one following you. He could be the killer."

"I doubt that seriously," Britt replied. "He's not the kind of person who blends in. He's an odd little gnomelike fellow. Believe me, I would have recognized Felix if he had shot me. And the police would have his description by now if he'd been in the vicinity of any of the crime scenes."

"But the FBI should be made aware of him."

"If the FBI comes into the picture, Felix will never be found. I don't even know his last name."

"Then how did you set up a meeting with him?" Romano asked.

Britt knew it would sound stupid even before she said it. "He told me I could contact him by having a bookstore in Vienna place a message in a copy of a specific book at least a week before coming to the city."

Romano leaned back and raised his eyes in mock amazement. "You've got to be kidding," he said. "This must be a joke."

Britt clenched her teeth. "Is it a joke that two priests are dead and I was shot?" she asked.

Britt could see the muscles in Romano's jaw tense, then relax, as he seemed to reflect on her question. She noticed Carlota and Charlie with frozen expressions staring down at the floor.

"No, that's certainly not a joke," Romano replied. "I want to find out who killed Father Ted."

"I'm convinced Felix can provide some . . . answers," Britt said. "If you want to find out the truth, why don't you come with me to Vienna and see for yourself. I suspect Felix may be a priest. Maybe you'll listen to him."

Romano's eyes went wide with surprise, blinked a few times, then he flashed a disarming smile. "I have a close associate in Vienna," he said. "He might know this Felix. What flight are you on? I'll meet you at the airport."

THIRTY-FOUR

THE MEMBERS OF THE COUNCIL OF FIVE SAT around the rosewood table, their eyes locked on to data scrolling across laptop screens. They were reviewing the research materials Philippe Armand had copied from Britt Hamar's apartment.

Christien Fortier grew more and more apprehensive as he waded through the computer files and digital images. He hadn't found any direct evidence that put the work of the Council in jeopardy, but there were citations dangerously close to the truth. Hamar made numerous references to *Rex Deus* but nothing directly incriminating. No names. Just the usual theories that had been bandied about for years: a shadowy dynasty whose members were harboring secrets of Christ and a possible bloodline; historical references to succession of the House of David to the throne of Jerusalem after the first Crusade.

"Here are references to archangels." The diminutive Scot cast a warning glance at the other members. "Mostly related to the high priests of the Temple in Jerusalem. She did a lot of research into the *Kohanim*. She even discovered the genetic signature."

"Any mention of the archangels relating to *Le Serpent Rouge*?" Fortier asked.

"There's no mention of *Le Serpent Rouge* or a bloodline in this section. She seems to be focusing on the Immaculate Conception. She's referring to the theory that Mary was impregnated by a high priest from the Temple in Jerusalem."

"Uh-oh, this is a problem." The burly Russian leaned forward and pointed to his laptop. "Here's a reference in which Hamar insinuates she might be able to crack the secret code of the *Rex Deus*." His chair creaked as he waved his finger across the screen. "She feels Felix is the key. He could provide the details if she can get him to open up."

Fortier jumped up and went over to the Russian. "Don't tell me she's been in contact with Konrad."

"Here's a note about an airline reservation to Vienna," the Englishman said. "It's for tonight."

"She could be going after Michael. We've got to stop her immediately," the Russian added.

"There's no question," Fortier said. "Felix Konrad must have steered Brittany in this direction. Maybe they're working together."

"Even if they're not, who knows what he might divulge that could bring her to some dangerous conclusions," the Englishman added.

"Philippe followed him for a year after we found out he had heard his uncle's deathbed confession and started his deviant behavior," Fortier said. "He gave no indication he knew any facts that could be dangerous to our cause. We concluded he had simply become part of the conspiracy-theory rumor mill. After the French magazine articles started referring to a secret James Gospel, I had Philippe investigate him again. He couldn't find any connection between Konrad and the articles. He broke into Konrad's house and found nothing relating to the gospel. At our last meeting, we agreed the magazine references were complete fabrications. The supposed translations weren't even close to being accurate."

"Well, it looks like Konrad's back on the radar screen and we better not take any chances," the Englishman replied.

Fortier returned to the end of the table and continued scrolling through a file. "Has anyone found any references that Hamar had anything to do with the deaths of Uriel or Raphael or that she has any evidence of the Inner Circle or our Council?"

The men looked at each other questioningly.

The Scot wriggled nervously in his chair. "No direct references."

"Philippe's report states that she could not have killed Raphael," the Russian replied. "He followed Hamar and Raphael to a tavern, and afterward she left him at the front door of the Jesuit center and returned to New York."

"But what if she had an accomplice, Konrad for instance?" the Englishman asked. "She could have set Uriel and Raphael up." His voice rose in agitation. "Do we know where Konrad was?"

"Gentlemen, we have another major problem," the German announced.

Fortier went over and stared at the data displayed on his screen.

"This entire file is on the James Gospel," the German said. "It's only a small portion of the text, but the translation seems accurate."

"That's not possible." Fortier bent down and flicked his finger across the touch pad, scrolling the data on the screen. "There's no way anyone could know about the real James Gospel, much less have a translation of it."

"Could someone have made copies of the manuscript before you acquired it?" the Russian asked.

"I was there when the urn was broken open," Fortier replied. "I took immediate custody of the manuscript. The Egyptian could only have gotten a mere glimpse of the first papyrus sheet. He could never have memorized any of the uncial writing."

Fortier straightened up and stared at the screen. "Besides, this translation is from near the middle of the manuscript."

"Could Uriel or Raphael have told Hamar's accomplice the translation?" the Scot asked. "If she set them up, maybe her accomplice tortured them or drugged them."

"I'd find it hard to believe Konrad could be capable of that," the Englishman added.

"This file was created a few months ago," the Russian said as he moved to the end of the file. "It says she made the translation from the original. There's also a notation about verification she got from carbon dating."

"Impossible," Fortier said. "The gospel is sealed in our vault."

The Englishman moved beside Fortier and reviewed the screen. "This is getting way out of hand. I say we take action immediately. Hamar is definitely a liability. And we should have taken care of Konrad a long time ago."

Fortier ran the back of his hand across his brow. It was creased with sweat. There was no way Hamar could have an original segment of the James Gospel. But she definitely had an accurate translation of a small section. He had to do something. Something drastic.

"I agree," Fortier said. "I recommend we have Philippe go to Vienna and eliminate Hamar and Felix Konrad."

The members looked uneasily at each other. The Russian nodded. Then the Englishman. Then the German. And finally the Scot.

THIRTY-FIVE

"WHA . . . WHOA, FATHER," CHARLIE STAMMERED after Britt was well out of earshot. His eyes were fraught with amazement. "You were kidding. Right?"

"You're not really going with Professor Hamar to Vienna?" Carlota added. She looked more shocked than amazed.

Romano found himself a bit puzzled about his reaction. He wasn't sure what finally made him blurt out that he'd meet Britt at the airport. Impulsiveness was not one of his normal characteristics. His fellow faculty had him pegged as somewhat of a stoic who was careful not to jump to conclusions. This hadn't been a jump so much as a leap.

"I told her I'd meet her at the airport," Romano replied. "You wouldn't want me to break a promise."

"But that's crazy," Charlie piped in. "Something I'd do. Not you or Carlota."

Romano let down his guard and flashed a short grin. "I guess two factors probably played a role in my rather quick decision."

Charlie smirked. "She is a good-looking lady."

Carlota smacked his arm before "lady" left his lips. "Charlie, you are sick."

"Now, now," Romano replied. "Charlie has a right to his opinion. And just because I'm a priest doesn't mean I relinquished my male chromosomes."

Romano saw Carlota's eyes bug out. "But that's not one of the reasons," he quickly added. "She seems to have done her fair share of research into the bloodline theory and I'd like to find out more about how she came to her conclusions. A long plane ride should give me a great opportunity. And I want to find out why Father Ted died. Why he was implicated in her research on a bloodline."

Charlie rooted around in his knapsack. He finally pulled out an electronic device that looked like a PDA with a built-in mini keyboard. He rolled his chair over to Romano's desk.

"Here, take my BlackBerry." Charlie held the device out toward Romano.

Romano held his hands up in rejection and shook his head. "Thanks, but no thanks. I told you I've given up on cell phones."

"This isn't just a cell phone," Charlie replied. "You can get and send e-mail messages twenty-four-seven. It's got quad band so it'll work in Europe through Deutsche Telecom."

Carlota's eyes lit up. "Take it, Father Romano. We'll be able to keep in touch with you. You can sneak us questions, and we can be your research eyes and ears."

Romano hesitated, then took the BlackBerry from Charlie. He glanced at his watch. "Give me some pointers on how to work this thing. I have to pack and get to the airport."

Charlie gave Romano a quick lesson and set up the Black-Berry to receive his e-mails. Romano sent a test message to Carlota in which he requested her and Charlie to look into some of the alternative theories relating to Christ's Crucifixion and Resurrection and to hold down the fort until he returned in a few days.

Charlie and Carlota huddled around one of the Macs and replied to Romano's e-mail. Within seconds, the BlackBerry vibrated, and Romano opened their e-mail. Charlie and Carlota high-fived each other.

"You passed, Father." Charlie leaned over and high-fived Romano. "You're back in the digital age."

Romano noticed the time on the BlackBerry. "If I don't get out of here right now, it won't matter if I'm in the digital age. I won't make the flight. That is, if I can even get a ticket."

Romano checked his daily planner then stuffed it into his shoulder bag and started for the door. "I don't have any meetings scheduled for the next few days. Tell the staff I've gone to Vienna. I can be reached through Father Heinz Müller at the Jesuit rectory. Or through this." He held up the BlackBerry as he went out the door.

THIRTY-SIX

Philippe Armand slowly swirled a glass of Château Lafite, held it up to the light, and observed the strong legs forming as the red Bordeaux slid down the sides of the bowl. He buried his nose in the crystal goblet and inhaled the deep complex almond and violet aroma, then took a long draft, savoring the firm, masculine flavor. Settling back in his chair, he dabbed his mouth with a linen napkin. Dining at the très chic Imperial Room in the Hôtel de Paris was a perquisite he treasured. Plush gold draperies swagged above the doorways, alabaster statuary stood on marble pedestals, magnificent gold-emblazoned chandeliers hung from the arched ceilings, and gold capitals topped elegant stone columns. At this time of evening, the dining room was a mélange of aristocrats, important financiers, famous artists and intellectuals, the social elite of the world.

Whenever Philippe was commanded to personally deliver reports to his mysterious employer, a room was reserved in his name at Monaco's Hôtel de Paris. The services of the hotel were at his beck and call. It was always the same routine. Leave the report at the desk when he checked in and settle into his room overlooking the manicured gardens lined with statuesque palms and wait for a call. This evening he had waited in his room for a few hours then enjoyed an exquisite meal in the Imperial Room. He had even treated himself to a serving of his favorite pâté de foie gras marinated in the finest aged Cognac and flavored with truffles.

On a few occasions, Philippe had been tempted to secretly follow the courier who came to collect his reports from the front desk and pay his bill in cash. He had a burning desire to know who his secret employer really was. But his father had warned him that was an option he should never consider if he wanted to live out his life in the same luxury his father had enjoyed—the focus being on living out his life.

Philippe's father, Carlos Armand, had worked in the same capacity for the same employer his entire career. After Philippe graduated from university, Carlos had trained him to follow in his footsteps. He taught Philippe all the skills required of a private investigator and a government agent. And one final skill. How to kill and vanish without a trace. His father had prepared him for the day when he would be required to put that skill into action, just as Carlos had to in 1967. In that year Carlos had to kill four men under very specific circumstances. The first was thrown from the Paris-Geneva express, killed to recover an important briefcase. He had to torture and hang three more men to recover secret documents relating to a privately printed work entitled *Le Serpent Rouge* they had deposited in the Bibliothèque Nationale in Paris.

Carlos had often warned Philippe that he was working for a secret organization that had deep ties to Christianity. Many of his surveillance jobs had strong religious overtones and involved secret documents or organizations critical of the Church. "Just do what you are told and don't ask questions," Carlos told him. "An inquisitive mind can lead to an early demise" was another phrase his father had drilled into him.

Shooting Hamar had not been as difficult as he had thought it would be. He had even experienced an unexpected thrill as he squeezed the trigger and her eyes popped open wide in shock and she crumbled to the floor. He had been on an adrenaline high as he merged with the fleeing crowd and jammed the box into the priest's hands. But now he was feeling apprehensive as he waited for the call. He had a hunch things could escalate very quickly and he could use a backup, but his father, who had been his backup, had faded out of the picture. Carlos had done a special job almost four years ago. He told Philippe he'd be gone for two months. He never returned to Paris and Philippe never found out what happened to him. He vanished from the face of the earth. In the back of his mind, Philippe thought maybe his father had breached the inquisitive limit.

As Philippe finished a final glass of the fine Bordeaux, he felt his cell phone vibrate. He quickly left the Imperial Room to take the call and found a secluded spot behind one of the stone columns in the vast hotel rotunda. Eerie flecks of sunlight reflecting through the polychrome glass dome splashed across him. The voice sounded as though it was electronically altered. Philippe could never tell if the calls were from the same person. He listened carefully to his instructions.

When his employer finished, Philippe felt a chill ratchet through his body. His stomach twitched. The day his father had warned him about had finally come. It stirred up an emotion that had lain dormant, one that he had sensed in his father's eyes when he was told about the events of 1967. He didn't know if it was fear or excitement.

Philippe collected his bag from his room and headed to the airport for the next flight to Vienna. There he would have to kill twice and vanish without a trace. But there was a catch . . . he had to take a priest with him whom he was to protect with his life.

THIRTY-SEVEN

FATHER ROMANO RIPPED OPEN ONE OF THE CARtons stacked about his new apartment at the America House. He rummaged through it and pulled out a leather knapsack he used for short trips. Then he dug his passport out of the desk drawer and began packing. On the way to the apartment he had tried to make sense out of why he was rushing off to Vienna. Everything came back to spur-of-the-moment impulse. He tried to convince himself it was intellectual curiosity, but there was another thought gnawing away at him. There was something about Britt Hamar he couldn't come to grips with. Something about her eyes. The way she spoke. It made him feel uneasy, nervous.

Romano stuffed his toiletry bag into the knapsack and did a final check to make sure he hadn't forgotten anything. He was intrigued by Britt's dogged fascination with a general philosophy that seemed hell-bent on disproving the canons of Christianity. But nothing she had discussed with him and his grad assistants came close to supporting such a controversial theory. Even if there was a document that could be authenticated from the time of Jesus, it could have been written by a radical or a Jewish high priest who was trying to discredit the fledgling Christian movement. There was a lot more to interpreting and validating ancient manuscripts than simple carbon dating. He also sensed there were factors she hadn't fully disclosed. Something got her on this track. Something she was either afraid of or embarrassed to discuss. And maybe that something could shed light on who, or what, killed Ted.

Romano was almost out the door when he remembered Father Cristoforo. He grabbed his phone and started to call the assistant to the father general when he realized it was late evening in Rome. He rushed off an e-mail on his computer updating Cristoforo about the shooting of Professor Brittany Hamar. He mentioned her visits to both dead priests based upon a mystery caller who provided their names and insinuated they had information about the bloodline theory. Romano stressed that Britt was startled when she heard Father Mathews was dead and that he was confident she wasn't directly involved in the deaths. He told him he was going to Vienna with Britt to meet with a priest who might have information that could be relevant to the deaths. He described the odd letter from Father Mathews urging him to contact Father Sinclair and said he would keep Cristoforo informed of any new developments. When Romano hit Send, he realized his stupidity. He had Charlie's BlackBerry and could have sent the e-mail while waiting in line at the airport.

Romano glanced at his watch and panicked. He'd need a lead-footed cab driver if he had any chance of making it to the airport in time to book a seat on Britt's flight and get through security. He threw his knapsack over his shoulder, rushed out the side entrance of the building, ran down Fifty-sixth Street to Sixth Avenue, and waved furiously at the first cab. The driver slid to a stop and beamed ear to ear when Romano mentioned JFK.

As the cab made a few quick turns to head toward the Queens Midtown Tunnel and the Long Island Expressway, Romano settled back and took a deep breath. He still wasn't completely sure why he was rushing off to Vienna with, as Charlie put it, "a good-looking lady."

THIRTY-EIGHT

GABRIEL PULLED THE BILL OF HIS NEW ORLEANS
Saints cap low on his forehead and headed for a pay phone on St.
Charles Avenue. An American flag fluttered in the afternoon
breeze in front of the Royal St. Charles Hotel. He dialed the hotel
and was immediately connected to Father Sinclair.

"I just arrived," Gabriel said. "I should be at the hotel shortly.
Did you have any problems?"

"Everything went smoothly, so far. I'll breathe easier when
you bring me up to date on what's happening."

"Sure you weren't followed?"

"I walked all the way to the hotel, didn't notice anyone. I even
doubled back on a few streets to be sure. Where are we going?
Is everything worked out?"

Gabriel glanced up and down the street. There was the usual
foot traffic heading to the French Quarter to get a head start on
happy hour. "We'll be fine," he said. "Everything is under control. I'll explain it all when I get to your room. What's your room
number?"

"Two-sixteen. Right next to the elevator."

"I'll be there in a few minutes."

Gabriel hung up, shouldered his carry-on bag, and headed up
the street to the hotel. He waited by the front entrance until a
woman in a flowered dress and a funky rose-colored hat and a
man with a "Ragin' Cajun" T-shirt entered the rotating doors. He
followed them inside, and when they turned toward the intimate
lobby bar, he headed straight to the elevators.

During the short ride to the second floor, he slipped the cigar
case out of his shoulder bag and tucked it in his inside jacket
pocket. As the elevator jerked to a stop, he reached into his side
pocket and wrapped his hand around a TASER.

He rapped once on the door to two-sixteen. The door opened

immediately and Gabriel rushed inside, jamming the TASER into Sinclair's chest. The startled priest's eyes bugged out, his jaw dropped open, and he crumbled to the carpet. His body convulsed as Gabriel locked the door and swung the security latch into place. Gabriel opened the cigar case, pulled out a hypodermic, and jabbed it into Sinclair's chest, slowly injecting the contents into his heart.

He put the empty syringe back into the case and pulled a small vial out of a second cigar tube. He opened the vial and dabbed a few drops of oil onto his index finger and made the Sign of the Cross on Sinclair's forehead, saying: "Through this holy anointing may the Lord in his love and mercy help you with the grace of the Holy Spirit." Then he anointed the palms of Sinclair's hands with the Sign of the Cross, saying: "May the Lord who frees you from sin save you and raise you up. Amen." He watched with his hands folded in prayer as Sinclair lapsed into a coma and died.

Gabriel carefully pulled the body into the bathroom, stripped it naked, and placed it in the bathtub. He then opened a third cigar tube and pulled out an iron spike with a head in the shape of a flattened cross. He took a small mallet out of his shoulder bag and pounded the spike through Sinclair's wrists and feet while intoning a creedlike recitation in Latin. After pausing to wipe beads of sweat from his brow with the back of his hand, he pierced Sinclair's side with a sharp blade and proceeded to prick the skin around the top of his skull.

When he was finished, Gabriel cleaned away any blood with tissues and flushed them down the toilet. Then he carefully lifted the body out of the tub and carried it to the bedroom, where he placed it on top of the ornate bedspread. He replaced Sinclair's briefs, folded his hands, closed the priest's eyes, and offered one last prayer. He washed the knife blade and spike in the tub and rinsed any evidence down the drain. Then he called the New Orleans provincial's office and told them to check on Father Sinclair, who may have had an accident at the Royal St. Charles Hotel.

Gabriel quickly left the hotel and walked to the nearby French Quarter, where he hailed a cab to the airport and the last leg of his religious quest. A strange calm enveloped him. It was as if he were entering the eye of a storm.

THIRTY-NINE

Brian Donahue entered the Strategic Information Operation Center on the fifth floor of the Hoover Building. The SIOC was the site where top-level cases were reviewed. Tom Cutler was briefing an elite FBI team on the priests' deaths. Donahue handed him an update and took a seat at the head table.

Cutler looked over the printout and placed it in a scanner next to his podium. A report from the Louisiana bureau filled the screen behind him. "You're all here because the stakes on the case I've been reviewing have just been raised. We've got a third dead priest. Same MO as the first two, but this time they found TASER marks on his chest. Brian, any autopsy results on the first two?"

"Still waiting. Preliminaries indicate some type of poison. They're performing additional tests and coordinating with Spain. We should have something by tomorrow."

Cutler scanned to a detailed photo of Father Mathews showing the marks of the stigmata. "At least we can most likely rule out divine intervention." There were scattered chuckles from the group. "Ladies and gentlemen, this is serious business. There is a serial killer out there, and we don't have anything solid to go on. Brian, what's the status on Brittany Hamar?"

"We have an agent at her apartment. She hasn't been seen. One of her neighbors thought he saw her leave carrying an overnight bag."

"I want her in this office for questioning stat."

"We're checking airline and train reservations." Donahue pointed to the screen. "There's no way she could have gotten to New Orleans for this."

Cutler banged his fist on the podium. "I don't care. Right now she's our only lead. I don't want any more priests killed in the U.S. on my watch. Marcia and Tim, I want you to coordinate with

New Orleans. I want to know everyone that priest met or spoke to in the past few days. The rest of you know your assignments."

The team dispersed. Cutler turned to his partner. "Brian, we're not leaving this building until we locate Brittany Hamar. I don't care if we have to pull an all-nighter. Push the staff checking reservations. I'm going to assign a couple more agents to interview her neighbors. I'm convinced there's some sick bastard out there, and we don't have much time before they discover another dead priest."

PART II

☩HE QUEST

FORTY

Father Romano was the last passenger to board the Austrian Airlines flight to Vienna. He located the seat he had requested just as the stewardess prepared to begin the routine passenger orientation and safety instructions.

"Excuse me, ma'am, I think I'm in the seat next to you." Romano smiled down at Britt.

She looked up and did a double take. "This is quite a surprise."

"It was a close call, but I'm here." Romano opened the overhead compartment and shoved his knapsack into a gap between two carry-on bags.

Britt unsnapped her seat belt and stood aside to let him by. "I would have put slim odds on you showing up."

He slid into the middle seat. "There's a lot I'd like to discuss, and you can't beat a long plane ride."

"That's if you can keep me awake." Britt sighed. "It's been a rough few days."

"It'll be between naps then. I admit I'm still recovering from the shock of Father Ted's death. But I'm convinced something in your research triggered the deaths and your shooting."

Jet engine noise filled the cabin and the Airbus A330 accelerated down the runway. Romano slid his hand away just as Britt planted a white-knuckle grip on the armrest between them. "I take it you're not a fan of air travel."

She shoved herself back into her seat as the plane picked up speed and lifted off the runway. During the sharp ascent, Britt took a deep breath and held it. When it started to level off, she seemed to relax a bit. "Sorry. I'll be okay."

Romano waited until Britt loosened her grip and had taken a few normal breaths. "I've given your suspicions about Church involvement some thought. Why would the Church kill its own priests? I can't even think of any bizarre justification."

"What if they were aware of facts that could be detrimental to the Church? If some group within the Church was following me and saw me meet with them, they could have sanctioned their death and my shooting to protect the Church."

Romano shook his head. "Believe me, I doubt if the Church has a secret agency that would go around killing people."

"Joseph, you have to agree that history shows the hands of the Church are not free of blood."

"You're comparing the Middle Ages to today. A lot has changed. And continues to change. There are no secret police forces and the Curia oversees the executive, judicial, and legislative authority of the Holy See. There are many checks and balances."

"But you must agree that the Pope, the cardinals, and the bishops wield a lot of power. And not too long ago there were murders relating to research similar to mine."

Romano looked skeptically at Britt. "Bloodline research?"

"Felix, the man I'm meeting in Vienna, warned me I could be in great danger if I continued my research. He referred to four murders related to *Le Serpent Rouge* that took place in 1967 in France. I investigated his claim and found that an Austrian dealer in miniatures, Leo Schidlof, involved with works entitled *Dossier Secrets*, purportedly had documents relating to a bloodline. Upon his death, a briefcase containing his papers was passed on to a man named Fakhar ul Islama, whose body was discovered on the railroad tracks after being hurled from the Paris-Geneva express. The briefcase was never found. A month after Islama's death a privately printed work entitled *Le Serpent Rouge* was deposited in the Bibliothèque Nationale in France. It contained one Merovingian genealogy and two maps of France in Merovingian times, as well as references to our familiar Poussin painting, *Les Bergers d'Arcadie*. It referred to a red snake uncoiling across the centuries through France, a direct allusion to a bloodline or lineage. All three of the authors of *Le Serpent Rouge* were found hanged. No documentation supporting their publication was ever found."

"That's a fascinating account, but you have to admit there's not one shred of solid evidence supporting a bloodline."

"That's my point," Britt said. "The people who may have had evidence are dead and the evidence is gone. I have part of a gospel that describes efforts to revive Jesus after the Crucifixion and refers to Mary Magdalene being with child."

Romano couldn't believe what he had just heard. "You're telling me the manuscript fragment you have goes into detail about the Crucifixion—and a child?"

Britt turned in her seat and looked straight at Romano. "That's right. It describes Simon Zelotes orchestrating the use of soured wine mixed with snake venom being presented to Jesus while on the cross to put him into a comatose state. The first time Jesus was offered a drink on the cross, he refused. Just before he died, a bystander soaked a sponge with wine, put it on a reed, and gave it to Jesus. After he drank it, he immediately said, 'It is finished,' and he bowed his head, and gave up the ghost. The passages I have state that he was taken to his family tomb, where—"

"Whoa." Romano shook his head and raised a finger. "What do you mean, 'family tomb'?"

"That's just another example of the Church conveniently failing to dig deeply into the meaning of certain scripture passages."

"I'm not following you."

"The Catholic Church has a distinct view that Jesus didn't have any brothers and sisters. In my opinion they're simply trying to justify the Virgin Mary being a lifelong virgin. They interpret the Greek for 'brother' and 'sister' applying Semitic usage from the time of Jesus and insinuate it could mean nephews, nieces, cousins."

"I'll grant that's a bone of contention with some scholars and other Christian faiths. How does that relate to a family tomb? The tomb Jesus was buried in belonged to Joseph of Arimathea, a distinguished member of the Sanhedrin."

"Some of the Gospels refer to Joseph as a disciple of Jesus."

Romano nodded. "But that's a long way from being family."

"Using the same logic of *language of the time*, I can show that Joseph of Arimathea could have been the brother of Jesus."

Romano couldn't follow Britt's rationale. "I don't see the connection."

"I didn't either, at first. But when I analyzed it strictly from the language and practices of the time, I started seeing a link."

"And?"

"Wouldn't it make sense that Jesus' family would be given the body for burial?"

"Maybe under normal circumstances for a thief or other common criminal. Jesus was charged with sedition. I don't see the connection to *language of the time*."

The cabin lights dimmed. The woman sitting on the other side of Romano reclined her seat and nestled her head against a pillow tucked between her seat and the window.

Britt twisted around until she faced Romano. The dim light in the cabin and flickering overhead displays showing the latest movie cast soft shadows across her face. "Bear with me, please."

"Believe me, I am." Romano dropped his voice and leaned toward Britt so he wouldn't disturb the other woman. "You've got my full attention. I just don't see where you're headed with the language interpretation."

"It relates to who Joseph of Arimathea really was. Many characters in the Gospels were not identified by their given names. Saint Matthew was referred to as Levi of Alphaeus, Levi the son of Alphaeus, or Levi of the Succession. The word 'Arimathea' is a combination of the Hebrew *ha ram* or *ha rama*, of the highest, and the Greek *theo*, of God. The composite would mean of the highest of God, *Ha Rama Theo*, or Divine Highness."

Romano still didn't see a direct connection. "But there's no reference to a Joseph except for Mary's husband, who was described as a carpenter or craftsman."

"I don't think it meant that Joseph. I think it relates to Jesus' brother, James, who had his own following among the ranks of the Hebrew community."

"That's stretching scholarly license. How do you get James to be interpreted as Joseph?"

"Most scholars agree that Jesus was the heir to the throne of David. The patriarchal title of Joseph was applied to the next in succession. With Jesus regarded as David, his eldest brother, James, would be designated Joseph."

Romano tapped the fingertips of his right hand into the palm of his left in a series of ceremonial claps. "I give you credit, Britt, that's an interesting theory. But you'll need a lot more than that to defend it as a credible theory to an academic jury of your peers." He thought for a moment. "What about Joseph of Arimathea as a respected member of the Hebrew community volunteering his tomb to the Sanhedrin and Roman authorities as a means of having it guarded against attempts to steal the body and any further unrest?"

"Isn't that more of a stretch of known facts than Jesus being entombed in a sepulcher belonging to his own family? And wouldn't it make more sense for Pilate to allow Jesus' own respected brother to take charge? That would support the women of Jesus' family accepting the arrangements made by James without question."

Romano scratched his goatee and raised his eyebrows. "I must say I credit your creative imagination and the depth of your research. You've piqued my interest. I'm looking forward to analyzing the gospel segment. That could nudge me closer to your theory. But, at this point, it's just that, a theory. You must remember I've researched my share of alternate theories about Jesus and Christianity. The end result is they all lack supporting evidence. The Gospels adopted in the New Testament were carefully culled over hundreds of years as being the most reliable."

"All I ask is an open mind. The last section of the document refers to the disciples secretly using aloe and myrrh as a purgative to resuscitate Jesus." Britt seemed to struggle keeping her eyes open. "Saint John verifies that Nicodemus delivered a hundred-pound weight of those plants to the sepulcher."

"But if Jesus died on the cross, wouldn't it have been resurrection, not resuscitation?"

"I told you the gospel segment refers to snake venom and Jesus being put into a comatose state."

"But wouldn't that have even exacerbated his death by asphyxiation? From what I recall, crucifixion stresses the chest muscles and diaphragm, which puts the chest in the inhaled position. In order to exhale, the individual had to push up on his feet to release the tension on the muscles. Eventually the person would become exhausted. Couldn't push. Couldn't breathe. If Jesus went comatose, he'd have suffocated very quickly."

"I came to the same conclusion until I looked more closely at the scripture account. When the soldiers came to Jesus after breaking the legs of the other two who were crucified with him, they saw that he was dead and a soldier thrust his lance into his side and blood and water flowed out. Medical experts believe that the water was fluid that would have collected in the membrane around the heart and around the lungs, speeding up asphyxiation. When the lance was pulled out, the fluid was released, which could have delayed asphyxiation."

Romano tented his fingers in front of his lips and nodded. "I must admit, that's an interesting theory, but what did the James Gospel say about the supposed resuscitation? Were they successful? And what happened to the body, dead or alive?"

Britt dropped her gaze. "Unfortunately, the gospel segment I have ends before that's resolved. It's why I didn't think twice about going to Grand Central to get the rest of it." She looked up at Romano. Her eyes were glassed over with fatigue, but she managed a weak smile.

Romano managed his own hint at a grin. "I did the same thing. And without having a clue as to what this so-called gospel might really contain."

"But there is a reference in my document to Mary Magdalene being with child. Twins, to be exact."

"Now there's a concept that keeps cropping up in every alternative theory." Another thought hit Romano. "You know, Mary Magdalene also adds support for your theory that Joseph of Arimathea could refer to James. I've read a number of scholarly works that claim Mary was really Miriam, who came from the fishing village of Magdala."

Britt reclined her seat a bit and settled back into it. "I guess there's a glimmer of hope that you may be coming around to supporting my theory."

"Oh, we're a long, long way from that." Romano reclined his seat to match Britt's. "I'd say we're at the stage of agreeing to disagree."

"Well, that's progress."

Romano noticed Britt's eyes were closed. "Why don't we get some rest and continue when our brains are not frazzled. I know mine is."

Britt mumbled, "Great idea," and her head slumped toward her shoulder.

Romano's eyes felt heavy. He realized he was fading fast but was glad he had made the trip. He was seeing Britt Hamar in a slightly different light. Even if her theories were based upon some questionable premises, at least she seemed sincere in her beliefs. But he couldn't rid his mind of the lurking anger with Britt that gnawed away at him for what happened to Ted. He shook his head. Maybe he was being too harsh in rushing to judgment thinking Britt was even indirectly responsible for Ted's death.

He glanced over at Britt. Her chest rose and fell in a deep, slow cadence. She seemed so innocent as she cradled her injured shoulder and drifted into a deep sleep. Suddenly, her body twitched and she slid closer to him. Her head inched lower until it rested against his shoulder.

Romano slowly blotted his sweaty palms on his pants legs and closed his eyes. A recurring image of Marta filled the darkness. No matter how hard he tried, he couldn't erase the picture of her etched in his mind or push away the thoughts of what his life would have been like with her. The anger against his mother was always there festering in the background. He tried to justify what had happened through the words Father Ted had told him, *Maybe it was an exercise by God to bring you into the priesthood, where you could make an impact on so many lives*. No matter how hard he tried, he couldn't accept what had happened.

Marta's smiling face faded into a darkening mist and Romano became aware of his own breath matching the subtle rise and fall of the warmth against his shoulder.

FORTY-ONE

AGENT TOM CUTLER GOBBLED DOWN THE SECOND energy bar from the stash he kept in his desk drawer for occasions like this. He was hunched over his computer, going over the latest reports from his team. His wife, Maggie, wouldn't be happy with what was turning out to be another very late night, or maybe an all-nighter. But Cutler had a hunch these priest deaths were not over, and he had to stop the momentum of whoever or whatever was behind them.

His agents had interviewed all of Brittany Hamar's neighbors, and only one of them saw her leaving with an overnight bag. She hadn't returned to her apartment, and so far she was the only direct connection to at least two of the deaths. And then there was her shooting. This was turning out to be one hell of a mess. As soon as the details about the deaths and the stigmata reached the news media, the scandal rags would have a field day. The bureau would be deluged with calls from every wacko and conspiracy nut.

Donahue entered Cutler's office clutching a stack of papers. "Tom, we located Hamar."

"Great." Cutler grabbed his jacket. "Let's go interview her."

Donahue held up a hand and dropped the papers on the desk. "Hold on, Tom, we're not getting to her tonight. She's on a flight to Vienna."

Cutler picked up his phone. "Vienna is near Washington Dulles International. Get some agents over there from the local field office to detain her when the plane lands. I'll get us a ride to Dulles."

"I'm afraid it's not Vienna, Virginia. She's on a flight to Austria."

"Shit." Cutler started to hang up the phone, then stopped. "Get me on the next flight to Austria. I'm going to call the National

Central Bureau and see if they can arrange for an Interpol agent to meet me in Vienna. We don't have enough for them to bring Hamar in, but at least they can locate her and keep tabs on her until I get there."

"Afraid there won't be any flights 'til tomorrow." Donahue pointed to the top sheet on the stack of papers he had put on Cutler's desk. "Take a look at this first." He traced his finger beneath a name on the copy of a flight manifest. "Father Joseph Romano is on the same flight."

"Hell." Cutler smacked himself on the forehead. "Don't tell me he's the next victim."

FORTY-TWO

CHARLIE CLOSED *THE LOST CHRISTIANS*, GRABBED his mug of coffee, and rolled his chair away from the table. "Wow, I thought we were done with cramming when we got accepted into grad school."

Carlota laughed. "I wouldn't call this cramming. I find it fascinating."

"Yeah, me too." Charlie took a long swig from his mug. "I think we agree Professor Hamar is on a slippery slope."

Carlota put the last of the articles by Britt Hamar on the stack next to her computer. "I took notes on our discussions. There's a definite trend of her slipping further and further from orthodox Church doctrine."

"I think it started with *The Lost Christians*," Charlie said. "It got her focused on the Gnostic Gospels and a fascination with rituals, the mysteries, and finding gnosis, or true knowledge, through Jesus' teachings."

"And that led to her last book." Carlota picked up *Saint Paul— The Apostle Who Never Walked with Jesus*. "This entire book questions the basic foundations of Christianity. It claims that Paul led the evolving Church away from the philosophy that salvation comes from knowledge through Jesus' teachings and good works to a belief that salvation comes only through accepting Jesus as savior through his Crucifixion and Resurrection."

Charlie finished the last of his coffee. "I think somewhere along the line Professor Hamar became a closet Gnostic."

"She wasn't hiding anything in her latest articles." Carlota spread out copies of five articles on the table. "She blatantly says the Church took a shortcut to simplify what Jesus was all about when it established the creed and offered blanket forgiveness of sins through confession."

"I hope Father Romano knows who he's really dealing with in Professor Hamar."

"I'm meeting with one of her students tomorrow. Evidently something happened that set her off in this direction. I don't think it's purely academic."

"I'm glad he took the BlackBerry. I'll send him a heads-up on what we've found." Charlie rolled his chair back to the computer and started typing.

FORTY-THREE

Bright sunlight flashed through the cabin as passengers slid up window shades and the flight attendants began serving breakfast. Romano smelled the unmistakable aroma of coffee, opened one eye, and squinted to get accustomed to the light. Britt was still leaning against him. She finally stirred from all the commotion and opened her eyes. Her look had a dreamlike quality, as if she were lost, not sure who, or where, she was.

Britt blinked a few times and glanced around the cabin. She rolled her eyes and shook her head. "It took me a moment to get my bearings. I was dreaming about being shot. I thought I was still in the hospital."

A flight attendant rolled a cart next to them and pushed the wheel lock in place with her foot. She smiled, handed them breakfast trays, and poured them coffees as they began pulling the foil off their egg platters.

"I could really use my morning espresso," Romano said after he downed half of his coffee in one gulp.

"I wouldn't have pegged you as an espresso man." Britt pressed her hand against her left shoulder and flinched.

"Are you okay?"

"Just a little sore. I'm not used to getting shot. I'll be fine. Is espresso a morning ritual?"

"Yes. It's one of my weaknesses. I love a piping-hot espresso to kick-start the day."

"Do you brew your own?"

Romano gave Britt a guilty look. "I do have a secret extravagance, my prized FrancisFrancis Italian espresso machine. I grind my own blend, tamp it to perfection, and after a twelve-second pour, it tops off with a delicious golden crema. After a few sips, my brain kicks in."

Britt chuckled. "You'll soon be in your glory, Vienna has outrageous cafés. But I've been told to be careful not to overindulge on their incredible pastries."

Romano chewed on a croissant and then finished his coffee. "I've been to Vienna a few times. My motto is, When in Rome, do as the Romans do, so I have espresso a couple times a day and gorge myself on the sweets. My old college roommate lives at the Jesuit rectory and is also a religious scholar. I'm hoping he can help us out about this Felix. By the way, is the meeting set up? You did get through to him?"

The corners of Britt's eyes turned down slightly and she brushed something off her knit top. "I said he was a very secretive man." Then she looked back at Romano with an uneasy smile. "I checked with the bookstore. Someone picked up the message."

"Did he get back to you? What did he say?"

"The arrangement was that my message was to include the time I was arriving in Vienna and the name of the hotel I would be staying at. He'll contact me when I get to the hotel."

Romano couldn't believe what he had just heard. He was on a plane getting ready to arrive in Vienna and Britt didn't even have a firm meeting scheduled with the mystery man. This was way more than he had bargained for. "You're telling me we may never see this Felix?"

"I know it sounds stupid, but I have confidence in Felix. I met him a few months ago under the same conditions. I left a message for him at the bookstore and flew into Vienna just to see him on my way back to the States and spent the night at the NH Hotel at the airport. There was a message waiting for me when I checked in, and he met me that evening at a nearby restaurant. That's when he warned me about stopping my research on *Le Serpent Rouge* and told me about the killings in France."

Romano decided to take advantage of the time he had with Britt to push her for more details about her book. Maybe something would trigger the discovery of a real motive for the deaths of the priests. If the Felix meeting fell through and he flew back to New York on the next flight, at least he might be able to dig up something from her that could help the FBI track down Ted's killer.

After the stewardess collected their breakfast trays, Romano looked at Britt and stroked his goatee. "Something still bothers me about the basic premise behind your book."

"That it contradicts the teachings of the Church?"

"In my office you stressed that you wanted to present a balanced view of historical data, folklore, mythology, as well as the canonical version of the Church. You seem to focus on limited facts and digging out isolated theorems to support those facts. I hope you gave appropriate weight to the preponderance of evidence supporting the canonical version."

Anger flashed across Britt's face. Her radiant eyes retreated behind a fearsome squint and her lips tightened. "And you stressed you were only interested in the truth. You'll find that I gave appropriate weight to that which deserved it."

"And what is the *truth*?"

"It may be what you're not ready to accept."

Romano felt his anger rising. "Try me."

"What if my shooting and the deaths of the priests were an act of God because the world is not yet ready to accept the truth?"

"That's ridiculous. Now you're acting like a conspiracy buff."

Britt's mouth hardened into an angry grimace. Her eyes radiated arrogance. "Maybe you have a better idea why your friend is dead. You said the reason may be hidden in my research. I've been telling you what my research found, and all you seem to want to do is label me as someone focusing on irrational theories, or worse, a conspiracy buff."

Romano realized he had stepped over a line. "Sorry. I'm not trying to discount your research. I'm just trying to better understand where you're coming from."

"I blindly followed Church teaching for most of my life and career until I realized maybe the Church wasn't telling the whole story. That maybe they molded Church doctrine into something that supported their human failings: hunger for power and control. That's what got me interested in Gnosticism and the Gnostic Gospels. Maybe you should give them appropriate weight."

Romano started to see a crack in Britt's veneer and decided to probe deeper. "I have done research on the Gnostic Gospels."

"Well, they certainly should have provided a lot of food for thought. For example, what makes you so certain Jesus was one single entity of physical and spiritual man? Is that a perception? Or are there consistent, synoptic theories and solid facts to support that concept?"

Romano tried to determine where Britt was going with her argument and decided it was best to cut and run. "Based upon our current level of science and technology, I'd have to say that we don't have a very good handle on the spiritual aspect of that question. But, on the other hand, for two thousand years, science has not been able to disprove the Church canons and the basic premises of the New Testament."

"You accuse me of not giving appropriate weight to the canonical version. You don't seem to even consider the alternatives. My faith has taken a dramatic shift in the past few years. I believe that Jesus could have been two separate entities, a physical being and a spiritual being. The physical being could have been crucified, dead, and buried, and the spiritual being could have been resurrected and ascended into heaven."

Romano nodded while trying to search for an inkling of what Britt's motivation could be to so doggedly try to disprove accepted Church doctrine. "I guess I'll have to borrow one of Charlie's favorite expressions. That puts us in a very tenuous *do-loop*. Because of the spiritual factor, science and physical evidence can't prove either position, or, for that matter, disprove them. So we're stuck in a never-ending circle. But just for argument's sake, how do you explain the empty tomb that was described in the Gospels or the latest evidence on the Shroud of Turin?"

"If you follow my theory about Jesus being buried in the family sepulcher supported by the declaration in the James Gospel, that opens a few options. Jesus could have died, and his body was hidden by his family or his disciples. Or he could have been resuscitated and spirited away with Mary Magdalene to the south of France, where they raised their adorable twins."

"And the shroud?"

"That was a pet project of mine and I think it puts the Church on rocky ground."

"How so?"

"Many scientists confirmed that the image on the shroud has a high probability of being that of Jesus, created by some physiochemical process that had taken place in the tomb. Medical doctors, radiologists, criminologists, and professors of forensic medicine agreed all indications pointed to an authentic representation of the crucified Jesus down to the wounds from the crown of thorns and the nails through the wrists rather than the hands, as in all other conventional medieval representations. Even the thumbs were rotated inward as a result of median nerve damage as the nails passed through the spaces of Destot in the wrists. The evidence also pointed out that the body was not washed in accordance with Jewish custom and law. Instead, it was anointed with large quantities of expensive ointments and swathed in a burial cloth. That seems to support the theory of an attempt to resuscitate Jesus using aloe and myrrh."

Romano raised a finger. "Allow me to play devil's advocate. If the tomb did belong to Joseph, a member of the Jewish council, and if the body was delivered by Roman soldiers, isn't it also possible that they wouldn't follow Jewish custom? After all, Jesus was looked upon by the Sanhedrin and the Roman authorities as someone spouting blasphemy and trying to incite rebellion. They mocked him as being the King of the Jews."

"We're back to competing theories and we'll get caught in Charlie's *do-loop*. Why don't we just look at what is supported by solid scientific facts."

Romano nodded. "Agreed."

"Microscopic examination of the fibers revealed that the cloth came from the area of Palestine around the Dead Sea. In 1988 independent carbon-dating analyses were performed by the University of Arizona, the Swiss Federal Institute of Technology, and Oxford Research Laboratory. They all agreed that it was ninety-nine-point-nine-percent certain that the Shroud of Turin had its origins in the period from 1000 to 1500 CE and ninety-five-percent certain that it dated from somewhere between 1260 and 1390."

"And that set the conspiracy buffs running amok."

Now Britt wagged a finger. "But don't forget, the Church was also relieved when the shroud was discredited because it proved that Jesus could have still been alive when he was taken down from the cross."

"That's still open to some speculation," Romano said. "I only bring that up because I know you'll be quoting the latest scientific findings. Either the sample tested came from a later repair to the fabric of the shroud or a fire in 1532 in the chapel where the shroud was housed caused the silver reliquary where it was kept to melt and altered the carbon dating."

"Don't forget the biogenic varnishes deposited on the shroud by bacteria and fungi that grew on the fibers over the years. What was in fact being tested was less than forty percent shroud and more than sixty percent living organism."

Romano raised his eyebrows. "I see you certainly have done your shroud research. Why don't we agree that the shroud is most likely from the time of Jesus."

Britt's eyes widened in surprise. "I don't believe it. We agree on something."

"I think our only disagreements are in the weights we assign to various theories. There's only one unquestionable certainty that I've found." Romano cocked his head and locked his eyes on to Britt's. "The idea of *eternal truth* is a myth concocted as we struggle to exist in an imperfect world."

Britt formed a half smile. "And I think God lives within our search for *eternal truth* and Jesus was sent to guide us to live better lives in the imperfect world."

"Ladies and gentlemen, please return to your seats and fasten your seat belts. We are preparing for our descent into Vienna."

Romano raised their tray tables. "Well, I guess you get the last word."

The jet banked into a turn. "Look at the view." Britt pointed to the window.

As the plane sliced through a puffy layer of cumulus clouds, the small farms surrounding Vienna suddenly appeared. The landscape looked like a carefully crafted patchwork quilt. It appeared almost unreal, with precise lines separating each verdant field. Romano knew as the plane swooped closer he'd see the details like finite brushstrokes, including all the flaws.

It reminded Romano of the story unfolding around him. Maybe he was caught up in seeing only the overall picture, guilty of not giving appropriate weight to all the facts. Like Britt, he might be seeing only what he wanted to see. He had to narrow his focus, to look for the details. He thought of the cross he'd been given by Ted, the same cross Britt had seen on Father Matteo. Maybe Father Sinclair had some idea of its significance. Maybe he should take a closer look at Ted's life. He knew nothing about his years in Switzerland, except that he had studied in Innsbruck with Father Hans Josef, the father rector at the Vienna Jesuit rectory. Maybe Father Josef could shed some light on Ted's death.

Now there was Britt. Romano sensed he hadn't seen the real Brittany Hamar, that she was hiding something. Her zeal for attacking Church doctrine was grounded in more than academic curiosity. She seemed to be a woman on a mission. So far, he didn't have a clue as to what that mission could be. He glanced at her left hand, which now had a white-knuckle grip on their shared armrest. No rings. He hadn't noticed that before.

FORTY-FOUR

THE TAXI MANEUVERED THROUGH THE MORNING traffic beside the brown waters of the Danube Canal toward the heart of Vienna. Britt was fascinated by the quaint charm of the city. She glanced through a tourist guide and map she had purchased at the airport. The descriptions of Vienna exuded an old-world serenity and order that was disappearing in America. It was even reflected in the taxi they were taking from Schwechat International. The pristine black Mercedes sported leather seats and the driver wore a black suit with a crisp white shirt and tie. A far cry from the banged and bruised yellow cabs that wandered the streets of New York.

Britt noticed that Romano's attention was still riveted to a PDA with a built-in thumb pad that he had dug out of his knapsack as soon as the taxi pulled away from the airport. He hadn't said a word during the twenty-minute ride. "I hope you're not playing a video game and missing the beautiful scenery."

Romano glanced up from the device. "I'm checking my e-mails. Charlie insisted I take his BlackBerry so I could receive messages twenty-four-seven and warned me to shut it off while we were on the plane." His eyes locked back on to the screen. "I'm trying to catch up before we get to the hotel. Unfortunately, I'm not up to speed on these electronic gadgets."

Britt wondered what could be so important as to cause him to miss the picturesque ride into Vienna after being cooped up on an airplane for so many hours. Romano had the BlackBerry tilted away from her so she couldn't get a peek at the screen.

The driver turned left across a bridge over the canal. They headed up a small side street toward the dense center of the city marked by the ornate spires of Vienna's many churches jutting into the crystal blue skyline. During the next few turns, Britt marveled at the contiguous rooflines of the multistory buildings that hemmed the streets and turned them into a veritable maze throughout Vienna's First District. The architecture was a mélange of Renaissance and Baroque styles blended with the clean lines of renovated buildings. The conservative Austrians maintained a seamless continuity of style that didn't conflict with the rich legacy of the Hapsburg reign.

At the next turn, they entered a wider street, and Britt noticed a blue-and-white sign on the corner of a building indicating it was Singerstrasse, the street her hotel was on. The map showed Singerstrasse ending at a pedestrian zone near the famous Stephansdom church that many referred to as the soul of the city. Her guidebook pointed out that the pedestrian zone ran along Kärntner Strasse, which attracted tourists like a powerful magnet to the myriad retail stores and small shops selling everything from designer clothes and jewelry to miniature statues of the Hofburg Palace, famous Mozart chocolates, and prints from well-known turn-of-the-century artists of the Jugendstil period.

Britt noticed Romano slip the BlackBerry into a pocket of his knapsack. Then he looked at her with a puzzled expression. "I've been thinking about this whole sequence of bizarre events and one factor keeps cropping up."

"And what's that?"

"I'm convinced your research is what got you targeted. And the only thing you've told me that sticks out as unique are your meetings with Felix and the calls from *The Messenger*. You told me you haven't confided details of your theory to anyone."

"I keep telling you, if Felix was involved with the deaths of the priests, someone would have remembered him. He's not the kind of person who blends in. And I definitely didn't see him when I was shot."

"Did the calls from *The Messenger* start after your meeting with Felix?"

"They started between my meetings with Felix. But, believe me, I would know if the voice of *The Messenger* was Felix." Britt raised her eyes in frustration. "It's not."

"Don't you agree that your being shot is related to something you've uncovered in your research?"

"I'm sure it's related to my research."

Romano's eyes narrowed into a look of confusion. "What makes you *sure*?"

"Remember, while I was in the hospital, someone accessed

my computer. It had to have been either the shooter or an accomplice. Nothing was deleted, so they must not have found anything incriminating. I'm hoping Felix can provide the final links that tie everything together, especially now that his life may be in danger."

"His life's in danger?" Romano said. "Am I missing something?"

"Felix's information triggered me to look more seriously into the bloodline theory. As you would be quick to point out, he got me to put more *weight* on that theory. If Felix is not involved with whoever shot me and killed the priests, then he could be in real danger and I must warn him."

"How would anyone know about Felix?"

"I referred to him numerous times in my notes."

"If he's as paranoid as you say, Felix is probably not even his real name." Romano's expression froze, then he turned to Britt. "Unless someone's been following you."

"Then we're all in danger." Britt shrugged. "But for Felix, it wouldn't matter. In my notes I described where I met him and what we discussed. Since he's such a memorable character, I'm sure they wouldn't have much trouble tracking him down."

"All the more reason to tell Felix everything. I think it's time for you to be totally up front with him. Tell him all that's happened. If he thinks he could be in danger, maybe he'll shed some more light on who could be behind this."

Or maybe he'll clam up and completely disappear. Britt decided to play it by ear with Felix. After today, she might not even need him anymore.

Then a shiver of fear gave her a reality check. If Felix was involved or being monitered, she and Romano could be in serious danger.

A few blocks away a massive stone-and-stucco building with ornate sculptures and columns jutted out into a plaza teeming with people. "We'll soon know if we're meeting Felix." Britt pointed ahead. "My hotel should be just before that pedestrian zone."

Romano glanced up the street. "Well, I see the world leader in fast food hasn't missed its chance."

Britt noticed the Golden Arches rising from the second story of a large Viennese storefront. As they got closer, she saw the giant neon letters of the Hotel Royal and beneath it another sign,

McDonald's, with an arrow pointing to the fast-food restaurant across the street. The street ended abruptly just past the hotel at the start of the pedestrian zone. Droves of tourists milled about, their necks craned as they searched for details of Vienna's regal past among the elegant buildings.

The taxi stopped in front of the glassed entrance to the Hotel Royal and Romano got out, retrieved Britt's bag from the trunk, and paid the driver. Britt went inside to check in and see if there was a message from Felix. As she was filling out the registration, the desk clerk handed her a sealed envelope with her name printed on the front in calligraphy. She stopped and immediately opened it. The message was also in a fancy script. *Ms. Hamar: I will ring you shortly after your arrival to set up our meeting. No need to worry; I'll be watching for you. You won't have long to wait. Felix.*

Britt felt an apprehensive twinge in the pit of her stomach as she turned her head and glanced through the glass front of the hotel. Romano was coming through the door carrying her bag. Beyond him she could see a throng of tourists and a small group of people sitting in a makeshift outdoor café surrounded by planters sprouting an array of manicured bushes, miniature trees, and seasonal flowers flowing over their edges. She didn't spot the gnomelike figure of Felix anywhere. She glanced down the street and around the plaza at the start of the pedestrian zone. There were countless places where he could be watching from and never be seen. Cars parked along the street, storefronts, the cluster of canopied pay phones on the corner, even a window on the second floor of McDonald's could be hiding Felix from view.

Romano set Britt's bag next to her. "Any message from Felix?"

Britt pointed to the note. "I think you should leave until I speak with Felix. He's a weird character, to say the least. I don't want him to refuse to meet if he sees me with a stranger. I'll go up to my room and contact you after he calls."

Romano scanned the note. "I'll go check in at the rectory and wait for your call." He wrote a number on the back of Felix's envelope. "This is the main number for the Jesuit rectory. I'll tell the person at reception I'm expecting a very important call."

Romano put on his backpack, left the hotel, and disappeared among the cluster of people checking out the pastries in the window of the Aida Café Konditorei on the corner.

Britt hoped she hadn't made a mistake including Romano. She desperately wanted to meet with Felix before the next leg of her journey and feared if he saw her with Romano he might be scared off. She was hoping Felix could provide details that could be critical to the final phase of *The Jesus Fraud*—and more important, he might be privy to secrets that could keep her alive.

Then the spector of fear gripped her again. If she was wrong, it could mean her death—and Romano's!

FORTY-FIVE

THE SUN PEERED THROUGH A GAUZY LAYER OF clouds scattered across the blue sky, and a strong breeze whipped down the narrow streets as Romano wound his way toward the Alte Universität. He had decided to take a brisk walk to the rectory next to the Jesuit church near the Old University rather than continue on with the taxi. He had missed running for the past few days and needed the exercise, even though he knew a few brisk walks wouldn't make up the lost miles. But his concern about his missed runs couldn't come close to the guilt he felt for missing his daily Examen of Consciousness. It had been over twenty-four hours since his last examen. He was always diligent in following the daily Jesuit ritual, which made him more focused and brought him closer to God and his calling as a priest.

He had intended to start his examen last night before he fell asleep on the plane. As he had closed his eyes and began the process by recalling he was in the presence of God, he felt Britt's head against his shoulder and was filled with a sense of confusion. He couldn't focus on the rest of the five steps. His brain flashed images of fear, weakness, despair, even anger. He finally focused on prayers of reconciliation and resolve, seeing his need for God's concern for him and his human weaknesses. Then he finally fell into a fitful sleep interrupted by snippets of dreams he tried to suppress but failed.

Romano had not been surprised at Charlie and Carlota's e-mail. His conversations with Britt during the flight had prepped him for the details about her steady drift away from orthodox Church doctrine. His grad assistants' solid research and well-thought-out interpretation of Britt's work gave him a better understanding as to where she seemed to be headed, which was down a very slippery slope. But he didn't understand why she had drifted so quickly toward a radical interpretation of the life and passion of Christ.

Romano decided to take a more direct approach with Britt and focus on what she was trying to uncover during her meetings with Ted and Father Matteo. He also wanted to press her for more information on *The Messenger*. Why did the mystery caller refer to himself as *The Messenger*? Since each of the priests had a code name based upon archangels, could *The Messenger* also be a code name? The archangel Gabriel was the heavenly messenger mentioned in the Old Testament and the Qur'an. Maybe the tie-in had to do with archangels?

Romano hurried along the side of the elegant Austrian Academy of Science building, turned the corner at Dr.-Ignas-Seipel-Platz, and entered a large cobblestone plaza. Directly in front of him was the imposing Jesuit church dedicated in high memory to the Virgin Mary and topped by two cupolas aged to a rich aqua patina. He headed to the entrance of the provincial rectory for Austria next to the church.

Once inside, he was greeted warmly by the receptionist, who wore a perpetual smile and asked him to please take a seat while she called a priest to show him to his room. She was a student from Poland and very proud to show off her command of English. She offered profuse apologies for his friend, Father Heinz Müller, and Father Rector Hans Josef, who had prior commitments at the university and would not be returning to the rectory until after lunch. He explained to her that posed no problem since he was awaiting a call for an important meeting that brought him to Vienna at the last minute.

The phone rang at the desk and the receptionist waved at Romano. "Father, your call." She pointed to a phone on the table next to him. "I will transfer it to that telephone."

Romano picked up. "Britt, that was fast."

"Felix must have been watching just like he said. It gives me the creeps."

"Is the meeting set up?"

"He got very defensive when I mentioned bringing you. I told him you were a colleague, another professor helping me with my research."

"I'm honored you raised me to the status of a colleague."

Britt laughed. "That was just to get him to agree to let you come to the meeting. I'll hold off on the final decision until I've seen your review of my manuscript."

"When and where is the meeting?"

"Ten o'clock at the café Zum Alten Blumenstock. He says it's on the corner of Ballgasse and Blumenstockgasse a couple blocks away from my hotel. I checked the map. It looks like a small side street off of Weihburggasse."

"I'll pick you up at your hotel in a few minutes."

Romano stood as a young priest came toward him with a hand outstretched in greeting. He shook hands with the priest and they exchanged pleasantries on the way to the room. Romano dug a lightweight cotton Windbreaker out of his knapsack and stuffed a notepad and pen into the inside pocket. He apologized for having to rush out to a meeting so quickly, grabbed the BlackBerry, and headed out of the rectory.

On the way to the hotel, Romano pondered the events of the past few days. The more he thought about it, the more he feared there were far-reaching connections to the Church itself.

FORTY-SIX

Romano stopped in his tracks when he and Britt arrived at the entrance to Ballgasse. On the map it had appeared to be a street that branched off of Weihburggasse not far from the Franziskaner church, but this looked like the entrance to a courtyard, not a street. It was a stone archway between two buildings with the face of an angel carved into the apex. The narrow, dark alley beyond was not what he had in mind for meeting Britt's mystery informant.

Britt shook her head. "This is not exactly what I had expected."

"Well, that makes two of us. You did say he was an odd fellow. I hope odd doesn't include dangerous."

Romano stepped inside the entrance to the narrow cobblestone passageway and checked out the row of signs on the wall beside the stone archway. They promoted a restaurant, antique shop, cabinetmaker, furniture restorer, and a café. He looked down the passage past the darkened entrance. Light spilled between the buildings, highlighting a café on the corner where the passage intersected with another alleyway.

Romano motioned to Britt, and they made their way along the narrow cobblestone path to a quaint café sporting chalkboards leaning against the front of the building listing the specials of the day. Three lighted cases on the outside wall displayed the full menu and drink list. Draped above the entrance was a string of colorful lights.

As they stepped inside, Britt stopped suddenly and Romano slammed into her and grabbed her by the shoulders to avoid knocking her down. When she regained her balance, she pointed to a stone sculpture jutting out of the wall next to a gilded Baroque mirror that had been transformed into a display for the café's extensive liquor collection. "That's Baphomet. I attended a

Gnostic mass at an *Ordo Templi Orientalis* ceremony yesterday in New York where they referred to Baphomet. He's one of the idols the Templars were charged with worshipping and the modern symbol of the devil."

"Please don't tell me you've woven the myths of the Templars into your bloodline theory." Romano walked over and took a closer look at the sculpture. "This is Bacchus, the god of wine. See the grapes and grape leaves surrounding his head."

Britt pointed to the horns. "Bacchus didn't have horns. Because of the danger involved in worshipping Baphomet, they often disguised his image."

"Now you're going to tell me that the venerable head of John the Baptist was the true Baphomet worshipped by the Templars." Romano slowly rocked his head from side to side. "Britt, that's pure unsubstantiated myth."

Before Britt could respond, a gnomelike man with the droopy face of a bloodhound walked up to them. He wore a tweed sport jacket and a gold silk ascot tucked into a brown dress shirt. "Sir, listen to her." He waved a finger at Romano. "Professor Hamar's right, she's right."

"Joseph, this is Felix. Felix, Joseph, the colleague I told you about on the phone."

Felix glanced warily around the café, then motioned to a small room off to the side of the bar. "In there. Take a table in there. More privacy."

Romano studied Felix as they walked into the empty room. He realized why Britt insisted Felix would be easily recognized. The little man could be a caricature from Madame Tussaud's who was hit by a blast of hot air. The skin of his face drooped in folds and his eyes were reduced to narrow slits by sagging lids.

When Romano sat down, he was surprised by the painting hanging on the wall behind Felix. It depicted a raven-haired woman emerging through heavenly clouds in a deep blue sky being kissed on the mouth by a cherub. The winged child with an innocent, rosy face caressed the woman's neck with his delicate fingers.

Felix made an effort to raise his brows and his eyes brightened a bit, almost into a droopy smile. "Aha, aha. I see you're fascinated by Sophia."

"That's something I haven't discussed with you," Britt said. "Felix is convinced that when Baphomet is decoded using the

Atbash cipher, it will be a perfect encryption of *Sophia*, Greek
for wisdom."

"Very fascinating," Romano replied. "How does that relate to
your bloodline theory?"

"Some researchers, Felix included, think the *Rex Deus* created the Knights Templar to protect *Le Serpent Rouge* and to recover a great treasure hidden beneath the Temple of Jerusalem.
They believe the Templars and the *Rex Deus* follow the original
teachings of Jesus relating to finding true knowledge, or gnosis,
from within. Baphomet is their symbol of the search for that
knowledge."

Felix made another attempt at a smile. "Well put, Professor.
I hope you are now a believer." He gave a wild look toward
Romano. "Are you, sir?"

"Let us just say I'm not as far along as Professor Hamar. She
told me you have done considerable research relating to the
bloodline theory." Romano turned his head toward Britt. "We're
hoping your information can shed some light on who may have
tried to kill her."

For the first time Felix's lids raised wide open and Romano
could see fear in his dark eyes.

"Someone tried to kill you, kill you." Felix's voice trembled.
"I warned. I warned. Those who control the bloodline, they'll destroy you, they will."

"That's why I wanted to meet. I need to know who would try
to kill me. The only thing I uncovered that could be a threat is an
original section of a secret document written by James, the
brother of Jesus."

Felix's head suddenly made small jerks in random directions.
His eyes blinked with each twitch, as if a gnat were attacking
him. Then he stared up at the ceiling and scratched at his jaw
with both hands, as if searching for a lost fact or a fading memory. Finally he looked across the table at Britt. "James? There's
no secret James document. That's crazy, crazy. The French papers. Lies, all lies. What secret document do you have?"

As Britt described the text, Felix rested his chin on his folded
hands and gave her a cold, wary look. When she finished, he
shook his head. "I uncovered those details from many different
writings. Yes, I did. There's no gospel. Where did you get it?"

"I suppose you could say from a source such as yourself."
Britt glanced at Romano. "An anonymous caller who refers to

himself as *The Messenger* contacted me a few months after the Saunièr Society meeting in London. He sent me the sample and said when the time was right I would see the entire document."

"You were shot. Who shot you?"

Britt told him about the call requesting her to go to Grand Central Station to get the manuscript. She described the shooting, then stressed that she was certain the caller was not *The Messenger*.

"I've been thinking about this caller," Romano said. "He gave you code names of Uriel and Raphael for the priests. The archangel Gabriel was known as the heavenly messenger, maybe—"

"Priests, what priests?" Felix's voice raised to almost a shout.

Britt described *The Messenger* telling her Father Matteo and Father Mathews had information concerning the bloodline and that the code names Uriel and Raphael might get them to be more cooperative. Felix leaned toward her, his attention locked on every word. When she mentioned the death of the priests and the stigmata, he jerked back in his seat, and fear crept across his withered face.

"Were they Jesuits, Jesuit priests?" Felix asked.

"As a matter of fact, they were," Romano said. "What significance is that?"

Felix sat up and glanced nervously back and forth, seeming to be deciding what to say next. "I was a priest, parish priest." His voice lowered to almost a whisper. "I heard a confession. Caused me great alarm. I researched the Jesuits. Hmm, hmm. I was suspicious. The *Rex Deus*, I think they sponsored the Jesuits. Yes, yes, I think so. That's why the Jesuits grew so powerful. Rapid growth, much wealth. The Templars found the riches. Oh yes. Beneath the Temple of Jerusalem. The *Rex Deus* used the wealth to protect their secret. Ignatius Loyola, he's the one." Felix kept nodding and nodding, "He's the one. He gave them what they needed. The Jesuit order. *Follow in the footsteps of Jesus*. What better place to hide the bloodline." Felix wagged a finger at Romano and Brit. "*Follow in the footsteps of Jesus*."

Romano was stunned by the mention of the Jesuits being involved in a conspiracy to hide a secret bloodline of Jesus. The Jesuits were accused of many things over the years, but this took the cake. Before he could respond, a waiter arrived and took their orders for two espressos, a weak coffee with cream for Britt, and an assortment of pastries.

"You haven't looked into the Jesuits. Do it . . . do it," Felix said after the waiter was out of earshot. "Do the research, you'll see."

Romano looked to Britt, who shook her head. "I found no references to the Jesuits," she said.

"And I'd say that's an enormous stretch," Romano added. "If anyone would have reason to suspect a shadowy history to the Jesuit order, it would be me. I'm a professor of religion at Fordham University and a Jesuit."

The folds of flesh around Felix's eyes pinched inward and his odd face seemed even more askew. At that moment, the dim light in the room seemed to converge inside the narrow slits of his eyes.

The waiter arrived with their order as thoughts of a Jesuit connection spun through Romano's mind.

FORTY-SEVEN

CHARLIE BARELY BEAT THE DAWN AS HE LOCKED his mountain bike to the rack next to the Fordham Lincoln Center Campus. He jogged to the main entrance and noticed the sidewalk food carts hadn't yet arrived, so he'd have to go without his usual steaming morning jolt. He'd run down later when Carlota came in and the campus officially geared up for the start of the school day.

He entered Father Romano's office and dug a CD case out of his frayed canvas book bag. He had the new software disk balanced on his index finger before his computer finished booting. Charlie had gotten the sophisticated program that developed anagrams from a friend majoring in computer science and had spent the past few days creating a database of Latin words. He was anxious to see if the program could come up with any new anagrams for the inscription *Et in Arcadia ego* on the tomb in Poussin's painting. So far he and Carlota had only been able to come up with *Et in arca Dei ago*, And I act on behalf of the Ark of God.

Charlie installed the program and imported his Latin database from another CD. He typed in the phrase and took the last sip of tepid spring water from yesterday's bottle while he waited for the program to do its stuff. Before he swallowed, their anagram came up on the screen followed by a second one, *I tego arcana Dei*. He almost choked getting the water down as he scrambled to get the Latin text sitting on Romano's desk.

After a few minutes of checking and double-checking the translation, Charlie wrote it in marker on the flip chart next to the others. *I tego arcana Dei*, Begone, I conceal the secrets of God. He leaned back in his chair and grinned with pride at his work. This could have a definite impact on their research. Up until now, he and Carlota thought the inscription was only a code relating to the work of the person buried in the tomb, or, at the most, directions to a secret Cathar treasure. This new anagram opened a whole new possibility. It could mean the secret itself was right under everyone's nose, buried in the grave depicted in Poussin's painting near Rennes-le-Château in France.

Charlie dug out the research files on Rennes-le-Château and did a Web search that generated hundreds of links referring to the tiny village high in the Pyrénées. He sorted out what seemed the most credible data and sent an e-mail to his BlackBerry alerting Romano of the discovery. Then he remembered Father Romano's comments about *being controlled by the phone* and *his time being his time*. He picked up the phone and dialed the Jesuit rectory in Vienna.

FORTY-EIGHT

FELIX DRANK HIS ESPRESSO LIKE HE WAS DOWNING a shot of whiskey. Then he took a deep rasping breath. "You will never discover the *Rex Deus*. They're hidden very deep. All over Europe. I tried for years. No, no, no." Felix shook his head like someone possessed. "I warned you, I warned you. You're too close, too close. They tried. They'll get you." He pointed a finger at Britt. "You'll cease to exist."

"Or could that be because the *Rex Deus* doesn't exist?" Romano asked.

"Believe me, Professor, they exist." Felix went through another bout of twitches. Then he nodded and added, "As does *Le Serpent Rouge*. There's an inn near Rennes-le-Château. The secret could be there. Oh yes, oh yes. Santa Maria, Santa Maria. She holds the key. Maybe even the Holy Grail."

"What is this secret?" Britt asked. "And what exactly is the Holy Grail?"

"No, no, no. I heard this during confession."

"Look." Romano leaned toward Felix. "This is not some game. People, good people, have died, and you may hold information that could prevent future deaths. Anything you know might assist the authorities in finding out who's responsible."

"Father, you're a priest. Yes, yes, you're a priest. Confession is sacred. No, no, no. I won't break the vows. What I heard will go with me to the grave. Yes, yes, to the grave."

Romano pointed to Britt. "Do you want whoever shot Britt to try again?"

Felix tapped his spoon nervously against his empty cup and looked away from both of them. "The secret I know, it won't help. They won't find them. Never, never. Professor Hamar, you should hide. They'll find you."

"Why don't you let the authorities decide that," Romano said. "One of the dead priests was like a father to me."

Felix looked back at Romano, suspicion etched across his face. His mouth dropped open. "Who was your real father?"

The question caught Romano as odd, but maybe it could be leveraged into finding out more about Felix and his secret. "My father was Gregorio Romano. He died when I was twelve. Father Ted Mathews was a close friend of his and became my mentor. He's the one who guided me into the Jesuit order. Now, how about sharing your family name?"

Felix stared at Romano as if he were looking right through him. "Where was he from? What did he do?"

"He was American, like me. A banker who represented a European banking group and established their U.S. banking division before he died." Romano returned Felix's stare. "Now it's your turn, Felix."

Felix abruptly stood. "I've already told you more than I should. Too much, too much." He pushed his chair aside and rushed out of the café.

Romano stuffed a hand in his pocket and pulled out some of the euros he had gotten at the airport. "See where he's going. I'll pay and be right behind you."

Britt rushed to the door and looked up and down the narrow alleyway. Romano struggled to read the amount the waiter had scribbled on the slip, left a crumpled stack of euros on the table, and chased after Britt. When he caught up to her, she was at the end of the alleyway looking up and down the next street.

Britt turned to Romano and shrugged. "I couldn't see which way he went. When I got here, there was no sign of him. Sorry."

"Actually, I should be apologizing," Romano said. "I don't know what we would have done if we had caught up with him. I don't think the Viennese would look too kindly on me grabbing an old man on the street."

Britt's lips twitched as if she were attempting to suppress a smile. "I guess you're right. But there are still a lot of questions I'd like to ask Felix."

"I'm sorry, but I've got to say this." Romano shook his head. "I wouldn't put much credibility in anything he says. That man has serious issues. I think he needs institutional care. I'm no psychologist, but I'd say he borders on schizophrenia or some other psychotic disturbance." Romano checked his watch. "Let's go to the Jesuit rectory. My friend may have returned from the university. He might have some idea who Felix really is."

Britt glanced at her watch and her expression changed. At that moment she seemed weak and fragile, as if she suddenly realized she may be hopelessly caught up in something way over her head.

"Are you okay?" Romano asked.

Britt frowned. "I'm fine. I know Felix seems like a kook, but I think his whole life revolves around researching alternative theories. Whatever he heard during a confession sent him off the deep end. That doesn't mean he's crazy. All I can say is that I found supporting research for most of what he provided me. At the Saunière Society meeting, he carried two briefcases filled with detailed handwritten notes complete with citations. He may be crazy, but when it comes to the *Rex Deus* and *Le Serpent Rouge*, he's more like a savant."

Romano felt sorry for Britt. She seemed to be grasping for anything that supported her far-out theory. But he couldn't lose sight of the fact that someone did try to kill her. "Well, we have another option," Romano said. "My friend, Father Müller, has done a lot of research on some of the fringe theories of Christianity. I think you'll find him interesting and he may be able to give you some additional insight into your theories. There's also a good chance he'll know something about Felix, or whoever he is, especially after we describe him."

Britt looked at her watch again. "Why don't you see if Father Müller knows anything about Felix and if he'd have some time for me. I have something I need to check into at the hotel. Meet me there at two and we can decide where to take it from here."

Romano walked Britt back to the Hotel Royal and then headed for the rectory. On the way, he thought about Britt and the episode with Felix. He had heard a lot of fanciful stories and odd-ball theories about Christianity, but he couldn't understand how an educated professor like Britt could have gotten hooked on this insanity. She seemed to have accepted anything and everything that fell her way. The more he learned about Britt's concepts, the more he realized how far she'd slipped away from the bedrock of historically accepted values. But then, maybe he was being naïve in dismissing them out of hand.

He thought about what Felix said about the Jesuit order and connections to the *Rex Deus* and a bloodline and the mention of the Templars. He couldn't get over a nagging suspicion that there was something he was overlooking . . . or not wanting to see.

FORTY-NINE

The receptionist was still all smiles when Romano returned to the rectory. "Father Romano, I hope your very important meeting went well."

"Thank you, everything was . . . as expected."

"Joseph!" A priest with a closely trimmed beard and black half-rimmed plastic glasses strode toward Romano. He looked like a finely groomed Robin Williams as he grabbed Romano in a bear hug. "I heard about Ted. You were in my prayers." He stepped back, his hands still gripping Romano's shoulders. "It's been too long. What brings you to Vienna?"

"Thanks for the prayers, Heinz. I still can't seem to come to grips with Ted's death. It's part of the reason I'm in Vienna."

Müller gave Romano a questioning look, his eyes studying him for an answer. Then he turned toward the hallway. "Let's go to an office where we can talk."

Romano followed Müller to a small, dimly lit office decorated in typical Austrian style with high ceiling, polished wood floor, and spartan furnishings. He brought him up to date with a condensed version of the bizarre events of the past few days. Müller sucked in a breath with the air whistling through his teeth when Romano described seeing Ted's body marked with the stigmata.

When Romano mentioned the gnomelike Felix, Müller let out a groan. "I'd say that your Felix is most likely Felix Konrad, a former village priest who is crazy, *verrückt*, as we would say in Austria."

"What do you know about him?"

"It's a long story, but I'll give you the short version for now. We can discuss the details about his questionable theories with your Professor Hamar. She should view any information he gave her with the utmost skepticism."

"I told her that. I'm hoping Britt will take your sage advice to heart more than she has my efforts."

"Konrad was always known to be eccentric, even when he was a priest. When he inherited his family home and a considerable estate, he left the priesthood and started getting involved with fringe groups and conspiracy theorists all over Europe. There was some talk about him hearing a confession from an uncle who was also a priest that set everything off. My personal view is that he didn't take to a vow of poverty very seriously. He spends his time traveling throughout Europe chasing after every crazy idea that floats by. Your Felix is nothing more than a crank, or how would you say, a crackpot."

"Does he live here in Vienna?"

"In Hietzing. I believe on Gloriettegasse. Quite a plush address. It's where the nobility spent their summers in Maria Theresa's time. It's across from the famous Gloriette arcade on the hill behind Schönbrunn Palace."

Just then the phone rang and Müller picked up. He spoke a few words in German, then looked over at Romano. "It's for you, Joseph, your graduate assistant. They're transferring the call." He handed the receiver to Romano and grinned. "You must be quite the taskmaster. It's very early in the States."

Romano listened to Charlie remind him to keep the Black-Berry turned on when he wasn't flying. It was set on vibrate so no one but him would know if he was getting a call or an e-mail. He pulled the BlackBerry out of his jacket pocket and turned it on as Charlie told him about the new anagram. After he assured Charlie he had received the lengthy e-mail, Charlie told him Carlota would be meeting that morning with a student of Britt's who had the inside scoop on why she had gone off on the radical side of the tracks. They'd e-mail him the information as soon as Carlota got to the office.

Romano handed the phone back to Müller. "Thanks, that was one of my grad assistants chastising me for not keeping this electronic gizmo running so I could get his e-mails anytime day or night."

"What would we do without modern technology."

Romano scrolled through the e-mail. "Probably have a lot less stress." He noted summaries of a series of Web searches on Rennes-le-Château focused on the local village priest, Bérenger Saunière, who accumulated great wealth and built many strange structures in the small, isolated mountain village. "Is there some way I could print out this e-mail?"

Müller jotted something on a sheet of paper and handed it to Romano. "Forward it to my address and I'll print you a copy." Then he turned to the computer on the table behind the desk and signed on to the Internet while Romano forwarded the message.

"I have to meet Britt in a few minutes. Can we meet with you later this afternoon? I'm sure there are many areas that Britt researched that you're a lot more qualified to discuss with her than I am. And you can warn her about Konrad."

Müller printed out the e-mail and handed it to Romano. "Actually, I look forward to meeting her. It's not every day I get a chance to try to persuade someone writing *The Jesus Fraud* to rethink the premise for her book."

"Believe me, that's going to be a tough challenge."

Romano glanced through the printout and noticed the many references to Rennes-le-Château. He wondered if the fascination with the small French village high in the Pyrénées might be taking on a whole new meaning.

FIFTY

BRITT AND ROMANO SAT AT A SIDEWALK TABLE under a red-and-white-striped awning in front of the Hotel Royal. They were enjoying coffee and fresh croissant sandwiches Romano had bought from the Aida Café on the corner while he had waited for Britt to come down from her room. He had found Felix's address in a phone book borrowed from the front desk at the hotel.

Romano handed Britt the printouts of Charlie's e-mail. "I think you'll find this interesting. Charlie used some new program to come up with the anagram."

Britt carefully read the e-mail, nodding as she reviewed some of the findings. "I've found references to this anagram and cite it in my manuscript. I believe the secrets of God refers to the Grail, or *San Graal,* and the bloodline of Jesus. Bérenger Saunière may have found the Grail in that tomb, and that could have been the basis for his wealth."

"Why didn't you mention that anagram when we were discussing the Poussin painting in my office?"

"It wasn't relevant at the time. We never really discussed my theory that involves Mary Magdalene being the *Graal,* G-r-a-a-l."

Romano gave Britt a sidelong glance. "The Holy Grail, or *Graal*, is not a topic I've taken very seriously. Enlighten me, please."

"There are a few schools of thought regarding the origin of the term 'Holy Grail.' Some Grail scholars see a derivation from the words '*sangraal*' and '*gradales,*' meaning cup or basin in the ancient French Provençal dialect. Some go a step further and break the word '*sangraal*' after the g to create *sang raal*, which means blood royal. My theory is that the Holy Grail was really Mary Magdalene, who carried the blood royal in her womb to the south of France. I think the Holy Grail is the bones of Mary Magdalene hidden somewhere near Rennes-le-Château."

"Are there any other secrets I should know about?"

"I've decided to check out the myth of the tomb myself. Who knows, maybe I'll be the one to find the legendary Holy Grail."

"You can't be serious."

"I've made arrangements to fly to France tomorrow morning."

"I'm sure thousands of treasure hunters have scoured that area over the years."

"But they were looking for a chalice or secret documents. I'll be looking for something that could have been right before everyone's eyes and which they didn't give a second thought." Britt's eyes flashed a sign of self-assurance. "Bones buried in a grave-yard."

"But there's no way to verify whether any bones could be from Mary Magdalene."

"I've given that some careful thought." Britt devoured the last of her sandwich, then smiled. "The bones can be carbon-dated to verify they'd be from the time of Mary. And remember Felix's comment about discovering information about an inn near Rennes-le-Château that he claims may hold the secret to the bloodline and the Holy Grail. He mentioned Santa Maria."

"I'm glad you brought that up. Maybe now we can put this whole conjecture about a bloodline to rest," Romano said. "Heinz is sure Felix is Felix Konrad, a former priest who came into a large inheritance and spends his time jetting around Europe hob-nobbing with conspiracy theorists. I have his address. We can visit him, and when he's aware that we know who he is, maybe he'll be less secretive. You can tell him about your theory, and see his response for yourself."

Britt took a large swig of coffee, dabbed her lips with a napkin, and stood. "Great, let's go."

Romano felt a glow of satisfaction that maybe he was finally taking a step that could get Britt to realize she was chasing false hopes. Maybe, if Felix wasn't delusional, he would finally admit that the reason he won't divulge his "secrets" is because there aren't any. The secrets are only in his warped imagination.

FIFTY-ONE

PHILIPPE ARMAND HAD THE TAXI DROP HIM OFF AT the main entrance to Schönbrunn Palace. He'd come to Vienna by train because he had a gun hidden in his briefcase. His employer had even provided his favorite weapon, a Glock 17 with an altered barrel and silencer; they had made it clear that time was critical, so Philippe hadn't been able to access the weapons he had hidden in safe-deposit boxes in key cities in the EU and the States.

He paid the driver, then blended in with the throng of tourists milling about at the entrance to one of Vienna's grand attractions. As soon as the taxi sped away with a new fare, Philippe walked briskly to a corner of the palace grounds and gardens and headed up Maxingstrasse. He knew exactly where he was going and only hoped that his first target was at home, or at least in Vienna, because the clock was ticking.

Philippe turned on Gloriettegasse and casually strolled past Felix Konrad's house. The large property was set back from the street and protected by an iron fence topped with ornate spikes. The main gate was ajar but posted with a bright yellow sign in German warning visitors to keep the driveway clear. There was no foot or car traffic that time of day. Philippe was tempted to go right up to the house and get the job done, but thought better of it when he spotted a video camera above the door. That was a new addition he hadn't counted on. He decided to check the neighboring streets in case there were complications and he had to make a quick getaway.

The last time Philippe was here a few months ago, Konrad didn't have an alarm system. He had broken in while Konrad was out of town and photographed the stacks and stacks of handwritten research papers the little man had neatly piled in drawers in his library. He had found it odd that some were written in German, some in French, and some in English. The little fellow was quite literate and a prolific writer.

Philippe remembered something else that gave him cause for alarm. It had to do with a neighbor on the next street. He walked around the block to Weidlichgasse, the street that ran behind Konrad's house. He noticed video surveillance cameras along a long, high masonry wall and two small guardhouses on either side of the entrance to the property. He passed by on the other side of the street and saw that both guardhouses were manned. He knew he'd have to be extra careful about any undue noise since Konrad's backyard neighbor was the U.S. embassy residence.

He decided to go back to Konrad's house and see if the old man was at home, preferably alone. If he wasn't, it could pose a problem since he'd be too obvious waiting around in this posh neighborhood. He was certain there'd be periodic police patrols. He'd have to check the house for any new addition of a security system to go along with the video camera, then break in and wait.

Philippe felt his pulse quicken as he approached the house. When he was a block away, he buttoned the top button on his suit coat and slipped the strap of his briefcase over his head so the soft leather case draped across his chest. He opened the briefcase and made sure his silenced Glock was in easy reach. Then he took a worsted wool cap with a short visor, a rectangular metallic pin tag, and a large envelope out of the case. He pinned the tag above his coat pocket, put on the cap, pulled it down to just past his scar, and headed for the house.

FIFTY-TWO

FELIX KONRAD PACED BACK AND FORTH IN HIS library chewing nervously on his lower lip. He shouldn't have met with Hamar and Romano. Had he only known Romano was a Jesuit. No, no, no, this wasn't happening. It was too confusing, too confusing, out of control. Hamar shot, priests dead, he was in trouble. They were evil. He knew it. Evil.

He never gave up the secret, never told. His uncle warned him. Take it to the grave, take it to the grave. He had spent years looking for others. Others who knew. He found no one. Some put together theories, bits and pieces. But no one knew his secret. Even Hamar thought she had cracked the code of the Holy Grail. The bones of Mary Magdalene. He had been tempted to tell her how wrong she was.

Felix's breath came in short raspy gasps. What should he do? Leave? He'd go away and hide. Hide somewhere they couldn't find him. But if they found Hamar, they'd find him. They could have seen him with Hamar. He couldn't think, couldn't think. His mind was speeding out of control. He had to breathe, had to breathe, had to breathe.

The bell! Someone was at the door. He felt his head jerk side to side, up and down. He saw flashes of light then his head felt as if it were gripped in a vise. It was a sign. His brain had sensed danger. He wasn't expecting anyone. The video camera. He'd installed the system a month ago when the fear had gotten to be too much for him. The evil hadn't come. No one had come, only deliveries and mail. He checked the monitor and saw a man in a suit with a cap and a leather case strapped across his body. There was also some kind of badge or name tag. He couldn't make it out. The man held a large white envelope.

Felix let out a breath of relief. Only a messenger. Maybe the latest Saunière Society reports. He swallowed a few times and went to the door. "Please, leave the envelope by the door, thank you," he said in German.

"I need a signature," the man replied.

Felix peered through the peephole in the center of the door and saw the man reach inside his jacket and pull out a pen. Felix unlatched the dead bolt, opened the door a crack, and kept a firm grip on the handle. He motioned for the man to hand him the envelope. The man reached inside and gave Felix the envelope, then thrust the door open, pulling Felix into the doorway, where he grabbed him by the throat and pushed him back inside, slamming the door behind him.

Felix felt a hand crushing his throat. Then something jammed into his chest. There was a popping sound and a sharp pain. He began to shake violently. Then sounds and flashes echoed within his brain and seemed to reverberate as a wet icy chill swept through him and everything turned black.

FIFTY-THREE

Britt and Romano descended the steps leading to the U-Bahn beneath the pedestrian plaza across from the hotel. They passed a glass-enclosed, high-tech command center, where technicians were focused on video screens monitoring the many stations and underground trains connecting key points of the city.

A large map on a nearby wall showed the station stops for each of the numbered lines. The trip to Hietzing looked like it would be easy on the U-Bahn, with only one transfer.

"Help me out here," Romano said as he stared at the ticket vending machine.

Britt reviewed the instructions on the machine. "I think you just punch Adult, Zone Four, and it'll tell you how many euros to insert."

Britt watched Romano punch and repunch buttons and fiddle with a handful of euros. Finally he shouted "Eureka!" as two tickets and some change emerged from the slot at the bottom of the machine.

Romano handed Britt her ticket and they headed for the doors to the U1 line. They inserted the tickets into the stamping machines and followed the color-coded signs to their platform, where they joined the crowd of commuters waiting for the next train. Britt was pleasantly surprised at the modern, spotless facilities of Vienna's underground rail system. The glass and stainless steel were polished, the floors were clean, and there was no graffiti. She had expected to see the typical European penchant for smoking, with every other person puffing on a cigarette, but smoking was forbidden on the platforms and trains.

As they waited for the next train, Britt had second thoughts about tracking down Felix. Who knew where a confrontation with him could lead. Romano was already plenty spooked about the whole scenario and seemed to doubt her more with each new piece of information. She wasn't sure whether it was a mistake for him to even be with her. But she did feel safer with him around. He gave her a hard time, but in the end he seemed truly concerned. She hadn't experienced someone being concerned about her for a long time. It felt good.

Britt had already gotten what she needed from Felix at the café. He had no idea who the *Rex Deus* members were, although he seemed to think they were hidden all over Europe. And the Jesuit connection—that was a shocker. If the bloodline was hidden in the Jesuit order, that would support the deaths of the priests. Maybe they knew who were members of *Le Serpent Rouge* . . . or could they have been part of the bloodline? That still left a big question—who was doing the killing and who tried to kill her?

A train came to a stop in front of them, the doors slid open, and commuters rushed out in all directions. Britt followed Romano inside and sat in the first open seat as he grabbed the hand strap on the rail above. At each stop a voice identified the station, and they had no problem making the switch to the U4 train at Karlsplatz. It didn't take long before the voice announced they had reached Hietzing. Romano hadn't said a word during the entire ride. Britt was convinced he felt another meeting with Felix would open the door to proving many of her theories were based on the fictional side of myth rather than fact.

Britt and Romano left the train with a crowd of tourists laden with cameras headed for Schönbrunn Palace. When the tourists made a beeline for the main entrance to the palace and gardens, Britt and Romano continued around the walled grounds to Maxingstrasse. There was a constant hum of cars and trucks on the busy street bordering the palace grounds.

Britt had to struggle to keep up with Romano's long strides. She noticed his shoulders had a casual droop, but he carried himself with an athlete's confidence. She hadn't thought about it before, but, except for at the hospital, all she'd seen him in were khakis, an open-collared shirt, and soft-shouldered sport jacket or Windbreaker. And the knapsack took the cake. Joseph Romano was definitely not the stereotypical bow-tie-and-tweed professor—or priest.

Britt caught up to Romano and linked her arm in his and slowed him down. "This is only to prevent me from going into oxygen debt."

Romano looked down at her with a wry smile. "Sorry, I sometimes get carried away. I try to run five to ten miles a day. If I don't, my body rebels and tries to make up for it. You set the pace, I'll follow. It shouldn't be too far."

As they neared Felix's street, they came upon a charming little house that looked like it was straight out of a children's classic. Romano slowed and pointed to a sign indicating it was once the home of Johann Strauss. "I wonder how many homes of Johann Strauss there are scattered around Vienna? Maybe he was like George Washington?"

Britt looked at him like he was a little crazy. "Now I think you're suffering from jet lag." Then she pointed up the street. "Is that Gloriettegasse?"

Romano squinted at the blue-and-white sign on the corner of a building up ahead. "If it is, we've just established that your distance vision beats mine by probably half a block."

After another half block, Britt unlocked arms and nudged Romano. "That's Gloriettegasse. Now we know you're in better shape, but I've got sharper eyes."

They turned onto Felix's street and Britt realized why Hietzing was known for the summer residences of the nobility. The ocher facades of the almost solid wall of buildings lining Maxingstrasse were replaced by large residential plots with elegant homes in pastel shades, many sporting ornate iron-railed balconies and beautiful gardens.

"Well, I guess this proves that Felix has come a long way from being a poor parish priest," Britt said.

"Well, Father Müller was right," Romano replied. "He said he believed Felix wasn't a fan of the vows of poverty."

Not far down the block they located the home of Felix Konrad set back off the street and surrounded by a tall, black, iron fence. The gate was not latched and Romano held it open for Britt. She cautiously followed him along a walkway through a small garden that looked like it was in need of a green thumb. As they approached the front door, she noticed that it appeared to be ajar. Her concern heightened as she peered up at the video camera mounted above the doorway.

Romano pushed the doorbell twice and glanced back at Britt. She heard the chimes ring inside the house, but then there was complete silence.

Romano put his head up to the opening in the door and peered through it.

"Do you see anything?" Britt asked.

"No, just the side of the vestibule. Mr. Konrad," Romano shouted.

Britt pushed the door open wider and stuck her head inside. "Felix. It's Brittany Hamar." She stepped into the vestibule and looked into the large living room beyond. That's when she spotted Felix Konrad. His silk ascot was jammed up over his mouth and his body lay twisted on the carpet at the entrance to the room. "Oh my God!" She pushed past Romano into the house.

Romano followed Britt, knelt down, and checked for a pulse. "He's been shot." He pointed to a bloody hole in Felix's chest.

"Is he alive?"

Romano shook his head. "I can't find a pulse." He went to a phone on a stand in the corner of the room. "Do you know how to call emergency?"

Britt grabbed his arm. "I have no idea. But I don't think we should call anyone."

"What are you saying?" Romano gave Britt a strange look.

"I don't think we should get involved. I visited Father Matteo . . . dead. I visited Father Mathews . . . dead. Now Felix . . . he's dead. There's nothing we can do." Britt let go of Romano's arm. "If you make a phone call, I'm leaving here, and Austria. Immediately."

"We can't just leave him here without doing something."

Britt realized she couldn't get caught up in another murder investigation. Especially not in a foreign country, and not for the next two days. Too much was at stake. After that, she'd let things fall as they may. "You're a priest. Say the appropriate prayers, then we leave. Someone will find him." She put her fingers up to her lips. "If you find that morally reprehensible, make a call from a pay phone."

Romano gave Britt an uneasy look, then folded his hands and dropped his head in prayer. Britt peered into the adjoining room, which had walls lined with shelves of books. While Romano prayed, she went into the room and found it was a library and study with old oak file cabinets and an antique desk. She opened the file cabinets and found stacks of handwritten reports. Each cabinet held writings in a different language. One in French, another in German, and one in English. The handwriting looked like it was done with painstaking perfection by fountain pen.

Britt leafed through the English documents and found that they were sorted by dates. She searched through the latest batch and found genealogies and notes on the Hapsburgs, Rennes-le-Château, and Abbé Saunière. One of the pages mentioned the Villa Santa Maria near Rennes-le-Château. In quotations was "conceals the secrets of God."

Britt grabbed the latest stack of pages and started stuffing them into her Coach bag.

"What in hell do you think you're doing?" Romano shouted.

"This is Felix's latest research. There could be something very important in here."

Romano rushed into the study and grabbed Britt's bag. "You're not taking anything from this man's house. I don't care how important you think it may be." He pulled the documents out of her bag, put them back into the file cabinet, and slammed the drawer. Then he pointed to the phone on the desk. "And unless you want me to start dialing numbers, we're leaving now."

Britt threw her bag over her shoulder and headed for the front door. She was dying to go through Felix's notes, but there was something more important she had to do. *The Messenger* had made it clear where and when they were to meet and she wouldn't let anything get in her way.

FIFTY-FOUR

Philippe Armand stood in front of the K+K Palais Hotel and carefully surveyed the surroundings. It wasn't the Hôtel de Paris but it had a unique blend of old-world sophistication and modern luxury. And the location provided him with what was more important, security and the ability to disappear quickly if he had to.

The historical building on Rudolfsplatz had once belonged to the imperial family and sat across the street from a park with dense trees and tall bushes. Beyond the park was the Franz-Josefs-Kai, a main thoroughfare that ran along the Danube Canal. Any of the side streets took him into the very heart of Vienna's First District. His father had always stressed having multiple avenues of escape if things got rough.

The entrance and lobby of the hotel had touches of black anodized steel and glass that gave it an Art Deco feel. Philippe had requested a room overlooking the park so he'd have a clear view of the street in front of the hotel. He wasted no time checking in and getting to his room so he could start the search for Hamar. He pulled the phone book out of the nightstand and opened it to the hotel listings.

Philippe didn't understand why his idiot employer had wanted Hamar wounded in New York and now dead in Vienna. He thought of another one of his father's admonitions and cringed at the irony. *It's not our job to reason why; it's just our job to do or die.*

He dialed the number for the first hotel in the listings and asked for Brittany Hamar.

FIFTY-FIVE

As they climbed the stairs exiting the U-Bahn station at Stephansplatz, Romano was still shaken by the harsh reality of Felix's murder and the fact that he hadn't called the police. He wasn't sure why he'd gone along with Britt's crazy insistence not to get involved. They were involved, up to their eyeballs. And now he feared they were being followed.

During the subway ride back to the First District, he'd checked everyone in each of the train cars, looking for someone who stood out as suspicious. In his paranoia, half the riders had been suspect until he realized that Vienna was a melting pot for Europe and the Middle East, and filled with tourists.

Romano spotted a cluster of pay phones on the corner of the pedestrian plaza. He walked over to an empty pair of stalls and picked up one of the phones. "Hold on for a second. I'm calling the police."

Britt got a panicked look on her face.

"Don't worry, I'll just tell them to check his address because I heard a gunshot and hang up. If you need anything at your hotel before we go to the rectory, now's your chance."

Britt stood in the empty stall next to Romano's as he dialed zero to ask the operator to connect him to the police. He got the impression Britt wasn't convinced he wouldn't offer too much information.

When he hung up, Romano felt partially relieved. At least the body of Felix Konrad would soon be getting proper attention.

During the walk to the rectory, Britt didn't complain about the pace. She seemed extremely eager to meet with Father Müller after Romano had mentioned Müller had a penchant for studying the less than authoritative versions of Church history and seemed to know a lot about Felix.

Father Müller was in the reception area when they arrived at the rectory and ushered them down the dim hallway to his office. Dressed in a black suit, crisp white shirt, and a narrow black tie, he presented a more priestly presence than the casual Romano. After the usual pleasantries they got down to business.

"Before I discuss Felix Konrad," Müller said, "I must tell you I'm fascinated about your upcoming book, *The Jesus Fraud.* I'm eager to get your perspective on what exactly constitutes the 'fraud.'"

"Unfortunately that would take a lot longer than we have," Britt replied. "Suffice it to say, many people have the wrong first impression. The premise of the book is not to insinuate that Jesus was a fraud. My goal is to correct some injustices when it comes to how Jesus and his teachings were presented to the world."

Müller folded his hands across his chest and leaned back in his chair. A smile spread across his face. "Am I to assume you subscribe to the school of thought that Jesus came to enlighten the world? That salvation comes through knowledge and good works, not only through accepting Jesus as savior through his Crucifixion and Resurrection?"

Britt returned the smile. "I should get you to write my book jacket, Father Müller."

"Just because I know where you're coming from doesn't mean I approve. I think that Gnosticism is an easy out for those who fear having their religious philosophies scrutinized." Müller made a point of adjusting his designer glasses. "And I don't agree with the anti-Paul school of religion."

"Heinz, don't get her started on Paul. Britt wrote *Saint Paul— The Apostle Who Never Walked with Jesus.* We could be greatly outgunned. Why don't we start with what you know about Felix Konrad. He provided her with materials that seem to have steered her to some of the theories she's pursuing in her book."

"Sorry." Müller grinned. "I'm sure Joseph told you I have a penchant for straying off point."

"Actually, I haven't divulged any of your, let's say, idiosyncrasies," Romano said.

"Then I better get on track before you do." Müller arched his eyebrows. "As I told Joseph, Felix had been a village priest who I believe you'd refer to in the States as someone who went over the edge. He gave last rites to his uncle, who had taken the last confession of Abbé Bérenger Saunière. Konrad is said to have started acting very strange after meeting with his uncle on his

deathbed. There were rumors that he was privy to the secret that
Saunière had supposedly discovered at Rennes-le-Château and
resulted in his acquiring considerable wealth. Konrad's parish-
ioners complained that his sermons started to include odd mystical references. Before the Church took steps to question his
actions, his mother died, and he was the sole beneficiary of a
sizeable family estate. As a diocesan priest, Konrad could have
inherited the estate and continued as a parish priest. Instead, he
requested Rome to laicize him. He no longer felt he could be obe-
dient to a bishop. Konrad was laicized, moved into his family estate in Hietzing, and started associating with oddball organizations
and making outrageous statements."

"Are his statements outrageous because they don't agree with
your Church's doctrine?" Britt asked.

"Not really. It's because they are fraught with errors and omis-
sions and blatantly inaccurate facts. I'd recommend that you ignore anything you heard from Felix Konrad unless you have
solid, substantiating proof. In the past few years he's gone further
and further off course. I wouldn't doubt that Konrad might claim
the Pope was the Antichrist or Mother Theresa was a direct descendant of Mary Magdalene."

"Look, I had been skeptical for years," Britt replied. "But after
wading through tons of research, I realized many of these stories
shouldn't be dismissed out of hand."

"All I'm saying is for you to get plenty of corroborating evidence before using anything from Konrad in your book. As we
say in Vienna, Konrad is *total verrückt*, totally crazy."

Britt eyed Romano. It was not a look of relief. "Could you
give us some examples? How about the secret discovered by
Saunière and his subsequent wealth? I've seen pictures of his
Villa Bethania and Tour Magdala. These were not the domain of
a simple village priest."

Müller's eyes brightened. He slid a file folder out of a stack on
his desk. "There have been so many stories about how Saunière
acquired his wealth. They range from finding Visigothic gold
from the treasure of Solomon to Dagobert's treasure from the
wars, the Cathar treasure that disappeared from Montségur, even
the results of pillaging convoys of money crossing the Spanish
border by the Lord of Rennes, and of course the Holy Grail, the
Menorah, the Ark of the Covenant, and secret documents that

Saunière used to blackmail the Church or the Hapsburgs. They all make fabulous fodder for conspiracy theorists."

Britt listened intently. Her eyes took on a glimmer of interest. "And which one of these do you subscribe to?"

Müller opened the folder and handed Britt some photocopies. "These are copies of material I hand out in one of my university classes. This set is for you. It includes documents showing that Saunière was removed from his parish by the Church and convicted by the diocesan authority in Carcassonne for trafficking in Masses. He may have been one of the first priests to catch on to the lucrative potential of selling Mass cards to devout Roman Catholics by mail order. He advertised in religious magazines and journals. That's were he acquired his wealth."

"But I found many books and articles discussing Saunière and they all allude to some secret that led to his wealth."

"What can I say?" Müller shrugged. "Secrets sell more books than simple facts."

"Britt is convinced that Rennes-le-Château may hold the secret to the Holy Grail," Romano piped in. "Britt, do you mind me telling Heinz your theory on the Grail and your evidence?"

Britt nodded. "Go right ahead. I'd be surprised if he didn't have a file there that disputes my theory."

Romano noticed Müller stiffen. "Britt has an original segment of the so-called secret James Gospel," he said quickly. "It's been carbon-dated to the time of Christ."

Müller's eyes bugged wide open. He grabbed his glasses, jerked them off his face with one quick tug, and gaped at Britt and Romano. "You can't be serious."

Britt held up the copies Müller had given her. "I'm as serious as you are with these."

"She tells me the translation indicates Mary Magdalene was pregnant with a child of Jesus at the Crucifixion," Romano said. "There were efforts made to revive Jesus in the tomb, but the segment she has doesn't present the outcome."

Britt leaned toward Müller. "I believe Mary went to the south of France, where she gave birth to twins, a boy and a girl, and a bloodline of Jesus was established. And that Mary Magdalene, as the vessel carrying the bloodline, was the Holy Grail. I believe the bones of Mary may be hidden somewhere near Rennes-le-Château."

Müller replaced his glasses and tented his hands, tapping his fingertips together. "Well, well, that certainly captures my attention. Joseph, have you verified the document?"

"Britt agreed to allow me to analyze it when we return to New York."

"If it's original, that would certainly give your theory a bit more bite. But I must add that I am very skeptical about a bloodline of Christ."

Romano saw Britt tense and her eyes flicker momentarily.

"Mary Magdalene and the south of France is another matter," Müller continued. "There are two strong theories supported by some historical references. One is that she accompanied St. John the Evangelist to Ephesus, modern Selcuk in Turkey, where she died. The other is that she may have settled in Provence, where she lived in a mountain cave for thirty years as a hermit before she died. If that be the case, her bones could be buried somewhere in the area."

"Then she could be buried near Rennes-le-Château," Britt said with a burst of enthusiasm.

Müller scratched his forehead. "I'd be very surprised. There are hundreds of stories about buried treasures, religious mysteries, secret societies. That area became a haven for treasure hunters and conspiracy theory buffs. For over a hundred years the locals have been tormented by people digging up graveyards and every conceivable plot of land that was mentioned in some off-the-wall book."

"But they weren't looking for a specific set of bones," Britt blurted.

Müller went back to his finger tapping and crinkled his brows. "I suppose you're right. I'm sure they were looking for some obvious treasure. But how would you verify that any bones found in the area were from Mary Magdalene?"

"Felix told Britt there's an inn near Rennes-le-Château that holds the secrets to the Holy Grail and the bloodline."

Müller shook his head and rolled his eyes. "That goes right back to the Saunière secret. Believe me, the whole secret scenario is nothing more than fantasy. And it's not just Felix Konrad. Many people have latched on to the concept of a valuable discovery, but usually for personal gain. You may have run into stories of a Frenchman, Pierre Plantard, who created a complex myth about the Priory of Sion and a relationship to Saunière's secret.

He even created counterfeit documents, all to gain notoriety and prestige."

"There's even a Jesuit connection," Romano added. "The original priory was absorbed by the Jesuits. Plantard insinuated his priory had a Merovingian connection to preserve secrets passed on by this line of descendants from the House of David." As he said it, Romano felt an eerie twinge, another connection between Jesuits and bloodlines.

Britt snapped her head toward Romano. Her expression was somewhere between confusion and amazement. "That supports Felix's claim that the *Rex Deus* supported the Jesuits as a means of hiding the bloodline."

Müller stiffened. There was no questioning his look of surprise. "Where did this come in? Was it before or after he declared the Pope as the Antichrist?"

"Actually, it was very creative," Romano said. "He tied the principle of *follow in the footsteps of Jesus* to be the perfect place to hide the bloodline. And he attributed the rapid rise of the wealth of the order to being financed by the *Rex Deus*."

The look of surprise on Müller's face melted to a quizzical gaze. He turned toward Britt. "I'd do some thorough research on that one before including it in your book. I'm sure you're aware that the Jesuit order was abolished by Pope Clement XIV in 1773 and—"

"You can be sure I'll do my research before anything finds its way into my manuscript," Britt blurted. "Before I take up too much of your time, I'd like your perspective on an Austrian issue. Earlier you mentioned the Hapsburgs. What's your professional opinion of the Hapsburg dynasty and the *Rex Deus* or the Merovingians?"

"As I'm sure you've gathered by now," Müller replied, "I don't give much merit to theories involving a bloodline of Christ. But that said, there are some fascinating myths surrounding the Hapsburgs. They were rulers of the Holy Roman Empire, although for many Hapsburgs, imperial coronation by the Pope never took place. There was speculation that the Church was concerned about the stories of the Hapsburgs' Merovingian connection claiming direct descent from the Old Testament House of David. In 1889 the thirty-year-old Archduke Rudolf was found dead with his mistress Mary Vetsera at the Hapsburg hunting lodge at Mayerling in an apparent double suicide. Archduke

Rudolf was an intelligent progressive heir to the Hapsburg throne who may have been tormented by the stories of his being a possible member of the *Rex Deus*, or even that he was part of the Davidian bloodline, or, to follow your theory, the bloodline of Jesus."

"That's a new twist I'd never heard," Romano said. "See, Britt, I told you Father Müller would be more knowledgeable about the areas you've been delving into."

"Ah, but there's another twist to the Rudolf saga," Müller continued. "He left a locked steel box for his cousin Archduke Johann, who renounced his title after Rudolf's funeral. Johann sailed to South America, and he and the box were never seen again."

Britt's eyes turned down slightly into a questioning gaze. "Now you're sounding more like Felix Konrad."

Müller grinned. "I'm just letting you know that I'm not blind to the myths that circulate about. That doesn't mean I believe them. If you want some physical evidence to support your theories, check into the mausoleum of the Emperor Maximilian the First at Innsbruck. He's said to have designed the mausoleum himself. It includes forty larger-than-life-size statues of his ancestors. There's Godfroi de Bouillon, the Merovingian King Clovis, Queen Elizabeth of Hungary, Archduke Sigismund, and King Theodric. These statues are seen as the crème de la crème of a possible bloodline of the *Rex Deus*."

Britt seemed intrigued. She pursed her lips and stared intently at Müller. "Do you believe that's myth or visible proof of a historical truth?"

Müller laughed. "I think I ought to defer to the master on that one. Joseph wrote a thesis on historical truths."

Britt turned to Romano. "Well, Professor, enlighten me."

Romano stroked his goatee a few times and tried to evoke a professorial air. "Basically, dogma and history are not necessarily the truth."

Now it was Britt's turn to laugh. "Are you telling me history is a mystical fiction?"

"Dogma and history are merely the interpretation of truth based upon available facts. As we accumulate more facts, or through improved technology find more accurate definitions of facts, dogma and history may change accordingly."

"Then we are living in a fantasy world," Britt said.

"In a way that's true. In my thesis, I suggested that we are best served if we acknowledge that dogma and history are fluid and change with the times."

"Then you're admitting that Church doctrine could change with the times."

Romano folded his hands and leaned his chin on his knuckles. "In blunt terms, I believe the dogma of the Church is the most probable truth until it is proven otherwise. That's why I keep referring to the fact that it has withstood the test of time and extreme scrutiny for over two thousand years."

Britt twisted in her chair so she was looking intently at both Romano and Müller. "Then since the Bible is heavily endowed with allegory, its interpretation is really up to the individual and the available facts as supported by current technology."

Romano was hoping the discussion with Müller would at least put a few cracks in Britt's determined approach to discredit accepted Church doctrine. He knew she didn't bend easily, but all he wanted was for her to put appropriate weight on the preponderance of evidence. "That about sums it up," he said.

"So if I discover a document that is verified by current technology to be from the time of Jesus and the content establishes that Jesus and Mary Magdalene had children, that would support a bloodline theory and require rethinking Church dogma?"

Romano and Müller exchanged concerned glances. "Rethinking, yes," Müller quickly replied. "But without additional supporting evidence, it probably wouldn't be taken seriously enough to change dogma. It could have been written by radical elements trying to contradict the developing support for the new religion or by that period's version of Felix Konrad."

There was a knock at the door and a portly man in a dark suit and a liturgical collar walked in. He carried himself with the distinctive air of importance and respect. The father rector had always reminded Romano of a slightly older, jowly version of Father Ted.

Romano immediately stood and greeted Father Hans Josef.

"I'm sorry to interrupt, but there's a very important call from the father general's office for Father Romano."

FIFTY-SIX

THE OFFICE DOOR OPENED AND CARLOTA ALMOST jolted Charlie out of his chair. He'd never seen her in such a state. She was out of breath and sweat glistened across her forehead and cheeks. Something had obviously shaken the conservative, laid-back, always-in-control graduate student from Topeka, Kansas.

"You won't believe what I found out about Professor Hamar."

Charlie spun around in his chair. "Come on, what's the scoop?"

"I spoke to her grad assistant. Well, former grad assistant."

"And?"

"Professor Brittany Hamar went through hell two years ago. She lost a baby boy to Tay-Sachs disease."

Charlie winced. "Sounds bad—what is it?"

Carlota shuddered. "From what Paula said, it's horrible. The disease destroys the central nervous system. The baby becomes blind, mentally retarded, paralyzed, has seizures. I can't even begin to relate to what she must have gone through."

"And then she gets shot. No wonder she's freaked."

"Charlie, that's only a part of it. Evidently both parents must be carriers of the Tay-Sachs gene and it's most frequently found in descendants of Central and Eastern European Jews."

"Hamar's Jewish and teaches New Testament classes?"

"That's just it," Carlota said. "She was adopted and raised Roman Catholic. She really didn't know her real parents. Her husband was French-Canadian and it turns out they're also at risk, along with Cajuns from Louisiana."

"Talk about the luck of the draw."

"Here's the kicker, Charlie." Carlota sank into her chair and let out a sigh. "Professor Hamar's husband felt so much guilt over contributing to the disease that killed their son that he committed suicide."

All items are credited
subject to final payment
and proof verification.

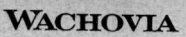

WACHOVIA

DATE: 08-21-07   TIME: 07:05AM
ATM: 1610 5   SEQ: 1 842
755 JEFFERSON DAVIS HWY
ARLINGTON   VA

CARD NUMBER: ************8886

WITHDRAWAL FROM SAVINGS

CASH RECEIVED $400.00
CONVENIENCE FEE $2.50
TOTAL AMOUNT $402.50

Charlie smacked his hands to his head so hard he knocked his cap off. "Man, that's so bad it's almost unbelievable. I wonder if she's in counseling."

"Paula said she totally fell apart after the husband's death. It was at the end of the school year, and Paula didn't see her until the next fall. Paula said she was like a different person. Up until all of this, she was very religious and heavily into the power of prayer, especially during the time her son was dying. When she came back to school, she was already working on this book concept and had Paula doing a lot of research into what Paula described as religious philosophies bordering on the heretical. Paula feels *The Jesus Fraud* is retribution for her religion letting her down. Professor Hamar was hung up on how a loving God could allow her prayers to go unanswered and kill an innocent child in such a horrible way."

"Who could blame her?" Charlie reached down behind his chair and picked up his cap.

"Her focus was on questioning everything and anything that related to Christianity, which led her to Gnosticism. She became convinced Jesus was a prophet sent by God as a teacher and guide to help man find inner knowledge. She became convinced Jesus was two separate entities. The spiritual Jesus came into the physical being when he was baptized by John. Paula said she was freaked by the new Brittany Hamar and was relieved when the school finally gave her a leave of absence to work on her book and probably to get some help."

"I wonder who she could have pissed off enough to want to kill her?" Charlie said. "And where does Father Romano fit into the whole thing?"

"I asked Paula if she had looked into any of Father Romano's work or research. She said his name never came up."

"Wow, this is really wacked." Charlie rolled his chair back to his keyboard and started typing away. "I'll send an e-mail to Father Romano. Who knows who Professor Hamar could have gotten involved with? She could have hooked up with some extremists who are into really weird stuff."

"Paula said she started attending all kinds of meetings of cult-like organizations." Carlota pointed to the Poussin print. "She even flew to London for that Saunière Society conference that had something to do with the area in France where that tomb is located."

"I'm getting a very uneasy vibe about this Professor Hamar," Charlie said. "I wonder what they're up to in Vienna."

"Father Romano's too nice a guy," Carlota said. "Too trusting." She shuddered. "I hope he's not in danger."

"The more I think about that mystery Felix fellow, the more I think he could be tied into the dead priests, the shooting, everything. I can't believe Father Romano flew off to Vienna like that."

Charlie finished typing the e-mail, rolled back his chair, and pointed to the screen. "Take a look at this. See if I covered all the details. And let me know if you agree with my recommendation to come back to the good old U.S. of A. and stay clear of Professor Hamar until this all gets sorted out."

Carlota scanned the e-mail, gave Charlie the thumbs-up, and he clicked Send.

FIFTY-SEVEN

"I WAS SHOCKED TO HEAR OF FATHER TED'S DEATH. He was a dear friend." Father Hans Josef put a hand on Romano's shoulder as they walked to his office. "I know how close you two were. He will be sorely missed."

Romano looked over at Father Josef. He noticed his grim expression but also sensed a deeper apprehension emanating from his eyes.

Josef opened the door to his office and pointed to the phone on his desk. "It's Father Cristoforo. He said it's vital he speaks to you immediately."

Romano sat in one of the plush brown leather chairs in front of Josef's antique mahogany desk and picked up the receiver. "Father Cristoforo."

"Father Romano, I'm relieved I was able to track you down. We've heard from Interpol. Did you meet with that priest?"

Romano felt a twinge of panic. This was not the time to divulge finding the body, and Cristoforo wasn't the person to confide in. "Yes. It was a very short meeting at a café. Turns out he's Felix Konrad, a laicized priest. Father Müller tells us he's a crazy conspiracy buff." Romano debated bringing up Felix's theory on the Jesuits but thought better of it. "There was nothing that could relate to Father Mathews's death. What have you heard?"

"I'm calling to warn you about Brittany Hamar. We've received word from Interpol that they're investigating her regarding the deaths of Father Mathews and Father Matteo."

"I don't think she was involved in the murders."

"Leave that up to the authorities. Where is she staying?"

"At the Hotel Royal near Stephansdom. Right now she's in Father Müller's office. We've been trying to convince her to reconsider her theories regarding her manuscript, *The Jesus Fraud.*"

"That's another reason you should be cautious. Let me know

if she moves from the hotel or leaves Vienna so I can advise Interpol."

When Romano hung up the phone, Father Josef was staring at him with a look of great concern. "Father Cristoforo told me this Hamar woman is a suspect in Father Mathews's and Father Matteo's deaths. How well do you know her?"

"Well enough to know she had no reason to kill them. And she was almost killed herself in New York on the day they found Father Mathews's body."

"No reason you're aware of. And I heard she visited both Father Matteo and Father Mathews the day before they were found dead."

"She thinks someone could be following her because of her research. She was told both of them had knowledge relating to a bloodline of Christ."

"That's absurd. You and I both knew Father Mathews better than anyone. He would not give a second thought to that kind of nonsense. And if she is involved with Felix Konrad, she could be unstable. I know Father Mathews would not want you to put yourself in danger."

"I intend to convince her to return to New York and meet with the FBI."

"I think that would be in everyone's best interest."

Josef stepped behind the desk and sat in his high-backed leather chair trimmed with gleaming brass tacks. "And I suggest you distance yourself from her as soon as possible." His look left no doubt that it was not merely a suggestion.

FIFTY-EIGHT

ROMANO POINTED TO THE ÍNIGO CAFÉ ACROSS THE plaza from the Jesuit rectory. "How about stopping for an early dinner? I'm famished. Airline food and a croissant sandwich haven't done it for me."

He saw Britt glance at her watch then scan the plaza. The only other people in the small plaza were an elderly couple wearing matching straw hats and carrying a guidebook. They craned their necks as they pointed to the elegant Baroque façade of the Academy of Science building next to the church. A few cars were parked along the square.

"I think the Inigo is a safe place for us to eat and talk about this mess," Romano said. He saw a look of confusion blanket Britt's face. "Mostly Jesuits, professors, and researchers frequent the place. And we'll beat the dinner rush."

Britt nodded and followed Romano to the café. The Inigo was just as Romano remembered it. An old upright piano with a bright paisley-clad swivel stool stood beside the entrance to a small back dining room. Recessed spots and wall sconces lit the main room, which was furnished with intimate tables sporting white linen tablecloths and vases of fresh flowers. Framed photographs and modern art adorned the walls and a small wooden cross hung behind the serving area.

A waiter in a crisp white shirt and blue apron came to greet them. Romano requested a table in the far corner of the main dining room, where he could see who entered the café but where they would still have some privacy. They ordered two glasses of red wine while they decided what to eat.

Britt glanced at the menu. "I'm going to need your help. I hope your German's better than mine."

Romano ran his finger down the opening page. "I may be able to get us through the daily specials." He let out a breath. "Thank

God there are only three, and I think I have a reasonable idea of what they are. There's a chicken dish in tomato and rosemary sauce with spaghetti. A turkey schnitzel. That's a cutlet baked with tomatoes and mozzarella served with herb rice."

"Stop right there." Britt raised a hand. "We're in Vienna. I'll have the schnitzel."

Romano pointed to the last item on the daily specials. "There's also a baked pig's head schnitzel."

Britt made a face. "No, thanks, I'll stick with the turkey."

"Great, I'll make it two and we'll be home free until dessert."

After the waiter brought their wine and took the order, Romano held up his glass. "Here's to getting this whole mess resolved and staying alive in the process."

A look of total apprehension blanketed Britt's face as she touched glasses and took a healthy drink. "Do you really think we're in danger here in Vienna?"

"I think someone's following you. Felix Konrad's dead and we still have no idea who's behind the killings."

"Felix was convinced the *Rex Deus* exists and is protecting the bloodline. But if they saw us with Felix, why not kill us all at the café?"

"Opportunity," Romano said. "They could have been watching from outside the café. They saw us meet Felix, followed him when he ran out, and killed him in the privacy of his home. No witnesses."

Fear replaced the apprehension on Britt's face. "That means they could be looking for me."

"That's why we should go to the authorities."

"Not in Austria," Britt snapped. "If they start checking my name, my meeting in Spain with Father Matteo could come up. I can't get involved with these murders. Not now."

"Look, this is getting way out of hand." Romano pulled a small leather case from his pocket, took out Cutler's card, and placed it on the table in front of Britt. "Here, call Agent Cutler. He's handling Father Mathews's case. We should leave for New York as soon as possible. You obviously don't want to get embroiled in a murder investigation here in Vienna. When they discover we met with Felix Konrad a few hours before he was killed, and if we were seen going to his house, believe me, you will."

Romano noticed Britt's lips tighten into the same expression she had when she dismissed him at the hospital. "You go back to

New York and meet with the FBI." Britt slid the card to Romano. "I'm flying to Marseille tomorrow morning and on to Rennes-le-Château."

Romano stared in astonishment at Britt. "Why?"

"You heard Felix yourself and saw the note about the Villa Santa Maria. It's a short flight to the Pyrénées, and I'm not going to give up this chance to uncover whatever is hidden there."

"Do you even know if there is a Villa Santa Maria? And you heard Father Müller. Felix Konrad was crazy. What could you find that hundreds of treasure hunters missed?"

Romano could see the muscles in Britt's jaw form taut ridges. "He's dead, isn't he?" she said. "If he was only crazy, why would someone want to kill him?"

"Because he met with you. Just like Father Mathews and Father Matteo."

Britt dropped her head and stared at the table. When she finally looked up, she pushed away strands of hair soaked in tears.

Romano reached out and put a hand on Britt's arm. "I'm sorry, but you seem to be caught up in some fantasy that is making you irrational and grasping at straws."

Britt dabbed away her tears with a napkin and slid her arm out from under Romano's hand. She took a few deep breaths and looked at him as if searching for a lost cause. He noticed a slight pallor beneath the natural glow of her cheeks.

"I can't expect you to understand," Britt said. "To me this isn't a fantasy. It's looking for an answer to why my life has been ripped apart. A justification for why all my hopes and prayers went unanswered." Her eyes welled up and she swallowed to hold back more tears. "This short flight to the Pyrénées is my chance to find answers to something that . . ." Britt's eyes radiated a new sense of determination. "I must go there for a very personal reason, even if it threatens my life."

The waiter arrived with their meals. After he left, Britt sat quietly and began eating. Romano felt a sense of frustration and confusion. He wondered what Brittany Hamar was hiding. This was not only about alternative theories of Jesus Christ. She had planned to go to Rennes-le-Château all along.

Romano felt the BlackBerry vibrate in his pocket.

FIFTY-NINE

Philippe punched the disconnect button and held his finger on it. She wasn't staying at the Hotel Römischer Kaiser. If he didn't find her by calling the hotels, he wasn't sure what his next step would be. He had worked his way from the area around the airport through the major sections of Vienna. He had called hotels in the Belvedere Quarter, Town Hall and Museum Quarter, the Hofburg Quarter, and now he was down to the Stephansdom Quarter in the center of the city.

Philippe dialed the number for the Hotel Royal. When he asked for Brittany Hamar, the clerk said, "One moment, please." He heard a click, then the phone in her room started ringing and he hung up. He looked at the map spread out on his bed and searched for number three Singerstrasse. He grinned when he saw it was near the corner of the busiest tourist area in Vienna: Kärntner Strasse, Stephansplatz, and the Graben. It was a lot easier to disappear into a mass of tourists than down a sparsely traveled side street.

Everything was falling into place. The cards were in his favor. Philippe decided to scout the area around Hamar's hotel and develop his strategy for the hit and escape. He had only used one round to take out Konrad so the Glock 17 still had sixteen rounds left in the magazine. More than enough to kill Hamar and protect the priest until he got him to the safe house in Monte Carlo.

Philippe didn't know how long he'd be required to keep the priest in hiding. He'd feel a lot better if his father were still in the picture. The two of them could protect the priest 24/7 without any glitches. His employer assured him the safe house was well protected. After he finalized his plans for Hamar, he'd make contact with the priest and arrange the meet and transport out of Austria. His employer had told him to use the phrase "I am the protector, it is time," and had given him the code word "Michael."

SIXTY

THE TAXI STOPPED IN FRONT OF THE HOTEL ROYAL. Romano and Britt were still shaken by the possibility that whoever shot Felix could be hunting Britt or both of them. Over dessert of mango torte with whipped cream and another glass of wine, Britt had pointed out again that whoever shot her may have broken into her computer and found out about Felix. Hopefully the shooter might think Britt was dead and they weren't being followed. They had agreed it would be safest for them to stay in their rooms that evening. Romano would meet Britt at her hotel early the next morning and share a taxi to the airport.

Britt cautiously opened the door of the Mercedes, then dashed into the hotel. Romano watched her disappear behind the reflection of the glass doors to the lobby and told the driver to wait. He looked around for anyone suspicious. Not a soul was in the immediate area of Singerstrasse, and the people in the pedestrian plaza were paying no particular attention to the hotel entrance. The outdoor café was shut down for the night and no one was near the bank of pay phones.

Romano told the driver to take him to the rectory. On the way, he opened the BlackBerry message he had received in the café. He was relieved he hadn't opened it while Britt was with him. He felt as if a dark cloud were drifting across his brain as he read the details of what Britt had experienced. As he went through line by line, a new vision of Brittany Hamar emerged: a very troubled individual who had literally been through hell.

He wondered if she had cracked under the pressure and had become delusional. What was her real reason for going to Rennes-le-Château? It was obvious Charlie and Carlota were convinced Britt was unstable and focused on *The Jesus Fraud* as retribution for her religion letting her down. Could she be suffering from a psychosis? Was there a hidden Brittany Hamar who could be killing priests?

Romano thought about Felix Konrad. She was with him when Konrad was killed—or was she? Between twelve thirty and two he was at the rectory while he assumed she was at her hotel. But where could she have gotten the gun?

Just as Romano finished the e-mail from Charlie, the Black-Berry vibrated. The new message from Charlie had the subject heading "911!" He opened the message and scrolled through it. TV news had announced another priest was found dead in a hotel in New Orleans under the same strange circumstances as the priests in Pennsylvania and Spain. They even referred to the marks of the stigmata. Romano stared in disbelief at the last line on the screen. *The priest was identified as Father Nathan Sinclair.*

When he arrived at the Jesuit rectory, Romano tried to find Father Müller and Father Josef. They were not in their rooms and no one knew where they were. And, so far, the news of Father Sinclair's death had not reached Vienna.

Romano tried to put the three deaths into perspective. One thing for certain was that Brittany Hamar couldn't have killed Father Sinclair. She was in Romano's office when the death occurred in New Orleans. The only factor that kept coming up was that they were somehow linked to a secret organization, *Rex Deus.*

What could the three priests have known that got them killed, and who wanted them dead? One priest came from Spain, one from Scotland, and Father Ted was originally from Switzerland. All three of them had done missionary work, and Father Ted had been a retreat director at Wernersville for the last ten years of his life. There was a European connection. They were all Jesuits. Britt said she was told the first two had information about *Le Serpent Rouge.* Why would these priests have information about a heretical concept of a bloodline of Christ?

There was an unnerving silence in the rectory as Romano settled into his room. A brown cotton blanket with a crisp white sheet folded over the top edge was stretched taut across the bed with military precision. Romano carefully lifted the intricately carved wooden cross off the pillow and placed it on the small desk in the corner of the room. He could smell the light scent of bleach as he sat on the bed and took off his shoes. Then he stripped down to his briefs and lay on the bed, his head settling into the down pillow.

As he closed his eyes and folded his hands, Romano saw a vision of Father Ted lying in almost the same position with the marks of the stigmata. He wondered if Ted had been doing his daily Examen of Consciousness when he died. Thoughts of Ted welled up inside him. He had so many questions for his mentor. His breath came in ragged bursts and his eyes filled with tears.

After Romano regained his composure, he began his daily examen, hoping to put into perspective what had happened. When he reached the step of examining how he was living this day and a survey of his actions, he realized he had been living in a dream since hearing the gunshot at Grand Central and getting the call about Ted. When he considered the context of his actions, he realized he could have made a number of disastrous decisions, starting with not taking the gun to the police. He rationalized he had made a mistake by not immediately notifying the Austrian authorities when they found Felix Konrad's body. But then he thought of Britt's struggle and her need for someone to stick by her.

Romano finished by praying words of reconciliation and resolve. He saw his need for God and remembered Ted always telling him that God made things happen for a reason. Maybe the reason he was in Vienna was to be there to support Britt until she could bring closure to whatever was trying to tear her and her religious beliefs apart.

As he tried to sleep, Romano was tormented by myriad thoughts flashing in and out of his consciousness. His torment about his mother, visions of Marta, Ted, Britt, even the twisted body of Felix. Then there was the claim by Felix that the Jesuit order could be hiding the bloodline of Jesus. That was unthinkable, but Jesuit priests were dying and people researching the *Rex Deus* and *Le Serpent Rouge* were dead or shot. And he couldn't ignore the obvious: Father Ted had directed him to Father Sinclair and now Sinclair was dead under the same bizarre circumstances as Ted. There was no denying there had to be a connection.

The last thought Romano had before he finally drifted off to sleep was the sickening feeling that maybe Father Ted had been involved in something above and beyond *Ad majorem Dei gloriam*, for the greater glory of God.

SIXTY-ONE

WHEN AGENT CUTLER WALKED THROUGH THE ARrival gate at Schwechat International Airport he couldn't miss his Interpol contact. The portly man with a beefy red face and bulbous nose that looked like it had been broken a time or two held a sheet of paper that had "Cutler" printed on it in blue ink. Cutler could tell by his dour expression that the Viennese Kriminalpolizei detective was not pleased to be at the airport at eight in the morning to meet him.

Cutler walked up to the detective, who fidgeted in his crumpled brown suit while staring at each arriving passenger. "Detective Braun, Tom Cutler, FBI. Sorry to get you out here this early."

"Ach, it's not a problem." The detective managed a gruff smile. "Actually, I think you can be of help to me. We had our own priest murder yesterday. Well, actually a former priest. Maybe it ties into your investigation. It was called in by an English-speaking man who didn't identify himself."

Cutler perked up immediately. "There could be a connection. The woman we want to question, Brittany Hamar, may be traveling with Father Joseph Romano, a Jesuit priest."

"Our victim was involved with crazy organizations. They believed in all kinds of conspiracies. He was shot in the heart at his home."

"My partner followed Hamar to a meeting of what you might call a crazy organization. They could be linked. I'll get our people to send your office the forensics on the bullet they took out of Brittany Hamar in New York a few days ago. I'd be shocked if there's a match, but it's worth a look. Maybe we've got the same shooter, but I doubt it's the same weapon. If it is, I'd sure as hell be interested in how they got the weapon from New York to Vienna."

Braun sped Cutler through Austrian customs and baggage claim to the lower-level exit. A white VW station wagon with

POLIZEI emblazoned in black letters was waiting at the curb. A uniformed officer dressed in Loden green sat behind the wheel.

When Braun tapped on the rear window, the officer popped the hatch, and Cutler tossed his overnight bag inside. After they were settled in the backseat, Braun turned to Cutler and gave another curt smile. "My detective division has been in touch with Interpol and we are ready to assist the FBI. What can we do for you?"

"I'd like to locate Hamar and Father Romano as quickly as possible."

Braun leaned back in the seat, reached for his cell phone, and punched a speed dial. "I already have my office trying to locate Brittany Hamar. I'll notify them to add Father Romano to the search."

"His full name is Joseph Romano. He's a Jesuit priest."

"That should make it easy," Braun said. "He probably stays at the rectory. If not, they will know where one of their own is staying."

The police car pulled away from the airport with siren wailing and headed for the city. Braun tilted his head a few times, eyeing Cutler from different angles.

"Do I remind you of somebody?" Cutler asked.

"Ach, I was only wondering if you got yours on the job."

Cutler gave him a puzzled look.

Braun tapped his own nose and shrugged.

Cutler chuckled. "I wish I could say it was in the line of duty. I was a boxer in college—and not very good at blocking punches to the face."

Braun let out a snort. "Wish I could say the same. A suspect opened the door to his apartment and when he saw I was a policeman, he slammed it in my snout." He let out another snort and jiggled his veined nose with a forefinger. "And my *Liebling* Austrian wine has left its signature."

Cutler laughed and settled back into the seat as the VW raced toward the city. It looked like Braun would turn out to be a good guy after all. He decided to ask him for a look at the file on the former priest who was killed yesterday in Vienna. Braun's remark about crazy organizations and conspiracies hit too close to the Mathews and Sinclair cases and Cutler wasn't one who believed in coincidence. In light of Donahue's report on the ritual ceremony Hamar had attended yesterday, she may not be the killer, but she sure as hell was high on the list of people in the loop.

SIXTY-TWO

GABRIEL DOWNSHIFTED THE SILVER GRAY CITROEN C5 and turned onto a gravel drive leading through dense woods. He had rented the car in Carcassonne and had driven through the Pyrénées to the last stop in his quest. The four cases in the trunk marked "Fragile—Computer Equipment" would help him close the final phase of his mission from God.

He pulled up to an enormous complex of stables and corrals nestled in a stand of pine. Two men carrying rifles appeared out of nowhere and stared through the driver and passenger windows. The men relaxed when they recognized Gabriel.

"We weren't expecting you till much later, sir," the man on the driver's side said.

Gabriel got out of the car and walked toward the trunk. "I need to update the computer systems before the Council arrives." He opened the trunk and pointed to the four cases. "Help me get these to the complex. Be careful, they're very fragile."

The men gently lifted the cases out of the trunk and followed Gabriel through a side door into the barn. They went to a far corner of the building, where Gabriel punched a code into a keypad and a door opened to a small vestibule housing a stainless steel elevator. The men placed the cases in the elevator and left through the door, which locked behind them.

Gabriel placed his thumb inside a sensor and the doors slid closed. As the elevator descended slowly down a deep shaft, Gabriel said a prayer giving thanks to God for providing him the strength to keep his quest on track. Soon the Church would finally be free from the heretical influence of these false prophets who had passed on their heresies through oral tradition since the Crucifixion. Tomorrow was the day celebrated by the *Rex Deus* as the true celebration of the death and rebirth of the spiritual Jesus. The Council would never miss the holiest of days. In twenty-four hours, his quest would be complete, and he would be able to rest for eternity in the greater glory of God.

The elevator finally jerked to a stop. Gabriel bowed his head in reverence as the door opened. He had tried to save the innocent, but their fate was now up to the will of God.

SIXTY-THREE

CUTLER WAS STILL GOING OVER THE REPORT ON THE Felix Konrad killing with an interpreter when Detective Braun came back into the office.

"We've located Brittany Hamar," Braun said, sipping from a coffee mug. "She is staying at the Hotel Royal in the First District. It is not far from Stephansdom in the ancient center of the city."

Cutler glanced at his watch, then realized he hadn't reset it for Austrian time. "Will it take us long to get there?"

Braun shook his head and grabbed his jacket off the back of his chair. "Our driver will take us there in no time."

"Anything on Father Romano?"

"He is not staying in a hotel. I think he is probably at the Jesuit rectory. I advise we go there in person after we locate the Hamar lady." Braun raised his eyebrows and rocked his head from side to side. "You know, if we call, he may not be there. If we go, maybe we find him. You know what I mean?"

Cutler nodded. "I'll follow your lead. This is your territory."

SIXTY-FOUR

ROMANO HEARD THE *BEEP, BEEP, BEEP* OF HIS wristwatch, and he jabbed the button to shut off the alarm. When he dropped his hand back on the bed, he realized he was still lying on top of the blanket. His eyes were closed, his lids heavy from a deep sleep. He hated this time just before his head cleared and jumbled thoughts faded in and out. Thoughts he couldn't get control of.

The snippets ratcheted from his mother to Marta to Britt to the dead priests to loneliness and back to anger with his mother, and with himself for not being able to forgive and forget. Why had Marta and her family disappeared? He knew his mother had sent them away. Marta had meant everything to him . . . and he'd never even made love to her. Wanting, caressing, closeness, the warmth of another body, loneliness, the dreaded fear of a life of celibacy; all those thoughts flashed through his mind and melted into confusion, desire. . . .

Romano felt the sweat ooze from his pores and fought the thoughts that ravaged his brain on more mornings than he even admitted to himself. His head began to throb, blocking the rampaging thoughts. He focused on Britt. What about her anger and rage? What could she be feeling? Could it have driven her to some religious cult that thought they were protecting a deep, dark, religious secret? Could they believe the priests, Britt, and Felix put their secret in jeopardy? Or was Britt an integral member of the cult, testing people to see who was a danger to them? Then why was she shot?

Romano opened his eyes. He sat on the edge of the bed and rubbed his temples. The sweats subsided. Nothing made sense; it was crazy. Then he spotted the cross propped against the wall on the desk and closed his eyes again. This time he took deep breaths and prayed for an end to the killing and to the torment that Britt must be going through. He prayed for Ted and finally asked for help in coming to terms with his own demons.

SIXTY-FIVE

PHILIPPE SIPPED THE COFFEE HE HAD BOUGHT AT the corner Konditorei and kept his eyes on the entrance to the Hotel Royal. He'd walked among the Viennese on their way to work, amidst the delivery vehicles and early tourists in the pedestrian zone, and up and down Singerstrasse, all within eyeshot of the hotel for the past hour. A young couple was all he saw leave the hotel.

He had the latest *Kurier* newspaper tucked under his arm as he moved to a bank of pay phones across from the hotel. He had a clear view of the entrance. He called the rectory again, worried he had not been able to contact the priest. He had called earlier and got no answer. This time a woman answered. She said she hadn't seen the father yet this morning and asked for Philippe's name and number. He said he'd call again later and hung up.

Sooner or later Hamar had to leave the hotel. When she did, he'd slip the Glock under the newspaper, walk up to her, and this time he wouldn't adjust his aim by six inches. By the time anyone realized the woman who'd fallen in front of the hotel was dead, he'd be long gone.

SIXTY-SIX

Romano showered, quickly dressed, stuffed his things into his backpack, and called Britt's hotel. When they transferred the call to her room, she picked up on the first ring.

"Joseph?"

"Are you expecting a call from anyone else?"

"No, no. I'm still edgy about our discussion. That someone may have followed me here."

"I'm ready to head over to your hotel. Why don't you check out and ask them to call a taxi to take us to the airport? Don't go out of the hotel until I get there."

"I'll be in the lobby watching for you."

Romano left the rectory and hurried up the side streets toward the Hotel Royal. A large street sweeper with DER SAUBERMACHER stenciled on the side rounded a corner and lumbered past him, scrubbing the gutter. He picked up his pace and turned onto the Wollzeile, where shopkeepers in white or green smocks were scouring windows, stoops, and sidewalks in front of their stores. It was not a sight he recalled seeing often in New York.

When he reached the area around Stephansdom, trucks and delivery vans were everywhere throughout the pedestrian zone bringing supplies for the shops along Kärntner Strasse and the Graben. People hurried in all directions heading to work. At this time of the morning there weren't many tourists gawking at the buildings. At the corner of Singerstrasse, there was an even larger crowd of people going in and out of the Aida Café Konditorei for their morning jolt of coffee and pastries.

As he turned the corner and headed toward Singerstrasse and the hotel, he saw waitresses in red-and-white-striped uniforms setting up the outdoor café. In front of the Royal, a taxi swung into the dead end near the pedestrian zone and stopped. He walked up to the driver.

"Are you here to take Ms. Hamar and me to the airport?"

"The hotel said two passengers. A man and a lady."

"That's us," Romano said. He turned and saw Britt wave through the glass doors of the lobby and then head toward him.

SIXTY-SEVEN

A man in khakis and a polo shirt carrying a backpack stopped and talked to the driver of the taxi that had just pulled up in front of the hotel. Philippe noticed something familiar about the man. Then it struck him; he wasn't wearing a priest's collar. It was Father Joseph Romano. What could Romano be doing in Vienna at Hamar's hotel?

Philippe felt a rush as his adrenaline spiked. Now there was someone who might recognize him from Grand Central Terminal blocking his access to Hamar. Romano turned and walked to the entrance. Philippe saw a blonde with a travel bag over her shoulder wave from inside the hotel and approach the glass doors. He pulled the Glock out of his jacket, slid it under the newspaper, and moved toward the sidewalk.

This wouldn't be the close-up heart shot he'd planned. He'd group three quick rounds into Hamar and disappear into the crowd clustered around the corner café. His finger was on the trigger as he raised the newspaper and moved into position.

The police car stopped in the pedestrian zone around the corner from Singerstrasse. Detective Braun and Agent Cutler got out and walked toward the hotel. As they turned the corner and headed past a group of people waiting to enter the outdoor café, a man cut in front of them.

Cutler saw the man pull a pistol out of his jacket and slip it under the folded newspaper in his other hand. He nudged Braun, who nodded and unholstered his weapon.

Romano saw someone moving toward him as he turned and pulled open the door for Britt. The man had a newspaper draped over his right hand. Something else caught Romano's attention as he looked at the man's face. His mind went into slow motion and flashed back to Grand Central.

The scar. It was the same man. He grabbed Britt and shoved her sideways as a gunshot rang out. Romano started running, dragging Britt with him. When they reached the corner, Britt got her footing and they ran along the shops surrounding Stephansdom.

DETECTIVE BRAUП KEPT HIS WEAPOП TRAIПED OП the man lying in the street behind the taxi.

Cutler kicked away the weapon next to the man's hand and knelt down and checked the body. He found no pulse. He looked up at Braun. "He's dead."

Braun holstered his gun. "Go after them. I'll handle this."

Cutler ran through the crowd gathering at a distance from the shooting. When he got to the pedestrian zone, he glanced ahead to the Graben, up Kärntner Strasse, then down toward Stephansdom. He wasn't sure which way they had run. He didn't see Britt Hamar's blond hair anywhere amid the throng of people and vans. When he spotted the blue circle with a white U designating the entrance to the U-Bahn station, he shook his head. Vienna's underground had trains speeding off like clockwork toward all areas of the city. As far as he could recall, Hamar had a bag over her shoulder and Romano carried a knapsack. They could be on their way to trains, planes, or even the Russian hydrofoils that sped up and down the Danube.

Cutler turned and headed back to Braun, who had been joined by the uniformed officer who had driven them from the station. The officer was motioning for people to stay away from the scene and Braun was talking on his cell.

Braun flipped the cell phone closed when Cutler approached. "My people are on the way. You didn't find them?"

"My guess is they ran into your underground train station."

Braun shook his head. "U-One and U-Three trains leave from down there. At this time of the morning, trains leave every few seconds. We'll have to give a description to my department and our uniformed officers."

"They both carried bags. Let's check with the hotel. I think they're on the move."

Braun flipped open his cell. "I'll have my department check with the airlines. If they're leaving by train we will be out of luck."

Cutler pointed to the dead man. "Who is this one?"

"His name is Philippe Armand. He's carrying a French passport."

The undulating wail of sirens could be heard in the distance. Cutler realized he now had to rely solely on the Austrian Kriminalpolizei to track down Brittany Hamar.

SIXTY-EIGHT

ROMANO PULLED BRITT'S BAG OFF HER SHOULDER and grabbed her hand as they ran around the back of Stephansdom. He followed the narrow street behind the church and turned right on the next side street. He glanced back a few times and saw no one following them. This was the route he took from the rectory, but under altogether different circumstances. He turned left at the next small street and breathed a sigh of relief when they reached the Wollzeile.

Romano tugged Britt around the corner onto the busy street and slowed to a fast walk. "We might find a taxi on the Wollzeile. If not, it takes us to the Ring, where I know we'll find one."

Britt was breathing like she'd finished a tough race. "This is not happening," she said.

Romano put an arm around her shoulder. "We may have lucked out. I saw a policeman rushing toward the hotel when we turned the corner. Maybe they caught the guy."

"I don't care. I just want to get out of here."

Romano saw a taxi and waved it down. "Don't worry, we're going straight to the airport."

"Schwechat International Airport," Romano said. He looked over at Britt. "I'm sure that was the same man who shot you," he whispered.

Britt looked at him, and he saw tears well up in her eyes. "How do you know? I thought you didn't remember what the man at Grand Central looked like?"

"It was the scar. He had a scar on his forehead and so did this guy. That's why I grabbed you. When I saw him, I had a flashback. I had seen that face before." Romano leaned closer to Britt. "Maybe we should go to the police."

Britt stiffened. "No, that's not an option. Not now. I've got to catch my flight to Marseille."

Romano couldn't believe the dramatic change in Britt. From tears a moment ago to anger and fierce determination. Her eyes said it all. There was something she was holding back.

"Don't you want to know if the police caught the man who shot you and maybe killed Felix? And maybe even killed the priests?"

"And what if they didn't?" Britt said sharply. "Should I give him another chance? If they caught him, we'll hear about it, and if they didn't, I'd rather be far away from here."

Her reply caught Romano off guard. Britt could really bounce back under pressure. From vulnerable to invincible. Whatever she was hiding, he'd bet it related to her bloodline theory. And now he was convinced it had something to do with Rennes-le-Château.

SIXTY-NINE

THE POLICE CAR SKIDDED TO A HALT ON THE COB-blestone plaza in front of the Jesuit rectory. Cutler followed Braun up the stone steps to a heavy, dark wood door. Braun opened the door and barged into the rectory's dim reception area, where a young woman looked up from the desk, smiled, and said something to them in German. Braun showed her his identification and they had a short conversation. Cutler heard the word "English" during the last exchange.

Braun looked at Cutler. "The young woman is a university student, and she speaks excellent English."

Cutler smiled and nodded to the receptionist. "Thank you, my language skills are not too good I'm sorry to say."

"Not a problem, sir. . . ." Cutler saw her ready her pen on the notepad.

"Sorry. Tom Cutler, U.S. Federal Bureau of Investigation." Cutler held out his ID as the woman jotted his name on the pad beneath Kurt Braun's.

"Could you please summon the father rector?" Braun said. "We are here on a matter involving Interpol."

A worried expression flashed across the receptionist's face. "Father Hans Josef isn't in the rectory. Could someone else help you?"

"When do you expect Father Josef to return?" Braun asked.

The young woman looked flustered. "I am not sure."

"Where is he?" Cutler asked.

"He . . . he really didn't say." The young woman's face flushed. "We haven't seen him today. It's not like the father to leave without letting us know." She picked up the phone. "Let me call one of the priests. They might have better information."

"We're actually looking for Father Joseph Romano from the States," Braun said.

The young woman seemed relieved and managed a smile. "Father Romano left this morning. I believe he's on his way back to the States." She punched a few numbers into the phone. "I'll get Father Müller. He spent a lot of time with Father Romano and Professor Hamar yesterday. Maybe he'll know more about Father Josef."

While waiting for Father Müller, Cutler had an unsettling thought. He motioned for Braun to follow him to the far side of the reception area, where a strange circular oil painting hung on the wall. The pebble-grained, dark tones of the painting were breeched by the subtle glimmer of a thin line of light emerging from a distant horizon.

As they viewed the painting, Cutler leaned toward Braun. "The painting is not why I brought you over here. The receptionist is nervous about Father Josef. I'm concerned the rectory doesn't know his whereabouts." He raised his eyebrows. "There are three dead Jesuits. I hope we don't have a fourth."

"Gentlemen, I'm Father Heinz Müller. What can I do for you?" A man in a well-tailored suit strode across the room.

"We're trying to locate Father Joseph Romano," Cutler said.

"I suggest you try the airport, but I recommend you hurry." Müller made a show of pushing back the sleeve of his suit jacket and glancing at what looked like an expensive watch. "He left the rectory a few hours ago. He might even be in the air by now."

"We're also trying to locate Brittany Hamar," Cutler added.

"Professor Hamar was with Father Romano yesterday. We discussed her research for her book. I'm sorry I have no idea where she might be. I assumed they'd be traveling back to New York together."

"We are checking the airlines," Braun said. "We were hoping you might know what flight they would be taking."

Müller shook his head. "Sorry I can't be of more help. May I ask what this is in reference to?"

Braun looked to Cutler and gave him a quick nod.

"We're investigating the death of three Jesuit priests and Ms. Hamar may have some information that would be helpful to us."

Müller blinked a few times then gave them a blank stare. "I was only aware of Father Matteo in Spain and Father Mathews in the States."

"Father Nathan Sinclair was found dead two days ago under similar conditions in New Orleans."

"Dear God. He was a good friend of Father Josef . . . and Father Mathews. Good Lord," Müller said. "We've got to find Father Josef. No one's seen him since early yesterday evening."

SEVENTY

BRITT SNAKED HER WAY THROUGH HARRIED PAS-
sengers in the terminal to the check-in line forming at the Air
France counter. She turned to Romano, who slipped her bag off
his shoulder and handed it to her.

"Well, I guess this is where we part company." Britt felt awk-
ward. She was tempted to kiss him on the cheek, but she had
never kissed a priest before, even as a thank-you. She smiled and
said, "I'll call you when I get back to the city."

Britt had mixed feelings about leaving Romano. On one hand,
he had saved her life, and she felt a strange inner peace with him
around. On the other hand, she was relieved he hadn't pushed to
join her trip to Rennes-le-Château. She feared what *The Messenger* might think if he saw her with Romano. She couldn't chance
scaring him off.

Romano was looking at her with what she could only regard
as caring, or respect, or compassion, or maybe a combination of
all three. Even though he didn't agree with the direction of her research, he wasn't threatening and didn't try to impose Church
doctrine on her. Maybe it was the teacher in him trying to get her
to see the light without shining high beams in her eyes. She
wished she could confide in him completely, but she was too
close to the final answers to take the chance.

Romano looked as if he were searching for the right words to
say good-bye. Then his face took on an odd expression. "You
won't get rid of me this easily," he said with the same quirky look
she had seen once before in his office. "I'm going to the ticket
line to see if there are any seats left on your flight." He shrugged
and gave a quick smile that may have included a hint of a wink.
"Do you have any idea the boost in credibility I'd get with my
students if I could say I was there when Professor Brittany
Hamar discovered the Holy Grail."

With that, Romano went to the Air France ticket line.

Britt panicked. This was not what she had anticipated. She thought about what *The Messenger* had said. There had been no demand to come alone, and he had never come across to her as a threat. Just the opposite; he had warned her of the danger she was in—"That both of us are in," he had stressed.

What could she tell Romano? She couldn't tell him the truth. He'd think she was crazy putting her trust in someone she had never met. But someone she nevertheless had a special bond with—a bond of blood.

SEVENTY-ONE

ROMANO FELT RELIEVED WHEN THE AIRCRAFT pushed back from the gate and no one was sitting in the third seat in their row. He was hoping Britt would open up about what she truly expected to find in Rennes-le-Château.

He watched Britt's white-knuckle grip on the arms of the seat until they were airborne. When they reached altitude, she twisted open an air vent and tilted her face toward the cool air. Then she rolled her eyes at Romano. "I'm sorry you have to see me go through this takeoff and landing routine."

"We all have our little idiosyncrasies. You just haven't uncovered mine."

Britt grinned. "There's still time for that."

Romano felt his face flush. He decided it was time to press Britt about why she was headed for this controversial village in the Pyrénées. "What exactly are your plans when you get to Rennes-le-Château?"

Britt didn't respond immediately, seeming to mull something over in her mind. "I want to take a look at Saunière's church, the church of Saint Magdalene. It supposedly contains a lot of symbolism that could tie into my research. I'm especially interested in the graveyard. Saunière is said to have erased the inscription on the Blanchefort tomb. Lady d'Hautpoul de Blanchefort was supposedly the source of the secret documents Saunière found in the Visigoth pillar, which held up the altar in the church of Saint Magdalene."

"What exactly are you looking for?"

Britt gave Romano a hazy look. "I don't really know. It's one of those things I just have to do. After all my research, maybe I'll see something that will tie some of the pieces together. Despite what Father Müller said, I'm convinced there is physical evidence in Rennes-le-Château that supports a bloodline and will substantiate my James document. Sometimes the answer is right in front of you."

"What about Mary Magdalene? You seem convinced she was the Holy Grail and her bones are somewhere near Rennes-le-Château."

"That's why I want to ask some of the people living in the area if they heard of a Villa Santa Maria. I'm also interested in information about a statue of Mary Magdalene that Saunière had placed in the Garden of Calvary in the village square. It disappeared years ago. So much is linked to Mary Magdalene that I am convinced she was the real key to the secrets held by Saunière."

"What's the significance of the statue?" Romano asked.

"There are so many claims of coded messages linked to Bérenger Saunière that I wonder if there wasn't a clue to the location of Mary Magdalene's remains somewhere on the statue. Saunière was seen collecting decorative stones in the valley of the Bals, and he brought them to his village in a hod. He set up a strange grotto in a corner of the garden using the stones, and in it he placed the statue of Mary Magdalene. I wonder if he carried more than stones in that hod. What if he found the bones of Mary and set up a shrine to her?"

"That's quite a stretch. A lot of speculation. There's no solid evidence for any of it. I hate to say it, but you're chasing windmills."

A look of annoyance rippled across Britt's face. "If you get enough pieces of a jigsaw puzzle in place, a clear picture starts to emerge. It's taken me years of doubt and research, but I'm beginning to see that picture."

Romano slowly shook his head. "But you've selected only biased pieces to fit your puzzle concept, and therefore you may be creating a clear picture of a myth of your own making."

Britt tensed. "But maybe it's a picture that needs to be created so people can make their own informed decisions. I'll admit it. I am sick and tired of the mystery, secrecy, and ritual of the Roman Catholic Church. I believe the early Orthodox Church established a bureaucracy that focused on creating power and wealth rather than sharing the teachings of Jesus and helping the flock to find self-enlightenment."

"You wrote a book on Gnosticism and I think it struck a nerve or a need in your life. You seem to be sliding away from Church doctrine toward Gnosticism."

Britt tilted her head back under the air vent. "Please don't label me a Gnostic. You don't understand." She took a deep breath. "After tomorrow, maybe you will."

"You're right, I don't understand. Are you so convinced you're going to have some revelation by wandering around in a village that you'll be able to disprove what has survived two thousand years of heretical claims, microscopic analysis, and daunting criticism?"

"Okay." Britt glared at Romano. "What about the research I discovered in legitimate journals? The early Jerusalem Church headed by James, who was *possibly* the brother of Jesus, who followed Jewish law and stressed the teachings of Jesus to find self-enlightenment."

"I'll give you the benefit of the doubt on James being Jesus' sibling and the early Church focus on self-enlightenment. But even that is difficult to support with any reliable documents from even close to that period."

Romano saw the spark in Britt's eyes. She was certainly passionate about her theory of a bloodline. But he also felt she wasn't telling him the whole truth. He couldn't buy a brilliant researcher going to a small village in the Pyrénées based upon a mere whim.

She hesitated, then continued. "But you must agree the early followers of the apostles didn't hold out Jesus as the Savior. And they didn't profess that faith in Jesus and confession would result in the forgiveness of sins without any additional good works."

"The Christian religion evolved over hundreds of years into what we have today," Romano replied. "Ten of the original disciples were put to grisly deaths for sticking to their faith. Surely someone would have recanted the accuracy of the information about Jesus if it were a myth."

"It's not the information about Jesus himself." Britt shook her head in frustration. "My problem is with the interpretation of what Jesus means to the world and his role in Christianity. The concept of Jesus as the Redeemer came from Paul. He believed that Jesus, having died for the sins of mankind, was now reserved in heaven as God's agent for the judgment. Those who believed in him and acknowledged him as Lord would have him as their deliverer on the Day of Judgment. Faith in Christ as the Redeemer became the foundation of Paul's preaching."

Romano shrugged. "And what was wrong with that?"

"Wrong with that? You can't be serious." Britt's jaw dropped. "I agree with Martin Luther. I'm disillusioned by the dogmatic theme of redemption. It leaves a lot to be desired. If an axe murderer believes in Jesus and takes confession, he's forgiven? Please!"

Romano raised his hands in a symbol of surrender. "I give up—for now. We're getting into areas that require at least a semester of serious academic attention."

Before he could continue, the plane dropped suddenly and then bounced a few times. The seat belt lights flashed on and the pilot's voice came over the intercom. "Please fasten your seat belts—we're heading into an area of turbulence. Sorry for any inconvenience."

Romano noticed Britt had resumed her white-knuckle grip on the armrests. Their discussion was finished for the time being. He checked his watch and realized they'd be landing in Lyon soon before the last leg of their flight to Marseille. He wondered whether the gunman in Vienna had been apprehended and if he was involved in the deaths of his fellow Jesuits. He was tempted to e-mail Father Müller or Father Cristoforo at the Vatican when he landed, but realized he didn't remember their addresses. Calling was not an option; he didn't know how he'd explain going to Rennes-le-Château with Brittany Hamar looking for evidence of a bloodline of Christ.

SEVENTY-TWO

The headquarters for the Vienna Kriminal-polizei was buzzing with activity when Cutler and Braun returned from the rectory. A uniformed task force had been sent to the Hotel Royal and, thank God, there was no dead priest in any of the rooms.

Father Müller had seemed relieved when they searched Father Josef's room and discovered his toiletries and favorite travel bag were missing. They interviewed the other priests, and no one had any idea where their father rector might have gone. He was last seen not long after Romano and Hamar met with Müller. One of the priests mentioned seeing the two of them eating at the Inigo Café across the plaza from the rectory, but Josef was not with them.

Müller told Cutler and Braun about the discussions concerning Konrad and Rennes-le-Château. He was visibly shaken when they told him Konrad's body had been found later that day in his home in Hietzing with a bullet to the heart. His voice cracked when he said he had mentioned to Romano where Konrad lived. He was concerned that he may have put them in danger—that maybe the killer saw them at Konrad's house and that's why he tried to shoot them at the hotel.

An officer motioned to Braun when they entered his office. After a short discussion, Braun looked at Cutler with a smug expression plastered across his face. "They just landed in Marseille."

"Do you have a map of France?" Cutler asked.

Braun rummaged through a file cabinet, pulled out a map that had seen a lot of use, and spread it across his desk. He jammed a pudgy finger near the bottom along the Gulf of Lions. "That's where they landed." He shook his head. "I am afraid it's too late to get the French authorities to detain them."

"I think I may know where they're headed." Cutler scanned the map until he found what he was looking for. Rennes-le-Château was a mere speck in the Pyrénées below Carcassonne. The only identifying symbol was a black dot with a cross designating that a chapel existed in the tiny village. "Father Müller seemed to think Hamar was focused on Rennes-le-Château."

Braun lifted his head and stared at the map through the bottom of his bifocals. "You might be able to fly into Carcassonne. I can have someone check on the next flight."

"Thanks."

"Not a problem, my friend. If you like, I can contact the French authorities and have them meet you." Braun raised his thick eyebrows and glanced at Cutler over the top of his glasses. "It might be easier for me than for an American. I have an associate at the French Interpol office who owes me a favor."

"I'd appreciate that." Cutler clapped Braun on the shoulder. "You're a good man, Herr Braun."

While Braun got busy on the telephone, Cutler thought about the priest deaths and the link between Romano and Hamar. He should have seen it before this. A priest living a vow of celibacy and, from Lieutenant Renzetti's description, a beautiful blond professor who has a bone to pick with her religion. Either Romano was somehow involved in a conspiracy the bureau wasn't aware of, or he was part of some bizarre rituals from that *Ordo Templi*, or Britt was playing him for a personal vendetta. Hell, she could have shot herself and left the gun in the manuscript box for Romano to retrieve when he came to her aid. No one reported actually seeing the shooter, and they never checked the victim for gunshot residue.

Cutler knew it would be tough to get the French to step over the line to detain Hamar and Romano since none of the murders took place in France. If they could just help him locate them, he'd do the rest.

Right now it was important to get as much as he could on the Vienna shooter, Philippe Armand, before he went to France. There was always the option that Armand was behind all the deaths and Hamar and Romano were on his list. But there was the question of motive and whether Armand acted alone. And there was still Father Hans Josef to worry about. All these priests knew each other. Hamar had visited each of them except for Father Sinclair. There had to be some common thread tying these cases together. And, right now, Cutler was betting on Brittany Hamar to know what it was.

SEVENTY-THREE

ROMANO AND BRITT NIBBLED SMALL BAGUETTE sandwiches and enjoyed a bottle of French burgundy in the café car on the train from Marseille to Carcassonne. On the short hop from Lyon to Marseille there hadn't been much time for discussion between Britt's panic attacks. Romano thought the train ride would give him an opportunity to get Britt to open up about the trauma that may have been the trigger for her anti-Church crusade.

Romano took a sip of burgundy and savored the soft sweet flavor. Father Ted had once shared a rare vintage with him. When they were about to finish the bottle, Ted raised his glass with a hint of a smile and said, "A good burgundy is like the fine face of a woman with good bone structure; it is beautiful." He always wondered whether Ted ever had the company of a woman with the features of a good burgundy.

Romano noticed Britt staring out the train window in a world of her own. She seemed at peace. Even after all she'd been through, she managed a soft smile. It seemed natural, nothing overdone. For that matter, there was nothing overdone about Britt, except maybe her zeal for her book.

"I know the Church isn't perfect," Romano said. "Nothing in life is, except maybe the life of Christ. You must agree that it's possible God sent Jesus to show us the way even if you question his role as the Redeemer."

Britt turned to Romano, her eyes still soft and radiant. "You know I don't have any problem with that. As you're so quick to point out, it fits with my Gnostic point of view." Her expression turned serious. "What brought you to the Church?"

Romano smiled. "Oh, that's a story for another time and place. My original motives were not the best intentioned. But I think the results turned out far better than I had dreamt they would."

Britt's eyes turned down slightly and she tilted her head. "So I take it you get great satisfaction out of being a priest."

"Do you get great satisfaction out of being a professor of religion?"

"I enjoy my *profession* very much. It gives me great satisfaction. But being a priest is not just a profession, it's your life. And a very prescribed life at that."

Romano topped off their wineglasses and took another sip. "I suppose it's about time for me to expose a layer of my idiosyncrasies. The culture of the Church doesn't make it easy to be a priest. I think about the love of a woman, about lonely last days, and about sex. A lot."

"Wow, I guess I never thought a priest would admit that he was first and foremost a man."

"First and foremost, I'm a priest. But, when you get right down to it, we're all human beings with all the trappings and frailties that go with it. I often reflect on the restrictions and rigidity of the cloth. Did Christ establish vows of celibacy—no, that came from the early Church fathers to address a human issue, a practical dilemma. As you made clear on the plane, you feel the early Orthodox Church established a bureaucracy that focused on power and wealth. I see it as establishing a structure that could survive in a less than perfect world. Christianity may not be perfect, but on the whole it has served a noble purpose for over two thousand years."

"If you clump people being massacred in the name of the Church in that less than perfect sector, I might agree."

"We all have our crosses to bear," Romano replied. "I . . . I'm sure you've had your share of disappointments and tragedies."

Britt gazed down at the small table. "We can usually find our own share of blame for our tragedies." She seemed to be fighting back tears. Then she looked up at Romano. "I lost my son and husband and I could have prevented it. My son died of Tay-Sachs."

"You can't hold yourself responsible for an unfortunate tragedy."

Britt nodded. "Yes, I can. I was adopted and didn't know who my birth parents were. If I'd been tested, I could have prevented it."

"There was no way you could have known."

"You could say the same for my husband. He was French-Canadian and totally unaware that his heritage carried a risk of the Tay-Sachs gene. He certainly felt responsible." Britt's eyes seemed to go void of all emotion. She stared through Romano as if he weren't there at all. "He killed himself."

Romano saw the tears pool in Britt's eyes but not a drop escaped down her cheeks. "I'm so sorry. I can't even begin to understand the grief you've been through."

"And if you haven't figured it out by now, I also blame my religion. I prayed and prayed for my dying child, and God didn't answer my prayers. How could a loving God allow an infant to die such a horrible death? Maybe that's what caused me to look beyond what my religion drilled into me. Beyond the hollow bounds of forgiveness."

"Is it possible you don't want forgiveness? Are you looking for a way to hold yourself responsible no matter what the outcome?"

Britt rubbed the tears from her eyes. "I don't understand."

"If you prove Jesus' Crucifixion and Resurrection didn't happen and therefore there is no redemption and forgiveness of sin, you win. Even if you're wrong and Jesus is the true redeemer, your rejection of your faith would guarantee that you would not be forgiven."

"Well that's a demon only I can confront."

"That's right. But I think it's important to understand what may be the motivation that has you looking under every pebble to discount the accepted basis of the many Christian faiths."

"But that first pebble came to me through my son's illness."

A confused look spread across Romano's face. "I don't understand."

"It was my research into Tay-Sachs that convinced me it may be possible to prove that the *Rex Deus* could exist and to identify its members. While looking into the genetic defect that causes Tay-Sachs, I found there was another genetic trace that links the *Kohanim* worldwide."

"You're referring to Jews of the priestly tribe descended from the high priest Aaron?"

Britt nodded. "Exactly. The same *Kohanim* that made up the twenty-four high priests of the Temple at Jerusalem. Only their male descendents could become *Kohanim*. In 1997 Israeli scientists found a unique genetic link in the Jews claiming to be of the priestly tribe of *Kohanim* worldwide. They found that they all shared the same peculiar Y chromosome carried only by men and passed down father to son."

"By now there are surely thousands, or hundreds of thousands, of descendants who carry that gene," Romano said.

"If my premise of Mary being impregnated by one of the high priests of the Temple at Jerusalem who was referred to as the angel Gabriel is true, then Jesus would have been a *Kohan*. As would be the members of *Rex Deus*. Some researchers claim that after the killing of James and before the final destruction of the Temple, the priests scattered throughout Europe. The survivors took the group designation *Rex Deus*, Kings of God."

This new puzzle piece of Britt's personal myth about a bloodline concerned Romano. "Who knows the details of your theory about the Y chromosome and the *Rex Deus*?"

"The only public knowledge about anything in my book is the general concept of a bloodline I alluded to in my interview." Britt finished her glass of wine. "Various individuals know details. But it's mostly related to what they provided me during my research."

"Whatever triggered the deaths and shootings is serious business to somebody."

The train slowed and Romano saw signs for Carcassonne. The more Britt told him about her book, the more concerned he became. She had strayed into so many offbeat areas she could have crossed the line with any number of fanatics. He still wasn't convinced someone hadn't been following Britt and also killed Father Ted and the other priests thinking they had some connection to her oddball theories.

Romano nervously glanced around the dining car. He'd feel a lot better if he knew the man with the scar and gun was in a Viennese jail. Even if he had eluded the policeman, he doubted if he could have followed them to the airport or knew what flight they'd be on, unless . . .

"Was there any airline booking information on your computer when it was broken into?"

Britt hesitated. She rolled the stem of her empty glass between her fingers. "I booked my reservations online. And I had notes about meeting Felix."

"You didn't have any information about a trip to Rennes-le-Château? You did decide to take this jaunt while we were in Vienna?"

Britt looked at Romano sheepishly. "The flight to Marseille was on my computer. But there was no train information." She looked like she was about to add something but stopped short and peered out the window. "We're coming into the station. What time is our next train?"

Romano wondered what else Britt was keeping to herself. He pulled a small leather wallet out of his front pocket and counted his remaining euros. "Let's check the cost of a taxi to Rennes-le-Château. We'll be going through some desolate areas of the Pyrénées. From a taxi, we'd be able to see if we're being followed. I'd feel a lot more secure knowing we weren't."

His instincts told him he should take the next train back to Marseille and fly to New York, but something else urged him to stick with Britt and find out where her quest finally ended.

SEVENTY-FOUR

Gabriel finished installing the last of the devices. He positioned his thumb on the sensor and the door to the small room housing the computer security system opened. He stepped inside, entered his personal code, and made the final changes. Everything was going according to plan. He felt his anxiety increase as he closed the massive steel door to the underground complex and entered the elevator. It wouldn't be long now. He was so close.

When he entered the interior of the barn, Gabriel inhaled the heady combination of horseflesh, straw, and manure. It was a pleasant shock to his nostrils. He was more accustomed to the exhaust fumes from cars on the Via della Conciliazione and the idling diesel tourist buses on the vast Piazza San Pietro. Gabriel picked up a handful of hay from a manger and tossed it into the air. How ironic, he thought. Jesus was born in a manger and the final act would take place here.

Gabriel left the barn and made his way past the stables through a stand of holly trees to the main building. He went to his room and out onto a tiled balcony overlooking the surrounding peaks, which were dappled in sunlight through wispy clouds. He positioned his chair so he had a clear view of the driveway and waited for Michael.

The two of them were the last remaining members of the Inner Circle.

Michael had his right arm wrapped over the leather carry-on bag next to him in the taxi as it wound up and down the narrow mountain roads. He was still panicked by the call from Gabriel to leave the rectory immediately and meet him in the sanctuary of the sacred complex. There was no time to waste. Someone was killing the Inner Circle and he could be next.

The taxi turned onto the gravel drive toward Hotellerie du Cheval. The tires crunched over the stone fragments as the driver shifted into a lower gear to negotiate the steep rise. Michael clutched his bag and prayed this horror would soon be past. He and his brethren were the last of the active members of the Inner Circle. The Council of Five had decided to embrace modern technology to uphold their sacred duty to preserve the holy order until the Second Coming. He had hoped to live out the remaining years of his life in peace and anonymity, until a few days ago when the horror started with Uriel in Bilbao, Spain.

Michael was relieved to see Gabriel standing in front of the main building when the taxi pulled up to the elegant inn and horse farm. Gabriel embraced Michael as the taxi turned around and headed down the drive.

"I'm glad you got here safely." Gabriel took Michael's bag.

"Not as happy as I am. What's the word from the Vatican? Do we know how they died?"

"Let's go to the complex, where we'll be totally secure." Gabriel started walking toward the horse stables and barn. "The Council will be here early tomorrow morning to celebrate our holiest of days. They will decide how we will proceed from here."

When they were safely inside the elevator, Michael turned to Gabriel. "Is there any information on how they died?"

Gabriel shook his head. "There was no obvious cause of death and the only physical evidence was that they were all found with the marks of the stigmata."

"Do you have any idea why Brittany Hamar and Father Joseph Romano were in Vienna asking questions about a bloodline, Rennes-le-Château, and the Hapsburgs? I'm afraid she's found something."

"That's why I urged you to leave immediately."

Michael felt a twinge in his stomach. "They're involved?"

"Brittany interviewed Uriel and Raphael the day before their bodies were found. I thought that was sufficient cause to get you out of Vienna and up here immediately. I'm sure the Council is investigating every possibility."

"She was very interested in Rennes-le-Château. You don't suppose she knows about this place."

Gabriel opened the elevator door and stepped inside. "I doubt that. I'm sure her research brought up the issues surrounding Rennes-le-Château, but I think we'll be safe here until the Council resolves this crisis."

As the elevator descended, Gabriel locked Michael in his gaze. "We must also be prepared for the possibility that the deaths may be an act of God. They could be preparation for the Second Coming."

A sudden chill surged through Michael's body.

DO YOU

GET OFF AT

SEABROOK

SEVENTY-FIVE

Romano glanced out the back of the taxi as it made its way up the winding road through the mountains. He could see for miles in this desolate region of the Pyrénées. There were no other cars. There were no towns, villages, hamlets—nothing. Only occasional herds of cows grazing in the grass and brush along the sloping hillsides.

"Do you think anyone's following us?" Britt asked.

"Not only is no one following us, but I'm beginning to wonder if anyone still lives in this mysterious village."

"From what I read, around forty families live there."

Romano turned toward Britt. "Do you really think you're going to find evidence to support your bloodline theory in this village?"

"I don't honestly know. But I know I'll find answers, and if nothing more, peace of mind."

"Answers to what?"

Britt hesitated. Romano saw that look again. Like she was hiding something. Then her eyes brightened. "Maybe to my own personal demons." Britt turned away from Romano and looked out at the looming peaks in the distance.

As they headed into higher elevations the surroundings became more and more barren. The landscape took on a quality that reminded Romano of early TV westerns—a haunting patchwork of sepia tones.

Britt turned back to Romano. "I admit I spent a lot of time researching myths about the Holy Grail. Maybe too much time. But I kept finding a common theme. From Saint Grail and earlier forms of *San Graal* and *Sangréal* there was too much pointing to an interpretation of blood royal to be simply coincidence. Do you realize how many people throughout history spent their lives, gave their lives, searching for this Holy Grail? It's given me hope. After losing Tyler and Alain, that's something I've had very little of."

Romano could see her pain. It was deep within her eyes, etched in the frown lines across her brow. "Even if you find something, let's say bones, female bones from the time of Christ. What will that prove? It's a long leap from there to a bloodline theory."

"Add that to the manuscript from the brother of Jesus stating that Mary Magdalene was with child at the Crucifixion and fled to the south of France and you open a window of doubt. Even for serious researchers like yourself."

Romano had to admit Britt's determination was starting to chip away at his own rational, scholarly outlook.

"And we can't ignore perception," Britt continued. "Just look at the disagreement over creationism versus evolution. This is the twenty-first century, and we still can't agree on what to teach in our schools. If there is an alternative to resurrection and redemption, don't you think it should be given equal consideration—or at least some consideration?"

The taxi slowed. Up ahead stood a dilapidated barn with half its roof caved in and a farmhouse that had seen better days. At the entrance to a weed-infested, dirt driveway was a mud-splattered sign with a picture of a horse and the words HOTELLERIE DU CHEVAL. The driver turned to Romano and Britt and shrugged his shoulders. Britt's face drained of color.

The taxi continued up the rutted drive to the house. Romano got out, walked to the door, and banged his fist on the weather-beaten wood. The place looked uninhabited. He heard nothing inside. He stepped through the weeds and thistle and looked through a window. A few broken chairs were scattered about and a rotted table leaned on its side. There was no one home and evidently hadn't been for a long time.

"This place is abandoned," Romano said to Britt, who was standing beside the taxi.

"That's impossible."

"Did you speak to the innkeepers when you made the reservation?"

Britt looked totally flustered. "I . . . I was told to come here, that a room would be reserved for me." She turned and leaned against the taxi.

"Who made the reservation? This doesn't make any sense. What are you telling me?"

"It doesn't matter now." Britt's eyes were blazing. She stuck her head inside the taxi. "How far is Rennes-le-Château? Can you take us there?"

The driver unfolded a map and traced his finger over it a number of times, then shrugged. "Maybe ten, fifteen kilometers. I will take you if you want." He checked his watch. "I cannot stay there long for sightseeing. I must return to Carcassonne."

A puzzled look came over Britt. "I don't understand. I was told the inn was only a few kilometers from Rennes-le-Château."

Romano jogged down the short drive to the sign. It looked fairly new. Why would a new sign be put up on an inn that had been closed for what looked like months or even longer? He bent down and scraped some of the mud off the bottom of the sign. He stood and called to Britt. "Because it probably is. There's an arrow pointing in the direction we were headed."

They got back in the taxi and continued up the road. When they rounded the next rise, Romano saw a higher peak in the distance with a small clearing near the top and a cluster of buildings. He pointed toward the horizon. "That's more likely to be your inn."

"Thank God. You don't know how important this is to me."

Romano appraised Britt for a moment then decided it was time to get at the truth. "Look, you've been planning to come here all along. Now you tell me you were told to come here. Someone booked a room for you. I think I deserve the truth. What's going on at Rennes-le-Château?"

Britt shook her head imperceptibly and looked at Romano. "You're right. You do deserve the truth. I was afraid if I told you everything you might call that FBI agent and tell him where I was headed and they'd stop me. This is too important for me to miss."

"Who told you to come here? What's too important to miss?"

"It's complicated and involves physical evidence that could support my theory. I'll explain everything when we get to the inn." Britt paused. "The answer may even be waiting for me at the inn."

Romano wasn't sure what to think. Britt looked concerned. Maybe even a touch of fear was lurking behind those wide olive eyes.

"I think this one is your *hotellerie*." The taxi driver glanced in the rearview mirror and pointed to a long drive with a sign for Hotellerie du Cheval.

The taxi turned up the tree-lined drive. They passed a large corral with a few magnificent horses frolicking in a lush grassy meadow. Near the top of the drive stood a large barn and stables behind a stand of trees. The taxi stopped in front of a grand stone structure with an orange tiled roof and a wraparound balcony topped with an elegant white balustrade. It seemed completely out of place in the stark rugged mountains.

Britt jumped out of the taxi and Romano asked the driver to wait while he checked to see if there was a room available. When they got to the entrance, Britt stopped and pointed across a meadow. Above the trees, Romano saw a nearby mountain peak and a circle of stone and stucco homes at the crown of what resembled a stagnant volcano.

"That must be Rennes-le-Château." Britt's voice brightened with enthusiasm. "Let's see what the situation is here at the inn. I'd like to get some research done in the village before it gets dark."

Britt went inside and Romano followed. The innkeeper spoke almost no English, but with Britt's limited French, she confirmed her reservation and managed to get a room for Romano. Britt seemed let down when the woman told her there were no messages or packages waiting for her.

"When are you going to tell me what this is all about?" Romano asked.

Britt gave him an uneasy look. "It's too late to change anything now. I really think we're safe here. Tonight over a bottle of wine on the balcony, I'll try to make some sense out of why we're here. I promise by sunset tomorrow, I'll either have the answers I've come here for, or we'll be on our way to the next flight back to New York."

They got in the taxi and headed for Rennes-le-Château.

SEVENTY-SIX

Braun came back into the office and lowered his large frame into the chair next to Cutler. "Well, at least I got something."

Sweat stained the armpits of Braun's white shirt. He had yanked his tie loose and draped it around his neck. Cutler figured the Austrian detective would breathe a sigh of relief when he left the next morning on the early flight to Carcassonne via Brussels.

Braun let out something between a sigh and a grunt. "Interpol could not get a lot of information on our Philippe Armand. It turns out he is not your typical hit man. He comes from a wealthy French family and lived in Paris his whole life. He and his father are listed as business consultants, but the authorities couldn't find who their clients were. Armand has a clean record. Not even a driving offense. He does a lot of travel throughout Europe and the U.S."

"Were they able to find out where he's been the past week?"

"That you will find more to your liking." Braun gave Cutler a self-satisfied smile. "He was in the U.S. when the two priests died and when Ms. Hamar was shot. And he checked into a hotel in Vienna when Felix Konrad was shot. They couldn't verify Armand's location when Father Matteo died."

"Well, that certainly makes him a candidate for the deaths and the shooting," Cutler said. "I'll e-mail my office to check flights to New Orleans from New York and Pennsylvania as well as car rentals. I'd sure like for this Philippe Armand to be our man."

"Our office is finalizing the ballistics tests on Armand's gun and the bullet that killed Konrad. I should have the results within the hour."

Cutler hoped that taking out Philippe Armand had put an end to the priest deaths. But that didn't take Brittany Hamar off the hook. She could have been working with Armand. For all he knew, Romano could have been the real target.

SEVENTY-SEVEN

THE TAXI SNAKED UP THE DESOLATE BACK ROAD TO Rennes-le-Château. When it finally rounded the top of the peak and headed toward the entrance to the village, Romano turned toward Britt with an odd expression. "Is this what you expected?"

Britt couldn't believe her eyes. "I certainly wasn't prepared for this. I had anticipated finding a serene country setting with Saunière's church maintained by the villagers and his estate inhabited by an eccentric Felix Konrad type."

What she saw was a line of cars with license plates from England, Spain, Germany, and France leaving through clouds of dust from a large unpaved parking lot. The road down that side of the mountain was teeming with vehicles.

At the top of the lot, a white iron fence spread across the property. A green arch over the entrance proclaimed in bold yellow letters, DOMAINE DE L'ABBÉ SAUNIÈRE. Next to it was a green booth. Above the window was printed BILLETERIE. People were lined up buying tickets to what Britt had thought was a private village.

This looked more like the entrance to an amusement park. Attached to the fence was a matching green bulletin board filled with ads for souvenirs and attractions. A freestanding sky-blue-and-pink ad board was plastered with pictures of ice cream treats. A few birds and squirrels scurried about fighting for snacks dropped by the tourists.

Britt gave Romano a dejected look. "So much for finding long-lost secrets hidden in an obscure mountain village." She noticed a few taxis parked at the top of lot. "We're here, so let's see what this is all about. The driver might as well return to Carcassonne. If we can't get a ride, I'm sure we can make it back to the inn on foot."

Romano paid the driver while Britt purchased tickets to

Saunière's domain. The tickets contained an alert in French, English, Dutch, Spanish, and German to *Keep your ticket: It entitles
you to a reduction at the two other sites*. At the top of the ticket
was a notation about *Catha-Rama* in Limoux and *Chateau de
Puivert*. She assumed these were other local attractions related to
other secrets and conspiracies. Attached to the ticket was a red
slip of paper titled "Rennes-le-Château *le trésor*," with a cartoon
sketch of a man in black inside a cave shining a lantern on an
elaborate chest. As best as Britt could make out, the French text
beneath the picture referred to the treasure Abbé Saunière found
near the end of the last century. There was something about secret documents and the house of Austria, an assassination of a
priest, and secrets hidden in a tomb.

Britt was totally dismayed. She had thought this would be her
ideal academic research journey through an old village in an area
that had seen man's presence for over three thousand years. The
little mountaintop stronghold had seen the likes of Romans,
Visigoths, Huns, Merovingians, and Cathars. Evidently someone
had seen the tourist potential and turned the little village into a
hot spot for European conspiracy buffs.

Romano caught up with Britt. "Lead the way. I'm sorry to
burst your enthusiasm, but I don't think we're going to uncover
any deep dark secrets."

"I'm shell-shocked," Britt said as she headed into Saunière's
domain.

Britt felt another dip on her emotional roller coaster when she
saw arrows directing visitors to a museum, café, souvenir shop—
even a boutique. The first place they stopped offered tapes,
DVDs, and books on every conspiracy theory hatched in the past
hundred years.

When Britt asked the shopkeeper about a Villa Santa Maria
and the statue of Mary Magdalene that disappeared from the
Garden of Calvary, he tried to sell her audiotapes that told the
"whole" story of Rennes-le-Château. To Britt it was like a bad
dream. She had visions of finding codes hidden on statues leading to tombs containing ancient ossuaries. She felt an urge to cry
but fought it back. She had shed enough tears in front of Romano.

Romano bought a visitor's guide flying the British Union Jack
and handed it to Britt. "Why don't we start with the Saunière Museum. There may be something there that could relate to your
theory."

Britt could tell Romano was trying to console her and she appreciated it. She considered telling him the truth about why she was there but decided she was too close to getting the manuscript, answers about the Holy Grail, and meeting *The Messenger*. Maybe she was overreacting. She hadn't really been told there was any link to Saunière or directly to Rennes-le-Château. She was only told to go to the Hotellerie du Cheval near Rennes-le-Château and all would be revealed. Maybe she had read too much into the mysteries surrounding Bérenger Saunière. Maybe the secret was no longer in this tiny tourist mecca.

The museum in the old presbytery next to the church contained copies of documents relating to many of the Saunière stories. There were references to the Cathars, Mary Magdalene, and secrets found by Saunière. The museum had been created by descendants of the villagers who were contemporaries of Saunière. The focus was on the oral tradition passed down through generations and referred to documents and secrets found in the tomb of the local "seigneurs" discovered in the church by Saunière.

A bulletin board labeled LES HYPOTHESES caught Britt's attention. "Joseph, take a look at these. It's a photograph of *Les Bergers d'Arcadie* and a photograph of a local tomb in surroundings with an uncanny resemblance to the Poussin painting."

They pressed up to the glass-covered bulletin board. Two printed sheets were stapled next to the photographs. The first, titled *"Les Documents,"* had an English translation. *Without a doubt the Abbé Saunière found certain documents in the church. They have since disappeared and their contents are totally unknown to us. Did the Abbé Saunière discover an "ordinary" treasure or was he, along with a few other priests from the Rennes, keepers of a sacred treasure?* The second sheet was only in French.

"I'm going to need your input on this one," Romano said.

Britt leaned in close to the small printing on the sheet. "I can at least get the introduction. This is from a letter from the Abbé Louis Fouquet to his brother Nicolas Fouquet, Minister of Finance to Louis the Fourteenth, April twelfth, 1656."

Britt struggled trying to translate the contents of the letter. The printing was faded and her French was rusty. Finally she looked at Romano and shrugged. "I can only translate bits and pieces. *He and I have discussed certain things of which I should be able to discuss with you . . . and that . . . through Mr. Poussin will give you certain advantages that even kings would not be able to . . . would be . . . in the coming centuries to recover . . . and these documents are of such importance that nothing on earth could ever . . . a fortune."*

Britt's eyes narrowed into a look of desperation. "Sorry, that's the best I can do." She opened her Coach bag and dug around until she pulled out a small digital camera. She took pictures of the bulletin board and close-ups of the documents. "At least this shows that the people closest to Abbé Saunière believed there was something to the theories supporting a powerful secret or a treasure that he had uncovered."

Romano rocked his head from side to side a few times and squinted. "Or they knew what would attract tourists to their little village." He moved on to some other documents presented in glass cases. "Here's something else that refers to a treasure."

Britt looked at the document titled "The Legend of the History of the Treasure of Rennes." At least this one was in three languages. *During the eighteenth century, the shepherd Paris, looking for a lost sheep, went down a hole that opened into a grotto in which were skeletons and piles of gold. He returned to the village with his beret full of gold pieces. Accused of theft, he was killed as he obstinately refused to tell where he had found his "treasure."*

"Maybe, along with selling Mass cards, this is how Saunière obtained his great wealth," Romano said. "You mentioned stories of Saunière carrying stones to the village in a hod. He could have found the gold and brought it to his rectory under the stones."

"Or it could have been the bones of Mary Magdalene. Or it could have been stones. Or it could have been the Holy Grail." Britt threw up her arms in disgust. "This is about as far from academic research as you can get."

"I know this is not what you had in mind, but it's not a total disaster. You're the one who said it's important to look at all the options and not just focus on the accepted dogma. We're here where some of the information came through people who lived with Abbé Saunière. Something of value could be hidden among the tourist attractions. Take pictures of everything of relevance. I'll even treat you to a few of the books and videos. When you get back to New York, go through it all and maybe the puzzle pieces will fit together."

Romano locked his eyes on to Britt's. "You've spent a lot of time developing your theories. If you don't find any concrete supporting material, then I hope you'll reconsider some of your conclusions."

Britt realized he was right, but she still had tomorrow and the promise of the full James Gospel and all being revealed. That is, if it wasn't all a ruse or some hideous joke. But it couldn't be. Priests were dead and she had been shot. So much didn't make sense.

Britt nodded in agreement. Then she looked at her watch and saw many of the tourists heading out of Saunière's domain. "We'd better get moving before they close up or it gets dark."

They visited the Visigothic Pillar in the Garden of Calvary that had been erected by Saunière. The visitor's guide noted that it was placed upside down, suggesting that the decoding of the enigma hidden within the church should also be worked upside down. On the base of the pillar was inscribed *May Christ protect his people from all harm*. There was also inscribed *Mission 1891*, which if read upside down became 1681, the date inscribed on the tomb of the Marquise de Blanchefort.

Britt handed the guide to Romano with her finger on the reference.

Romano looked at it. "This is what I mean about finding secrets and conspiracies under every rock," he said. "The restoration work took place from 1887 to 1896. The inscription *Mission 1891* could just as well relate to when the pillar was erected as to a code for the tomb."

Britt took photos of everything in the garden and then they rushed to catch the last tour through the church of St. Magdalene. The tympanum at the entrance to the church was framed in gold roses with a cross in the center and the inscriptions "This place is terrible!" and "It is the house of God and the Gate of Heaven." Britt didn't know what to make of the inscriptions, other than being another example of Saunière's eccentricity.

When they entered the church, Britt stopped short. "Don't tell me this is a statue of Bacchus and not Baphomet." She pointed to a statue of a hideous devil holding up the holy water stoup surmounted by four angels.

Romano laughed. "I think I have to go along with you on this one."

Everywhere they looked in the church they found mysterious features. The sign of the Rose+Cross that could refer to Rosicrucianism on either side of the confessional, Jesus crouching in the inverted position of the devil in the church entrance and being baptized by John the Baptist, a bas-relief of Mary Magdalene in tears kneeling in a grotto in front of a cross formed by two branches and a skull, and the tenth station of the cross showing Jesus being divested of his clothes and a soldier gambling for his tunic by throwing two dice, one die showing an impossible three and four on adjoining faces and the other a five. The tourist guide even pointed out references to cryptograms relating to the black-and-white floor tiles and anomalies added to the stations of the cross that supposedly described a precise location to be found in the stone circle around Rennes-les-Bains.

There were so many bizarre features throughout the church Britt found it mind-boggling. Rather than answering the many questions she had generated during her research, there were now many more.

Britt snapped as many pictures as she could that related to the claims in the visitor's guide, then turned to Romano as they left the church. "I'm beginning to think Saunière was as crazy as Felix. In his paranoia he created these codes and diversions, and in the end they may all be meaningless."

Romano had remained relatively quiet during the tour. "It seems as though Abbé Saunière was quite the character, to say the least." He pointed to a page in the guide. "The only theory I keep finding that's supported by a number of references is Saunière and gold. Let's take a look at the Villa Bethania and Tour Magdala before we head back. It says the half sister of Saunière's housekeeper maintained she saw gold ingots laid out on a shelf in the cellar of the villa."

Britt followed Romano toward the Renaissance-style house while he continued glancing through the guide.

"This is interesting," Romano said. "When Abbé Saunière died, his housekeeper, Marie Denarnaud, inherited his entire estate. And it's bizarre that he named the villa Bethania. That was the name of the house belonging to Mary Magdalene's brother Lazarus. And it looks like the local bishop wasn't a fan of Saunière. He filed legal proceedings to prevent the Villa Bethania from becoming a retirement home for priests as expressed in Saunière's will."

Britt took a quick photo of the villa. "Are you starting to have second thoughts that Saunière may have been involved with religious secrets after all?"

Romano pointed ahead to the Tour Magdala perched on the edge of the plateau. "I haven't taken that large leap of faith, but based upon this opulent villa and that magnificent tower, I'm becoming more convinced that your village abbé had gotten his hands on incredible wealth and used it to feed a growing hunger for power and living in grandeur."

Britt had mixed feelings about what she was seeing on this mountaintop. She had been convinced she'd find answers in the quiet little village in the Pyrénées that could have been harboring religious secrets for centuries. All the books she had researched, and even crazy Felix, had led her to believe the answers were here. Maybe it was only all myths, religious conspiracy theories, and the ramblings of people who, as Father Müller had said, were *total verrückt*.

Britt remembered something her husband had told her. *It's not the questions that get us into trouble, it's the search for answers*.

She turned to Romano. "I think it's time to go back to the *hotellerie* and regroup."

By sunset tomorrow, she'd know for sure whether this was all crazy.

SEVENTY-EIGHT

MICHAEL SLEPT PEACEFULLY IN ONE OF THE PLUSH rooms set up for the Inner Circle during their annual pilgrimage to the Holy Site. Once a year, each member spent a few days of prayer and remembrance with the Holy Grail.

Gabriel pressed his thumb on the sensor and the door slid into the stainless steel wall. He entered the conference room and placed the last of his supplies on the gleaming rosewood conference table. Two chairs upholstered in deep burgundy leather stood on each side of the table, while one was at the head reserved for the Council chairman. This room was only used for the meeting prior to the annual celebration of the holiest of days. Here the Council of Five voted on critical matters relating to their holy duty.

Gabriel moved three of the chairs away from the table, placing them against the wall. He repositioned the remaining two near the head of the table. He spread a red satin cloth over the table and another across it and the chairs to form a cross, and carefully smoothed the fabric. He chose red because it was the color of celebration, and tomorrow he would be celebrating the rebirth of the Church, a rebirth that would allow it to continue unthreatened by the blasphemy that had existed for over two thousand years.

Gabriel carefully placed a religious icon in its velvet case on a table in the corner of the room along with a small mallet. Beside them he placed a vial of blessed oil, gauze pads, and a bottle of alcohol. All was ready for the next to final act of his religious quest.

SEVENTY-NINE

A DUSTY GRAY RENAULT PULLED UP BESIDE ROMA-no and Britt as they left Saunière's domain and headed to the parking lot. The driver lowered the window. His dark hair was slicked back with pomade and he wore a brown-and-black hound's-tooth jacket and an open-collared shirt. A large gold cross dangled from his neck. The strong scent of sage and bay rum wafted through the open window. He briefly introduced himself in French, English, and Spanish as Leone, with a car at their service.

"Thank God," Britt said. "We need a ride to our inn."

Leone's eyes lit up. "Where do you stay?"

"We are at the Hotellerie du Cheval."

The enthusiasm on Leone's face faded for a moment then returned. "You are in luck. I will take you to Limoux or Arques. You will see wonderful Cathar ruins and have a *magnifique* dinner." He brought his fingertips to his lips and kissed them in a grand manner. "The finest wine from the Limoux region." He wagged his index finger in the air. "Do not worry. Enjoy the evening, then I will take you to the hotellerie for a low, low, all-inclusive fee."

"That's very kind of you," Britt said. "But we must get back to the inn."

Leone jumped out of the car and opened the rear door for them. Romano was tempted to jog back while Britt went with the driver but decided he'd better stay with her. There was no telling where she might end up if he didn't.

The Renault wasn't out of the parking lot before Britt leaned toward Leone. "Do you know of a Villa Santa Maria?"

Leone glanced at them through the rearview mirror and shook his head. "No, I'm sorry, I do not."

"What do the local people think happened to the Statue of Mary Magdalene from the Garden of Calvary."

Through the mirror, Romano could see a smile cross Leone's lips.

"My family has lived in the village for over two hundred years. We have heard all the stories. The statue was probably stolen by one of the many people who come to the village looking for Abbé Saunière's secrets. They even dig up our graveyards."

"What does your family think Saunière found?" Britt asked.

"Most older village people are, how you say, fifty-fifty. Some say he found gold, others are sure it was secret documents. My grandmother was convinced it was a marriage certificate of Jesus and Mary Magdalene."

Britt almost jumped out of her seat. "Is there any evidence to support that claim?"

"No, no. Just talk. Fantasy. Probably from the stories of Mary Magdalene living in the south of France. You know she is revered by many in the Languedoc region."

"What about the stories of the abbé selling Masses?" Romano asked.

Leone turned his head and looked back at Romano. "Oh, he was doing that for sure. My grandmother's aunt worked for Abbé Saunière. She prepared the letters sent to the faithful all over Europe. He advertised in many religious magazines."

"Could that have been the source of his great wealth?"

Leone laughed. "Hardly. My auntie said they received maybe a hundred or so each week. Some weeks it was only fifty or seventy."

"But who knows how much the rich in cities like Paris were willing to pay for the blessings bestowed through Mass and prayer," Romano replied.

Leone laughed again. "You saw what the abbé did in our village. Even the rich wouldn't give that much for a piece of paper promising a prayer at Mass. And the sale of Masses only lasted for a few years. The Church finally put a stop to it." Leone glanced back again in the mirror. "Abbé Saunière was even stripped of his rights to administer the sacraments. My auntie stopped going to church because of it. Then the new Pope Benoit the Fifteenth lifted all the sanctions on Abbé Saunière, and he was back to being the grand master of Rennes."

"What do you think was the source of Saunière's wealth?" Britt asked.

"I vote for the secret documents. Something that the Church and wealthy aristocrats in Europe were willing to pay to keep secret."

"What do you think they were?"

"I have no idea. But I think they were hidden in our old church and the abbé found them during the rebuilding. I think it started with Abbé Bigou, who received the secrets from Lady d'Hautpoul de Blanchefort in the late seventeen hundreds. He hid the documents in the church and passed on the secrets to other priests. During those days and through the time of Abbé Saunière, in a small village like ours, the priest was king. There are many stories about the documents and secrets in the books about Rennes-le-Château, but nobody knows for sure what they are or where they are now."

The car pulled up to the inn and Leone jumped out and opened the door for Romano and Britt. As Britt stepped out of the car, he said, "You are the first visitors I have driven to Hotellerie du Cheval. They cater to a very select French-speaking clientele who have their own drivers. Very strange for a *hotellerie*."

When Romano paid him, Leone handed him a card. "Please call me if you want to visit some of the other sights. It will be my pleasure to drive you." He winked at them. "And I can provide answers to questions about the many secrets hidden in the land of the Cathars."

Leone didn't waste any time spinning his tires on the loose gravel and speeding back toward Rennes-le-Château to get another fare.

Romano thought about the stories of documents and secrets passed on by priests. Secrets the Church would pay dearly to keep hidden. Maybe somewhere within Britt's tangle of myths there was a truth—a truth that was killing priests.

Romano was getting an uneasy feeling that maybe Father Ted had known something that led to his death—something he kept hidden because he didn't want to put him in the same danger.

EIGHTY

ROMANO WAS STANDING ON THE GRAVEL WATCH-ing the car disappear down the long drive. Britt walked up the steps to the inn and wondered if he was as confused as she was about all the stories of secrets and treasures. He finally turned, came up to her, and opened the door.

Britt smiled. "I wasn't waiting for you to get the door. I know by now that you're the perfect gentleman. I was just wondering why you were staring at Leone driving away."

"Just reflecting on all the crazy things we ran across in Rennes-le-Château and on Leone's perspective."

"I hope you're starting to see that there's got to be something tangible hidden within all this muddled mess," Britt said as they entered the lobby.

The desk was tucked into a small niche beneath the stairs. There were vases of fresh flowers and plants everywhere. What was missing were people. There was no one anywhere to be seen in the inn. She stuck her head through the open door to a small dining room, and that was also empty. The tables were set for dinner. Burgundy napkins blossomed from stemmed glasses on each table. Lush greens were draped across the stone archway leading to a second, more intimate room with two tables and a large fireplace.

Britt went back to the desk, where Romano was holding up two keys attached to large metal shafts with rubber bumpers on the ends.

"Found these hanging on the end of the desk." Romano handed a key to Britt. "It looks like they have ten rooms, and all the other keys are still hanging there. Either we're the only guests or the others followed Leone's advice."

"At least we won't have any trouble getting dinner reservations." Britt pointed to the dining room. "They're all set up for dinner, but there's not a soul around."

"You would like dinner?" A man appeared out of a door next to the front desk and walked toward them puffing on an unfiltered cigarette. Smoke trailed behind him like a steam engine.

Romano turned to Britt. "Would you like to eat now or come back later?"

Britt hung her key back on the hook. "I'm beat and would like to turn in early tonight. We might as well take advantage of the empty dining room to discuss our great discoveries in Rennes-le-Château."

Romano hung up his key and turned to the man. "We'll have dinner now, thank you."

Just then, Britt noticed a photograph on the wall behind the desk. It looked as though it could have been the inn years ago, before the current renovation. Next to the front door was a large statue of Mary.

The man went behind the desk and stubbed out his cigarette in an ashtray. "I am Remy. Follow me, please."

"Excuse me." Britt pointed to the photo. "What was this place before it became an inn?"

Remy seemed shocked at the question, then his eyes narrowed into a look of confusion or defiance; Britt couldn't tell which. When he finally opened his mouth to speak, Britt noticed rows of stained, uneven teeth.

"Sorry, my English is not good," he said with a heavy French accent.

Britt leaned over the counter and waved her finger at the picture. "What is that picture?"

"Ahhh." Remy said. "Hotellerie. Hotellerie du Cheval."

Britt pushed her hand back and forth in the air as if pushing back time. "A long time ago. Before it was a *hotellerie*."

"It was villa. Private villa."

"Was it Villa Santa Maria?"

Remy seemed annoyed. "No, no, not a home for a saint." He started toward the dining room. "Please. Follow me."

When they were seated, Britt leaned toward Romano. "Do you buy his not good English and explanation of the picture?"

"To be honest"—Romano shook his head—"I have never been very good at understanding the French. They live in their own world, and it's not completely in tune with ours."

"I got the impression he was hiding something when I asked about Villa Santa Maria."

"I think you may be reading something into his reaction. Leone's family has been here for generations and he wasn't familiar with a Villa Santa Maria. I'm sure there's somewhere you can search local property deeds and see if a place with that name ever existed."

Remy returned with a pad and pen and handed menus handwritten in French to Britt and Romano. Britt struggled through the elegant printing and finally looked up at Romano. "My French is bad enough, but this script makes it extremely difficult. There are some filet of beef and chicken recipes. If you like chicken, I'm thinking of having the *Poulet au Porto*—it's a roast chicken steeped with port wine, cream, and mushrooms and served with risotto and asparagus tips."

Romano laughed. "Since my French fades after *boeuf* and *poulet*, I yield to your choice."

Remy took their orders and returned moments later with a bottle of white Burgundy Montrachet. He presented it to Romano, who nodded acceptance, then uncorked it and poured them each a glass.

When he left, Romano took a small sip and smiled. "Very good." He held up his glass across the table toward Britt. "Here's to both of us finding the truth and getting back to New York in good health."

Britt tapped her glass to his. "I'll drink to that. And that our truths will be one and the same."

Romano smiled and they took a drink. This was just what Britt needed to take the edge off the insanity of the past few days. The dry white wine filled her palate with a seductive bouquet. She took a second drink and felt an immediate tingle as she inhaled deeply. Then she looked at Romano, who was staring intently at her. "Be honest," she said. "Do you think I'm crazy following a theory to substantiate a bloodline of Christ?"

Romano eyed Britt with concern. His lips formed a half smile. "I certainly wouldn't go as far as to say crazy, but I would say your desire to discredit accepted doctrine is tainting your objectivity. What exactly do you expect to find?"

"The only objective evidence I have is linked to the secret James Gospel. What if the gospel was the document that was hidden in Rennes-le-Château and used by Saunière to blackmail the Church and European aristocracy supporting the Church?"

Romano put his hands together and leaned them against his lips. Finally he said, "We've heard and seen a lot of strange theories today, but it's been almost ninety years since Saunière died and no one has been able to discover what his real secret was. That's the only conclusion I've come to today."

"Someone obviously discovered the gospel or I wouldn't have a segment of it. And I was told to come here to receive the rest of it. Doesn't that—"

"You were what?" Romano stared wide-eyed at Britt. "Who told you to come here?"

"Before you go ballistic, hear me out. I think he must be a priest or maybe even a member of the *Rex Deus*. He discovered the secret gospel and wants to correct a terrible religious wrong. If the truth comes out, maybe Christianity will change its focus from blind faith for unbridled redemption to following the teachings of Jesus and doing good deeds."

Romano's jaw dropped. "Now I think you may be crazy. Who is this person?"

"I don't really know. I've never met him."

"He could be the one killing the priests, for God's sake. Is it *The Messenger*? Why didn't you tell the authorities about him?"

"I know he's not killing anyone. He sent me the manuscript segment, and it proved to be authentic. He sent me to Father Matteo and Father Mathews. They knew something about *Rex Deus* or some religious secret that brought about their deaths. You weren't there. I saw their responses. He warned me someone might try to stop me. When he called to make sure I was coming to this inn, he warned me to be careful that the man who tried to kill me in New York would most likely try again. He also told me you had nothing to do with the attempt on my life. Right, right, right. Why should I not believe him?"

"Because you have no idea who he is. You have no proof that he's not behind all of this."

"All I ask is that you bear with me until sunset tomorrow. You can leave right now and go to Carcassonne. I'm sure Leone would be happy to take you. By sunset tomorrow, I'll either have my proof or I won't—or I'll be dead."

"Don't talk like that. This is too serious. People are dead and you were shot, almost twice."

"Then go to Carcassonne."

Romano rolled his eyes. "I'm not leaving you here alone."

Remy arrived with their meals. Before he left the table, he refilled their wineglasses.

Britt raised her glass to Romano. "Then here's to a great meal and putting up with my obsession."

"I'll drink to that." Romano clinked his glass to hers. "But I'm not going to stop trying to get you to redirect your focus."

After the toast, they settled down to enjoying the meal. They were alone in the dining room and the only sounds came from the occasional plaintive cry of a bird or a horse neighing in the distance. The food was cooked to perfection. Britt detected a hint of brandy in the chicken roasted in port wine, the risotto was not too dry, not too moist, and the asparagus tips were done *à point*. She wondered if Remy was host, waiter, and chef for this intimate little inn.

Romano didn't waste any time finishing the meal. He gave Britt a guilty look as he downed the last forkful of risotto and emptied the remaining wine into their glasses. Before she could comment, Remy arrived with another bottle, uncorked it, and topped off their wineglasses.

"Coffee? Espresso?" Remy asked.

"Could we have our check, please?" Britt noticed Romano giving her an odd look.

Remy's smile bordered on a smirk. "Your stay is complimentary. All included." His eyes diverted to Romano. "And for the father, it is our pleasure."

"Who do I have to thank for all of this?" Britt asked.

Remy's expression switched to one of confusion. "You would have to ask the owners. They gave the order." He took the empty wine bottle and quickly disappeared around the corner of the entrance to the dining room.

Britt gave Romano a concerned look. "I was just about to ask you to elaborate on redirecting my focus, but I have the strange feeling we're not totally alone in this dining room."

Romano glanced around the room a few times. "You know, it's odd, but I'm afraid I agree with you."

Through the window, Britt saw the glimmer of the sun setting over the horizon. Pink and lavender bands swirled across the dimming background of deepening shades of blue.

"Let's finish this bottle of wine out on the balcony," Britt said. "I'll share the steps that got me to my current *focus*, as you so aptly put it. I'm sure you think I'm obsessed and, as you said, crazy. Maybe if you follow the steps that got me here, you might better understand why I feel so strongly about a possible bloodline of Christ."

Romano slid the stems of their wineglasses between the fingers of one hand and picked up the bottle in the other. "Lead the way."

Britt snatched their keys from the rack at the desk and started up the stairs that led to their rooms and the balcony. The wine and fatigue of two days of hell had definitely mellowed her. Maybe after another few glasses of wine she'd tell Romano the truth about *The Messenger*.

EIGHTY-ONE

GABRIEL LOOKED UP FROM THE VIDEO MONITOR AS Britt and Romano left the dining room. He had been tempted to sneak up to the *hotellerie* and see the real Britt. The video feed didn't do her justice. He couldn't see the brightness in her eyes, the glow of her cheeks. He couldn't feel the emotional connection he knew was there. He had sensed it during the calls. She had exuded an almost religious zeal, especially after she had learned the truth about their special bond.

Remy's image came onto the monitor as he started to clear the table. Gabriel shut off the video surveillance system. He was supposed to be with Britt tonight enjoying dinner and wine while they reminisced about their separate lives and common feelings. He was torn about what he had to do, but there was no other option. No compromise.

Gabriel felt a strange rush of energy flush through his body. Heat seared his brain as he thought of tomorrow. It would be the end of his quest and the beginning of something wonderful he couldn't even begin to comprehend.

EIGHTY-TWO

The last of the limousines arrived at Christien Fortier's château outside of Carcassonne. The former Villa Santa Maria had been transformed into a magnificent summer residence for the chairman of the Council of Five after the bones of Mary Magdalene had been moved to the Hotellerie du Cheval to join the Holy Grail. Fortier and the rest of the Council turned as the massive oak doors swung open and Egor Ivanov entered the main hall.

"We were worried, Egor. Why were you delayed?" Fortier asked.

Ivanov settled into his designated seat. "Sorry, gentlemen, there were mechanical difficulties with my plane. In light of what's been happening, I didn't take any chances. I had a second team of mechanics go over it." He smiled to the rest of the Council. "I'm here in one piece. Isn't that what's important?"

"Indeed," Fortier said. "Then let's get started."

"What is the status of Gabriel and Michael?" Walker asked.

Fortier turned toward the Englishman. "I have been in contact with Gabriel. He's safe in the complex at the *hotellerie*. Michael has left Vienna." Fortier scratched his chin before continuing. "I have not heard from Philippe, and he and Michael haven't arrived in Monte Carlo."

"Then we don't even know if Philippe took care of Konrad and Hamar." Ivanov smacked his hand on the table. "I don't like this at all. His father would have had things under control by now. Have you contacted Carlos?"

Fortier felt a tightening in his chest. He had feared someone might bring him up. "Carlos has been out of the picture for a few years. He's retired in the south of Thailand. He made it very clear that Philippe was able to handle any complications. He hasn't let us down yet."

"This is not some routine maintenance operation. Three of our Inner Circle are dead and we're not certain a fourth is safe."

"Egor is right," Rahn said. "We don't even know for sure who's behind the deaths. In the 1960s, Carlos was on top of the leaks that led to *Le Serpent Rouge* fiasco. He put an end to the threat immediately, and there were no repercussions."

Fortier had to defuse this before it went any further. "Philippe is convinced it's Hamar and Konrad who are behind the deaths, and I agree. There could be a third person. Possibly someone in the Saunière Society. I have a list of the key players and I'll have Philippe track them down once Michael is safely in Monte Carlo. I have someone checking the Viennese news media for reports. By tomorrow we'll know for sure what took place and we'll take appropriate action."

"Do we have the luxury of waiting till tomorrow?" Henderson's eyes made the rounds of his fellow Council members. The little Scotsman nervously flicked at the corner of his notepad. "If whoever is behind this knows the identity of the Inner Circle, then they know who we are."

Fortier saw the concern on the faces of the other Council members. He too had considered that frightening scenario. "That's why we flew here individually and this villa is under extra security. Early tomorrow morning three separate limousines will take us to the Holy Site. That's our most secure location. We'll be safe there until we know what happened in Vienna and whether Michael arrived safely in Monte Carlo."

"I hope you're right," Rahn said. The German stared coldly at Fortier. "I still can't determine justification for the killings. If Hamar and Konrad discovered the truth about our holy order, why wouldn't they simply publicize it? Hamar has already made insinuations to the media about her ridiculous *Jesus Fraud* book. Why kill the Inner Circle?"

"That could have been Konrad's doing or a third party," Fortier said. "I think they were using Hamar as a ploy to cover up their real agenda. Maybe they thought that by eliminating the Inner Circle they could eradicate any threat to the Church."

"But there's still the Grail and the James Gospel," Walker replied. "That physical evidence is the real threat."

"We all agreed that going forward with the preserved embryos was the safest way to protect the holy order." Rahn wrung his hands. "You recall I was not enthusiastic about allowing the living bloodline to be depleted." The German's right eye began to twitch. "Our charge is to preserve the bloodline for the Second Coming. I interpret that to mean a living, breathing, physical being, not some embryos in a cryogenic chamber."

"If someone has targeted the Inner Circle, then we should be bloody well relieved that we have the embryo project," Walker replied.

"Gentlemen, gentleman," Henderson shouted. "At this point we don't know how the three died. We can't rule out that this isn't the beginning of the Second Coming and that God is delivering us the one true Lord who will lead the world into the new kingdom of God."

The Council members stared at the Scotsman.

A chime rang and Fortier felt a chilling sense of relief. "Blair is absolutely right. We can't rule out anything until we determine the causes of death and hear from Philippe." Fortier stood. "Dinner is being served in the main dining room. This is a difficult time for all of us, but until we have more facts, we can't make an informed decision. Tomorrow is our holiest day. I'm sure God will guide us to make the right decisions."

As Fortier started to the door, the other Council members stood and followed. He couldn't push aside the fear that his decision to use the James Gospel to support the oral history of their holy duty had been a mistake. Luckily the only one who knew the truth was Carlos Armand—and his body would never be found.

EIGHTY-THREE

Romano placed the wine bottle and glasses on a small table next to the alabaster balustrade. The vista from the balcony was breathtaking. They were above the treetops and had an unobstructed view of mountain ridges as far as the eye could see. The nearest peak, topped by Rennes-le-Château, was already draped in dark shadows. Each receding ridgeline grew hazier and the setting sun splashed the sky with subtle shades of color.

Britt moved their chairs closer together and sat down. Romano topped off their wineglasses and joined her. They leaned back and took sips of wine. This was the first time Romano had seen Britt really relaxed. In the dwindling twilight she exuded an inner beauty highlighted by a softness in her eyes he hadn't noticed before. It was as if the veil of pain and distrust had drifted away.

Britt turned to Romano. "What motivated a handsome man like you to become a priest?"

The question stunned Romano. He was about to put her off with a stock answer about following a calling but decided to share his true feelings with her. Maybe then she'd be more forthcoming about the mystery surrounding why she was in Rennes-le-Château.

"I'm embarrassed to say that my reasons for entering the priesthood were tainted, to say the least. You might say I became a priest to spite my mother."

Romano saw Britt flinch, then appraise him with a look of fascination. "My father died when I was twelve and left my mother and me with substantial trust funds," he continued. "We had a maid and houseman for as long as I could remember. I fell in love with their daughter Marta during my first year of college. We kept our relationship secret because we both knew my mother would probably not approve. During spring break, my mother found out. After an initial outburst telling me I could do better and that Marta was below my station in life, she dropped the subject. Then a week later Marta and her family vanished. My mother said they had decided to move to the West Coast and she didn't have any forwarding address. I went ballistic. I tried to hunt them down and found nothing. They left no trace. I was sure my mother had paid the family to disappear. I never forgave her. I turned to Father Mathews and spent my summer vacation with him at a Jesuit retreat. It was then that I decided to become a priest. I knew in my heart that a good part of the decision had to do with spiting my mother, who wanted me to find a woman of our status and raise a proper family. Well, now that will never happen."

Two globes on the wall behind them lit up as the sun dipped behind the last of the distant ridges and cast their table in dark shadows.

"Do you regret entering the priesthood?" There was a slight hesitancy in Britt's voice.

Romano leaned back and ran his fingers through his hair. "Oh, there are times when I wonder if I made a dreadful mistake. I still think about the wonderful feeling of holding Marta close to me. That's a warmth I'll never feel again. From time to time I still try to locate Marta and her parents, but I've never even come close to finding them. I think they moved out of the country. But I've come to find great satisfaction in teaching. My students have become a never-ending family. I guess you could say I've got God and my students."

A faint breeze drifted across the balcony. Britt's eyes took on a mournful air. "At least I got to experience the love of my husband and son even if it was short-lived."

Romano finished his wine, poured a little more for himself, and topped off Britt's glass. He decided it was time to change the discussion. "What do you think will happen tomorrow? Or maybe I should say, what do you want to happen?"

A look of determination spread across Britt's face. "I want closure. Satisfactory evidence that will give me the faith to finish my book with a focus I can live with. I honestly don't care whether it supports a bloodline or provides me sufficient doubt to define the bloodline theory as a myth."

"I'm glad you brought up faith," Romano said. "I have faith in the dogma that you seem to be doubting. But I admit my faith is based upon the wisdom of many before me." Romano took another sip of wine. "The Old Testament was a product of Israelite faith and culture for over a thousand years or more. The New Testament evolved in a similar manner for over a hundred years after the death of Christ. Most of the books of the Old and New Testament circulated orally before they were written down and involved many people—storytellers, authors, editors, listeners, and readers, all bound together by one thing: faith."

Britt shook her head and smiled. "We both know that faith is complete trust without supporting proof."

"Depends on what you accept as supporting proof. For a century after Christ's Crucifixion, those who were closest to him passed on the stories that became the New Testament. They never recanted even when faced with horrible deaths." Romano squinted and wrinkled his nose at Britt. "I'd say that provides a good measure of credibility."

"You know by now that I don't reject most of the values of Christianity." Britt took another drink. "My problems are with unmitigated redemption for believers and the promises of prayer. Of course there's the new question I've struggled with since receiving the gospel segment—did the physical Jesus die and rise from the dead?"

"I think that no matter what this secret James Gospel turns out to be, it will still boil down to some elements of faith."

"Won't it depend on what it says?" Britt asked.

"Unfortunately, today we tend to believe everything we read. Y2K, global cooling then global warming, bigfoot sightings, weapons of mass destruction. Mark Twain said it best, 'I've seen a heap of trouble in my life, and most of it never came to pass.' Whatever you decide to write, some people will buy it and some won't."

"All I want to do is present the truth."

"Because we mere mortals can't begin to comprehend what God really represents, whatever you find can only be presented in terms of what people are able to comprehend today. What happens when our intellect can't go any further? We reach the end of our comprehension. That's when faith enters the picture and takes over. The bottom line is, there's something bigger and greater than all of us. That's God."

Britt stared intently at Romano. "I had faith in God and the interpretation my religion put on Jesus for almost all of my life. But when I put my faith to the test, it failed me."

Romano saw the pain and sorrow drift back into Britt's eyes. "I'm sorry for your pain. Life doesn't always follow a fair path for even the best of people. But you seem to have found faith in your phantom caller, *The Messenger*. What supporting proof do you have that he's legitimate?"

Britt hesitated, seeming to ponder what she was willing to share with Romano. She finally pursed her lips. "After the deaths of my son and husband, I admit I became obsessed with discrediting the Church. I looked into every conspiracy theory I could find. I know you'll think I'm crazy, but I want you to know how I came to my conclusions and ended up here."

"Britt, please, I have no intention of being critical. I honestly don't know how I would have responded in your situation. But there's something we're both missing, and I'm afraid your zeal to prove your theory of a bloodline has clouded your vision. People are dead and someone tried to kill you. There's a lot more to this than you and I know."

Britt stood, leaned against the balustrade, and stared out toward the bright orange glow at the end of the horizon. She turned back to Romano. "The more I dug into research about the Knights Templar, the more I realized there had to be direct links between the Temple of Solomon, the Templar excavations, the rapid growth of the Templars' wealth and power, and finally the siege at Montsegur not very far to the west of where we are now. Many researchers think the Templars found great riches under the Temple along with the Holy Grail. I think the Holy Grail ended up in the hands of the Cathars, who were thought to have secrets that threatened the Roman Church. When the Cathars made a last stand against the papal crusade at Montsegur, they asked for one last night before giving themselves up to be slaughtered. The crusaders thought they were going to have a final ritual, but during that night four men escaped down the sheer cliffs with a Cathar secret and the Grail. They could have made their way to the area around Rennes-le-Château, where they hid whatever they had spirited out of Montsegur, possibly in the tomb depicted in the Poussin painting, until the Abbé Bérenger Saunière uncovered it."

Britt sat down and took a sip of wine. "Even your grad assistants came up with the same anagram, 'Begone! I conceal the secrets of God.' Whatever the Holy Grail is, it must hold the answer to the truth about Jesus Christ. I think *The Messenger* is involved with the *Rex Deus* since he had access to the secret James Gospel and promised to provide me access to the Holy Grail itself."

Romano leaned toward Britt. "And that's why you have faith in him?"

"No, I have a much more personal reason. *The Messenger* is my brother."

Romano drew in a deep breath. This was a twist he had not seen coming. "But . . . you were adopted. You don't even know who your parents are. What brother?"

"My twin brother. We were separated at birth."

"Who is he?"

"I don't know. We've never met. I don't know his name. I didn't even know I had a brother until *The Messenger* sent me the manuscript segment and a vial containing strands of hair for a DNA test."

Romano realized he was gaping. "And you were able to verify that he is your brother?"

"We're fraternal twins. I had the hair sample tested and compared to my DNA. That's why I'm sure he's involved with the *Rex Deus*. He has the defective gene of the *Kohanim*. It's a mutation that results in a probability of error of less than one one-thousandth of one percent. If my brother isn't a member of *Rex Deus*, I'm positive he's at least a descendent of the high priests of the Temple at Jerusalem."

"Why wouldn't he tell you who he was? What's he trying to achieve?"

"He said he's trying to correct a horrible wrong, and I'm his conduit to the truth. He was very evasive. All he'd say was for me to come here and he would bring me the complete James Gospel and show me the secret of the Holy Grail before sunset tomorrow."

"But how can you be sure your brother isn't involved in the deaths of the priests? You have no idea who your brother is or what he's done with his life."

Britt got a faraway look in her eyes. She stared over Romano's shoulder out across the darkened landscape at the last remnant of a purple glow in the sky, as if searching for divine guidance. "I know you'll find this crazy, but when I speak with him, I feel a connection, a sense that somehow we're on the same wavelength. I trust him. Maybe that's the twin connection."

Britt stood up, leaned over, and kissed Romano on the cheek. "Thanks for staying with me. Let's meet at eight for breakfast." She started toward her room, then turned and smiled at Romano. "One way or the other, we'll know tomorrow."

EIGHTY-FOUR

"AGENT CUTLER, IT'S YOUR OFFICE." KURT BRAUN reached a beefy hand across the desk and handed Cutler the phone. Then he went back to chewing on one of the Wiener schnitzel sandwiches his aide had brought to tide him and Cutler over until they could put the Philippe Armand case to rest for the night.

"Tom, we can forget about acts of God," Donahue said. "The autopsies on the priests determined the cause of death for all three was a fast-acting poison mixed with snake venom."

"What the hell?"

"I know, it's screwy. The priests were comatose for a short time before they died. The medical examiners claimed each stigmata was created after death. Therefore the killer had to wait until their hearts stopped before puncturing their wrists, feet, and sides. The wounds were caused by a spikelike object made of iron."

"How was the poison administered?" Cutler asked.

"In the first two deaths, the priests ingested the poison in wine and scotch. The priest in New Orleans was zapped with a TASER and then injected with the venom. Our profilers think we're looking at a ritualistic serial killer with some vendetta against the Church or the Jesuits."

"Brian, I'm heading to France in the morning hoping to catch up with Brittany Hamar and Father Romano. A former priest who Hamar and Romano were asking questions about was shot and killed in Vienna."

"Could they have shot him?"

"We've got the shooter. Unfortunately, Detective Braun had to take him out. When we arrived at Hamar's hotel, he pulled a gun on her and Romano. The guy's name is Philippe Armand, a Frenchman. I was just about to e-mail you the details. He had flown into New York before the priests were killed. He could have easily gotten to Mathews. I want you to check out if he could have flown to New Orleans when Sinclair was killed."

"Was this Armand a priest?" Donahue asked.

"No. Why do you ask?"

"The autopsies found oil on the foreheads and palms of each victim in the sign of the cross. It's the same oil used in the Catholic rite of Anointing the Sick. Formerly known as the Last Rites or Extreme Unction. It would indicate the killer could be a priest or former priest."

"I'll let Interpol know," Cutler said. "We only have preliminaries on Armand. So far they couldn't find any evidence he was in Spain when the first priest was killed. If he was, and if you can link him to New Orleans, there's a good probability Philippe Armand was the killer. And when I catch up with Hamar and Romano, maybe I can get some answers that will put these priest murders into some perspective."

"At least there haven't been any more."

"We're not totally out of the woods on that account," Cutler replied. "Yesterday a Jesuit priest went missing here in Vienna."

EIGHTY-FIVE

BRITT BARELY MADE it into her room when the tears started flowing. She sat on the edge of the bed, head bowed, shoulder throbbing, eyes swelling. She didn't understand what was happening to her. Romano was right. People were dead and someone was trying to kill her, and maybe him. What had she gotten him into?

During her graduate studies at Harvard, Britt had access to file cabinets filled with gospels and apocrypha written during the first centuries after Christ and unearthed near Nag Hammadi in 1945. The myriad Gnostic texts left so much to the mind of the reader because they had been focused on finding inner knowledge. Many of the sayings suggested other dimensions of meaning. Did Jesus have a secret twin, Judas Thomas? Were the virgin birth and the bodily resurrection naïve misunderstandings? It was all so rife with references that were ambiguous, highly symbolic, and subject to widely varying interpretations. After years of study, all she was left with was confusion and doubt.

When she lost Tyler and Alain, it was as if a toxin had spilled across her life and contaminated every part of her being. She had felt so alone. Then she received the segment of the secret James Gospel and the vial from *The Messenger* along with his claim of being her twin brother. When the DNA and carbon-dating results came back, it was as if a veil had been lifted from her eyes and she could see what others couldn't. She even had dreams that, maybe, Tyler's death had been part of God's plan to push her to find the truth that had been hidden for so long by the leaders of the Orthodox Church.

But now priests were dead, she'd been shot, and someone had tried to shoot her again in Vienna. In spite of all of it, Father Joseph Romano seemed to have faith in her. Well, at least he hadn't branded her a heretic. She didn't know exactly what to make of the lanky Jesuit with thick dark hair, a goatee, and a ragged mustache. But she was petrified that she may have dragged him into danger. What if her brother was responsible for the deaths of the priests? Romano was right: She had no idea who her brother was or what he'd done with his life.

Britt crawled between the cool sheets and pressed her fists against her eyes. She laid there quietly and let the sad dreams come, as they always had.

EIGHTY-SIX

Dim blue light bathed the room in an eerie luminescence. Romano lifted his head and squinted at the alarm clock on the nightstand. The blue numerals glowed 5:15. This was the fourth time he had awakened. Maybe he had never really slept, just drifted in and out of semiconsciousness throughout the night. His mind kept flashing from Britt and a mysterious twin brother to strange theories about a bloodline of Jesus to Father Ted to the man with a scar. What did it all mean? It didn't make sense. He couldn't put the disjointed pieces together.

Romano flipped on the nightstand light and sat on the edge of the bed. He opened the BlackBerry to send a message to Charlie and Carlota and saw there was no signal. He got up, threw on a pair of running shorts and a T-shirt, and went out on the balcony. All the rooms were dark. The only light was from four white globes mounted between each of the large patio doors leading to the rooms and the soft gray glow of the emerging dawn. The mountain air was refreshingly cool. There were a few random lights twinkling in the distance in Rennes-le-Château, as well as in the nearby valley at Rennes-les-Bains.

Romano decided to jog down the winding mountain road toward the small spa village only a few kilometers from the inn. He went back to his room, put on his running shoes, and stuffed some euros and his passport into his fanny pack. The inn was totally quiet and he didn't see a soul as he hung his key on the hook at the front desk. He noticed Britt's key was the only one still missing. He found it odd that they were the only guests at the inn. He wondered if Britt's mysterious brother might be the owner.

The horse barn and corrals were eerily silent as Romano headed down the gravel driveway in a light morning mist. A black van was parked at the end of the drive. He glanced through the window and saw no one in the front seat. A steep trail led into the woods toward an outcropping with what appeared to be a hunter's stand.

As he jogged down the narrow mountain road, Romano thought about the repercussions if Britt's theory had any credibility. A lot depended on the validity and content of the secret James Gospel and whatever supporting data *The Messenger* had that could take it out of the realm of a conspiracy hatched by Jesus' detractors.

Romano was conflicted by his need to find out who killed Father Ted and why, and concern that he might be trying unconsciously to protect the Church, or maybe Britt. He was worried about her blind faith in a twin brother she had never met—or even if there really was a twin brother.

The landscape changed dramatically and the mist faded as Romano picked up his pace down the winding road toward Rennes-les-Bains. The hillsides grew more lush and green the closer he got to the spa village nestled along a stream in the Pyrénées.

When he rounded a sharp curve, Romano stopped abruptly. There at the bottom of a sharp embankment of dark rock was what looked like the entrance to a cave. Water dripped off the overhanging rock above the opening and trickled through a narrow path in the thick grass and tangled vines.

Romano looked up at the outcroppings of Rennes-le-Château high above him through the swirls of mist. He wondered how many of these caves were scattered throughout the myriad peaks surrounding Domaine de l'Abbé Saunière. And what secrets had been, or still were, hidden deep within the underground channels.

EIGHTY-SEVEN

THE ALARM SHRIEKED IN THE CONTROL ROOM. Gabriel sat up on the cot he had erected in the small security center deep within the complex. He scanned the wall of LCD displays and focused on the one with a blinking red light. It monitored the front door to the *hotellerie*. He watched Romano exit and jog away from the building. How convenient that Romano was going out for an early run. It would be much safer to bring them to the Holy Site one at a time.

Gabriel picked up the phone and called Britt's room. She seemed dazed and had trouble finding the right words, but agreed to meet him in fifteen minutes. After a quick shower he put on his custom-tailored Italian black suit and adjusted his crisp white clerical collar. He had looked forward to this meeting for as long as he could remember. It was never supposed to happen because Britt had been terminated from the *Rex Deus* at birth because she carried the Tay-Sachs gene and could not be used to carry a new generation of the Inner Circle. By order of the Council, she was put up for adoption. For all intents and purposes, she ceased to exist and would never know the importance of her heritage. That was about to change.

Before Gabriel left the security center, he picked up the TASER and slipped it into his jacket pocket. He hoped he wouldn't have to use it.

EIGHTY-EIGHT

Romano passed a second and a third cave entrance as he got closer to Rennes-les-Bains. The treasure hunters must have had a field day scouring the area for the source of Bérenger Saunière's wealth. He wondered how many died crawling through the myriad tunnels or drowned in underground streams. There could be literally hundreds of caves scattered throughout this area of the Pyrénées. He was sure the stories of gold and secret treasures were too much of an allure for many who didn't know the dangers of crawling around in unexplored caves.

As a child, Romano's father and Ted had taken him on many spelunking adventures in caves from Tennessee to Maine. After his father's death, Ted continued their jaunts to challenging caves to develop his skills. They spent memorable weekends exploring the bowels of the earth. Ted was a great teacher, always stressing the importance of respecting the elements and keeping track of the options for escape in case of an emergency. There had been some hair-raising adventures crawling through the damp, dark confines of narrow passages that led to magnificent caverns.

Romano felt pangs of remorse thinking about his father and Ted. The two men he looked up to and, whether he realized it or not, tried to emulate, were gone. It hadn't really hit him until now. Those relationships were gone forever and he'd never be able to pass on his experiences to another young man. There were students like Charlie he mentored and was able to see grow and set off on their own life journeys. But it wasn't the same as being there and seeing a young boy go through the trials of becoming a man. Now he didn't have Ted's shoulder to lean on, and if Ted were still here, he probably wouldn't be in some godforsaken mountains in the south of France.

The sound of rushing water filled the air as Romano jogged

around a sharp curve. Up ahead the landscape flattened out along a stream that dropped off into a small waterfall. A few stucco homes with red-tiled roofs marked the beginning of Rennes-les-Bains.

Romano checked his running watch and realized he'd better head back to the inn. It was going to be a much tougher run up the mountain road than it was coming down. He didn't want to be late for breakfast with Britt and finding out whether her "twin" was fact or fiction.

EIGHTY-NINE

FORTIER GOT INTO THE FIRST OF THE THREE LIMOU-
sines and settled in for the ride to the Holy Site. He had spoken to
Gabriel; everything was under control. Gabriel was in the underground complex and the security team was awaiting the arrival of
the Council. Guards were posted at the entrance to the drive leading to the *hotellerie*. No one, not even delivery personnel, would
be allowed anywhere near the main buildings.

Fortier had been tempted to postpone the annual pilgrimage to
the Holy Site, but that had never been done. Today was the celebration of the life and death of the Savior. The time for the Council of Five to renew their vow to preserve the bloodline for the
Second Coming. Throughout history many had given their lives
to maintain that commitment. In the thirteenth century, an entire
community of Cathars had been slaughtered at Montsegur to preserve the Holiest of Holies, the Holy Grail, and the lives of four
of the Inner Circle.

As the long black Mercedes left the Villa Santa Maria in Carcassonne, Fortier knew he was doing the right thing. Theirs was a
sacred duty to God, and he would protect them.

NINETY

Romano arrived back at the inn drenched in sweat. The early-morning sun had dissipated the light mist on the mountaintop when he'd left, and the steep, winding road on the way back had stressed his leg muscles to the limit. There were no horses in the corrals and no cars in the parking area in front of the inn. The black van was still parked alongside the entrance to the drive.

Britt's key was still missing from the rack at the front desk and the inn was quiet when Romano went back to his room. He showered and changed into his khakis and a polo shirt, then put on the cross Father Ted had given him. He had twenty minutes before he was to meet Britt for breakfast, so he packed his knapsack and tried the BlackBerry, but again it didn't indicate a signal. He'd try again tonight when he got to Carcassonne. He took Leone's card from the nightstand and stuffed it into his pocket. He decided he wouldn't be spending another night here. He'd either be in Carcassonne or on his way to a connecting flight to the States. If Britt had other plans she hadn't confided to him, she'd be on her own.

There was a loud knock on the door and Romano opened it expecting to see Britt. He stared in total astonishment. Standing there dressed as if he were about to attend a formal meeting at the Vatican was Father Dante Cristoforo, the assistant to the father general in Rome.

"Sorry to startle you," Cristoforo said. "I should have called, but time is critical."

"What are you doing here?"

"Please, come with me and I'll explain it all. We don't have much time."

Romano grabbed his knapsack. "Where are we going?"

"You won't need that. We're only going to the barn. Or I should say to a complex beneath the barn."

Nervous panic tore at Romano's gut. He suddenly realized

that there could be a Church connection. Was the Vatican involved with the deaths of the priests, with the attempt on Britt's life? "Where's Britt? Brittany Hamar. She's here with me."

"No need to worry. Brittany is safe. She's waiting for you at the Holy Site." Cristoforo stepped back into the hall and slipped his hand into his pocket. "We have to hurry. The Council is on the way. I must get both of you to safety before they arrive."

Romano grabbed the key to his room, stepped out into the hall, and closed the door. "Just tell me where we're going. What complex? What Council? What's this all about?"

Cristoforo started down the hall. "I'll explain it all to you and Brittany when the time is right. There is a lot to see. Believe me, Joseph, this is beyond anything you've ever dreamed of."

Romano followed Cristoforo through the horse barn to a door in the far corner, where Cristoforo punched a code into a keypad. When Romano was inside the vestibule, Cristoforo closed the door and they entered an elevator. Cristoforo positioned his thumb on a sensor and the elevator started dropping.

Romano stared intently at Cristoforo. "Who killed Ted? And why?"

Cristoforo's expression tightened. He appraised Romano coldly with his deep olive eyes. "There are some mysteries that defy logic and reason. Ted and Juan and Nathan were part of one of those mysteries. They are now joined with many blood brothers who went before them. They left this earth in the same manner as their Lord, who will return in glory to set the world free. They were part of a holy cause."

"Holy cause? What's this all about?"

The elevator slowed then lurched to a stop. "I'll explain it all to you and Brittany. Just follow me."

Romano estimated they were at least a few hundred feet underground. When the doors slid open, they entered a sleek stainless steel hallway. Immediately to their right was a large doorway with another electronic scanner. Cristoforo headed down the long hall past two more doors. One of them was ajar and Romano saw a wall of monitors inside. He noticed some of them displayed images of different views of the inn. They continued to a door at the end of the hall. Above it was a gold globe with silver metallic rays radiating out from the upper half.

"Brittany is in here," Cristoforo said. "Along with our most sacred relics."

Cristoforo inserted his thumb inside a scanner and the doors slid open. The walls and ceiling of the large room were a dull black metallic substance. Three areas were bathed in eerie funnels of light emanating from the ceiling. Britt was leaning over a large glass case in the center of the room. Her head snapped toward them as they entered.

"Joseph, you won't believe this." Britt was beaming. She rushed over to them and grabbed Cristoforo's arm. "Would you ever in your wildest dreams have thought that my mystery twin brother was Father Dante Cristoforo?"

"In my wildest dreams, I never would have believed any of this." Romano looked around the room. In one corner was a pedestal with a glass case containing a scroll. In the other corner was what looked like the missing statue of Santa Maria. In the center of the room was a large glass case containing an intricately carved small wooden sarcophagus with sections gleaming in gold leaf. The headpiece was a golden globe with rays similar to the one above the door. "Dante, what does all this mean?"

"You are in the Holy Site that has been maintained by the *Rex Deus* ruling Council of Five." Cristoforo pulled a small electronic device out of his pocket and checked it. "They will be arriving within the hour for their annual pilgrimage to pay respect to what you would refer to as the Holy Grail."

Romano was stunned. This was more like a dream than reality. "What exactly is the Holy Grail?"

"It is the holiest relic of the *Rex Deus*." Cristoforo gestured to Britt. "Actually, Brittany has done a remarkable job in researching her book, above and beyond my help. The Council had her shot and copies made of her manuscript and research notes. She had it right. The *Rex Deus* are descendants from the twenty-four high priests of the Herodian Temple in Jerusalem who, for ritual purposes, were known by the names of archangels. The high priests were not only responsible for the instruction of the children in two separate boarding schools for boys and girls, but when the girls reached childbearing age, their impregnation as well. The girls were found suitable husbands among the higher-class men of the community. Any children born of this union were, at the age of seven, returned to the Temple school for their education. This is especially important when one looks into the young life of Jesus Christ, whose only scripture reference relates to him talking with the high priests in the Temple."

Romano stared at Cristoforo in disbelief. "As a learned priest and respected biblical scholar, you can't honestly believe that all the Gospels are wrong. What proof is there to support such a myth?"

Cristoforo stepped over to the glassed-in sarcophagus. "The oral tradition that has been passed on to members of the *Rex Deus* tells of Mary, the mother of Jesus, being impregnated by the high priest known as Gabriel after he had a vision directly from God. Thus the reference to the angel Gabriel in Luke, 'And the angel came in unto her, and said, "Hail, thou that art highly favoured, the Lord is with thee: blessed art thou among women." ' "

Romano joined Cristoforo and Britt in front of the intricately carved sarcophagus that looked like something out of a King Tut exhibit. In front of it was a kneeling rail. "Are you saying that Jesus Christ wasn't the Son of God the Father?"

"No, not at all," Cristoforo replied. "We were initiated through oral tradition to believe that Jesus was both a spiritual Son of God and a physical man so he could relate to humankind. Christ was divinely guided, because the Father willed him to be so, therefore the physical being was not God, but a messenger of God. Even the Gospels refer to the spiritual Jesus. The *Rex Deus*, for all intents and purposes, is a Gnostic sect that passed on the initiatory teachings of Jesus and the commitment to preserve the bloodline of Jesus."

Romano pointed to the scroll in the glass case. "I take it that's the infamous secret James Gospel?"

Cristoforo nodded. "James originally denounced the work of his brother and only after Jesus' death did he accept the mantel of Christianity to lead the Church in Jerusalem. But even then, he followed the laws of Judaism and fought against the principles espoused by Paul that eventually gained acceptance by the growing Christian community. That papyrus roll is written in Aramaic and has been carbon-dated to the time of Jesus. The Council believes it was written by the hand of James describing what really happened at the Crucifixion and Resurrection. It is the first physical evidence to support our teachings and responsibility to maintain the bloodline."

"But if James denounced the work of Jesus, wouldn't his writing contradict the words of the Apostles?" Britt asked. She glanced at Romano and smiled. "See, Joseph, I do listen to your rebuttals. After all, death and resurrection were not something easily believed by the masses. Just think if the claim were made in this day and age."

"Is there any proof other than that document that Jesus was really the son of a high priest? Or that a bloodline exists?" Romano asked.

"The James document was only discovered three years ago in Egypt by the chairman of the Council. Up until then, our history was passed on through oral tradition to the initiates who became the Council of Five and were responsible for preserving the most important relic of all." Cristoforo pointed to the mummy case.

The device in Cristoforo's hand began to beep. He rushed to the doors. "They've arrived. I must prepare to greet them. You'll be safe here." He stepped through the doors and they slid closed.

NINETY-ONE

THE FIRST LIMO PULLED AROUND THE BACK OF THE horse stables next to the barn. The driver pushed a remote and a large corrugated steel door slid open, revealing the inside of a pristine garage that already housed two dark vans and a silver gray Citroen.

"I'll stay in the car until the others arrive," Fortier said to the driver. He was not a fan of the horse farm, or farm animals for that matter. He much preferred the ocean breezes of Monte Carlo to the stench of animal dung. But he agreed this was a perfect cover for their underground complex. It had served its purpose well for over a century. It was impenetrable and easily protected.

After the third limo entered the garage and the door slid closed, Fortier joined the other four Council members and headed into the barn to the elevator leading to the complex. The men all carried briefcases and laptops containing the latest data on their banking empire and the crisis to their holy order. When they arrived at the underground complex, Fortier activated the security lock on the conference room and the door slid open.

Fortier didn't know what to make of what he saw. Draped tautly above the table and chairs was a large red satin sheet with a gold cross down the center.

"What the hell is this?" Rahn said.

"It must have been something Gabriel did." Fortier grabbed a corner of the sheet as the rest of the Council approached the table. "He's the only one who could have accessed the room." He yanked the sheet off the table. The Council cringed in horror at what they saw. Laid out on the table covered in red satin in the shape of a cross was the pale, gray-blue body of Michael. Father Hans Josef's arms were spread, his feet crossed, and he was marked with the stigmata. His eyes stared toward the ceiling as if pleading to God.

Fortier turned quickly and rushed to the door that had closed behind them. He shoved his thumb into the reader but nothing happened. In a panic, he punched in the emergency code—still nothing. He noticed the lights on the system were dark. He pulled the emergency manual override handle. The door did not budge.

He wondered if Gabriel was lying somewhere in the complex in the same condition as Michael—or was he the one behind the killings?

NINETY-TWO

"Do you have any idea what's going on or what Cristoforo intends to do?" Romano asked Britt.

"All I know is he said he was going to eliminate the threat that the *Rex Deus* poses to Christianity."

"He could destroy what's in this room, but what about the gospel segment you have in a safe-deposit box?"

"He told me it's a forgery made with papyrus from the original gospel, but written with ink from the current century. He said he sent us both letters revealing the process. When the ink is tested, it will prove that it's a fake."

"But you and I will know the truth. Everything he's told us so far seems to support a bloodline theory. And this Council of Five knows the truth. Is he going to kill them?"

Fear shredded Britt's optimism. She sucked in a breath. "Do you think he killed the priests?"

"He'd certainly have had easy access to them in his position as assistant to the father general in Rome. And what is his role in this *Rex Deus*?"

"I have no idea," Britt replied.

Romano went to the door and quickly found there was no way out unless someone had the right fingerprint or code. "We're stuck in here until Cristoforo returns." He looked down. "This is not good. Cristoforo is a rigid conservative when it comes to Church doctrine. Even more so, considering he's a Jesuit. There are jokes among some of the Jesuit professors that he's positioning himself to become the father general someday so he could bring back the concept of the Black Pope and challenge the papacy. He's an extremist in his thinking. The only thing that makes any sense is that he thinks Fathers Matthews, Matteo, and Sinclair were part of the bloodline."

Britt moved closer to the light bathing the glass case in a golden hue. Her normal glow changed to pallor. "Then what about us—if we know the truth, we're also a threat."

NINETY-THREE

CRISTOFORO SHUT DOWN THE SECURITY COMPUTER and smashed the module that controlled the exit doors. The monitors flashed and went blank. Earlier he had disabled the manual override system and locked down the manual emergency exit from the outside. There was no way to leave the complex. He reached beneath the desk in the security room and clicked on a timer. The rhythmic beat of the seconds ticked away as he headed back to the Holy Grail. There was something comforting about taking the last step of his holy quest with his twin sister.

THE HEAVY DOOR SLID OPEN WITH A GROAN. GONE was the soft hum of servomotors. Romano immediately turned to Cristoforo. "What's going on? What do you intend to do? And what about us?"

Cristoforo walked up to Britt and put an arm around her shoulders. "I am known to the Council of Five as Gabriel. I am the last of the Inner Circle, the bloodline of Jesus Christ that Britt described in her manuscript. We were originally known as the *Desposyni,* or the descendants of the Master. Later we were referred to as *Le Serpent Rouge,* or the bloodline of Christ that snaked through the south of France."

"That can't be," Britt said, visibly shaken.

"Oh, yes, dear sister. And twins were common in the bloodline. Just as there are references in the apocryphal Gospel of Thomas and The Acts of Thomas, Jesus could have had a twin, the disciple Thomas, since the name Thomas was a sobriquet in Hebrew for 'twin.' Mary Magdalene gave birth to twins. A boy and a girl."

"How can you be so sure that's true and that the bloodline is real?" Britt inched away from Cristoforo.

"Oh, the bloodline is real. The *Rex Deus* has been quite careful over the centuries to maintain its purity." Cristoforo pointed to the scroll. "I believe that the physical Jesus died at the Crucifixion as was passed down through the oral history of the *Rex Deus* and verified in that James Gospel. But his bloodline that evolved through Mary Magdalene, who was pregnant at the Crucifixion, was, and is, that of mere mortal man. I'm convinced that God intended for Jesus to leave the world with his words for mankind to follow in his footsteps. The *Rex Deus* passed on the legend that it was their responsibility to maintain the bloodline of Christ for the Second Coming." Cristoforo threw up his hands. "If God could create the universe and everything in it, he wouldn't need a *Rex Deus* to maintain a bloodline."

"But why hasn't anyone before you questioned the bloodline?" Romano asked.

"I believe the whole concept of maintaining a bloodline for the Second Coming was a creation that evolved from the mind of man, not from the will of God. God gave man the power to reason and the power of imagination. The mind of man put its 'spin' on the concept and thus the *Rex Deus* established itself as having the prime responsibility of maintaining the bloodline. The enormous wealth controlled by the *Rex Deus* was the real force behind perpetuating this myth."

"What wealth are you talking about?" Britt asked.

"The Knights Templar were created by the *Rex Deus* to uncover the secrets of the Holy Grail and the enormous riches hidden under the Temple of Solomon. With this wealth they established the banking system in Europe and financed the Jesuit order to hide and maintain the pure bloodline for the Second Coming. That's why the Jesuits became so powerful so quickly. The *Rex Deus* created the perfect hiding place within the flock to follow in the footsteps of Jesus."

"I don't understand," said Britt. "What if the legend is true? You will destroy what you're trying to save, the will of God."

Cristoforo shook his head. "That's exactly why I'm doing this. If it were the will of almighty God, I couldn't destroy it. The uncovering of the secret James Gospel three years ago caused me to rethink our cause and the potential danger to Christianity. The gospel says God came to James and told him to preserve the Holy Grail and the male bloodline for the Second Coming. The physical Grail plus the James Gospel supported by the testimony of five of the top European bankers and descendants of royal lineage would be evidence enough to put the Church in serious jeopardy."

Romano pointed to the sarcophagus. "What is this Holy Grail? If it is the bones of Mary Magdalene as Britt theorized in her manuscript, what's the great importance to God?"

Cristoforo pointed to the statue in the corner. "That statue of Mary Magdalene is the ossuary for Mary's bones." He made a grand sweeping gesture across the top of the glass case housing the sarcophagus. "This chest holds the real Holy Grail. The word *'Sangraal'* was mistranslated to be Holy Grail when it should have been *Sang Raal*, which in Old French means blood royal. The real Holy Grail is the preserved mummy of Jesus Christ."

Romano and Britt looked at each other in disbelief.

"Jesus' apostles wrapped his body in oils and linens and secreted it to Egypt, where it was mummified and later hidden under the Temple in Jerusalem. It was unearthed by the Knights Templar along with untold riches and preserved by the *Rex Deus*. This is what four members of the Inner Circle carried down the sheer cliffs of Montsegur during the siege of the Cathars. They hid it in a cave near Rennes-le-Château until the eighteenth century, when it was buried secretly under the tomb of a noble family. The Abbé Bérenger Saunière uncovered the secret and held the Holy Grail up for ransom to the *Rex Deus*. Key members of the European Council of Five visited Saunière and paid him for the return of the Grail and his silence. They then created this secure complex to house their holy treasures."

"Have the remains been tested?" Romano laid his hand on the glass case. "What proof is there that this could be the body of Christ?"

"The latest Council of Five considered analyzing the Grail, but Christien Fortier, the leader, was against disturbing the remains, as that would be blasphemy. After the James Gospel was found, the Council agreed it wouldn't be necessary because the gospel supported their oral history."

Cristoforo checked his watch and moved to the opposite side of the case from Romano. "Now it doesn't matter anymore. I am convinced the tradition of the *Rex Deus* was based upon lies, or at least a misinterpretation of the truth. Father Juan Matteo, Uriel; Father Ted Matthews, Raphael; Father Nathan Sinclair, Barachiel; and Father Hans Josef, Michael; and myself, Gabriel, were the last of the bloodline."

Romano was astonished. "Father Hans Josef's in Vienna," he said.

"He flew here immediately after you met with him. I told him to get here for his safety." Cristoforo smirked. "The Council of Five is now probably staring at Michael's body lying on the conference room table. He died the same glorious death as the other members of the bloodline." Cristoforo glanced at his watch. "There is not much time left until I, as the last member, will join my brothers, and the Council of Five and these sacred relics will be destroyed."

That's when Romano saw it in Cristoforo's eyes—an intensity and focus almost manic in nature. His pupils were dilated. It was as if he was experiencing a vision, not unlike that described by those who claimed to have been visited by the Holy Ghost. Romano glanced at Britt and knew she had come to the same conclusion—they were not getting out of here alive.

NINETY-FOUR

Britt felt the adrenaline hit her in a rush. Her brother was another David Koresh and this could end up another Waco. He was going to take his life and the lives of those who could jeopardize his warped image of a twisted religious myth. It wasn't unlike the Church in the Middle Ages massacring the heretics or burning witches at the stake. She had lost her son and husband because she was ignorant about her genetic history, and now Joseph would die for the same reason. But Cristoforo was her twin; maybe she could convince him he was making a mistake.

"What about the future bloodline?" Britt asked. "Where are the children of the next generation?"

Cristoforo looked into Britt's eyes with a thin smile. "You, my dear sister, are a perfect example of what was happening to the bloodline. Due to the inbreeding, genetic problems arose. You would have been an ideal carrier of a new generation, but you were eliminated and given up for adoption because you carried the Tay-Sachs gene. More and more of the Inner Circle were born with serious genetic defects and had to be weeded out."

"Then why not let God and nature take care of the problem?" Romano asked.

"Because embryonic research and the wonders of cryonics have resolved that issue for the Council of Five. They decided that future generations of the bloodline would be embryos stored in cryonic chambers until God was ready for the Second Coming." Cristoforo cocked his head and looked straight at Romano. "You knew one of the three female descendants chosen to provide the embryos. As a matter of fact, you caused the Council quite a scare when you and Marta became an item."

Romano flinched. His jaw dropped. "What happened to Marta?" His voice trembled.

Cristoforo shook his head. "Only the five men in that room know what happened to her and where the embryos are stored. Only they have memorized the codes to access those embryos. There are no existing records, and when those men die, the future dies with them."

"But you're breaking God's commandment not to kill," Britt screamed. "There is no rationale to kill to save the Church. If the Church is God's will, it will survive. It's been through its share of hell over the past two millennia."

"If you destroy these artifacts, there'll be no evidence to support any of their claims. There is no way to prove that you, or the embryos, descended from Jesus. Stop the killing," Romano pleaded.

"It's too late. There's no escape from this complex. In a few minutes, the explosives I planted will destroy what is left of this heresy. Believe me, it will be painless." Cristoforo stared coldly at Britt and Romano. "It will be like Armageddon." His eyes grew larger, filled with a sinister energy. "Maybe it is Armageddon. Maybe it will signal the beginning of the day of judgment. Maybe this *is* God's will."

A wave of nausea swept through Britt. She inched closer to Romano.

Cristoforo reached both hands over the glass case toward them. "Please join hands with me and pray over the body of our Lord."

Britt experienced a strange mixture of anger and fear. She stared at her twin, and the fear drained from her, replaced by sheer rage.

NINETY-FIVE

Romano was still in shock over the revelation about Marta, but right now he had a more pressing problem, keeping Britt and himself alive. He reached over the glass case for Cristoforo's hand and looked around the room, focusing on the vented door that blended into one of the black walls.

"Are you crazy," Britt screamed. "We're about to die."

Romano took a firm grip on Cristoforo's hand. The coolness surprised him. He yanked hard, pulling the smaller priest across the case, grabbed his hair with his free hand, and smashed his head into the glass. Cristoforo jerked violently. Romano used both hands to pivot Cristoforo's head back and then jammed it a second time into the case. This time Romano felt the body go limp and slide off the case headfirst.

Romano kicked the kneeling rail free from its base and used it to smash the glass case holding the manuscript. He stuffed the papyrus roll into his shirt.

Britt stood over Cristoforo's body. Blood oozed from a gash on his forehead. She looked at Romano, terror in her eyes. "What do we do now? He said there's no escape."

Romano grabbed Britt's arm and dragged her toward the door at the far side of the room. "There's got to be a way of getting fresh air into this complex." He yanked open the door and pulled Britt inside what looked like a sophisticated climate-control room. "Our only chance of escape is to find the air vent."

The only light in the room was from green and red indicator lights on the air handler and filtering equipment. Romano pulled out his key chain, which had a small LED light attached to it, and shined the dim beam around the room. In the far corner, a duct from the air handler attached to a vent on the wall. He took off the iron cross Ted had given him and slid the end of one of the shorter arms into the slot of a large screw on a corner of the vent.

Using the long arm of the cross as leverage he removed all the screws.

Romano helped Britt climb into a large galvanized duct and followed her with the small light. "Crawl like you've never crawled before," he said. "I have no idea how much time we have, but we have to get to the outside air source before this place becomes an inferno."

The duct joined another and then ended a few meters farther at a dark tunnel carved into the rock.

Romano grabbed Britt's foot. "Let me take the lead. This could get difficult real fast." He slithered past Britt in the narrow confines of the tunnel. "I've done a lot of caving in my time but under much different conditions. I'll warn you of any problems. Stay right behind me."

Britt tugged on Romano's pant leg. "Don't worry. I'll scream if you get out of arm's reach. I don't do well in the dark or cramped places."

"Don't even think about it. Let's get moving. I saw a number of entrances to caves during my jog to Rennes-les-Bains this morning. We'll get out of here." Romano started crawling. He didn't want to be anywhere near the complex when the explosions started.

The tunnel opened up into a small chamber. Stalactites hung like icicles from the sloping roof that dipped to a dark crevice in the far corner. Romano could almost stand, and he pulled Britt to her feet so she could rest while he looked for a way out. The feeble bluish light from his key chain wasn't much good for illuminating the dark crevices. He knew these cave systems could extend for miles beneath the surface of the earth and have many outlets—and just as many dead ends.

"Stay here and rest," Romano said. "I'm going around the perimeter of this chamber to find the best passage out of here."

"Don't leave me here in the dark." Britt's voice cracked.

"Don't worry, you'll see the light at all times."

The cave floor shuddered. A loud rumble followed. Romano grabbed Britt, dragged her to the far corner of the chamber, pushed her down, and covered her with his body. A series of explosions accompanied flashes of light out of the tunnel from which they had just emerged. The noise was deafening. A few stalactites fell to the cave floor, shattering into tiny fragments that skittered across the limestone.

Romano had his arms and body wrapped around Britt, who was shaking beneath him. He rolled off her and helped her sit up. "Are you okay?"

Britt ran her fingers through her hair then clasped her head with both hands. "I guess, since we're both alive, I'm as okay as can be expected."

Romano stood and worked his way around the chamber, shining the LED light back toward Britt every few feet. He only located one exit. It was pretty narrow but it beat his fears of finding only fissures in the subterranean chamber. "Over here." He shined the light on the chamber floor for Britt to make her way to him.

Romano hoped the narrow passage didn't take them deeper into an underground labyrinth. He noticed small grooves in the dusky brown limestone leading to the opening. It was a probable indication that the groundwater drained down that passage into an underground stream. He hoped that stream eventually made its way to the one he had seen in Rennes-les-Bains.

Romano slid on his back through the narrow opening then turned over on to his stomach. He breathed a sigh of relief when he shined his light down the passage. It seemed to widen as far as he could see in the glow of the faint beam. He pulled Britt through the opening and they crawled down the tunnel. Before long Romano heard the gurgle of an underground stream. The tunnel merged alongside the stream and they followed it until the tunnel shrank to a mere slit above the water with no passage on either side of the flowing ribbon of water.

Romano crawled into a sitting position. "Don't panic. I'm going to shut off the light for a few seconds."

Britt kneeled next to him and wrapped her arms around one of his. "What can we do?"

"Pray that this underground stream connects to a larger tunnel real close to here. Or, better yet, merges under bright sunshine with an outdoor stream." Romano flicked off the LED.

The darkness was palpable. Britt clutched Romano's arm tighter. He felt her nails dig into his skin. He strained to adjust his eyes and stared down at the stream. There was nothing but inky blackness and the soft ripple of the flowing water. The stream didn't merge with the outside world—at least not close enough to transmit even a glimmer of light into their hellhole.

Romano flicked the LED back on. He felt Britt's grip loosen

on his arm. "There's only one option." He handed the light to
Britt. "I'm going to check out this stream and see if it leads to a
connecting tunnel."

"You're not going in that water."

Romano pulled off his Nikes. "You have any better sugges-
tions?" He took off his cross and polo shirt, wrapped the shirt
around the papyrus roll, and handed them to Britt. "Here, hang
on to these. I'll be back in a minute."

Romano slid into the stream. He shuddered from the shock of
the cold water that came up to just above his waist. Fear gripped
him, squeezing his gut like a vise. He had always been afraid of
underground streams. He dipped under water to get more accli-
mated to the cold and tried not to show his fear as his head
splashed out, and he smiled one last time at Britt.

Romano knew this was a great risk, but he had to take it.
There'd be air pockets between the water and the tunnel, but he
couldn't chance locating one in the pitch blackness if he needed
it. The current was weak, but it would be a major factor if he had
to turn around and return before running out of precious oxygen.
He took three deep breaths and submerged under the surface of
the dark water.

NINETY-SIX

Britt held her breath as Romano disappeared beneath the rippling current. A renewed fear gripped her as the seconds ticked away. She was suddenly aware of the cool dampness of the cave and the feeling of being trapped. She began to tremble as the terror of her situation became all too real. She held the dim light close to the water, hoping it would be a beacon for Romano to find his way back to her.

Britt stared at the faint glimmer of light as it dispersed quickly in the dark water. She didn't even blink, hoping to see Romano emerge from the dark tunnel of water at any second. She realized she had lost all track of time and wasn't sure how many seconds or minutes Romano had been gone. It seemed like too many. She clenched her teeth—he wasn't coming back.

Suddenly there was a loud splash and Romano pulled himself half out of the water and lay gasping on the rock shelf with his head plopped against Britt's knee. After he managed to catch his breath, he looked up at Britt. "What kind of a swimmer are you?"

"I didn't spend my summers at a beach or swim club, and my home didn't have a pool. I can swim, but just barely."

Romano crawled the rest of the way out of the water and sat next to Britt. "The stream goes a good distance underground, but near the end you can see dim light from the connecting passageway. There's got to be access to the outside."

Romano took the laces out of his Nikes and slipped the shoes on. Then he took the shirt and cross back from Britt. He opened the heavy chain holding the cross and tied one end of it to one of his belt loops. Then he knotted one of the shoelaces to the chain and tied the other end around the bottom of the shirt holding the scroll. He knotted the other lace around the collar of the polo shirt and tied it to a belt loop on the side of Britt's pants. He smiled at Britt. "This is so you don't get away from me with the manuscript."

Britt felt the panic attacking her muscles. She stiffened. "I don't know if I can do this. You looked like you barely made it back here."

Romano took the light from Britt and clipped it to his pants. Then he grabbed her by the shoulders and looked her straight in the eyes. "Believe me, you can do this. We'll get in the water. It's a bit chilly, but that's good—you'll swim faster to get out. We'll take three deep breaths, hold the last one, then stay with me under water and stroke and kick like you've never done before."

Britt nodded and Romano slid into the water and held out his arms. Britt turned around and he lifted her in beside him. The water was a lot colder than Britt had thought. She was shaking when Romano let go and said, "One." She sucked in as much air as she could, held it, and then exhaled along with Romano. "Two." This time she took a deeper breath. "Three."

NINETY-SEVEN

The two French Renaults were still kilometers away from Rennes-le-Château when Cutler heard the first rumble coming from a nearby peak. It was followed by four more in rapid succession.

A confused look swept over the French agent as he slowed the car, craned, and scanned in the direction of the sounds.

Cutler pointed to smoke rising from the area. "Those were explosions. What's up there?"

"The Hotellerie du Cheval. It's a horse farm and inn. It's one of the few places your suspects could be staying."

"Let's hope it still exists."

The agent sped up and headed toward the smoke that was now billowing above the trees.

Cutler was shoved against the shoulder harness as the Renault skidded around the first turn. He wondered if Romano and Hamar had become another statistic in his case.

NINETY-EIGHT

Romano dragged Britt sputtering and coughing out of the water and onto the tunnel floor. While she regained her breath, he untied the shirt and cross. He relaced his shoes, wrung out his shirt, and put it back on. Then he carefully squeezed the water from the dripping papyrus roll and placed it inside his shirt.

Britt's hair was plastered to her face. She pushed the strands away from her eyes, puffed out her cheeks, blew out a deep breath, and finally looked up at Romano. "I sure hope there's not another water tunnel. You don't know how close I was to losing it."

Romano shut off the light.

"Please, don't do that," Britt pleaded.

Romano wrapped his arm around her shoulders and pulled her toward him. "Look, look. See the dim haze down at the end of this tunnel. That's our ticket to getting out of here." He squeezed her shoulders. "There's no more swimming, I promise." He switched the light back on and started crawling. "Just stay close."

"You don't have to worry about that." Britt's hand grabbed Romano's shoe.

Romano crawled toward the growing light. After a few minutes he turned a narrow corner and saw a shaft of sunlight streaming onto the tunnel wall. When he got to the opening, it was overgrown with grass and vines. He ripped through the vegetation and crawled out onto a steep hillside.

Romano turned to help Britt, but she had already scrambled out. She grabbed his arm, pulled herself up, then wrapped her arms around him and buried her head in his shoulder. She shivered from the cold water and the chill of the cave and slowly increased her embrace. Romano rubbed her back and shoulders as they stood in the warming rays of the morning sun.

Finally Britt looked up at Romano, slowly shaking her head. "What the hell just happened? This can't be real."

"I wish it wasn't, but it is. At least the killing is over, but I'm afraid many questions still remain."

"What do we do now?" Britt asked.

Romano looked up and saw smoke rising above the peak in the area of the inn. He looked down the hillside and spotted a narrow, winding road. There was a loud wail of sirens, and a fire engine and red emergency vehicle shot past followed by a few cars.

"Let's get down to the road," Romano said. "We can't be too far from the inn. Maybe the building survived and our passports and bags are still intact."

They climbed down through the underbrush until they reached the road. Then Romano turned to Britt and patted the papyrus roll stuffed inside his shirt. "I don't know about you, but I still think there are many unanswered questions relating to what Cristoforo told us. All I ask is that you and I take a look at all the evidence and evaluate it carefully before we jump to any conclusions. There seems to be a lot of mystery surrounding the history of the *Rex Deus* and the bloodline. Remember, Cristoforo felt that one of the main motivators of the Council was wealth and power."

"As long as you agree that I won't go along with hiding the truth."

Romano gently squeezed Britt's forearm. "With what we've been through, I don't think either of us wants to hide the truth. Too many things in life are an illusion. If the *Rex Deus* was perpetuating myths, I just want to be sure that we don't continue them."

"No matter the outcome, some very troubling facts are going to come out of this."

"I think your book will be the perfect venue for putting all the pieces into perspective." Romano looked at Britt but felt his serious expression slipping. "I'm confident you'll give the appropriate weight to all your theorems based upon the preponderance of evidence." He patted the manuscript in his shirt. "This is yours. I'll be happy to contribute my knowledge of Aramaic to the translation."

A brief smile appeared on Britt's face. "You're hired. And I hope you'll be willing to give me your professional comments if I bring you my final draft."

"You can count on that, if you don't mind my biased opinion."

They started hiking to the inn. When they got to the driveway, they could see the main building was undamaged. The smoke rose from one end of the horse barn where firemen aimed hoses on the flaming structure. A few cars were parked in front of the inn, and people stood staring at the fire crew.

Romano and Britt were halfway up the drive when two men jumped into a Renault, which sped away from the inn and came to a screeching halt next to them.

Agent Cutler got out of the car and held out his ID.

"Father Romano, I hope you remember me. Agent Tom Cutler, FBI." Cutler motioned toward the driver, who walked toward them cautiously. "This is Agent Guy Raison, the French representative to Interpol." He looked at Britt. "And I assume you're Professor Brittany Hamar."

Britt nodded.

Cutler motioned toward the car. "Let's get you back to the inn so you can dry off. I'm hoping you can fill us in about what happened here."

"That we can certainly do," Romano said. "I just wish you would have arrived here a few hours ago. It might have saved six or seven lives."

Cutler appraised Romano with a questioning look. "I hope the two of you coming here wasn't responsible for those deaths."

"Actually, we were supposed to be numbers eight and nine," Romano said as they got into the car.

They drove back to the inn, where Romano and Britt were allowed to shower and change. They were given hot mugs of coffee and interrogated separately by Cutler, Agent Raison, and two other French agents. After an hour they were brought into the dining room of the inn.

Cutler and Raison were waiting for them. "Interpol has agreed that both of you be released into my custody," Cutler said. "We'll go to Marseille, where they'll take your official statements, then I'll escort you back to the U.S. and we can sort this all out."

Britt formed a half smile, but that was enough for Romano. This nightmare was finally coming to an end. But he felt uneasy, as in the minutes immediately after a thunderstorm; there was a strange calm but he was waiting for the next lightning strike or clap of thunder. There was still the James Gospel, the *Rex Deus*, and the bloodline to sort out. How much was fact, and how much was fiction?

Romano felt a tremor through his body. He couldn't block out the unnerving thought that his saving the James Gospel could be the catalyst that threatened the sanctity of the Church.

NINETY-NINE

ROMANO, BRITT, CARLOTA, AND CHARLIE arrived at the Jacob Javits Federal Building. The stone and concrete structures surrounding 26 Federal Plaza were striped with columns of tiny dark windows shooting toward the skyline. Silver-trimmed black pylons lined the sidewalk along the street, and rows of steel barricades blocked some of the stairs to the entrances. Uniformed officers monitored the comings and goings of those without federal IDs.

Romano noticed Carlota and Charlie shoot each other uneasy glances. These security measures added a shocking new dimension to their private little world of Manhattan. Terrorism had left an indelible mark on the country's more visible institutions.

One of the officers stopped them at the top of the stairs leading from the sidewalk to the entrance. Romano showed her Cutler's card. The officer spoke into her radio, then directed them inside.

Agent Brian Donahue met them in the vast lobby. He took them to an upper floor, where Agent Cutler was waiting in a small conference room with a man in a navy suit with reading glasses hanging out of the breast pocket. The man's gray hair and wrinkled eyes gave Romano the impression he was one of the more seasoned agents. Romano was surprised the room looked more government-issue than he had anticipated.

When they were all seated at the conference table, Cutler handed Donahue a stack of documents. "Before we get into the analysis of the manuscripts, you'll be relieved to know that we've uncovered evidence that links Father Cristoforo to the deaths of the priests. His travel itinerary puts him in each of the cities and his fingerprints were found at each of the scenes." Then Cutler turned to the man sitting next to him. "I'd like to introduce Agent Carl Landis, the head of our forensic unit. He'll discuss the results of the carbon-dating tests."

Donahue passed reports to everyone at the table.

"These are the tests on Professor Hamar's document seg-ment," Landis said. "You'll notice that the papyrus is dated from the time of Christ. It verifies Professor Hamar's test. The ink, however, isn't more than a year old. The document is a forgery."

Donahue handed out two more reports.

Landis held up a plastic case containing the papyrus roll from France. "This one's a different story. Both the papyrus and the ink are from the time of Christ." He motioned to Romano. "And, as Father Romano has verified, the Aramaic writing is authentic. Therefore, we must conclude that the document is genuine."

There was an audible gasp from Britt and the grad students. Romano was silent. He had hoped it would have been that easy to prove the document was a fake. But with the vast resources of the *Rex Deus*, he had doubted it would be. Deep in his gut he had feared the gospel could be the real thing.

"Before we agree on the authenticity of the document, there's one more factor we should consider," Romano said. "I've done some research into fake antiquities. There are some very skilled forgers in the Middle East, especially in Israel. Not long ago an ossuary was found that had an inscription indicating it was 'James, son of Joseph, brother of Jesus.' It created quite a stir when scientists authenticated that it was from the time of Christ. Only after much debate and careful analysis did they find that the patina in the grooves of the engraving for the last part of the in-scription was different from the patina on the first part and the other surfaces of the ossuary. They also found that the letters of 'James, son of Joseph' were vertical, while the letters of 'brother of Jesus' were slightly slanted."

"But this isn't an engraving," Britt said.

"I uncovered a similar process to evaluate the age of written documents," Romano replied.

Landis looked puzzled. "I'm sorry, but I don't see how we could analyze the material underneath the ink."

"That's not necessary," Romano said.

All eyes were now glued on Romano.

"What do you suggest we do?" Landis asked.

"First of all, there's a process for tricking the carbon-dating of the ink. Skilled forgers have discovered that by burning papyrus sheets from that time period and mixing the ashes with ink re-sults in a false carbon date."

The eyes turned to Landis. The forensic scientist scratched his chin and seemed perplexed by Romano's statement. "I'd have to run some experiments to verify it, but it seems plausible."

"Now you've caught us in another assumption scenario," Britt said. "Authentic versus fake—take your pick. And on this one I'd rather not go the preponderance of evidence route. Unless you can prove that it's fake, all you can do is attack the credibility of this author who claims to be James, the brother of Jesus."

"That won't be necessary," Romano said. "Agent Landis, could your lab analyze the papyrus roll to determine if any previous writing had been scraped off?"

Landis paused for a moment. "It would probably depend on the process used to remove each character. There could be minute particles of ink or the impression from the original writing implement. Under special lighting conditions and digitally enhanced microscopic analysis, we might be able to re-create anything previously written on the roll."

"How long would it take to do that analysis?" Romano asked.

"I'd have to call our Questioned Documents Unit. If they're not backed up, they could verify any evidence of previous writing fairly quickly." Landis picked up the phone on the conference table and punched a few numbers into the keypad. "Enhancing any results to verifiable characters could be another story, especially since our software isn't programmed to identify Aramaic or Greek text." He raised a finger then talked to someone on the phone. When he finished, he picked up the plastic case holding the James manuscript. "Do you want to observe the testing? Processing documents this old is not something we normally do in this lab." He shrugged. "Maybe you can teach our techs some new techniques."

"Oh, I've never performed this type of analysis," Romano replied. "My specialty is researching historical documents, analyzing writing techniques, the formation of characters, language, that sort of thing."

Landis snapped his head toward the door. "Come on, at least you can see the lab. State of the art. It's my pride and joy." He charged out clutching the document, followed by Cutler. Charlie and Britt weren't far behind them.

Carlota looked at Romano. She slowed up until she was directly beside him at the end of the entourage. "Do you believe Charlie is actually wearing a shirt and tie?" she whispered. "He even left his beloved Rams cap in the office. You don't think he might be a closet federal agent wannabe trying to worm his way in for an internship."

Romano leaned toward Carlota and grinned. "Actually, I think you're more their type."

As they entered the elevator to take them to the lab, Romano felt a pang of remorse. Could his saving the manuscript have set into motion the very same chain of events that Father Cristoforo feared enough to start a killing spree?

ONE HUNDRED

THE LABORATORY TURNED OUT TO BE MUCH MORE impressive than the conference room. Romano was pleased to see that tax dollars had at least gone to supporting technology rather than décor.

After preparing a section of the manuscript for analysis, the technician brought the magnified image up on a large LCD monitor. As he zoomed in on an area, small dark random dots began appearing within the pithy texture of the papyrus.

"I don't think that's part of the plant material," Landis said. "It could be remnants of ink. Matt, change the angle of the light and the scan. See if we can identify any impressions in the area of those particles that could have been made by a writing implement."

Five heads closed in on the high-definition monitor mounted on the wall. The technician caressed a large trackball with three fingers, slowly defining an area of the image with the cursor. Then he typed a command on the keyboard. The computer did its thing, and the texture of the papyrus melted into a smooth dimensional surface with a distinct indentation that contained the random dark dots. The surrounding area was free of dots.

Landis pulled glasses out of his jacket pocket and put them on. They exaggerated the wrinkles around his eyes as he leaned up to the monitor and carefully perused the image. "Matt, do a progressive scan over a contiguous section and print out the results. I think there may have been something written on that scroll before the current text. By printing out a contiguous section, we'll be able to get a better idea of what it was."

Landis turned to Romano. "If there is something that looks like it could be a kind of text, you'll have to work with Matt to identify it letter by letter." He shook his head. "That could end up being a long, drawn-out project."

"We may not have to go to that extreme," Romano said.

"I don't follow. How will we determine when the text was written?" Landis's voice was shaded with wariness. "To determine the current text is a fake would require identifying the previous writing contained information that dated it."

"Dating can also be determined by the style of writing," Romano replied. "The Institute for Basic Epistemological Research in Paderborn, Germany, developed very successful analytical techniques for manuscript dating that involve careful scrutiny of writing styles."

Landis eyed Romano with growing skepticism. "How do you carefully scrutinize writing if you haven't identified the text?"

"You focus on the style of writing for specific time periods," Romano replied. "Uncial writing, which contained only Greek capital letters, was used around the time of Christ up through the ninth and tenth centuries. Miniscule writing, which contained Greek upper- and lowercase letters, came into use in the ninth century."

Matt stepped over to the printer, picked up a stack of papers, and carefully lined them up on a table. "I guess there's no doubt about these results," he said.

Landis slid his glasses down his nose and moved along the line of printouts. "I have no idea what these shapes represent, but they seem to contain upper- and lowercase characters."

Romano approached the table with renewed optimism. He carefully analyzed each of the shapes. He pulled out a pad and made some notes, then reviewed the shapes a second and third time. When he was satisfied, he turned to Landis and Cutler. "I can recognize some of the Greek characters without further enhancement. This was definitely miniscule writing that wasn't used until the ninth century. Anything written on top of it had to have been done after that period."

"There's no margin of error in that conclusion?" Britt asked.

"I don't see how there could be," Romano replied. "That style of writing definitely was not around during the time of Christ. Even if the research into dating the onset of miniscule writing was in error by one or two hundred years, that's still a long way from any time period that a brother of Jesus would have been alive."

"Well, I guess we have to agree that Father Cristoforo could have been right," Britt said. "I suppose Christianity's not faced with a radical reversal of accepted wisdom."

"I'm sorry. I don't follow you," Cutler said.

"Father Cristoforo believed that the supposed foundation of the *Rex Deus* was based upon centuries or even millennia of flawed philosophy." Britt pointed to the manuscript. "That fraudulent document proves he was right."

"There still remain many great questions that I'm afraid will never be answered," Romano added. "What was the real basis for the *Rex Deus* and Inner Circle or *Le Serpent Rouge*? The *Rex Deus* took extreme measures to control the bloodline. The big question is, whose bloodline? What elements were based upon fact and what elements were based upon fiction? Since Father Cristoforo destroyed all the initiated members as well as the crypt containing any physical evidence, the final answers may never be known."

"There's one thing you've managed to drill home to me," Britt said. "There's so much we think we understand, but in the final analysis, we really don't."

"I can't take credit for that. I think it was more a result of what we both experienced in the past few days. Much of what we accept as fact is based upon perception, which may be a skewed version of truth."

"The *Rex Deus* may have been the first 'spin doctors,'" Charlie said.

Everyone laughed.

"Charlie, I'm afraid that concept has probably been around since the beginning of mankind," Romano replied. "The mind of man has a tendency to present things to its best advantage. But remember, in order to put a spin on something, there's got to be some element of truth."

"But isn't faith the unwavering constant?" Carlota added. "You always stress that, in the end, we follow our faith whatever that may be, no matter what the 'spin doctors' might say."

"Amen," Romano said with a smile. "I know the past few days have tested my faith." He was proud of his grad assistants. They were good critical thinkers. Always eager to dig in to any new challenge. They'd make an outstanding research team, but sadly, he knew once they graduated they'd be snapped up by different companies or universities and go their own ways. No matter where they ended up, he hoped for Charlie there'd be another Carlota and for Carlota there'd be another Charlie.

Donahue returned to the lab. "Sorry to break into your discussion, but I thought you'd like to know. The father general of the Jesuit order just issued a statement that Father Cristoforo had suffered extreme emotional distress and had developed an irrational fear that the five European businessmen and some of his fellow priests were threatening the Church. His theory was based upon delusions, not fact. There was no mention of any supposed bloodline of Christ. We've also received confirmation from Interpol of the names of the men who died in the explosion." He handed the list to Cutler. "Interpol found no official record of any organization called *Rex Deus*. The men were heavy hitters in the European banking community, heads of some of the largest banks in France, Scotland, Germany, England, as well as a Russian aristocrat with large land holdings."

Suddenly a dark feeling shrouded Romano's thoughts. His father had moved from Italy to establish a branch of a German bank in the United States, and he'd had a close associate in England. "Could I see the list of names?" he asked.

"Have these been officially released?" Cutler asked Donahue.

Donahue nodded and Cutler handed the list to Romano.

Romano read the list: Christien Fortier, Blair Henderson, Egor Ivanov. He paused in shock when he saw the last two names. . . . George Rahn and Rexford Walker had been business associates of his father.

ONE HUNDRED ONE

ROMANO STOOD IN THE FAR CORNER OF THE PORCH on the front entrance to the Jesuit Center for Spiritual Growth. He stared through the stone archway at the majestic trees lining the driveway. The silky gray sky cast them in subtle shadows as they swayed in a soft breeze. Nature had spread a gentle reverence across the morning of Father Ted's funeral.

Romano had spent the past few days at Wernersville helping prepare for the service. During the entire time, he was haunted by thoughts that his father and Ted had been part of the *Rex Deus* and questions about what really happened to Marta. He spoke daily with Britt, who shared her extensive research on the secret society. Much of what she had uncovered was bizarre, to say the least. She e-mailed him many of her research notes. They included references to Egyptian Gnostic sex rites, the murder of John the Baptist so that sorcery could be performed with his head, aliens from Sirius establishing the Egyptian civilization, and plots to overthrow the Arab nations to possess the Holy Land, or overthrow the Pope, the Roman Catholic Church, and Western Christendom.

The only consistent factors that kept cropping up in Britt's research were references to the *Rex Deus* believing they were preserving a bloodline that would one day establish the kingdom of God on Earth, and that their mystical traditions, known as "The Way," were passed on orally through a lengthy initiation process. If Cristoforo was right, the only initiated members were dead—and "The Way" had died with them.

Interpol hadn't been able to find a shred of evidence indicating there had actually been a modern-day *Rex Deus*. The families of the dead European businessmen insisted there was no secret organization. They claimed the *hotellerie* was used for business meetings and family horseback riding vacations. The underground bunker had been built during the Cold War as a safe haven for the families in case of a nuclear attack.

Romano had resigned himself to the fact that he would never know the whole truth about his father and Ted. But he had come to accept that it wasn't important. He had the memories of the two men who helped shape his life, and that, after all, was what really mattered.

There was still the matter of Marta and his mother's involvement in her disappearance. He had decided it was more important to mend his relationship with his mother and keep Marta as a fond memory of a first love.

A black limousine came up the drive. Romano walked to the entrance and started down the steps as the limo came to a stop in front of the center. The driver held the door as Regina Romano stepped out of the backseat. She wore a black chiffon dress and dark glasses. Her dyed black hair was pulled back into a chignon. When Romano gave his mother the customary kiss on each cheek, he could see, even through the darkened lenses, the result of tears that had ravaged her eyes and smeared her heavy makeup. He couldn't recall his mother reacting with so much emotion even at his father's funeral.

Regina grabbed Romano's arm and squeezed it. "I'm so relieved you're okay. I don't know what I would have done if I had lost Ted and my only son."

Romano hugged his mother, something he hadn't done in a long time. "Mother, I'm safe; the danger is past. Unfortunately, we're left with the deep sorrow of Ted's death."

Regina took a handkerchief out of her purse, tilted her glasses, and dabbed her eyes. Romano saw, by the stains, that her handkerchief had gotten plenty of use on the drive from New York. He took his mother's arm as they started up the steps.

"Mother, why don't you come to my room and freshen up. We have plenty of time before the service starts."

Regina gave him the closest thing to a smile since the episode with Marta. "I suppose you still know your mother pretty well. I would feel embarrassed going to Ted's service looking like this."

When Regina came out of the bathroom, she looked like a new person. Many of the wrinkles on her face had vanished and the pallor of her skin was replaced by a soft glow. She had shed the tinted glasses. Her eyes were made up with a model's perfection.

"Mother, you look radiant. Ted would be pleased."

Regina looked embarrassed but quickly recovered. Then her eyes glassed over. "You know, that's the first real compliment you've given me since . . . well, in many years."

"That's something we have to talk about." Romano drew in a deep breath. "Ted left a letter to be given to me upon his death. In it he urged me to repair my relationship with you. I believe his death has given me strength to finally try." He felt his eyes well up. "I hated myself all these years for not having the courage to get past my feelings about what happened with Marta."

Regina's hands started trembling. "You don't know how often I wanted to tell you the truth but was afraid."

"Afraid? Afraid of what?"

Regina sat on the edge of the bed and lowered her head. "When I said I didn't know what happened to Marta and her family, I was telling you the truth. What I didn't tell you was what happened before they disappeared."

Romano leaned against the desk and stared at his mother.

"I never knew exactly what your father and Ted were involved in, but I knew it was much more important than his banking business. He told me that if anything ever happened to him, Ted would help me prepare you for some future role." Regina looked down at the floor. "I thought your father may have been involved in something illegal." She looked up. "But I couldn't understand what role Ted played."

Romano sat next to his mother and put an arm around her. "Father and Ted were not into anything illegal. They were part of an organization that thought it had a high spiritual calling to protect secrets of God. They were good men with good intentions. For whatever reasons, their perceptions were based upon centuries-old myths relating to mystical teachings rather than facts."

A look of anguish spread across Regina's face. "I was actually happy when I found out you had been seeing Marta. She was such a kind and gentle girl. But when I told Ted, he was furious. I'd never seen him that way. I couldn't tell if it was anger or panic. He said Marta was special and had a unique calling in life and that she and you could not be together. She was pledged to someone else. I never understood what he meant. He told me to do whatever I could to get you to stop seeing her. When I told him how you responded, he said he'd take care of it. A week later Marta and her family vanished without a word."

Romano stared in astonishment at his mother. He felt as though the air was sucked from his lungs. His own words flashed in his mind's eye: *Much of what we accept as fact is based upon perception, which may be a skewed version of the truth.* He pulled his mother to him. "I'm so sorry," was all he could say.

ONE HUNDRED TWO

After the service and burial in the small cemetery on the center grounds, Romano walked his mother to the limo. Before she got in, he held her close. "I'm staying here for the next thirty days on a retreat with a group of Jesuits to go through the spiritual exercises. After all that's happened, I have some serious soul searching to do." He looked down at her and smiled. "When I get back to New York, let's have dinner. I'd like for us to become a family again."

Regina squeezed his shoulder. "I think we both deserve that."

Romano waved to his mother as the limo headed down the drive. When he turned to go into the center, he saw a blonde walking toward him from the parking lot. As she got closer, he realized it was Britt.

He rushed over to her. "I wasn't expecting you. I thought you were burning the midnight oil working on a redraft of your manuscript."

"Your loan of Carlota and Charlie paid off." Britt held out a manuscript box. "They're one heck of a team. We managed to restructure the material into a new format. Here's a rough draft, mostly in outline form. They felt it was important to get your expert opinion before I go to the next step."

Romano took the box. "Your timing couldn't be better. I'll need breaks from contemplating my Ignatian spirituality." He felt a nervous tremor as he looked down at the box.

"You don't have to feel guilty in front of your fellow Jesuits," Britt said as she reached over and lifted the lid.

In bold letters on the title page was *Unholy Grail*.

"What happened to *The Jesus Fraud*?"

Britt pointed proudly at the manuscript. "It still needs a lot of work, but I think you'll find I gave 'appropriate weight' to each of the theories, especially to the danger of myths based upon faulty perception leading to a quest to preserve what turns out to be the 'Unholy Grail.' "

Romano smiled. "Did Carlota or Charlie have anything to do with the title change?"

"No, that was all my doing." Britt let out a laugh. "Charlie did offer a line to explain the theories relating to Christ not dying on the cross. He recommended I refer to the early Christian mystics who had interpreted the *crucifixion* as the *crucifiction*."

"I guess it didn't take you long to get a good dose of Charlie."

"He's got a sharp mind. But I don't want to leave out Carlota. She countered Charlie's comment with, 'It is so easy for us to take snippets of history and weave them into a tapestry of our own design.' That has a good shot at making my final draft."

"I'm happy you're enjoying them."

"That brings up another question. I got an advance of research money from my publisher. If you approve, I'd like to hire Carlota and Charlie while you're on retreat to do some research and be my sounding board."

Romano beamed. "You certainly have my blessing. They'll be in their glory." Then he raised his arm and held up a finger. "But only on one condition—that I get them back."

"You don't have to worry about that. They worship you." Britt cringed. "Sorry. I guess that wasn't the best choice of words."

"With what we've been through together, you have carte blanche when it comes to word choice." Romano motioned toward the center. There was a large group gathered on the porch. "Would you like to come to the center? I'm sure they wouldn't mind if you joined us for dinner this evening."

Britt shook her head. "Thanks, but you've got a lot of guests to mingle with. Honoring Father Mathews deserves your full attention. When you're back in New York, we'll do dinner. I'm really looking forward to your comments."

Britt turned to head back to her car, then stopped and turned toward Romano. "There's something else you should know." She glanced up at the porch full of people and shrugged. "I'd like to give you a hug and kiss, but I don't think this would be the appropriate place. Being with you for those few days got me to realize that I had been totally focused on the pain of my past. I was ignoring my future. I'm sure Alain and Tyler would want me to move on with my life. To make something worthwhile out of it. God gave us the gift to live our lives as we see fit. Sometimes there are some rough 'spots along the road. You've helped me to get past my worst. Thanks."

As Britt walked toward her car, Romano felt as if a part of him were leaving too. He turned and started back to the porch and Ted's friends and colleagues. He realized he had reached one of those rough spots.

During his spiritual exercises he'd have to decide whether, in the next chapter of his life, he'd continue to follow his final vows—or whether he'd make a detour and follow his heart.

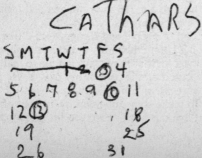